THE GOWKARAN TREE IN THE MIDDLE OF OUR KITCHEN

ALSO BY

SHOKOOFEH AZAR

The Enlightenment of the Greengage Tree

Shokoofeh Azar

THE GOWKARAN TREE IN THE MIDDLE OF OUR KITCHEN

The translator has chosen to remain anonymous for security reasons. Translated from the Farsi.

Europa
editions

Europa Editions
27 Union Square West, Suite 302
New York NY 10003
www.europaeditions.com
info@europaeditions.com

This project has been assisted by the Australian Government
through Creative Australia, its principal arts investment and advisory body.

First publication 2025 by Europa Editions

Original title: درخت گوکرن وسط آشپزخانه ما

Library of Congress Cataloging in Publication Data is available
ISBN 979-8-88966-097-2

Azar, Shokoofeh
The Gowkaran Tree in the Middle of Our Kitchen

Cover design by Ginevra Rapisardi

Cover image: detail of a painting by Shokoofeh Azar

Prepress by Grafica Punto Print – Rome

Printed in Canada

CONTENTS

To the Dead Lovers
And Also
To Those Who Do Not Know
Love Leaves Behind More Dead than War

THE GOWKARAN TREE IN THE MIDDLE OF OUR KITCHEN

Book One
The Womb of Destiny

A love story may begin like this: "It doesn't matter whether you belong to me, it doesn't matter whether you belong to him, what matters is that you belong to poetry." That is, if the narrator of this story were Nizar Qabbani who, after years of loving and being in love, had transcended the beloved and drowned himself in the pure concept of love. Or it may begin with, "Even the birds help one another. Come here. Close, closer. Help me kiss you," if Tess Gallagher had wanted to write this story when she fell in love with Raymond Carver.

But let me see how I, a woman fifteen years old at the time, might begin . . . Perhaps like this: "The night you were leaving, I wanted something simple to happen. For you to get lost. For a cuckoo to coo and for the rusty key to fall to the ground from the cranes' empty nest. For it to rain. For me to wake up. For me to wake you up and for you to have told me the rest of this dream." Yes, I could have begun my story with this poem of Vaheh Arman[1]*. Instead, do you know what I will do? I will begin my story not with poetry, but with ambiguity: the ambiguity of life . . . the ambiguity of the tree. Because as I was repeating his name under my breath, I suddenly reached the conclusion that the story of our love has no beginning*[2]*, and that therefore I should remember that the Shahnameh, for example, did not commence with the reign of Keyumars, just as it did not end*

[1] Iranian poet.

[2] The national epic of Iranian literature, written by Abol-ghasem Ferdowsi between 970 and 1010 CE

with Yazdegerd III's defeat against the Arabs. Stories succeed stories, just as one human succeeds another, time succeeds time, and no death has ever commenced with birth, and no being has ever been the continuation of non-being. I close my eyes and take out the first book my hand touches from the shelf. It is Vladimir Mayakovsky's collected poems. I use it for divination:

The drum of war thunders and thunders.
It calls: thrust iron into the living.

Chapter One

As you know, I'm not a poet or a writer. I write simply and give everything away right at the beginning, but perhaps it's your fate not to be able to stop reading me, you who will inherit the sacred fire and the secrets of this great dynasty and this immense mansion, the white notebook of my memoirs with its two hundred pages is but one of the 1,763 dusty notebooks of memoirs sitting in the rusty iron trunk in the corner of the attic you have chosen to read. You certainly know by now that I am obsessed with the idea that everything in this world begins in ambiguity and that nothing in this world has a definite beginning. In the same way, no question in this world has a definite answer. Everything depends on everything. For instance, it would be naive of me to think that it all started that day when I saw him in the mansion courtyard. No! How do we know everything didn't begin with those two notebooks on love? Or much earlier, with the smells and colors, or, for example, the taste of wild raspberries in childhood? With the things that put me in a good mood, while at the same time a cry within me summoned him, he who would be the symbol of all the pleasures, joys, and beauties of this world, without me even knowing his name. Or who knows, perhaps even from much, much earlier . . . from a previous life or lives. Whatever the case may be, I have concluded that in life either everything begins from everything or that nothing begins from anything. And is it even possible to say with which bud, which shoot, which tree spring begins? Or autumn with which yellow leaf? Which forest? My love for him began in the same way; calmly, beginningless, vague, and the size of the blossoming of the first blossom in spring, the size of the fall of the first yellow leaf in autumn, in silence.

When I think about our family's many and winding adventures, the situation seems similar; sometimes it seems to me that everything started with the revolution and my uncle's assassination and my aunt's execution, yet when I think about it carefully, I see that's not the case! It's as if everything started when I met the twelfth prophet in my dream, or then again, maybe not! Perhaps it would be correct if I thought everything started with the tree; when the tree appeared, twelve of us emerged from the forest and the palace, and then the temple was discovered, and Leyla disappeared and the revolution happened and war came and Mehrab was lost. It's as if everything began with the tree. When the tree appeared, I fell in love and Eblis[3] descended upon me, he left and I went off to war. It's as if everything started with the tree; when the tree appeared, the revolution happened, and we were scattered. When the tree appeared, we came face to face with our true selves, yet we could not endure. In the chaos of life, we lost much, until only the most real parts of us remained.

Perhaps then we can begin what happened, starting with the tree; on the very day of the year, Nowruz 1976, the big dining table in the middle of the kitchen, together with all its dishes of fesenjaan stew and herbed rice with fish and their accompaniments, was flung into a corner, and all of us, terrified, half stood up and stared at the vast tree that had sprung from the kitchen floor, split the chandelier that hung from the high ceiling, and thrust itself up into the sky. The cooks dropped the dishes full of food, Jamshid Khan and Khanom Joon and Auntie Malek stood open-mouthed and stupefied by the girth and height of

[3] The devil, Azāzīl, the Iblīs who is the leader of the devils according to the Quran and God and the incarnation of love according to an ancient Iranian myth.

the still-growing giant tree, and the two servants froze by the door. Once the tree had settled, it was my Only Brother who asked, "Is it the magic beanstalk?" "Isn't it Zarathustra's tree?" Khanom Joon, with her permanent tear on her left cheek, asked. Mom cautiously picked a red apple from it and then stated with confidence, "It is Eve's Tree of Knowledge." I, who had had religious studies recently at school, jumped on a chair and from the nearest branch picked a mango, something I had not seen until that day, and said, "It's the Tuba Tree." Dad examined the enormous, blessed tree's various leaves and fruits and said, "it's the Bas-Tokhmeh Tree,"[4] but it was our Leyla, the smallest member of the family, who with her usual powers of intuition, as if she was already predicting the disasters that would occur in two years' time, had the final word. "It is the Tree of the Incident," she said.

We were still stupefied by the ever-growing giant tree when the mansion began to shake and hundreds of pairs of birds, each one a different shape and color and size, broke the windows and knocked down the doors, and, singing, perched on the branches of the tree, their noise turning our mansion into a wild woodland orchestra. This was not all; we saw that the branches that had broken under the birds' assault quickly grew back and were restored to their original shape. Our breath was trapped in our chests until Dad finally came to his senses and, pensively straightening the glasses that were askew on his face, inspected the leaves on the tree, not one of which resembled any of the others, before correcting his opinion: "this is both the Bas-Tokhmeh Tree and the Gowkaran Tree; it is the tree of life and eternity."

From the very first day we were worried about how people would react. We were waiting for them to come and make

[4] The tree of life. A tree from Iranian myth reckoned to heal all illnesses. The "Many-Seed' Tree is the source of all the plants on earth; all species of plants grow from it. The Simorgh, the bird of Iranian myth, has its nest in this tree. This tree is located in the Sea of Farakhkard, the endless cosmic sea.

enquiries, or even for them to report to Rasht and Tehran about the giant tree which we had henceforth decided to call the Gowkaran Tree. Dad was worried that the inhabitants of Zorvan, our village, would want to cut the tree down so they could build the big mosque that was supposed to be erected next to the rundown school in the middle of the village, yet the days came and went and nobody asked anything about the tree. At first, we thought that people would talk about the matter discreetly amongst themselves and would write letters in secret to the towns and capitals of the province and the country, but a week and a month and a season passed and finally we were convinced that people couldn't see the tree at all. Even the servants, who were constantly moving between the villages and towns of the surrounding area, assured us that nobody ever made enquiries about the tree. This fact set our minds somewhat at ease, and yet we were still a little concerned. The first to wonder was Only Brother. "You mean this tree doesn't actually exist?" Dad, despite all the books he had read, books of history and philosophy and literature, both old and new, was unable to respond to this enquiry. To be or not to be, that is the question! Then the two Big Sisters, who, even though they weren't twins, always talked at the same time, got hungry and fell asleep at the same time, asked at the same time, "You mean we don't actually exist?" When matters had reached this point, although the question was shocking, we laughed, and everyone thought to themselves, "So the school doesn't exist either? What about other people and our classmates? What about this little border village and our five- or six-hundred-year-old mansion?" And old Little Sister suddenly said, "Either nothing exists, or everything exists." That day we all laughed at what she said, but I suddenly realized that in our mysterious and historic mansion a prophet had been born.

Everything was ready for us. The cooks, on Mom's orders, extracted oil from the olives, grapes, avocados, and coconuts that grew on the tree, and I ate so many sour cherries and black mulberries that my teeth turned numb. Our Only Brother, Mehrab, ate so many bananas, which, as all Iranians know, is a "hot" food, that his entire body broke out in a rash from the heat. My big sisters, Mina and Mandana, ate pineapples and coconuts one after the other, whilst Reza and Nader, the two house-servants, on Dad's orders made wine, and distilled arak from the red and white grapes, and left them to settle in the big earthenware vats in the attic or in the store behind the house. That left my little sister, Leyla. She was the only old child, the only albino member of this great sprawling dynasty, and had gotten so used to not eating that she looked thin and yellow and frail. Every day, Maryam, one of the three mansion cooks, before picking several baskets of fruit on Mom's orders for her own household and for the other servants and cooks, picked a dish full of nutritious fruit and put it in front of our white-haired little sister so that she might devour it, yet she didn't touch a thing.

Though at the time Dad was only with us on weekends and the rest of the week would stay in Tehran and attend to his University affairs, he had no choice but to get stuck in, and along with Only Brother and Nader and Reza and Hasrat, our gardener, repair the glass in the windows, the ceiling, and the attic. Although it had now been confirmed that apart from the mansion residents, nobody could see the tree, Dad was afraid that if he were to hire some workers to repair, they would see it. He spent several weeks repairing, after which it occurred to him that, instead of the big old table in the center of the kitchen which the tree had split in two, they might build a round table around the trunk of the tree. That is exactly what they did. A big, twelve-person table. In this way the Tree of Knowledge, the Tree of Life, the Bas-Tokhmeh Tree, the Gowkaran Tree, the Tree of the Incident, became the kitchen's center of gravity. Of the kitchen, which was the mansion's center of gravity. Of the mansion, which was Zorvan's center of gravity. And, God knows, perhaps the center of gravity of the province and even the country. A clear order was given to the cooks and servants that, until further notice, they should be careful to admit absolutely nobody to the mansion and the courtyard, even individuals who usually came and went every week in the execution of their duties, such as the postman, the florist, the tailor, and taxi drivers. All these activities would have to be carried out behind the mansion gate. It didn't occur to anybody, however, that this order would very soon be infringed with the entry of all sorts of close and distant relatives for the annual votive food-giving ceremonies.

Khanom Joon always used to say that before this mansion, there had been others in that very garden, in the very same place, and that if you were to dig under the walls or the building, you would find the remains of eleven other mansions. She always said with pride: "this garden is at least three or four thousand years old. The roots of our family stretch right back to that distant time." She once took me up to the balcony of the upper story and told me to look into the great blue pool in the middle of the courtyard. I did. "Can you see the reflection of this mansion in the water?" she asked. Yes, I could. "Look again," she said. "You must be able to see the reflections of the eleven other mansions?" No, I couldn't. "Because you don't have the eye of the heart," said Khanom Joon. And she herself used to sit, every afternoon before sunset, in a rocking chair on the balcony and stare at the reflection of those eleven other mansions in the great turquoise pool.

The idea that nothing in this world has a definite beginning occurred to me as I was thinking of the mansion. In the little time he had to spend with us, Dad used to say that based on this reason and that reason, this house is four hundred years old, whereas Dad's grandfather, Jamshid Khan, used to say that exactly for this reason and another reason, this house is five or six hundred years old. And the only person who had more precise information than everybody was Khanom Joon, Dad's grandmother, the mansion's principal heir and our extended family's custodian of the Zoroastrian religion, who always left important questions without response. It was at just those times that I would think to myself, "What if, just like I think nothing in this world has an exact beginning, Khanom Joon thinks that no question in this world has an exact answer?" At the time, I had just finished reading Bozorg Alavi's novel *Her Eyes* and was thinking about love. On the question of what love really is, I was asking myself why, despite Farangis's devotion, did Master Makan belittle and ignore her love.

I had just turned fifteen and the world about me was not only interesting and strange but was also an endless labyrinth. Or worse, it was an encyclopedia, each of whose entries could only be understood by consulting several others. Despite all these words, all these entries, I had all the same come to doubt the meaning of love. Why is it, I asked, that in every story love appears in a different color and shape. And this was how it came about that I picked up a two-hundred-page notebook bound in red cloth from Dad's study and started to write down important love scenes and dialogues from stories and films so that I could understood a little more about love. The moment where Rhett Butler says to Scarlett O'Hara, "No, I don't think I will kiss you, although you need kissing, badly. That's what's wrong with you. You should be kissed and often, and by someone who knows how." Or when the Gatsby and Daisy are alone together for the first time: "His hand took hold of hers, and as she said something low in his ear, he turned toward her with a rush of emotion. I think that voice held him most, with its fluctuating, feverish warmth, because it couldn't be over-dreamed—that voice was a deathless song."

The two hundred pages were quickly filled up, but this didn't mean I grasped anything new about love. On the contrary. I was even more perplexed. I tossed and turned in bed, keeping sleep away by thinking of lovers in novels quarrelling over love. I turned from this side to that and imagined that everyone was invited to a grand soirée in our mansion on a moonlit night and that I pulled each one of them into a corner and, while pointing out the lovers from the other films and novels to them, asked them, "How come you fell in love with this one and not, for example, that one over there? Mr. Rick, despite all that love for Ilsa who right now is looking at you from the corner of the verandah with those big, round, sad eyes, how come you chose morality? Is love superior or morality? Or Leyla, you timid traditional girl, why did you not stay in love with Saeed? Look at handsome Saeed, in the corner thinking of you with these sentences constantly turning in his mind: "One hot summer day, on exactly August 13, at around a quarter to three in the afternoon, I fell in love. The many bitternesses and the poison of separation I have tasted have made me wonder time after time whether, if it had been the 12 or 14 of August, maybe it would not have turned out this way."

Each question led to another one in my mind, until in the end I jumped out of bed before sunrise, convinced that I had to start the second notebook. For the second two-hundred-page notebook, bound in green cloth, I would have to talk to real people and ask them about their real experiences of being in love. It would be better to start with members of the family and then I would get to Zorvan and Rasht and school. I would have to ask, "Have you ever been in love? What is the point of falling in love? Whatever love might be, it's not water or bread that not having it will kill you! Just one simple question, kind sir: what, from your point of view, is love?"

So that was how I set off about the house, notebook in hand, to find out everyone's opinion on love, although I quickly ran into the fundamental problem: not one of the mansion's adults was prepared to talk comfortably and clearly and transparently about love, or explain what love was from their perspective. Everyone dealt with the matter at great length by means of hints and allusions, or with generalities and laughter and jokes and tales and sarcastic remarks, and after all that sent me on a wild goose chase. Some of them, like Dad, brought issues of morality and social custom to the fore, while others, like Jamshid Khan, took matters in the direction of old and instructive tales. When I asked the servants about love, one by one they turned red and shy and embarrassed, took refuge in hidden corners of the mansion. Only Shafiqeh, before running out of the kitchen, said that in Zorvan when someone talks of love to another person, it means they want to kiss that person and do other sorts of things with them. But before I could ask her what other sorts of things she meant she ran out of the kitchen. Meanwhile, only the Sisters and Only Brother listened seriously to my questions, but in the end they all said that these are the same questions they had themselves. Just like me, they too were novices when it came to love.

Out of all these people coming and going night and day in the sprawling mansion, it was only Khanom Joon who caught me unawares by telling me about the family's love affairs. Khanom Joon was well informed about the details of the past loves of the individuals of this great dynasty, and said, "This family has two madnesses, inherited by each generation from the previous: one is the madness of love and falling in love, the other the madness of memoir-writing." Then she referred me to the rusty old trunk in the corner of the attic, in which up until the present day 1,762 notebooks containing the memoirs of our ancestors had been gathering dust. Some of them had even used other languages, or made-up languages, so that the secrets of their love would not be revealed. Like the Zargari or Morghi languages, or languages that did not even have names. "Then why did Jamshid Khan say something else?" I asked. Khanom Joon wiped away the permanent tear from her left cheek and laughed but said nothing. "So, you definitely know what love is?" I asked. Yet even while recounting the long stories and adventures of our amorous ancestors, she was not able to utter a single exact sentence about the meaning of love. She simply said, "Love is something you understand once it has got you, and by that time it's already too late for you to escape it." "But is it some sort of plague or cholera that you'd want to escape from it?" I said. "It's worse than that," she said with the utmost seriousness.

When I wanted to take leave of Khanom Joon, she looked at me with one of those serious and severe expressions of hers, something I had rarely seen before that day, and said, "I am giving you a clear order not to ask Auntie Malek this question." I didn't ask. I was in no rush . . . I would let information about this great dynasty reach me, as always, in its own time. It reached me . . . when it was already too late and I was already afflicted with that mysterious and fatal plague and cholera.

That day as I was going back to my room after seeing Khanom Joon, it occurred to me that in this family, everyone talks of love as ill-reputed and ill-omened, and yet every one of them has at least once or twice secretly sacrificed themselves for love. Like Jamshid Khan, a few scraps of whose own ill-reputed adventure in love I had heard about, the full version of which would much later pass from mouth to mouth in the family until finally reaching me. Or the ill-omened amorous adventure of Hasrat and Zomorrod[5]. The story went that Hasrat, our gardener, and Zomorrod, the only girl with emerald eyes in the whole of Zorvan, who died at the age of sixteen from a mysterious illness, were in love and besotted with each other but, according to Hasrat, one of the neighbors, a girl who was jealous, bewitched Zomorrod, or alternatively, according to the Zorvan fortune-teller, Zomorrod was caught by the Illumination of Love. For as soon as her innocent heart had fallen in love, she woke up one morning and not only did she see everything as endlessly transparent, but she saw things, people, and beings that others could not see. One day she awoke and realized that her hearing had grown so strong that not only could she hear sounds from a long way off but she could also hear the voices of people and beings others could not see. Eventually, one day, her speech

[5] The Farsi word for emerald.

became so powerful, penetrating so deeply into the minds of others, and she talked so much to the people of Zorvan about the weird and wonderful things and people and beings she saw, that they set aside whatever they were doing and like metamorphosed beings followed her everywhere, asking her to talk to them more and more, until one night she went to sleep and never woke up. The following day her body disappeared, as if it had turned into steam and vanished into thin air. Hasrat, who had up to that point been called Hamid, changed his name, to Hasrat; a name that means deep regret, and spent the rest of his days deeply regretting Zomorrod. The people went back to their work and life, and gradually forgot Zomorrod, her supernatural abilities, and her penetrating speech.

Time passed and the only new thing to happen in our family was that one day our white-haired sister Leyla, whose voice was rarely heard around the house, brought a long rope and, with her small hands and feet, with great effort, yet noiselessly, hauled herself up onto the kitchen table and then, amid the chirping and cawing and cooing of the birds, whose presence and incessant noise in the mansion and garden we had got used to, set up a swing. The cooks protested that the kitchen was no place for a swing, but when we sisters and Only Brother saw her beautiful long white hair bouncing up and down with the movements of the swing, we were happy that our little sister of prophetic manner was busy doing something other than staring blankly with her colorless eyes. So, it came about that, when we sat around the table eating breakfast, lunch, and dinner from the produce of the tree, our little sister used to play on the swing alongside us. Gradually we all came to accept that she fed herself on air and that only sometimes, for the sake of amusement, would she pick an astringent medlar and suck it in a corner of her cheek while muttering things that were more like the ambiguous poems or scattered predictions of a banished prophet. One time, after a few days' silence, as we were eating breakfast, she turned to us from the swing and said, "Once that day arrives, it will be too late." The food got stuck in Mom's mouth, and Khanom Joon, who, with her own eyes, had seen God knows how many births and deaths in this mansion already, with complete calm said to the latest being born into this family, "Which day, my dear?" Leyla, looking at her with her white eyelashes and pallid pupils and swinging back and forth, answered, "The day when he falls among the sheep next to the nomads' tents and doesn't stand up again." Jamshid Khan frowned deeply and asked, "Who? What?" Leyla came calmly down from the swing. She stood on the table next to my glass of milk and, with that small frame of hers looked meaningfully at all of us, and in a tone which seemed to say, don't you know? said, "Uncle. To say goodbye." Whereupon she jumped down from the table and left the kitchen to go off into one of the snug corners of the mansion to talk and play with someone the cooks and servants called her "birthmate."[6] But before she did, she stopped again and turned to me and said, "To be honest, nobody knows what it is exactly, but everyone behaves as if they did." Then she turned and left the kitchen. Everyone looked at me in astonishment, but I knew what she was talking about. She was talking about love.

There were still two years left until the revolution, but later it occurred to me to ask why, if, as it was rumored, people were able to see Khomeini's face in the moon, why couldn't they also see the enormous tree stretching up to the sky in our mansion. And so it was that one day when all five of us, on our way to school, saw a village girl with a red umbrella ascend into the sky and stop there, we were not surprised, but we were unsure whether other people could see her or not. Nader, our driver,

[6] Birthmate, *hamzād*: in folk belief, whenever any human is born, a being perfectly resembling them but made of the stuff of a jinn or peri is created, growing alongside them; it is possible that they sometimes meet. In popular belief, the birthmate possesses supernatural powers such as access to underground treasures.

pulled over, and in a heat so intense that it was roasting our eyeballs, stared at the girl in astonishment. The locals later tried to explain what happened by saying that on a hot day, on account of the high-tension electricity transmission wires, it may have been possible. But for us the why wasn't very important. For us it was important to know whether anyone else apart from us could see the girl up in the air, one hand holding the strap of her bag and the other her red umbrella. This is what we were thinking when the girl dropped the bag and it fell on top of us and Nader as we were watching her open-mouthed. When we ran under the burning sun to the village coffee house and recounted what had happened, though nobody believed what we said, they came with us and stood under the high-tension wires and saw the girl still hanging there, umbrella in hand. Phew . . . great! So people could see her. This came as a tremendous relief to us but did not solve another of our problems. People persisted all the same in not seeing the giant tree in the middle of our kitchen.

That day people from the surrounding paddy fields and orchards slowly gathered and eventually concluded that they should build a very long ladder and bring the girl down. Under the hot sun, which had been wearing everyone out for three whole months now, twenty men together sawed oak planks, hammered in nails and wound rope, until finally a ladder with several stabilizing legs was made. The inhabitants of three villages gathered under the high-tension wires next to the great paddy fields and held the ladder so that they could bring down the girl, whose name we had understood to be Ehteram. But they never got that far. As everyone was watching her and her red umbrella, she waved a hand at her family who were standing apprehensively underneath, and then she rose up, higher and higher, passing in between the high-tension wires before disappearing into the blue sky above.

The long ladder stayed where it was, between land and sky, people holding it and looking in shock at the spot where, only a few moments earlier, Ehteram had been waving at them. It was only when a bewildered stork came and sat on the top step of the ladder, making it totter, that they came to their senses, and Ehteram's family lowered their hands, which had until then been suspended in the air, and opened their mouths, which had until then been open in shock, still wider, and screamed and cried. There was uproar, but before that, the first person to come to their senses and move away from the crowd was the Zorvan's fortune-teller. As she moved away from us, she muttered, "It's a good thing that the innocent girl went off to fairyland, because otherwise I'd seen in her horoscope that they were going to marry her off very soon, that her husband would take a second wife, and that afterwards her daughter would fall into a big pot of votive gheymeh stew and burn, while she herself would go mad." This utterance reminded Maryam and Shafiqeh and Shahnaaz, the mansion's three cooks, who had been drawn there by all the commotion, of this year's votive food, which had been erased from everyone's mind on account of the affair of the Gowkaran tree in the middle of the kitchen and that summer's burning heat.

We kids were glad of this reminder of the annual votive food, because if things had carried on the way they were, it would have been impossible to go on with our daily lives. We eventually had to resort to finding an excuse to extricate ourselves from the tree's circle of influence, because all our thoughts and attention and time had been devoted to it: in the morning we awoke to the deafening birdsong from its branches; when it was time to play we climbed up its trunk and went on the swing; when hungry we ate its various fruits; and once or twice when far from the gaze of the adults we fried or made omelets with the eggs of its weird and wonderful birds. In bed we talked about the tree together, its secrets and mysteries, as well as imagining fantastic things about the Simorgh who, it was said, had its nest at the top of it. Asleep, too, we dreamed of it. From our perspective, it wasn't fair things should go on like this. There were still too many things in this world we needed to devote time to: studying, the Communists on the other side of the border and the people who fled there in secret wishing for a classless society, the murmurings of discontent with the Shah from religious folk and leftists, and the televisions and telephones which were just then arriving in the surrounding villages and which people were talking about excitedly. We still had to devote our time and thoughts to many more things so that we might perhaps, before dying, succeed in at least having an overall picture of this world in our minds.

If we didn't take care of ourselves, we too would be caught in the grip of that ancient fever which the ancients had called the Fever of Objects, except that after seeing the tree we realized that this fever not only concerned objects but also trees. Like the Kyrgyz man who one day many years earlier turned up in town, left the city in the direction of Zorvan on the forest road, and made his way straight to our mansion, set on the highest hill overlooking all the surrounding villages. He approached the gardener, who was picking roses and irises and verbenas, as he did every morning, to put in vases in the rooms, and asked after Dad. As soon as he saw Dad, the Kyrgyz stranger told him he had to come with him to the depths of the forest. Years later when he told us the story, Dad said that the man, without even knowing him, had come straight up to him and addressed him using his first name, "Fereydoun Khan." And in his broken Persian the man had said that behind this mansion, to the north, five kilometers deep into the forest, well before the frontier river between Iran and the Soviet Union, there was an ancient wild medlar tree which they had to get to before its blossoms faded. The old Kyrgyz man also ordered that no servant or assistant should accompany them. Dad told us that despite not liking the Kyrgyz man's commanding tone, he didn't say no, and indeed he was curious and trusted him and kept on walking him until he realized that the path was repeating itself. The compass was showing the right way, and the sun was setting in the west without veering from its path, but the trees, mosses, black hawthorn, and common medlar and greengage blossoms on the route ahead of them kept repeating. At first Dad thought that they were going around in circles by mistake, but no, they were moving ahead and yet they were not moving ahead . . . They made marks with red mud on the trees and mossy stone slabs and soon saw that they were moving ahead, that they came across no red marks, and yet they were not moving ahead. Eventually the Kyrgyz man said, "This is as I dreamt it. We move ahead but the forest doesn't."

"So, what should we do then?" Dad asked.

"We must make a sacrifice. We should cry together."

"What does that mean?" Dad said. "Why?"

"I don't know either," the man answered, "but this is what I dreamt, that we have to cry at the foot of the medlar tree with fragrant white blossoms."

"Look around you. It's spring. Every single tree in the forest has white blossoms."

"That tree, it's old," the man said. "It has blossoms on it but it also has fruit."

They went on their way, scrutinizing all the medlar trees until finally they found it. The wild medlar that had both blossoms and fruit on it. They sat at its foot and wept a floodtide of tears. Dad said that at first he couldn't cry at all, but the old Kyrgyz man was so saddened that they had not yet reached the tree that tears began to wet his cheeks and ran down their deep and narrow furrows. Then when Dad saw that he was crying, he was reminded of the River of Tears in the World of the Dead[7], and he too started to cry. The more they cried, the more the petals of the blossoms fell on their heads and shoulders. When a petal fell on the Kyrgyz man's right eyelash, he wiped away his tears

[7] A river beneath the Chinvat Bridge in Zoroastrian mythology, it overflows with the tears of those who mourn the deceased and prevents the deceased from crossing into paradise.

and tapped Dad's shoulder, indicating it was time to get going. Their sacrifice had been accepted. Then they moved ahead to their right and the forest too moved ahead until they reached an old black hawthorn tree laden with blossom, under which they saw a great, mossy stone slab with the carved symbol of a tortoise. The old man stopped and took a piece of shiny green crystal from his knapsack, placed it on the ground next to the tree and under the great stone slab and started to pray and supplicate, singing in Kyrgyz. Dad sat down in a corner and held a cigarette in his hand. He said that the wrinkles on the man's face were so many and so deep that it was as if each one of them had been precisely created by each life-sapping event or instance of suffering in the man's life. When the Kyrgyz prayers and supplications were over, the man dug a hole, placed his shiny green crystal in it, threw soil over it, before finally opening his flask and pouring water on it. A few moments later his sad and thoughtful face suddenly loosened up and became joyous, and he turned to Dad for the first time and laughed and said, "It's ooooover! I'm doooooone with it. The curse has been lifted. Now we can go back."

Upon their return, without resting in our house for a minute, the man bid my father goodbye and left. Dad only had the chance to ask, "Why did you bury such a gorgeous crystal?"

The Kyrgyz man gazed penetratingly at Dad. "Never once allow yourself to think of retrieving that crystal, because otherwise you too will come down with the Fever of Objects, and you will never be able to leave its baleful circle of influence, unless years and years afterwards it is told you in a dream where and how you might bury it so that its baleful effect might be cleansed from your life."

So it was that, as soon as Ehteram was far off in the sky, we all suddenly sprang into action, because we remembered that very soon fifty or sixty relatives, be they close or distant, would be heading for our mansion just as they did every year at this time, so that we could be together for the mourning days, Tasua and Ashura, in accordance with Mom's family tradition, and at noon on Ashura offer votive food in the village mosque to a thousand people from the village and the surrounding settlements. Given Mom's complicated recipes for gheymeh stew with rice, fesenjaan stew, chicken and plum stew, and sour chicken, the cooks and servants were, like every year, busy preparing and purchasing the necessary ingredients. They bought a hundred and seventy kilos of best quality Taram rice from our own paddies, a hundred mesqals of Qayenat saffron, a kilo of Indian cinnamon, a hundred local chickens, fifteen kilos of home-made tomato paste, twenty kilos of Azarshahr split peas, ten kilos of Omani lemons from Shiraz, twenty kilos of Bukhara prunes from Kharv, and the rest of what was necessary, and found space for them in the ice chests and the shelves and sideboards of the back courtyard storeroom, and following the annual custom, covered the vats of wine and arak for those two particular days.

Two or three weeks later, all of my maternal and paternal relatives descended, one by one, two by two, group by group, on our mansion and garden, our mansion with its two stories, its four tall columns at the front, its ten big bedrooms decorated with hunting scenes and lovers drinking wine and nature scenes from the Safavid, Afsharid, Zand, and Qajar periods, which had for years been host to dozens of friends and relatives and the greats of the country's culture and arts, and for one week before Tasua and Ashura, and one week afterwards, became the annual gathering place for celebration and dancing and wine-drinking and eventually for religious mourning. These ceremonies had as many fans in our mansion as did the Sadeh and Chaharshanbeh Suri and Nowruz and Mehregan Festivals. It was an excuse for our weird and wonderful family to get together, a family which, like this mysterious tree, had made space for every kind of political and religious and ethnic belief and taste.

The Safavid period was one when, as family documents show, we became prominent as rice merchants, gradually also finding our way into politics, although certain oral accounts take our history back further still. But this is only the appearance of the matter. Certain parts of the truth are concealed among the scattered leaves and notebooks of memoirs half devoured by termites in that old rusty trunk in the corner of the attic. Dad says that, based on the evidence of those handwritten pages, the Safavid era was the worst of times for our Zoroastrian ancestors. For that reason, the builder of this magnificent mansion, Jamshid Khan I, who, they say, was an intelligent and ambitious merchant who knew how to enjoy life, had little choice other than to use one of the tools Muslims use—*taqiyyah*, pious dissimulation and abstinence from religious duties—in order to first cement and then extend his economic and political influence and power. They relate that Jamshid Khan I did his best impression of the devout pillars of the community by day, bending and prostrating in prayer and forever fingering his prayer beads, while at night he could be found in the mansion's underground fire temple, seven paces by seven paces of purified ground, casting sandalwood, frankincense, and other incenses into the sacred fire and with a bloody heart reading the Aeyo Srauthram night prayer: "I believe in the Mazda-worshipping religion brought by Zarathustra. I am a follower of the Ahuran teachings which are far from the devil of lying and worship of duality. I am a Zoroastrian monotheist, and I only see Ahura Mazda in the divine light of praise. I praise and declare worthy and make happy the guardian angel of night, the pure Aeyo Srauthram. I praise and declare worthy and make happy all the walkers on Zarathustra's path of paradise, as well as the Lord of the Paradises."

While Khanom Joon is always proud of our being Zoroastrian, unlike others, she brims over with joy at the thought that distant or close relatives might connect and join in union with other peoples or the followers of other religions or beliefs. With her personal encouragement, members of our extended family have married Shiites, Nimatullah Sufis, Jews, and Baha'is, hailing from all the different peoples, Lor, Bakhtiyari, Turkoman, Kurd, and Baluch. Khanom Joon insists to the many generations of her descendants that by, for example, marrying Sunnis and Ismailis and Mandaeans and Assyrian Christians and Yaresanis from every city and land, they turn this family into the symbol of Iran. Some people in our family find fault with her for this, but others say that perhaps what Khanom Joon does has meant that the Zoroastrians of this extended family have remained so emphatically Zoroastrian. Khanom Joon would particularly like to find someone in the family to marry a Yazidi. Whenever the discussion turns to marrying with other peoples and followers of other religions, Khanom Joon beams with joy, and after a detailed conversation about the history of the peoples and religions of Iran and the Middle East, finally sighs and says, "If only people were still Gnostics or Mithraists or Manicheans." And then she plunges into thought and imagination and goes on, "Just think if the Zurvanists or followers of the Wisdom of Khosro were still around!"

Yes, Dad's grandmother, our Khanom Joon, Khosro Khan's Faranak, Auntie Malek's mother, is that kind of woman. That is why in our mansion, the sacred fire of Azar Borzin Mehr has been kept, since the days of Reza Shah's, when Zoroastrians suffered less harassment and bother, in a room with a glass wall on the upper story, and is shown with pride to those guests with a desire to see it, so that they might recall that they live in an ancient land.

All close or distant relatives, friends and acquaintances and strangers that find their way, in whatever fashion, to our mansion, are sooner or later, with Khanom Joon's encouragement, taken to see the sacred fire which, according to her, as of 1976, has been burning without interruption for 4,583 years. Whenever someone asks Khanom Joon where she gets this figure of 4,583 from, she replies with great seriousness, "Sorry, but that is a family secret." And it seemed that this really was a family secret, since it had been arranged that in the future the secret be communicated to the five of us children, or at least to one of us who would become custodian of the sacred fire. The more I think of Khanom Joon, the more I realize that she treats religion like art, and the sacred fire like an ancient work of art.

As soon as the guests arrived from all over the country, I recognized him straightaway. Tall and thin, with straight black hair that kept falling over his forehead and hands that were often in his pockets lest they be polluted by this world. He was exactly how I had imagined him, like he was in my dream. Which dream? I don't remember . . . By the great pool in the middle of our tree-festooned courtyard, exactly at the moment a fearful sparrow jumped off a branch, and the light coming through the branches quivering under the pressure of the sparrow's feet fell on his straight hair which he was pushing aside with his right hand, my breath was taken away, my left eye twitched and my heart stood still for three seconds so that I could keep the breath of virgin madness, full of trepidation, within me. "Will I dare to ask him about love?" I thought.

I looked at my feet, which, just like the bronze boots of Reza Shah in Saadabad Palace I had seen on a postcard, had glued me to the ground, deprived of will. In the midst of all the commotion, all the cheek kissing and hugging and I've-missed-yous, he had still not caught sight of me, meaning I was able, with a resolution I had not at all suspected in myself, to get my bronze feet to move, turn my back on him and everyone else, crawl up the first and second flights of stairs and take myself into my habitual hidden corner in the mansion's hot and steamy attic, to my spot on the mouse-gnawed Russian armchair that stood beside the moth-eaten English one, which lay next to the decrepit American one, left over from the Second World War, where only occasionally tired ghosts of distant relatives kept you company. Whenever I sat on one of these faded, cobwebbed armchairs, I felt as if I were sitting on the Persian Corridor train, the history of oil, of Russian and American and British soldiers and the corpses of five million Iranians. On the three armchairs on which, as Dad says, the Churchillian Churchill,[8] Stalin the Terrible, and the fickle Roosevelt sat, unbeknown to the Shah, on the verandah of the Soviet Embassy in Tehran and from up there posed for the foreign journalists while in their minds plotting how to put the noose around the Persian cat's neck.[9] Dad always said these three chairs—exactly how they ended up in our attic I don't know—are a reminder of the fate of Iran after the discovery of oil.

Curled up in the chair, I let history go and breathed in the air of love and suddenly realized that from now on I was caught. That said, in my dreams I had seen that this madness would grip us both, neither of us knowing when it began or how long it would go on. Just like this mansion and this timeless tree and the history of foreigners' incursions and invasions in this country.

The commotion of the new arrivals mixed in with the hullabaloo of the birds still drifted up to the attic. As the noise they made moved from one room to the next and finally reached the kitchen, I thought of the tree and the birds on it. Could the new arrivals see the tree? Could he see it? At that very moment, an invisible hand squeezed my shoulder and brought calm streaming back into my veins. No doubt it was one of those kind distant family ghosts. One of those who had died of cholera during Great Famine, or one of those whose body had been host to a Russian, British, or American bullet.

"I'm scared," I said.

[8] In Iran the epithet Churchillian implies two-faced and malicious.

[9] A reference to the shape of Iran national boundaries, which resembles a sitting cat.

The gentle voice of a young man answered, "I was scared too."

"When falling in love?"

"No," he said, "when dying. They're similar."

"What's going to happen then?" I asked, doubtfully.

"Nothing," he said, "at first you feel like you've just come to life, but after that you die every day from sadness."

Suddenly it crossed my mind that, if this is my fate, then what is the point of being all sorrowful and afraid. Sooner or later, I would have to face it. I got up from the chair, shook the dust off my clothes, went over to Dad's vats of wine and opened the lid of one of the oldest ones, on which was written my date of birth: November 10, 1962. I plunged the earthenware bowl into it, and for the first time in my life, I drank wine. Wasn't it only a few days ago that Mrs. Mohammadi, our literature teacher, had been teaching us Attar? "If a man dare to beat a path, he must pass through blood, /And onward go though he fall or die, / Step thou too on the path, asking nothing, / For the path itself will tell thee how thou shalt go." I thought that they had written these poems for me and for us . . . After all, they hadn't written them just to be set down in history! This was how I set off, a little tipsy, full of a false self-confidence given to me by the wine, and headed down the attic stairs to come face to face with him.

The rooms were full of laughing people, excited people, loquacious people. Hellos and kisses and bursts of laughter and murmurs bumped against each other in the air of the rooms and embraced. Amid all this hubbub, Auntie Malek, inheritor of the family madness, who had lived all her life in this very mansion, went quickly to greet Naser Khan, a decrepit old man who was so distantly related to my father and grandfather that we always forgot how. It was the two of them who were supposed to pass on the mysterious madness to one of us wretched children. You see, in our family tree, which Auntie Malek was drawing up with what remained of her fantastical mind, it was evident that this inherited madness might also be contagious. We didn't believe it! We were waiting to see if these relatives, close and distant, both the sane and the crazy, could see the tree and the birds on it or not. As it happened, the sane ones could see the tree but behaved as if they were crazy and couldn't see it at all. Unlike the crazy ones, who acted in the sanest manner possible and did not take their eyes off the tree. As if whether the tree existed or not was not even a question for the sane ones! Uncle Esmail, Mom's brother, plucked a ripe tangerine from the tree and ate it and went back to the living room without asking a single question. Uncle Bijan, Dad's brother, picked a peach from the adjacent branch and, as he took a great bite from it, addressed himself to Uncle Ebrahim, another of Mom's brothers, and the two of them took themselves off, conversing all the while, to the store behind the house so that they could wet their lips with Dad's vats of wine. Our maternal grandmother and grandfather acted as if no tree with a girth of three or four meters that had split open so high a ceiling and whose crown was lost in the clouds and whose birdsong had turned into the background music in our house existed at all, or, if it did, that was as it should have been. The children too, as far as they were able, climbed the tree and ate its fruits and got stomach aches and twisted and turned while queuing for the mansion toilets. That's it. Amidst all this commotion, only he plucked a red apple from the tree and moved past the crowd so that he could get to where I was, behind everyone else, leaning on the kitchen wall, and as always observing others in silence. In disbelief I saw him standing opposite me; he took my right hand in his, placed the red apple in it, turned his back on me and was once more lost in the crowd. Nobody looked at the tree anymore, and nobody said anything about it. Only my restless heartbeat against my ribcage like an imprisoned sparrow hopping furiously about, wanting to jump through the bars, screech, and announce, "So you recognized me? So, you recognized me? So, you recognized me?"

For the newly arrived guests, the matter of the tree stopped there. Only a week later, on the Day of Ashura, when all the dishes were cooking on the wood stoves in the back courtyard, Mom's grandmother, being the expert on votive stews, tasted the gheymeh and realized the Omani lemons had not made it sour enough. This led her to immediately order that ten or twelve giant bergamot sour oranges be picked from the tree, their juice extracted and poured into the big pots full of the gheymeh stew devoted to Imam Hoseyn. That is all.

But the crazy ones in the family reacted more sanely; Old Auntie Malek, the most beautiful, proudest, most amorous, and the maddest woman we knew in all of our father's family, noticed the tree in the middle of the mansion kitchen the moment it appeared, but that day she behaved as if she were seeing it for the very first time. She took out her wedding gown, whose stains had survived every wash, which had been kept sixty or seventy years in the wardrobe, put it on, and, laughing uproariously, plucked the pink and white blossoms and made herself a great fragrant crown which she placed on her long white hair. Then, crown on head and wearing her stained wedding gown, she danced and danced so much around the broad trunk of the tree in the middle of the kitchen, amidst the votive saucepans and the sacks of onions and potatoes, that she eventually passed out and fell asleep on the spot. But before sleeping, she moaned, "Did you see I said so? Did you see I said so?"

On the other hand, ninety-three-year-old Naser Khan neither danced nor laughed nor even touched the tree. What he did was place a chair in the furthest corner of the kitchen and stay a whole day and night awake staring at it. He didn't have a single bite to eat, and despite the commotion of people and pans, he didn't speak a single word. Only in the last hour of his sit-in did he draw near to it, frowning and pounding the floor categorically with his cane, passing through the people and pans and sacks of potatoes and onions, climbing over the table built around it, and, in the midst of the marvelous and bewitching smells of the foods being cooked and the spices being used, undid the zip on his trousers and relieved himself at the base of the tree. From amid the uric acid steam, he turned to everyone else and said, "You only think of your own food, you selfish lot. From now on I'll feed this child."

Chapter Two

A few days before Tasua and Ashura, amid all the commotion of the adults' to-ing and fro-ing, we children had to sit beside the rice and the split peas for an entire day, cleaning each grain by grain under the rain of Arabic words that our maternal grandmother and grandfather took it in turns to recite from the Quran in order to purify the votive food, before throwing them in the enormous pots, in just three of which all of us children would fit. The time would have gone by painfully slowly had we let the two of them keep on forcing us to labor like that. So it was at sunset, as soon as they got up to recite the Sunset and Evening prayers, we all fled. Mehrab and I mounted our horses, Afsun and Shabro, and everyone else ran after us. We had only time to put a few apples and kolucheh and bottles of water in our knapsacks. As soon as we had made it to the woods and hid ourselves under the trees, we stopped and breathed a sigh of relief and started laughing and dancing and playing. We danced and played so much and made so much fun of Grandmother and Grandfather and their compulsory Quran recitation, that we didn't realize when it had become properly night, and that thick fog had surrounded us. At that very moment when we all felt we were lost, our hairs stood on end with fear, and we fell silent. Then all at once and all together, we started shouting, but soon enough the wall of trees reflected our cries back to us. Nobody answered. The birds had fallen silent, and the breeze stopped blowing. Occasionally Afsun and Shabro pawed the ground and snorted. A far-off bird sang briefly, while nearby a sheltopusik hauled itself across the dry leaves and moved off.

The first to come to his senses was Only Brother. “I’ve got matches,” he said, taking out a box of matches and a cigarette that he had filched from one of the paternal uncles or aunts. A dried leaf caught fire with the first match. A few moments later, we fixed our eyes on each other and counted one another. Including Azadeh, our seven- or eight-year-old cousin on our father’s side, and Mahsa, the spirit of our four-year-old cousin on our mother’s side, who had gotten themselves to the woods by following us, how exactly it was unclear, we numbered twelve. My attention went to Leyla, my little albino sister, who did not take her eyes off the fire, holding tight on to my top with her left hand. Once the light and heat of the fire had warmed our hearts and made us hopeful, we took a vote. Out of the twelve of us, the oldest of whom was nineteen or twenty, seven of us voted to start walking and see where we got to. I was one of those opposed. Mina and Mandana objected: “You know the forest like the back of your hand!” With my hand I gestured to our surroundings as if to say, “But can’t you see?” It was night and we were besieged by the fog that was getting thicker by the second. Only Brother said, “We’re not too far away.” He made a torch by ripping up bits of his sleeve and set off in the direction he guessed was home. I knew it wasn’t.

That night, we pressed on for two hours through the fog and the dark and in anxious silence, squeezing one another’s hands that were sweaty from fear until finally a faint light appeared before us. By the time we had reached the fort, Leyla had fallen asleep in my arms on Shabro, Azadeh our eight-year-old cousin in Mehrab’s arms on Afsun, and Mahsa’s spirit in the arms of her brother Bahman. When we got closer, we saw that the light appearing and disappearing in the fog emanated from a tall stone fort, cylindrical in shape, which we had never seen anywhere near the mansion. Perhaps that wasn’t so strange after all, since ferns and creepers had grown around it and so covered it that the mansion could easily have remained concealed from gaze. It was now very cold, and the fog was so thick that if we drifted a little apart, we quickly lost one another. We were all worried and tired, and all we wished for was to find somewhere safe and warm to sleep. So it was that we tied Afsun and Shabro's reins to an oak tree and all together pushed and shoved the fort's great heavy wooden door until it opened with a loud "creeeeeeeak-kkk." In the profound darkness, a sharp pain shot through my back with the sound of the creaking. The darkness was weighty that night, pressing its heavy hands around my throat. On the door, snakes and creepers of the twelve-petalled flower were depicted in intricate relief. Together with everyone else, I was pushing at the door to open it, and for an instant I felt that the snakes and creepers on the door were moving under my fingers and winding around one another. I drew my hand back in fear. The door opened.

Under the torch's dim light, what we saw in front of us plunged us into minutes of open-mouthed, stunned silence. Our breath was trapped in our chests. Eventually Little Sister, in a trembling and breathless voice murmured, "But . . . this is our own house."

Inside the fort, it was exactly our own house that was before us: in the middle, a living room with a round mahogany table and vases of yellow roses and purple irises and verbenas which a whistling Hasrat had picked that very day and arranged in the vases. With the same mirrorwork on the walls and the same tiled ceiling with Qajar-era images of women bearing wine and the same ten-meter handwoven Nain silk carpet on the floor. On the right-hand side, the grand drawing room with its ebony table in the middle, its set of green French armchairs and sofa for six people, its thirty-meter handwoven Nain silk carpet, its Weber piano made in 1945, and its great bookshelf that covered an entire wall.

Exactly like our own house; two bedrooms on the other side of the drawing room, and the tree in the center of the kitchen. Even the birds from the tree in the middle of the kitchen were busy flying around and singing, some of them perching on the bookshelves and pecking at the books. I walked forward and inspected the books one by one. They were our very own books: Saadi's *Golestan* and *Bostan*, Hafez's complete ghazals and Vahshi Basqi were leaning on Khayyam's quatrains and Baba Taher and both the Moscow and the Beirut editions of Ferdowsi's *Shahnameh,* and the complete poems of Saeb-Tabrizi, Hazin Lahiji, and Iraj Mirza. A little higher up was the row of holy books. The Avesta and the Gathas next to the Torah and the Quran and the Gospels and the Aqdas, the Triple Basket next to the Vedas, the Sikh Adi Granth, the Living Gospel, the Tao Te Ching and I Ching, the Book of Revelation, and the Black Book.

The two Big Sisters inadvertently cried out at the same time, "Mom? Dad? Isn't anybody home?" The sound wound its way around the rooms and returned to us in the silence. Opposite, the twelve steps ending with a twist into the landing and leading, via two rows of semi-circular steps, to the upstairs floor with its eight bedrooms. Even the chandeliers, the dagger, a memento of Jamshid Khan's youth, on the wall, the vases of flowers with pictures of the kings of the Safavid, Afshar, Zand, and Qajar periods with their long moustaches, the multi-colored orosi windows, sleeping porch, family paintings and photographs were also exactly like those of our own house.

We went upstairs in disbelief, and each of us five siblings opened the door to our own bedroom, lay down on our bed for a few minutes, and ran our hands over the table and chairs, books, cassette tapes, and school exercises that we had abandoned an hour before our flight to the forest. When we had all come out of our bedrooms, we stood in silence and confusion in the middle living room and looked at the staircase that would take us up to the floor above. In our house, there was no floor above the first two. But here there was. A few moments later we were all heading up the mysterious staircase like beings radically transformed.

On the floor above, the architecture was more or less the same as the mansion's, but the decoration and the objects found there were completely different, as if they belonged to a far remoter epoch. Here and there a few lanterns and round oil-lamps were lit. We picked them up, and in fear and trepidation, but also with a vague hope, opened the doors one by one. The rooms were full of sumptuous cushions and backrests and large, inlaid wooden thrones covered by silk carpets. In a niche stood a mirror, a handwritten Quran, and a candle. In another niche, a row of handwritten books with leather bindings. I looked at the books: Hafez and Saadi and Baba Taher and Nezami and Attar.

We ascended from floor to floor and encountered objects that were ever older as we went. When, from the third floor up, we saw all the paintings, glazed statues, incense burners, splendidly carved tables and chairs, and silk carpets of extraordinary beauty, we all became convinced that from now on we should call this place "the palace," not "the fort."

In one of the rooms on the fourth floor we broke the wax seal of marqueted wooden chest. A large, handwritten book, bound in leather and with gold-embroidered cloth covers, had been kept in the chest. I opened it. It was the *Shahnameh*. In the hand of, and signed by, the Sage Abolqasem Ferdowsi himself, along with striking and magnificent images inlaid with gold and silver. My hands trembling with excitement, moved by an uncontrollable desire, I picked the book up and opened a page at random for the purposes of divination, choosing according to tradition the seventh verse from the top on the right-hand page: "Look upon this swift-revolving dome / Whence healing and pain come alike." I put the book in my knapsack. Only Brother squeezed my arm, as if to say, *Don't pick it up*. I picked it up. I did not know what lay in store for us during the remainder of the night, but if we made it alive out of this mysterious palace and back to our mansion, I wanted, by seeing this book in my hands, to be able to recall what had befallen us this foggy night in a forest so close to home, in a palace so far away.

We reached a room all around which were arranged great

ancient stone statues and large earthenware vats filled with ancient wine, and beside them musical instruments that resembled tars, ouds, and tombaks. We were thirsty and hungry. We sat down and took out the food we had in our knapsacks. As he, Iraj and Bahman started drinking the wine, we too plucked up the courage, and soon enough it was a cup of the heavy centuries-old wine that was being passed from hand to hand between us. We even gave a mouthful each to the little children. We rapidly warmed up. We were filled with jokes and laughter and without sadness. Only Brother lit some cigarettes, giving us each one so that we could have a drag for the first time. That night, if wine was permitted to all of us, then why shouldn't cigarettes be as well? It was as if the wine and cigarettes were our joint signature on an unwritten agreement stipulating that henceforth the twelve of us would be bearers of common secrets. Secrets we had had no idea of before entering the palace. The roar of our laughter gradually wound its way through the dark corridors, past the rooms with their closed doors and the grand living rooms, moving over the paintings of kings and princes and over the statues, before returning to us once more. One of our cousins on our father's side, Mahin, picked up an old instrument resembling a setar. She wiped the dust off it with sympathy and tenderness, tuned it, and played a melody that had us all swooning. We had no idea that she could play an instrument. "A Souz-o Godaz Figure," she said, closing her eyes and playing. Even as I was transfixed by the mournful sound of Mahin's instrument, I saw that sometimes she opened her sorrowful eyes to stare in front of her, at Iraj, whose attention, it seemed, was on Mozhgan, Mahin's older sister. The world was once again jolted into motion by this gentle and mournful music, reminding us that we were lost, far from home in an unknown and mysterious palace in the depths of the forest that we had, until a few hours ago, thought we knew like the back of our hands. Sorrow, deep regret, solitude, and bewilderment—in short, Iranian traditional music—had built their nests in our hearts. First it was the smaller children who could hold it in no longer and burst into tears. Then we too hugged one another and a few of us also started to cry. As if we had remembered that the drunkenness and the laughter were only an excuse by which we could conceal our anxiety and worries. Between the tears and the mournful music, we were gradually falling asleep when the melody suddenly changed. One of the cousins on our mother's side, Bahman, in irritation, took up a tonbak, and in protest at Mahin's sorrowful music, struck up a comical 6/8 rhythm of the type that would set people's hips dancing, and while staring at me, sang, "Why don't you wear velvet? Why don't you join the fun with us? How much is golden velvet anyway? You have fun with someone else . . ." Mahin then quickly swapped her instrument for a tar and joined him in playing the same tune, and with this cheerful light music, this *takhteh-hōżi* music of the kind that once rang out in the courtyards of humble homes all over the country, excitement and playfulness and joy came back to our hearts. The smaller children jumped into the middle and started bouncing around to the music and roared with laughter. Iraj too leapt up and started dancing. Wasn't it him who was destined, in some future God knows when, to go mad? Then he pulled at Mozghan's hands so that she would dance with him. She danced and we all laughed. I couldn't understand how I then came to find myself there in the middle beside him, his black eyes aflame and fixed on me, me once again, heedless of the world, and the ancient statues with their clay eyes, the night and the forest and the palace, laughing and fooling around and dancing. He, Behnam, meanwhile, hastily took my hand, brought his head close to my ear, and uttered to me the most shocking sentence I had heard until then, or would hear till the end of my life: "I am your restless lover."

In that very moment I felt like my heart had jumped from its seat, a hiccup was caught in my throat, and my lower lip leapt. My legs stopped dancing. I quickly removed my frozen hand from his, and standing amidst all this jostling and bouncing up and down, I stared at him, astonished, for a few brief moments. He stared back. For the first time among the great many first times, their dates and whereabouts unknown, I was unsure what I had heard, nor was I sure what the thing I had heard meant. He didn't tell me, "I love you." He didn't say, "I've fallen in love with you." He said, "I am your restless lover." There was a certainty in the words "I am," as if he was introducing himself. As if, for instance, instead of saying, "I am Behnam Rostami," he had said, "I am your restless lover." And in this "I am" there was a sort of continuity that suggested he had been in love with me for years. As if this love, like his name, had been with him from birth. There was a sort of definite, eternal stillness in the "I" and a sort of continuity in the "am." If he had said, "I've fallen in love with you," there would have been no feeling of definiteness or continuity. If he had said, "I've fallen in love with you," it would have felt more natural, since we were meeting one another for the first time, and whatever was happening had to be new: "I've fallen." Meaning, "I've just fallen in love with you," or "I've just realized that I've fallen in love with you." But he had said, "I am your restless lover." As if in this "I am" were concealed "I was," "I am," and "I will be." Like me, then, had he seen me before, in his dreams? Like me, then, does he think that our love story began a long time ago, and, God knows, perhaps before we were even born? Like children condemned to bear a name that their parents gave them even before marriage or pregnancy? Are we also condemned to our love?

Perhaps because nobody was paying attention to us, he dared to take a step toward me again, bringing his head against the hair close to my ear and telling me, in a commanding tone, "If I hadn't been so afraid tonight, and if I hadn't got so drunk, there would've been no chance I could tell you this. So now that I'm both afraid and drunk, let me say this to you again: I am your restless lover. I am your restless lover. I am your restless lover . . ." The vibration of his voice repeating itself burnt the skin behind my ears and set my heart shaking.

It's not clear why my body then reacted by demonstrating a desire to dance and to flee. Perhaps because my dancing exempted me from having to reply to him or meant that both of us were distracted by something that wasn't as heavy as what he had just been saying. Perhaps it was just an excuse so I could escape from him. I went a little way away from him and, standing amidst all those vats and children, started to flail around. Dancing and drunk, I realized that dancing is the struggle of the soul to leave the body. As if something wanted, with all its force, to leap out through the pores of my skin and be free of the evil of the limits of the bones, muscles, and veins. It was that night and at that very moment that I first felt, with all my being, that other me. I heard its voice. The me who had transcended the limits of the bodily form and yet was haplessly caught in it, and who when I danced or perhaps under the effects of hearing that mysterious sentence or, what do I know, of drinking wine, was struggling with all its limbs to leap out of me, flee, and say to me, "Run . . . get away . . . escape."

We had to come to our senses eventually. An hour later we were once again wandering in the living and other rooms, and by distancing myself from him, I was able to endure his deep and burning gaze weighing on me from beyond the light and shadows and people and ancient statues. While searching through the rooms on the sixth floor, I opened the door of one of them and saw before me a view that froze me to the spot: Iraj and Mozhgan, who had at some unknown point profited from our neglect and inattention and were now, in this room, under the dim light of a tallow lamp and surrounded by ancient clay and stone statues, wrapped around one another, sighing and moaning and moving. I had never in my life seen two half-naked bodies stuck together. Didn't they always say that girls and boys next to one another were like cotton wool and fire? It couldn't be that what Shafiqeh meant that day by "other such things" was this?

They didn't notice me, and with my heart thumping against my ribcage and filling my ears with the noise of its beating, I watched them for a few moments that felt like years. Mozhgan was sitting on a large wooden chest and Iraj in front of her pressed her against himself, and her waist moved away from him and stuck to him again and again in a rapid and monotonous movement . . . I felt like hot blood was surging up into my head and face and ears and my ears were buzzzzzzing. Hearing Mozhgan's protracted sighing, I finally came to my senses and left the room, but as soon as I tried to take refuge in the dark hallway so that my thumping heart would calm down, I caught sight of Mahin, tears in her eyes, supporting herself on the wall beside me. When our eyes met in the half-darkness of the hallway, she said, "With the opening and shutting of this door, the era of our childhood innocence came to an end forever." Then she turned her back on me and disappeared into the darkness of the hallway.

Eventually, on which floor I do not know, I reached yet another room, of how many I do not know. A room completely in ruins, with a broken door, filled with royal jewels and magnificent, decaying, dust-covered clothes; jewel-studded crowns and bracelets and necklaces large and small of ruby and diamond and brilliant, lying next to shaliteh skirts, with moth-eaten headscarves and shawls of termeh cloth in silk and gold thread, silk scarves with mirrorwork and filigree, handwoven woolen cloaks and silken Paisley tonban trousers, faded and decaying, which seemed to have spent centuries on their hangers watching people sleeping and whispering and courting and holding magnificent assemblies with wine-drinking and dancing and music.

How everything was at once familiar and alien. I remembered what Khanom Joon had said. Weren't these the remains of those same eleven mansions which she saw reflected in the water of the pool in the courtyard every day? The walls, floor, and even the ceiling of this room were made of mirrors, and we mistook each other in the bronze mirrors and amid the play of faint light and vague trembling shadows. It was obvious that the effects of drunkenness had not yet worn off; the boys had started clowning about, and if they hadn't been, doubtless they would have set upon the royal jewels. The boys pressed women's clothes up against themselves and did impressions of the women of old, and the girls choked with laughter. Like everyone else I was laughing loudly until, between the forms of the others and of those magnificent, decaying clothes hanging shapelessly from our bodies, I caught sight of the image of me and him staring at one another in the mirror above me, which together with the mirror beneath our feet had created an infinite reflection, and without knowing it, I screamed, "This is exactly the same scene I saw in my dream!" The two sisters, horrified, put their hands over my mouth and said, "Shhh!" Yet I was so frightened by that living image, those two shining, astonished eyes that were fixed in the ceiling mirror, the living flicker of light and shadow in the mirror, that even if they had not covered my mouth, I would have had nothing else to say. Except, probably, for the futile repetition of that one sentence among the repeating, dusty mirrors: "This is exactly the same scene I saw in my dream . . . This is exactly the same scene I saw in my dream . . . This is exactly the same scene I saw in my dream!"

In the silence I remained fixed on the mirror above me, and I wondered whether I was dreaming that I was awake, or rather was I awake and could see that I had fallen asleep and was dreaming? Are the mirrors looking at me, or am I looking at them? As the four of us—me, the mirror, dreaming and waking—stared at each other, unable to distinguish ourselves from one another, Little Sister pulled my arm and took me out of the room, even as I was still sunk in thought as to what the destiny of the four of us in that room was and which one of us it was that came out of it in the end.

With my involuntary scream, our drunkenness wore off and

we were clear-headed again. We sped up. The sound of our fear-afflicted breath snaked through the room, mixing with the cool, stale air in the absolute darkness. From every corner of the palace a wave of agitation and anxiety assaulted our little hearts, and suddenly, we thought it would be better to escape from there. Perhaps if we slept under the trees, surrounded by jackals and wolves, we might feel more secure? As we were walking, we lit two or three more of the tallow lamps attached to the walls and took them with us so that more light might warm our inexpert hearts and make them hopeful. As if, in the sanctuary of light, fear of the dark and of the objects would plummet and ominous feelings would retreat once more into the dreadful shadows. In a cold and empty living room, the sound of our feet reminded us that we were the only ones in that mysterious palace. We looked up. The light was still higher. Terror pierced our burning hearts when with our swollen eyes we came face to face with enormous ancient statues that stared at us with clay eyes from across the ages: the effigy of a lion tearing into a cow's shoulder; the effigy of a winged horse in ebony, and the head of a cow with a human body. Had they not seen us before? Had the clay left eye of this statue not previously been the index finger of some ancient king? In another room, ancient inscriptions on stone and clay in unknown letters had been arranged on top of one another on tidy, long shelves that reached the ceiling. Waiting for somebody to come someday who would be able to decipher them. In one room, next to the open fireplace, lit some unknown time ago, a clay cylinder had been kept on a wooden table as if it were a sacred object. Only Brother ventured hesitantly, "Isn't it the Cyrus Cylinder?" We didn't know. History was not yet our favorite subject.

With every floor, the architecture and the items found there became more basic, simpler, and more dilapidated than the previous, meaning that we were, little by little, obliged to be heedful of the ground beneath our feet if we didn't want to plunge down into the holes in the rotting floorboards, or have the walls and doors fall on us. Whenever I was walking behind the others in the hallways, I meditated on time as I continued to attempt to forget and to quell my rebellious imagination. It occurred to me that time is a mysterious thing. Sometimes, as on that very night, it loses its distinctive quality, and it is not at all clear whether it is passing quickly or slowly or if it even exists. When I looked at the long, spiral staircase that went all the way down to the obscurity of the ground floor, I was struck by the feeling that I could never again know the staircase of the past. Just like that it had been erased, become subject to doubt, unfamiliar under the lanterns' mysterious light. I felt like the passing of time, even so short an interval, clarifies nothing, but rather conceals things within itself, and that what Dad thinks is not all correct when he says that time solves things. No. That night it was proved to me that time swallows things up. All the same, when I looked once more in front of me, at my relatives, close and distant, moving forward hopefully but hesitantly in the direction of the sound of the birds and the mysterious light, I felt like something heavy and numb had alighted from my heart and something light and cheerful taken its place. As if passing through those dark twists and turns and endless, decaying rooms, we had all suddenly grown up. More importantly, we had become the bearers of a great secret. The great secret which we, all of us and all at once, felt was more pleasurable in the keeping than in the revealing. The secret that none of us twelve knew exactly what it was.

At last, we found ourselves opposite the final stairway. The noise of the birds, which came as if in waves, was louder than before. The stairs were so rotten that they disintegrated beneath our feet, the pieces plunging into the vastness of the darkness below us. Only Brother calmly whispered into my ear, "The twelfth floor. We've gotten to the end." As we set foot on the last step, we were certain that there was no route back, since all the steps had collapsed behind us, vanishing into the darkness, their whereabouts now uncertain. Before us was a vast room, and the first thing to catch our attention were the birds. Many-colored birds of many species flew past us in the half-light of the room, singing and flapping in our ears before disappearing into the darkness. What lay before us was in fact a large library. The farther we progressed, the dwindling and flickering light of the tallow lamps illuminating a modest space in front of us, the more we understood the vastness of that library. The library bookshelves were so large that whichever angle we looked at them from, they appeared endless. The library might be named the Library of All Eternity, and one might wander lost among its rows of books until the end of one's life. Some of the books were so old and fragile that it was possible to see their skeletons. With the tallow lamps we were holding, we wandered like fireflies lost and transfixed among the dark rows and shelves of books, books asleep, books awake, books old and new. They gave off a pleasant smell. The smell of yellowing, decaying, inky paper. The smell of old leather bindings. The smell of moist earth. The smell of ebony and sandalwood and saffron and cinnamon.

Some of the writings were inscribed on stone and clay tablets, while others were written on animal skins and tree bark. There were some books so old that if we merely pointed to them, they turned to powder, their words getting mixed into the air and entering our lungs as we breathed in, before returning once more to the air when we exhaled, and there continuing their mysterious existence. There were books that were evidently new, their bindings, the way they were printed were modern, they still gave off the scent of the lead and petroleum and ink of the printworks. And there were some books which seemed to belong to the future; to times that had not yet come to pass. One section of the library was devoted solely to 24,000 heavenly scriptures belonging to 24,000 prophets who had, before Muhammad, given people the good news of the existence of the Unique Sustainer and of eternal salvation in paradise, but to whom people hadn't listened. For a moment I pitied the futility of God's efforts, but then my concentration was broken by the collective laughter that came from behind me. When Bahman had caught sight of the books of the prophets, he had started to joke about. As I drew near them, I heard him say, "Once Mo and Moses and Zoroaster and Ab and Noah and the rest of the lads was sitting together in paradise and talking about the heavenly houris when Jesus pitches up in the latest model of Rolls and parks it in a corner, its tires squealing. Mo said, "Damn my luck . . . This Jesus was the apple of God's eye right from the start." Without batting an eyelid, Moses said, "Well, if your Mom had put out for God like his, then you'd at least have got your hands on a Jaguar by now." Bahman always talked like this, like a rogue with no manners, but everyone loved him and counted the seconds until they could see him again at one of the family parties.

We, all of us, had completely forgotten the Gowkaran tree in our kitchen on account of the night and the mysterious palace and now because of Bahman's jokes, suddenly found ourselves face to face with it. With its trunk just as wide, its branches and foliage covering the ceiling, and all the fruits and birds of the world parading themselves on its boughs. In fact, the harder we looked, the more we realized that the top floor had no ceiling except the branches, leaves, fruits, and blossoms. When I looked closely, I could make out our kitchen chandelier all askew and broken, hanging from a branch, a bird having made its nest on top of it. So thick and tangled were the branches and foliage that not even a breeze or a gust of wind could pass through them, let alone the light of the stars. So tired was everyone that nobody could be bothered to ask a question. After all that anxiety and astonishment and walking and drunkenness, everyone pulled down a branch to pick the fruit they fancied and start eating it. When I looked up, he was sitting opposite me, staring at me as he ate a red apple. His gaze irritated me and made me want to get farther away from him. Mozhgan and

Iraj were sitting a little farther along, next to one another, from time to time exchanging meaningful glances with each other. Mozhgan's younger sister Mahin was amusing herself with Azadeh and Mahsa and giving them fruit. Bahman was sitting between the Two Sisters and Mehrab, telling them jokes again and making them laugh. I looked carefully at everyone sitting around the table. Was anyone among us thinking of love and love affairs at that moment, except me and Behnam and Iraj and Mozhgan? What about Mahin? We were all so tired and hungry that we had even forgotten about the faint light. So it was that a few minutes later the faint light that had drawn us towards itself from down below, from the depths of the forest, came towards us and sat down beside us at the round wooden table that had been built around the trunk of the tree, picked a bunch of grapes and began eating them. Whilst eating, the light smiled at us and looked at each one of our faces with enthusiasm and curiosity.

That light, that faint light, was nothing other than a young woman with long hair carrying a lamp with whom the boys, their gaze stunned and devastated, fell in love right away. All the same, nobody screamed when they saw her dressed in old silk clothes of unsurpassed beauty. Nor did she cry out when she saw us. Only once we were all full of both looks and food did she get up and take herself off in the direction of the dark spot she had come from. She walked on the rotten floorboards as if they couldn't possibly creak under her footsteps or from time-to-time crack and break and disappear in the darkness of the depths below. We set out in pursuit of her, yet cautiously. It was possible that at any moment our own feet might plunge into a hole, or that we be thrown down into that black abyss. When we caught up with her and gathered around her, she was sitting at a large old desk and writing something with a long peacock feather, in a fine hand, in a large notebook. The woman's study was flooded with light, yet I saw nothing except a single window covered by a thick curtain. Things appeared transparent under the mysterious light, and I wanted to enquire about its source, but as soon as I opened my mouth, Only Brother squeezed my arm. "Be quiet," he meant. In one corner a wood fire was burning, and the warmth and agreeable smell of burnt firewood and yellowing books spread through the air. So it was that right there we sat down on the woolen rugs and hardly a moment had gone by when, amid the warmth and gentle crackling of the wood fire, we fell asleep.

When we awoke, she was still writing, and the light had made everything in the room translucent, including her infinitely beautiful face. I felt that if I were to touch her translucent face, my hand would pass right through it. "How could anyone be this beautiful?" I thought. At that very moment the woman raised her head. She looked at each of our twelve tired faces. She stood up, opened the heavy, dusty curtains, and, gesturing with her hand to the library, the table, and then the forest outside the window, said, "This is the land of my ancestors." As she gestured with her hand to what lay outside, it was as if the sun and clouds and sky were likewise included in her gesture. We got up and went over to the window. The forest had surrounded us and under an ancient cypress, a spring of limpid blue bubbled away. The sky too was limpid blue and the birdsong outside was so close that it was as if the birds were singing right beside our ears. We looked at each another doubtfully and in surprise, for it was now obvious that the building had but a single floor, and that we could immediately go outside and wash our tired and sleepy faces in the spring under the ancient cypress. Where, then, were those eleven other floors, that maze of a palace, corridor after corridor, with its rotten spiral staircase? Those rooms filled with clothes and mirrors and statues and wine? I would not wait any longer, and asked, "But last night there was a tall palace here. Full of corridors and with several floors and dozens of rooms. What happened to them?"

The woman raised her curved eyebrows in surprise. She

smiled and said, “I don’t know. It’s a strange world, one might see anything at all in it.”

Mandana and Mina said at the same time, “But we all saw certain things; we were together. Things that are no longer here!”

The woman moved away from us with a calm and thoughtful mien, returning a few minutes later, and stood by her desk.

“All the same, that’s no reason for people not to see different things in the world,” she said.

“I’ll tell you a story, then, since no doubt you all turned up here for a reason, and perhaps the next time you come here, you won’t see my house.”

“Is that even possible?” one of us asked.

She answered simply: “That depends on you.”

I think we were all, or almost all certain we wouldn’t understand what she said, but she began regardless:

“For years, my father’s ghost has been living in the ghost of his house, but neither fully exists anymore; in the very rooms and hallways that he built with his own hands and that were, years afterwards, buried and destroyed under the weight of the snow. It was Nowruz in 1200 on the Zoroastrian calendar, and my father, who was one of the great sages of his day, had no wish except a vain one: He wanted to know when he would die. People used to ask him: ‘What kind of wish is this you have anyway?’ And he used to say, ‘Even if humans are born unawares, and, on a date unknown to them, why should they not have the right to know when they will die? If this were the case, wouldn’t we manage our affairs in this world better?’ And so it was that one day my father suddenly fell asleep, in his fathers’ mansion in Zorvan, while playing chess with his sister’s husband, the rook he wanted to castle with still in his hand. At that very moment he dreamt that a beautiful woman holding an astrolabe came into the mansion. She sat down opposite him and looked at the astrolabe, and after making calculations using numbers and *abjad* letters on its surface, wrote on a piece of paper: 'Die with Bibi Gharib, / come alive with Bibi Gharib, the Strange Lady,' and handed it to my father. At that very instant, my father started from sleep, and saw that in front of him, rather than the chessboard, was a large astrolabe, and the very same woman was sitting there scrutinizing him. My father said, 'Are you dreaming of me or am I dreaming of you?' Taking no heed of his question, the woman once again wrote on the paper, 'Die with Bibi Gharib, / come alive with Bibi Gharib,' handing it to him once more, but before my father could grab her clothing and ask her what this meant, the woman left the mansion. My father ran out after her, this way and that, but his sister's husband grabbed hold of him from behind, now up to his knees in the turquoise pool in the courtyard, and he suddenly started from sleep, the piece of paper still in his trembling hands."

Not one of the twelve of us so much as blinked, let alone plucked up the courage to ask what all this meant and what it had to do with us. Wasn't her fathers' mansion ours too?

The beautiful woman, light of great gentleness radiating from her back, endowing her with a spiritual aspect, came towards us and sat on the floor opposite us. She pulled her knees into her chest and, looking with kindness at each of our faces, continued:

"After this dream, he used to sit night and day by the orosi window of the sleeping porch and gaze at the mansion's wooden gates, waiting for the woman to arrive. The days and weeks passed, and without suffering the ill effects of sleeplessness, he sat expectantly. My mother gradually came to suspect that he had fallen in love with the woman, but when she eventually saw that he was visiting, mobads, fortune-tellers and writers of talismans and astrologers and was on the lookout for an astrolabe of a particular kind and quality she realized that he hadn't fallen in love after all; rather, he had caught the Fever of Objects. A dream interpreter told him that this was the very same astrolabe that would be made hundreds of years from then by two brothers from Isfahan named Ahmad and Mohammad, and that so many weird and wonderful events would take place because of it that it would be stolen many times, and passed around so much that in the end not a trace of it would remain. Another fortune-teller gazed into their mirror and told him that because this astrolabe would bring fever and sleeplessness and madness to its possessors, it would, two thousand years hence, be finally flung into the depths of the Southern Sea by Nader Shah. A mobad astrologer performed divination with sand and told him that right now the astrolabe lay on Mount Alborz which, many years hence, the followers of a new religion will call 'Qaf,' while a writer of talismans looked into a copper bowl full of the urine of a pre-pubescent boy and announced that it was demons who concealed and revealed it. Little by little, my father came to the conclusion that there was no hope of his laying hands on that astrolabe, and that it would be better to find the key to deciphering the abjad letters, since the mobads, fortune-tellers and writers of talismans and astrologers talked about it constantly, or made use of it in their strange and outlandish calculations. He thought to himself, 'Even though the woman hasn't come to see me and I haven't found the astrolabe, I might at least be able to understand what the woman said by using knowledge of the *abjad* codes.' So it was he started to learn the different codes of *abjad*: *havvaz, ḥoṭṭy, kelman, sa'faṣ, qarašat, Þaxað, żażağ*. It was said that the Prophet Enoch or Edris had invented these letters in Mesopotamia and that he had a specific meaning in mind for each word. *Abjad,* 'began'; *havvaz* 'attached'; *ḥoṭṭy,* 'obtained knowledge'; *kelman,* 'began to talk'; *sa'faṣ*, 'freely learnt'; *qarašat*, 'arranged'; *Þaxað* 'held'; *żażağ,* 'finished." And in this way, he likewise learnt that each letter stands for a number.

"My father calculated the whole of the sentence the woman had written on the piece of paper several times, forwards and backwards, but found no clue or anything else meaningful in it. He mixed the words up and turned them into *abjad* letters once again, but still found nothing meaningful. He lost hope. He became a recluse. He no longer paid any attention to daily affairs, any more than he did to my mother's protests or to the needs of us children. His beard and hair grew long, and many days and nights passed without him coming to the mansion; if he did, he would shut himself up in a room with his books of geography and history and esoteric and secret sciences and his talismans. A little later, he became a vagabond, wandering through towns and villages in search of the name of Bibi Gharib, among holy and famous personages and places. This was the last arrow in his quiver. Many days and nights he shut himself up in the chambers of tombs and sacred fire temples and temples of Anahita in the hope that the nickname of a holy woman in one of those places, in a time perhaps far off in the past or the future, would be 'Gharib, Strange,' and that through inspiration or revelation the meaning of the dream would be made clear to him."

The beautiful woman sighed and fell silent. We were open-mouthed, enrapt by her. Eventually she resumed:

"There was no use. Everything was pointless, like running after the wind. After he had followed every possible path without results, with the help of the villagers in a distant village in the hills around Mount Sabalan, he built himself a humble dwelling of mud and wood. He no longer sought anything. He had entirely forgotten about us. He had dismissed from his mind his fathers' mansion, the long evenings sitting with sages, scholars, mobads, poets, storytellers, and khiyal-bazan,[10] Zorvan and its ancient winding streets and alleyways, its mages and ancient fire temples. He wasn't even looking for the woman and the astrolabe and the fire temple and the *abjad* letters and how to interpret the dream anymore. He had surrendered. He eventually concluded that perhaps he had squandered the entirety of those twelve years in a futile search, that perhaps the dream was

[10] Animators of a kind of ancient shadow puppet show.

after all just a dream, like the hundreds of other meaningless dreams he had never bothered to follow up on, that he had forgotten. Until one day he woke up and saw that the mountains and hills and forests were entirely blanketed with snow. An excitement and ecstasy hitherto unknown to him filled his being. With great difficulty he cleared the snow from in front of his door so he could go out. All that whiteness and the untouched quality of nature made him feel cheerful. However hard he thought, he could not call to mind when he had last been filled with joy at the scent of a flower, the sight of a butterfly, or when reading a poem. With a childish joy that seemed odd for a man of his age in that village, he threw himself on to the snow and rolled down the hill, his loud guffaws slowly bringing the aged inhabitants of the village out of their warm and smoky houses. Gradually they gathered around him and joined in his laughter. Toothless old women and old men, cheeks rosy from the cold, clapped for him as, like a child, he leapt this way and that on the snow and flung it at them, then started to dance.

"In the middle of dancing he began to laugh. As he laughed, he spun around and around and around and drunkenly thought how such joy had been available to him all these years and yet he hadn't realized. Then, all of a sudden, as he grasped the stupidity of those twelve long years, of the wasted life, he began to cry. The sound of his laughter and weeping wound its way around the mountains and valleys of Sabalan and came back to him. Eventually, while turning around and around and weeping, he fell to the ground. He was blind drunk. Drunk with the indescribable pleasure of that moment. Drunk with the thoughts that had occurred to him in that same moment and which he had squandered his long life in trying to understand. Drunk with all the pleasures he felt in that moment but was unable to express. He threw a fistful of snow into his hot face. He cooled down. He laughed and thought that he had forgotten about time, and in the middle of the bursts of laughter he asked, 'What day of what year is it today?'

"An old woman took a small astrolabe out of her coat pocket, and, putting its strap around her neck, started calculating. Then she laughed vigorously and said, 'Today is Bibi Gharib, the Strange Lady. A day that will never again be repeated.'

"The smile on my father's lips froze. He flung himself toward the old woman, looked at her face and recalled her much younger face from the dream. He shouted, 'What does it mean? What does "the Strange Lady" mean?'

"The old woman, tall of stature, though bent, laughed toothlessly as she put the astrolabe back in her pocket, and said, 'Today is 12/12/1212 in the Zoroastrian calendar. I did warn you twelve years ago. In *abjad* letters this date is written *B-I-B-I Ğ-A-R-Y-B*.'

"The world spun around my father's head, he fell to the ground and at exactly 12 noon on 12/12/1212 his warm heart stopped beating—having reached the date that the woman had warned him about in the dream twelve years earlier, a terrible cold seized his heart, and he died. Only as he died did he say, 'It's odd. As if my entire life were nothing but a dream.'"

The beautiful woman sighed. Her eyes darkened and filled with sorrow at the remembrance of what weighed on her mind. "My father was buried an hour later, having gotten so close to the meaning of the poem but never understanding it until the last breath of his life. The villagers, who knew nothing about him, on his gravestone simply wrote, 'The Strange Lady.' The strangest date that any people's calendar might ever see."

We all stared wide-eyed at the tall-statured woman. The world stood still. The fire had stopped giving off warmth and the sun's light had frozen on our faces. I noticed that even the dust from the curtains, rugs, and books was suspended motionless in the air, transfixed by the woman's tale. Eventually respiration resumed. I understood that I was still alive . . . Even though I didn't understand anything precise about it.

The woman looked at us and said, "And my father, in seeking the interpretation of a dream that could have bestowed fresh excitement on his life, wasted it. If only he had understood that this dream was the answer to a question that he had always wished to know, perhaps he would have realized that he should have dedicated the time that remained to him to joy and poetry and philosophy and drunkenness. He had asked a question of his fate whose answer contained nothing but ruin for him. That question was fundamentally mistaken, even though it came out of the mouth of a sage."

On the table stood an earthenware cup and a bowl for wine. She poured a little wine into the bowl. She tasted it and her countenance was suddenly piqued; she aged. Her hair turned white, her teeth rotten, her cheek drawn and wrinkled. She sighed, but then as if she had remembered something pleasant, she took another draught of wine and, her face now young and cheerful, resumed:

"My father still lives and strives to uncover the secrets of life in the ghost of the mud house that neighbors his stone grave, constantly appearing in both my waking and dreaming hours, telling me stories of the lives of merchants, landowners, heroes and kings and Zoroastrian mobads. As if, because he so bitterly regrets his own squandered life, he wants to constantly see and hear the lives of others. I write down the stories that my father recounts to me. Stories without end and full of wonders."

We were still watching her when she said, "Yes, that's the situation, that it isn't possible to find the connection between events so easily. I know right now you are asking yourselves, 'What can this tale have to do with us?.' But know that in the world you will be confronted by all manner of things that you can see, feel, and understand yet not explain, or grasp how they are connected to each other, even as they are definitely, but mysteriously, related to one another. This is to grasp the truth and the meaning of life."

Then suddenly, as if she had just remembered something, her eyes lit up like the eyes of an excited child, and a joyful smile made her face still more beautiful, and she asked: "Would you like to know what my book is called?"

He said, "Very much."

The beautiful woman said, "The Shahnameh."

The five of us siblings looked at each other in surprise. Didn't I have a handwritten manuscript of the Shahnameh right there in my knapsack? And didn't we have the Moscow and Beirut editions of the Shahnameh in our library, and didn't Dad used to gather us in the living room on long winter nights and read us stories from it? And didn't Dad remind us every time, proudly and severely, that we weren't allowed to touch those thick quarto volumes with their Safavid-style pictures and deer leather bindings? Dad had told us that this was a one-of-a-kind handwritten edition of the Shahnameh that he had purchased, one winter night when he was young, from a hungry and bewildered passer-by, for a considerable sum of money and a couple of pieces of warm bread.

With one voice, Mina and Mandana said, "But if we have handwritten and printed editions of this book at home, that means that its writer was Ferdowsi and he wrote it hundreds of years ago."

The woman replied with a determined look. "It was written, it is written, and it will be written. Who knows? Perhaps you yourselves are the heroes of a Shahnameh without even knowing it."

Then without warning, with the earthenware bowl from which she was sipping wine still in her hand, she got up and disappeared between the shelves of the library. As if she had turned into a book among the thousands in the library, or a tale among the hundreds in the Shahnameh . . .

I don't know how long it took till we came to our senses and stood up. We had to find our way back home before it was too late and tell each other about the events of that night and day, like an incomplete secret, elusive in meaning. However much we looked for the woman among the shelves, we were unable to find her. We had no option but to leave without saying goodbye, and before that house with its mysterious library and Gowkaran tree collapsed under our feet or disappeared altogether.

It was not yet noon. Next to the spring by the house stood an earthenware bowl, turquoise in color, on which was depicted an ancient cypress tree and a water channel that reminded me of Sadeq Hedayat's *Blind Owl.* Further on Shabro and Afsun were busy grazing, still tied by their reins to the same tree as last night. We drank some water and washed our sleepy faces to freshen up. Only Brother climbed up the cypress tree to locate the path home. It was unbelievable. We were much closer to the house than we had imagined. We could have just headed east and crossed some modest hills and a stream. We set out in the direction of the mansion. Before we got too far away, we turned to look back at the other house. Where we had gotten lost in those many hallways, landings, rooms great and small, and its dark library, there was nothing but a small village cottage with an earthen roof. It hadn't, or so it seemed, contained those twelve mysterious floors after all, or the room of mirrors, the books, statues, musical instruments and ancient royal jewels, that tree of such great size, that woman of such great beauty and so full of mystery.

Back at home everyone was happy to see us. Mom and Dad hugged us tight, and Mom's relatives chanted blessings for the Prophet and said that our being found was one of Imam Hoseyn's miracles, while Dad's relatives gathered around the sacred fire and prayed: "Yazdân panâh bâd. In dudemân shâd bâd. Tandorosti niknâmi, tandorosti zendegâni, tandorosti farâkh ruzi, tandorosti shâdi va râmeshni. Dir bedar. Shâd bedâr. Tandorost bedâr. Idun bedâr. Sâl khojastah bâd. Ruz farrokh bâd. Mâh farrokh bâd."

We kids had nothing to say to them. We just wanted to be alone. Each one of us took refuge in a cozy corner until noon on Ashura, so that we could digest all we'd seen and heard. Could it be digested? When we saw each other the day after, it was as if we had been struck dumb. Nobody had anything to say. Only Khanom Joon, having emerged from the isolation of her room when we got back, as she stood by the door and looked at us with a penetrating and self-satisfied gaze, inspecting us from head to toe, smiled, shook her head as if to say that she knew about everything, and before closing the door behind her and disappearing, said, "So you met *her* at last!'

At noon on Ashura, the weather was warmer than it had been. The inhabitants of the five neighboring villages, bearing with them the *alam* and *kotal*[11] and sweating, assembled in the Zorvan village mosque, and smote their chests and wept as they mourned on the anniversary of the martyrdom of Imam Hoseyn and his seventy-two companions. They did so in the same village which, according to research carried out by Dad and his colleagues, had survived since the age of Mithraism, without its inhabitants having any memory of those times. Without them even wanting to know that their farmer ancestors, thousands of years earlier, had in that very same spot shed holy tears in ceremonies of the same ilk. Those ceremonies had, however, commemorated the disappearance of Mithra and his twelve companions in the cave, or during a later period, had marked the death of Siavash or sought rain from Anahita.

As we gathered in the mosque and watched the lines of mourners, who were clad in black and striking themselves on the back with chains and beating their breasts with their hands and weeping, all twelve of us turned our eyes to the sky and then to the mansion on the hill. The sky, clear blue until a few minutes earlier, was suddenly filled with black clouds, and it

[11] A heavy wooden or metal banner decorated with religious symbols carried in religious processions.

started raining and hailing so fiercely that the ranks of mourners could not decide whether to continue to weep and wail or shout out in joy and dance with happiness at the rain which for months they had wished for. As people ran from this side to that under the driving rain and chunky hailstones, conversing in loud voices between tears and laughter, the twelve of us stood and looked at the tree on the hill whose massive trunk stretched from the middle of our mansion up into the sky, and which, before disappearing into the clouds, thrashed around in the air like some hundred-armed monster and shook in the wind and the storm. We were all soaked and yet we did not stir from our place. Then Leyla let go of my hand, and as she walked back to the mansion, head down and moving away from us with steps of unprecedented determination, she said, "I want to climb the tree." Then, with her slight body and her long white hair on which drops of rain and hailstones sat like dew and wintersweet, she disappeared into the twists and turns of the lane leading to the mansion, and not one of the eleven of us remaining tried to dissuade her.

When a day and a week and a month had passed, and all the vows and crying from Mom and Dad and the rest of the family had led nowhere, the police search parties had turned up nothing, after scouring all the orchards and pastures and woods with the inhabitants of the surrounding villages and still there was no sign of Leyla, who had disappeared just like a drop of dew in her thick white hair, in despair they held mourning ceremonies for her on the third, seventh, and fortieth days in accordance with the custom of Mom's family, and then the Porseh, on the fourth, tenth and thirtieth days in accordance with the remembrance rituals of Dad's family. In one night, Mom and Dad turned old and silent. As for Khanom Joon, however, with the Ball of Light bouncing up and down in her pocket, she merely stared at us and kept quiet. She neither cried nor laughed. She just kept staring in astonishment. The remaining eleven of us cried along with the rest of the family, and though dread had seized us, our lips remained sealed. What we did not do was give permission for the swing to be removed from the Gowkaran tree in the middle of the kitchen, because we all agreed, without having to announce the fact, that she would one day return, which indeed is what happened. Although so late that by that time she had become a beautiful young lady and the swing had become too small for her to sit on, and we, meanwhile, were nothing more than ghosts, as much dead as alive.

Do you remember? On an ordinary hot summer afternoon, a few weeks before my and Behnam's wedding celebration, as you and we four siblings and Mom and Dad and Khanom Joon and Jamshid Khan and Auntie Malek were sitting around the table, as we had always done in bygone days, eating the produce of the tree in accordance with ancient custom, we heard the sound of feet that had jumped two-footed from the trunk of the tree on to the mansion's brick-colored sloping roof. The feet then seemed to walk along the roof toward the front of the building, eventually stopping at the edge. The food still in our mouths and staring up above, we followed the sound of the footsteps so we could see who it belonged to. Leyla, sitting at the edge of the roof, her long locks white and flowing, feet hanging down, wearing a sky-blue shirt and a gold belt, waved hand to us, smiling merrily. The food got stuck in Mom's throat. Dad started coughing and we stood staring, open-mouthed, as if we were all deaf and dumb. Eventually the servants came to their senses and swiftly brought a ladder, Leyla coming down and standing beside us, all the while exuding poise and elegance and an indescribable inner beauty. As our silence prolonged itself, she smiled, shrugged, and went silently toward the kitchen where she sat at the table in her usual chair. And us following her with eyes wide and round. The sound of Jamshid Khan grinding his teeth filled the kitchen, while Khanom Joon took hold of her Ball of Light, hiccupping. Once Leyla had found herself a comfortable position on the chair, she said, in a merry voice and an intimate tone: "It's really me. That's right." And she took a little bite from a medlar and with her pallid shining eyes looked each of us in the eye until finally Only Brother broke the silence, saying, "You've grown so much and become so beautiful!"

"I know," said Leyla, her eyes joyous.

And I, sitting beside her all the while thought: "And you look so like that woman!" I watched her as she slid her hand furtively under her shirt and brought out a slim volume, placing it on my feet. *Hekmat-e Khosravâni.*[12]

[12] Meaning "The Wisdom of the Kings. A collection of teachings, philosophies, and principles that became prominent during the reign of Khosrow I Anushiravan, the Sassanid king (529–579 CE). It was essentially an ethical and philosophical system based on reason, fairness, justice, and morality, emphasizing these as the core elements of governance and social life."

Chapter Three

Once the votive fesenjaan, chicken and plum, and gheymeh stews had been eaten in the mosque, the lamentations of Tasua and Ashura were over, and Leyla had disappeared, but before the discovery of Mithra and the Sacred Bull, after the conclusion of both the Islamic and Zoroastrian mourning ceremonies, the rest of the family and relatives gradually went back to their homes and daily lives. He went, Bahman and Iraj and Mozhgan and Mahin and the rest of them went, although before he left, Bahman punched his father in the face and told him he was a drunken bastard, Mozhgan and Iraj in a note that they left on the kitchen table announced that they had fallen in love, that they were Communists, and had fled to the Soviet Union, whereupon Mahin immediately announced that she wanted to go to Sistan and Baluchestan province and join the government's Literacy Corps. Meanwhile, before his departure, he, Behnam, came to my bedroom one night, woke me up, took me firmly by the hand, and, all the while careful not to wake anyone else up, led me out of the mansion, and without a word took me to a spot under the oak and common hornbeam trees in the middle of the forest. Then, as moonlight fell on his face he stood and said, "I couldn't sleep at all . . . Your voice kept echoing in my ears. Your voice that had echoed in the mirrored room, 'this is exactly the same scene I saw in my dream!'"

At breakfast, he takes tea with a single spoon of sugar, but for afternoon tea, without sugar. He loves cream and honey but doesn't like honey in tea. He has long, slender fingers which distract me and claw at my heart every time they move. Dark blue suits him better than any other color, while white makes his eyes and eyebrows and shiny black hair stand out more against his light skin. When he talks, he sticks his hands in his front trouser pockets, as if to make sure that the restless birds of his hands don't fly away. In large gatherings, he listens, in small ones, he talks. I had understood all of this, but not how beautiful he is . . . When he talked in a smaller gathering, I would stand near enough for me to hear his warm, gruff voice, but not so close as to attract his attention. I had heard him talk of the working class and social justice, without excitement, but in a confident voice. I had seen him go for a walk in the forest, at exactly 7 A.M. and again at 7 P.M., without drawing anyone's attention, returning an hour later, hands in pockets and whistling. I had learnt that until he was fifteen, he had lived in London and Paris with his family. He was in his second year studying journalism at the University of Tehran, his father was Dad's colleague and friend from their student days. I had come to realize that when he walked quickly, his right shoulder was a little lower than his left one. Once when I was out riding Shabro in the forest, I saw him leaning on a tree, inhaling oxygen mixed with cigarette smoke with deep and pleasurable breaths. That day I slowly dismounted from Shabro and sat down behind a raspberry bush, without taking my eyes off him; a little ray of light was falling on his left eye. By the time his cigarette was finished, a sparrow had come to rest next to his right foot, a crow cawed above his head, and as he looked up to the crow, the sky, and the light, a leaf from a Persian ironwood tree fallen on his high forehead, as if it were God's signature. That day as he dragged on his cigarette, he had a smile on his lips that seemed to be saying, *ah it is good to be alive*. There was something about his black, intelligent eyes that took away my courage to look; gleaming, with long lashes and sharp corners. His gaze was penetrating and meticulous. He knew how to talk with his eyes, to question with his eyes, to laugh with his eyes. I had known all of this, but how had I not realized how beautiful he was? That night, for example . . . On that most particular of all nights in the palace, I had realized that with those eyes there was no limit to the disasters he might inflict on me . . . I had realized this precisely in the wine and dancing room when he told me, "I am your restless lover," but at the same time fired bullets from his eyes that wounded and killed me.

Despite all this, during all those long days he had been with our relatives, close and distant, in our mansion, I had not uttered a single word to him. At the mere idea of talking to him, my entire body came out in blisters because of the heat, my hair caught fire, and my cheeks were roasted with shame. Even the one time he walked past me and our shoulders were less than a centimeter apart, I started hiccupping out of shame and fear, the hiccups not stopping for three days. During that time, he, Behnam, had tried to get close to me and had even addressed a few words to me, but each time without even speaking I had found an excuse to slip away, like a fish, like the wind, like the mist, losing myself in nooks and crannies hidden from people and walls and trees. Just like that night in the palace when I had lost myself among the hallways and rooms and children. As that day in the forest, timid and lacking in self-confidence, I watched him take pleasure in blowing smoke rings up into the air, I told myself that that night in the palace, that fearful night, he had certainly said what he had said to me only because he was drunk. I had no doubt about this. No, it wasn't to be doubted at all. Wasn't it? Now that he had taken my hand on this moonlit night and placed it beside him underneath the wide-awake trees and sleeping sparrows, I was once more unsure what he wanted to tell me. He would surely not speak of love. No! No! Because he wasn't drunk. Surely? Whatever the case may be, I had to say something, but nothing came to mind. As usual when he was around me, my mind hesitated and my thoughts began hiccupping. But in a gentle motion, he took my hand in his and squeezed it as gently. Gripped by shyness, short of breath, frightened and inflamed, I fixed my eyes on the ground, and if I hadn't lost the use of my legs, I would have run behind the oaks and hornbeams. My heart was beating rapidly, like the hearts of the sparrows we used to trap on snowy winter nights, until he drew his hand back in a swift movement and the sparrow of my heart stood still with shock and died.

I looked at the palm of my hand in surprise. There was a cavity. A vacuum. I was then so raw a lover, not having tasted all the separations of the years to come, that I imagined that this vacuum was an infinite one, because just a few weeks earlier in our science lessons I had learnt that vacuum could be divided into five types. If I had known that day that I would experience the vacuum in this way, and so soon, then I wouldn't have expended so much effort in the school yard at break-time in memorizing the five types of vacuum: the low vacuum, the medium vacuum, the high vacuum, the ultra-high vacuum, and the extreme-high vacuum, the infinite one . . . Ahhhhhh! Had I known that this vacuum would be a prelude to a life lived with the different types of vacuums, I would have known just how far off that infinite vacuum lay. That vacuum of vacuums. My hand froze from dread, pain shot up my back, my left eye leapt, and loud hiccups sprang forth from my mouth: "hic!"

Fortunately, it appeared he hadn't heard.

"Maybe it'd be better if we just looked at the moon," he said. "I can never get to sleep on moonlit nights."

I'm the same, I thought. But the emptiness of my hand without his in it, that vacuum, that sudden cavity, had shaken my spirit so unexpectedly that rather than saying "me too," without realizing I turned to him, so that I might be able to conquer my shame for the first time and look into his penetrating black eyes and ask, "Why did you let my hand go?"

But behind Behnam I caught sight of the ghost of the gorgeous lady of tall stature, leaning against a tree under the silver light of the moon, a peacock in her arms, staring at me with her bright face, elongated, black eyebrows and eyes of infinite beauty. A little scream escaped my mouth, and I drew back, terrified. "What happened?" Behnam asked, concerned. As I pointed to the tree, where now leaned no ghost, a sentence sprang from my mouth and for years afterwards I could not understand why. I said, "For a moment Eblis the Beautiful and I were looking into each other's eyes."

A playful sparkle shone in his eyes, the puffiness under his eyes increased, and he said, smiling, "So you've said something to me at last!"

Until then I had not heard anybody say, for instance, that their lips or hands or heart are maladroit, because if I had, I would have told myself, told my lips not to be so maladroit, that they should at least start moving. Smile. React appropriately. Talk. But it didn't happen. Not a single word came out of my mouth. The smile that I eventually presented him with was exactly the sort of smile maladroit lips offer, lips that had lost control once confronted by him, by those playful eyes of his. Then a miracle took place as he took my hand in his once more and pulled me to my feet. This time he held my hand very tightly, as if he were worried I would remove mine from his. We walked together in the moonlight forest. Then he asked, quite simply, "In your opinion, what is love?" It crossed my mind—ahhh, so this is his question too?

Despite having filled a two-hundred-page green notebook with summaries of romantic adventures from novels and films, as well as the twenty-three not particularly successful or useful interviews on the topic of love carried out with relatives and the inhabitants of the mansion recorded in the two hundred pages of the red notebook, I knew of love as much as I knew of life—something elusive and indistinct, a mere whisper of nothing. Wouldn't it have been easier if he'd asked me the names of Iran's rivers or to list all its peaks above 3,000 meters? Doesn't he know that they don't teach us anything about that in our schoolbooks? Love is one of those categories that doesn't fit in science lessons, nor in religion and literature, nor in history and geography. It's an interdisciplinary subject and all the sciences have evaded responsibility for defining it. Our math and science and history and geography lessons generally pay no attention to love. As if love had nothing to do with them. When, of course, it does. For instance, if Marie and Pierre Curie hadn't fallen in love, would Marie Curie have managed to discover those things for which she was in part indebted to Pierre? Or if Shah Jahan hadn't fallen in love with Arjomand Banu, would the Taj Mahal ever have been built? The Gathas talk constantly of wisdom and the Quran of obedience. The rest of the religions pass over love with hints and allusions, and most of them consider it sinful and forbidden anyway. In literature, meanwhile, they only talk about the happy state of union with the beloved, or the sadness of separation. Meaning that none of the subjects we study in school explains what love itself is. In our mansion, although there is sometimes talk of someone's love for someone else, or there are constant allusions to love and the lover and the beloved in Hafez's poetry, or it appears in the *Shahnameh*'s stories about Bizhan and Manizheh or Rostam and Tahmineh, nobody has ever explained what love itself is, that it occasionally afflicts people like the plague or cholera, or that because of it, like Majnun, they leave off sleep and food and living, or like Dash Akol[13] they die, or even, like Macbeth, kill.

I looked at him shyly out of the corner of my eye, he who was looking at me with that same kind smile that made the puffiness under his eyes bigger.

"I like the fact that you don't talk much," he said. "Although it's confusing. Even though you're always around for our discussions and you listen very carefully, or you're there behind a raspberry bush even when I'm having a smoke . . . you never talk. But the bad side of this is that I see you do sometimes talk to other people, but you never talk to *me*." He said "me" with great emphasis, as if this had really got to him. Then he asked, again emphatically, "Why?"

[13] A story by Sadeq Hedayat.

"Wouldn't it have been easier to answer his first question?" I wondered. The thought made me smile.

"What are you laughing at," he asked.

I put my head down and shrugged. No doubt I had gone red to my earlobes again. He put his hand under my chin and gently nudged my head back up, then asked me once again, but this time insistently: "You have no choice but to answer one of these questions: one, in your opinion, what is love? Two, why do you always run away from me?"

For the first time I looked at him from that breath-arresting close distance where our warm breaths collided. The same thing happened again; pain shot down my back, my tongue stammered, and my thoughts hiccupped. My chin still resting on his hand, I looked at the surroundings out of the corner of my eye. I had either really to run away and lose myself behind the trees, or finally give an answer. The trees and bushes were far off, so I mumbled an answer. "The answer to both questions is the same: I don't know."

I gently moved my head away from his hand. He sighed and stood staring at the surrounding trees, then after a brief pause said, "But I am starting to realize certain things. For example, the first thing I realized was that when I see one person, without me knowing, my heart starts beating like this . . . " He pressed my hand on his heart. I was flushed, hot. I looked at the surroundings out of the corner of my eye. If only I could run behind the trees, a little that way, over there . . . He continued: "Another thing I realized is that I cannot breathe when I'm far away from her. What's worse is that I can't breathe properly when I'm next to her either."

I'm the same way, I thought to myself helplessly.

"In my opinion love is a kind of state of uncertainty," he said. "A sort of state of suspension, restlessness, indecisiveness. Love is living on the border; the border of life and death, the border of dreaming and waking, the border of truth and illusion." Then he stuck his right hand into his hair, sighed unhappily, and said with irritation, "Mostly it has the symptoms of a chronic illness."

I thought that I must remember to note down the things he said in my second notebook. But perhaps I might not remain alive so long . . . I felt like I had caught fire inside and was going to die . . . It felt like my heart was not so much beating as pounding and breaking and spewing molten lava everywhere like a volcano. At last he went on.

"It's as if love confronts you with loneliness and the massive vacuum inside you. As if you suddenly realize how empty and meaningless your life was until now without that particular person . . . you . . ."

The vacuum . . . the vacuum again . . . I must remember to name today "Vacuum Day" on my desk calendar.

"Has anything occurred to you yet?" he asked.

No . . . nothing had occurred to me. He continued.

"Something else I've realized is that I had no say in choosing that person. My heart"—with his right hand he tapped a few times on my hand which he was still holding over his heart with his left—"fell in love of its own accord."

Without thinking, I looked up at the sky above me and, to distract my attention, to distract his attention, from those intense feelings, those eyes, those words, those two volcano hearts . . . "Shall we look at the moonlight?" And I calmly took my hand away from his, but he took it back, and as he brought his face closer to mine, and from his black eyes flung arrows and fire and bullets and stones and shells and all manner of other cursed things at my eyes and heart and soul, he said imperiously, "No!" And he pulled me towards him, placed his lips on mine and kissed them.

Pyiouufff . . . my skin was torn into pieces, my heart melted, the warp and weft of my being unraveled, and my lips . . . oh, my lips! Is this what a kiss is? Ahhh! You birds who stand in witness, do you realize what just happened? You crows? You sparrows? You owls? Did you see how in an instant my heart melted and forever lost its shape and essence? Moon, moon, O moon . . . Did you see how my soul was wrenched from my body and would not return? It occurred to me that my lips were extremely small and knew nothing of kissing.

He took his lips away from mine, looked at me with his innocent, besotted eyes, and murmured softly in my ear, "Are you alright?"

Was I? I felt so good, I felt bad. There is always one bird singing and flying solo in the still of the forest night, passing by. As if to say, "Why are you asleep? Wake up. Help me. Don't you realize what's happened to me?" That night I was that frightened bird of the night.

Eventually I managed to control myself and a hesitant smile appeared on my lips, its meaning unclear to me. Pleasure? Embarrassment? Fear? Security? Love? So, was love this kiss? I must remember to write in my second notebook that love was a kiss. As simple as that.

I wanted us to keep walking. For that reason, I turned my back on him so that we would get moving, because otherwise I would have out of haste once again said, "Shall we look at the moon?" My breathing had not yet gone back to normal. I looked up. I was trying to catch sight, between the branches and leaves, of that one wandering night bird, or perhaps I was on the lookout for my fugitive heart and soul . . . Where are you? My heart? My soul? The innocence of before the discovery of the kiss? Will I ever control you fully again? But he stood there without moving. He was still holding my hand in his. I turned around and looked at him inquiringly. The ghost of the tall-statured woman carrying a peacock appeared behind him again. This time I could make out the head of a snake on her left shoulder, emerging from between her long black flowing hair. A smile was on her lips. How beautiful the woman was, and how reassuring her smile . . . Even though her beauty was otherworldly, and was mingled with sadness . . . Yes, this time I could make out a certain, deep sadness in her wide eyes. When

I saw that sadness in her eyes, I lost my fear of her, and unlike the previous occasion, my heart felt strong. As if with those infinitely gorgeous and sorrowful eyes of hers she was reassuring me that I should set out with all my being on the path of no return. I calmly took my eyes off her. Without even realizing it myself, in between taking my eyes off Eblis the Sorrowful and looking into Behnam's eyes, I turned into another person; into somebody that had grasped exactly and swiftly that her life was henceforth divided between before and after that kiss. I turned into that bird who, in the nocturnal solitude of the alien forest, feels itself at its destination. I looked at Behnam, who pulled me towards him again; he kissed me firmly and with complete conviction that that was what he wanted to do. We sat down on the dry leaves and let our kisses become so passionate, dizzying, and natural, that not even the air could pass between our lips, between the outlines of our faces, through the distance between our young bodies. We had killed distance. We slaughtered the sheep of fear beneath the feet of Eblis the Sorrowful.

In the breaking light of dawn, when we reached home, he escorted me in silence to my bed, hand in hand, he gave a goodnight kiss to the end of a tress of my long hair and left. Before leaving, he whispered in my ear, "I shall see you again here soon." But I came down with a fever in that very moment of saying goodbye and was unable to get out of bed for another three days and nights. I could not even bid him and the others goodbye the following day. As usual, Dad, who was yet to be cruelly killed, sent for the doctor, while at Mom's behest Maryam burned wild rue over my head. "Wild rue, grain by grain. Wild rue, thirty-three grained. May the jealous and envious and stranger eye burst!" But it was Khanom Joon who, as soon as she came into my room, ordered everyone else out and sat by my bed for three days and nights and recited ancient Zoroastrian prayers over me. I was delirious and in my half-waking state probably calling on Behnam or Eblis as Khanom

Joon washed my feet and forehead with cold water and moved her Ball of Light around my body again and again so that she might heal me with its mysterious energy.

On the third day, in a delirious dream I saw Behnam being taken into the mouth of the snake, the snake taken into the mouth of the peacock, the peacock into the mouth of Eblis, and Eblis the Beautiful kissing me, and as she did, she had *his* eyes, the peacock's beauty, and the snake's mysteriousness. I woke up with a jolt and in the darkness of my room, my body drenched with sweat and shaking with fever, I turned to Khanom Joon and cried out, "Wasn't this the meaning of love?"

Chapter Four

Once more it was just us, and the tree, and Leyla's empty chair, and the swing that nobody sat on anymore, although sometimes it would start moving of its own accord. With Leyla gone, the four of us remaining siblings used to sit on Leyla's bed at nights and think sorrowfully about how we had never imagined that out of the five of us it would be our little sister, of poetic manner, who would be struck by this mysterious family madness. If Leyla hadn't been mad, would it have even been possible for her to have wanted to climb the tree and disappear, and what's more, on such a stormy day? Whilst it was only a few days later that Mehrab did something that from my point of view meant he was undoubtedly the inheritor of the family madness, not Leyla, nobody would accept what I said until years afterwards.

What happened was that a few days after the mansion had been emptied of the guests constantly bickering about politics and religion, when on one hot, slow morning, the buzzing horsefly of boredom left Paapi, our eight- or nine-year-old dog, and alighted on my cheek, my patience finally came to an end. I picked up a pick and shovel and went to the forest. I didn't know what I wanted to do exactly, but I knew I had to do something. Something that would make sweat drip from my body, my muscles ache, and cause me to stop thinking about that woman, Leyla, the tree, him, the kiss, the palace and its adventures. Or who knows, perhaps after all I did want to think about that woman, Leyla, the tree, him, the kiss, the palace and its adventures. I was only fourteen or fifteen and I had all these insoluble problems before me, and I had to figure out what I was supposed to do about them. And then what about Eblis . . . Eblis the Beautiful . . . Eblis the Sorrowful . . . How had that name occurred to me that night anyway? Why Eblis and not someone else? Why not Anahita?[14] Why not Death? Why not God, or Doghduyeh,[15] for example? Eblis, really? So, was Eblis actually a woman and I just didn't know? Eventually I would have to decide whether I would think about these things for the rest of my life, or rather avoid thinking about them. To think or not to think. That is the question. As I wandered aimlessly in the forest, pick and shovel over my shoulder, I concluded that the reality of the matter was that if I thought about these things, these problems would remain as insoluble and complicated as if I avoided thinking about them. Was it even possible to understand who the woman up the tree is? Where Leyla went? What that palace was? Or what those feelings between me and him were? And that Eblis, and the peacock, and her snake? All these things were as unexpected and inexplicable as the growth of the Gowkaran tree in the middle of our kitchen. I thought about how the world I was living in was inexplicable, even as on the surface it appeared that everything could be convincingly explained.

In the forest I walked and walked, and searched and searched, until I reached the place where we had kissed each other that night. No! Not there . . . Some things should be left untouched . . . One of those is the site of the lovers' first tryst . . . Even if that love should lose all value in the future. That place, that sacred place which calls to mind that holy time, must remain forever untouched so it may be recorded in the history of my feelings. The history of my feelings? I had to remember to write about this in my love notebook too. About whether it

[14] Anahita was the goddess of water, fertility, and nature, revered as a symbol of purity and life.

[15] Zoroaster's mother.

wouldn't be better if, instead of teaching us the social sciences, they taught us the history of social feelings? Or, for example, the history of love? I left that spot and went wandering in other parts of the forest. I didn't know what I was looking for exactly, but I knew it had to be somewhere I could take the pick and shovel off my shoulder without thinking about it, put them down on the ground and then start digging. Perhaps I could build a greenhouse? I love flowers. I love green leaves. Especially when rain is beating down on them, or narrow rays of light dwell on them. Or how about I dig a tunnel underground, like the ancient tunnel of Neyasar we visited a few years ago? A few minutes later I arrived back in the same place. At the patch of ground that had that night witnessed me and him and the kiss, and Eblis. Once more I moved on. There were many places that could have tempted me. Yet they didn't. It was as if the ground there had a magnetic force which, however much I moved away from it, drew me back to it again. In the end, I surrendered. Why not, anyway. I should move on from thinking that the sacred place and time are recorded within me, in my mind and in my memory. The place and time where those looks, those hot and virgin kisses had been exchanged, had been forever erased. Who was it anyway who said that time dies but places remain forever untouched? Even if nobody had interfered or tampered with that place, it was no longer that place where we had kissed each other in the middle of the night on the 10th of July, 1977. Haven't those dry leaves that were crushed beneath our restless bodies moved since then? And where now is Eblis of the beautiful countenance? Have the green leaves above us that were a week or two ago witness to our restlessness not altered in the intervening period? Whom does the moon now light up at night? Where is he now? The crows? Where are the sparrows and owls who witnessed us? Which valley and which mountain has the air we breathed at that very moment now reached? Is it not being inhaled and exhaled by the lungs of some fox? How many times has the earth rotated around itself since that night?

Sacred place is as fleeting as sacred time . . . Just like that moment when the first kiss wet our lips. That kiss . . . Ah! Where is that kiss now? Do those birds who stood in witness recall our kiss? I put the pick down and, leaning on the handle of the shovel, stood staring at the same tree the tall-statured ghost had leaned against that night, then looked at the ground again. For an instant I focused on my own thoughts. Wasn't that the same me a few minutes ago, thinking that the sanctity of the sacred place should be preserved? And wasn't it the same me who thought just a few moments ago that sacred place is as fleeting as sacred time? How was it that in such a short space of time my mind had made, presented, and confirmed these two contradictory thoughts? Which of them was trustworthy? Which thought am I, exactly?

I sat down, undecided. I looked around me. Just like that night, the dry leaves crunched beneath my feet and the green leaves above stirred in the breeze. There was a circular clearing in which I was sitting, and the surrounding trees cast their shadows over it. I remembered suddenly that Khanom Joon had said something about this little piece of the forest where no tree, bush, or flower grew. She had said that for as long as she could remember—and Khanom Joon remembers very, very many things from very, very many years ago—here had always been like this. Trees, bushes, and flowers grew everywhere but here in this little spot where the shadows of the other trees fell on it and concealed it from view. I looked up at the shady green canopy above me. At the gentle breeze that stirred the branches and leaves . . .

I lay down on the dry leaves. I fixed my gaze on the drops of rainlight falling through the leaves above me and let the smell of the humid earth and of the forest that reminded me of his wet, numbing kisses crawl over me. A smile covered my face and my eyes closed. A deep, satisfying breath entered my lungs and departed. All at once a strange feeling of elation took hold of my entire being, as if I had suddenly discovered how good it is to be alive . . . How delightful it is to see those dancing leaves under the sunlight . . . How wonderful the air is . . . How sweet a kiss is . . . How enchanting he is . . . And how marvelous it is to simply be . . . Could this be the trysting place of Eblis and her lover too? A crow took flight from a high branch, and as a fleeting beam of light, wavering through the leaves beneath its wings, settled upon the earth, I rose. I seized the pick, raised it high, and with strength brought it down upon that sliver of light; A squirrel leaped, a pheasant took flight, and a fox pricked its ears in keen alert.

On the first and second days, I dug, on my own, with my pick and shovel, a circle of five- or six-meters diameter. I sweated profusely and let the muscles of my body work till they ached, till the murmuring of the forest filled my ears, and myself be distracted from thinking about him. On the fifth day, Only Brother, biting at a peach and without asking any questions, came for a few minutes and stood over me, walked around me and the circle a little, finished off his peach, spat out the stone to one side and finally picked up the shovel and began digging. On the seventh day, Two Sisters came along. The two of them at first lurked for a few minutes behind the foliage imagining they could watch us that way. Then, as we pretended not to notice, they gradually came forward. They stood watching us, hands on hips. Then they went home, returning a few minutes later with pick and shovel. As we dug, nobody either asked or said anything. It was as if we all had a single objective: we wanted to drive away the anxieties of the adventures of recent weeks through our sweating bodies and aching muscles; we wanted the sweat of anxiety to pour out.

The second week, something broke under Only Brother's pick with a great crack. We all stared. It was a piece of green and cream glazed pottery. We all fell to talking, like chattering sparrows at five o'clock on a summer's morning. What was it doing there? Was it old, or ancient? Was there more of it? Who were they, these people who used to live in our fields and forest? Our own ancestors? Ancient Zoroastrians? The Medes?

Only Brother shot these names out in rapid fire. After the adventure of the palace, he had been the only one out of the five of us to have taken to books about the history of ancient Iran, whereas Two Sisters had taken to weeding their radish bed, and I to thoughts and fantasies of romance.

The piece of green and cream glazed pottery was a shard of a plate. The thick plate had been whole and unbroken before being smashed under Mehrab's pick. We found the other fragments and placed them side by side. Two Sisters ran home and brought glue. We cleaned the pieces carefully, as if they were sacred objects, put them side by side and glued them together. How simple it was, how beautiful, how without defect. Before we found the plate, we had had no goal in digging other than to empty out our feelings and our confused and contradictory thoughts, whereas now the picks and shovels were moving with the hope of getting somewhere. As if something down in the depths was calling us, waiting for us, and whispering about us.

I said, "Imagine that a beautiful woman with long black hair has been waiting for this moment for four thousand years, for us to bring her out from under there."

"Imagine if that woman, sitting on a pile of gold and ancient jewels, stretches out her arms to us as we are digging above her, smiling once the first ray of light strikes her face," Mandana said.

"Imagine if she has an ancient, four-thousand-year-old book in her hands and that book is the *Shahnameh*," Mehrab said.

"Shhhhh!" said Mina, frozen where she stood. "Listen, she's calling us."

And all of us really did fall silent for a moment, eyes wide open and a little afraid. Then Mehrab laughed loudly and said, "Wow, what idiots we are." And we really were. All the same, on the twelfth day these idiots reached a chunky and sizeable stone slab which they soon guessed was the ceiling of somewhere, because through the cracks along its sides, one could see that beneath it was empty. Was it really possible that our fantasies would turn out to be correct? The ceiling of a four-thousand-year-old house, complete with a long-tressed woman, book in hand, perched on a pile of gold and jewels? A woman who would turn to smile at us and at the sun with her four-thousand-year-old lips?

It was indeed a ceiling, but not of a house. That chunky and sizeable stone slab was a small part of the ceiling of a place which we would a few days later come to realize was a temple. We no longer distinguished between night and day. By night we dug, lantern in hand, by day, book in hand. That very first day when we had come across the stone slab, I had gone and found the *Illustrated Encyclopædia of Ancient Gilan* in Dad's library. In this way it became clear that thousands of years ago the plain of Gilan, as the wettest region in the whole of the Middle East as far as India, was so covered in marshes and thick rainforests that humans were unable to penetrate it and settle there until the Neolithic. It was a land that had only just emerged from underneath the Caspian Sea, whereas in the neighboring regions, where mountains, grasslands and wide valleys met, archaeologists had found the traces of pre-Neanderthal human beings dating to three hundred thousand years before the present.

Two Sisters shouted as one: "Three hundred thousand years?!'

"So that's why our forest is still full of seashells," I said.

And right then I reached out, picked up a small, white shell from among the dried leaves and branches, and put it on the plate.

Only Brother said: "Prehistory has entered history."

We all laughed. As we dug, and took turns reading from the book, it became clear that about three or four thousand years earlier, the marshlands had slowly dried out, giving way to agricultural land, while the dense forests became a place to hide from Assyrian invasions. Then the Marlik civilization emerged. A wealthy and peaceful civilization. Next, the Median Empire came to power in the western regions of Iran and the

Marlik civilization withered away. Afterwards, local religions and traditions emerged as well as the great religions of Zurvan, Mithraism, Zoroaster, and finally Islam. The book described the attacks of the Mongols and Arabs, and it was clear that that mysterious, wooded region south of the Caspian Sea, the plain of Gilan and Mazandaran, together with the snowy mountains, the narrow and winding passes, the misty, unconquerable forests, and the endless rains, was so unpredictable and impenetrable to those invading peoples that they were unable to conquer it for hundreds of years. The plain of Mazandaran and Gilan was for centuries a safe place for its inhabitants, as well as for political and religious refugees of the surrounding regions.

As we dug, we thought of our ancestors and we told ourselves to remember, the next time that our relatives came from Tehran and other cities, to show off our exciting history to them. It was as we were reading those sections of the book that a large swathe of the stone ceiling was cleared. Were we now supposed to lift up one of the stone slabs to see whether that woman was waiting for us down there, book in hand?

What happened was that once we had managed, with tremendous effort and much huffing and puffing, to move the extraordinarily heavy stone slab all of half a meter, a warm draught of dank, millennia-old, dark-depth-dwelling air rushed out and struck our sweaty, dirty, curious faces. A smell of soil and mold and the humidity of the forest and an indescribable scent. It was in that moment that it occurred to me that smells are among the most mysterious and least explicable things in the world. As Two Sisters and Only Brother were bickering about who would go down first, I gazed into the darkness of the cavity beneath me and thought about how it is impossible to describe a particular smell to someone, to him for example. Things are simpler when it comes to music. You can hum music for someone who has never heard a particular piece, but smells are confusing, profound, and indescribable.

The scent that wafted up to my face from the dark depths of

several thousand years, just like the unique and giddying scent of our first kiss, or of wild raspberry and primrose, insinuated itself into the capillaries of my body and remained trapped within me.

Eventually we called heads or tails to decide who would be the first explorer lucky enough to to descend. The luck was mine. The lot fell to me. The drop was not inconsiderable. Something like four meters, or more. We tied a knotted rope and threw it into the hole, and with everyone else holding torches and oil lamps, I descended. Before that, though, Only Brother placed his hand on my shoulder, and turning to each one of us said, "We have to promise each other something, right here. Let us swear by the life and soul of Khanom Joon that we will never ever ever speak of what we discover here to anyone." We all looked at each other . . .

I smirked. Another secret was being added to the collection.

Two Sisters said in unison, "But how long can we keep these secrets to ourselves? We'll have to tell them everything some day!"

"In that case, Mom and Dad will tell their families, and they'll tell their friends," Mehrab said. "Just imagine people who can't get their heads round these kinds of things, these secrets, these mysterious beauties, invading this forest . . . here . . . that palace . . . It's not even obvious what's under there anyway. Maybe there's nothing, but whatever there is needs to stay between the four of us, to the end of our lives." Mehrab spat on the palm of his right hand and extended it to us, looking at each one of us with great seriousness. Then I spat on my right hand and placed it in his. After a little delay and hesitation, Two Sisters did likewise. We placed our hands together and swore on Khanom Joon's life and soul, even though in that moment we did not know that so many unexpected events would come to pass in our lives that we would completely forget that there was this temple concealed in a corner of the forest.

I grabbed the rope and descended. When I got to the end of the rope, I let go. It was high. My ankle gave way a little and pain shot through it. It was pitch black down there. Cool and stuffy. They threw a candle and matches down to me. I lit the candle and under my feet and on the walls I could see thick tree roots that had made their way inside from all directions, twisting around one another. I moved ahead into the darkness. The space seemed large. Perhaps ten meters long. Was there no sign of the woman with her long locks? What about the pile of jewels and gold? The book of the secrets of life? No . . . There was nothing around me. Neither ancient pottery bowls and plates, nor treasure chest. The walls and floor were covered in large, rough, white stones, the roots had forced open the cracks between the stone slabs and become entangled as they grew downwards. There were no objects lying on the ground. I made out two arched niches on either side, on which there stood the remains of something like tallow burners. A little further on, at the end of the space, my eyes were struck by a white object. This large object was made of uniformly white stone and sat in a large recess, the upper part of which was arched like the mehrab in a mosque. The Sisters and Only Brother were still on their way down, one by one. I advanced and lay my hand on that stone, which seemed outsized to me. I held my candle higher and was lost in its great majesty and beauty.

At the end of the great ancient space sat no long-haired woman on a heap of gold, book in hand, but there was instead a stocky and handsome young man sitting on a splendid bull, his right hand grasping a dagger that he plunged into the bull's throat, his left hand meanwhile pulling the bull's head up. Underneath, under that chunky stone slab we had moved, there lay waiting for us after four thousand years a bulky statue of Mithra and the Bull: the ancient god of love, pacts, loyalty, and secrecy.

I stayed there, candle in hand, mouth open, rooted to the spot until the others arrived. As soon as Mehrab, two meters away, caught sight of Mithra and the Bull, he fell, stunned, onto both knees, and did not stand up again for another three days and nights, and when he finally did, crying and in a state of trance, he repeated madly, "Raven, Occult, Soldier, Lion, Persian, Sun, Father! Raven, Occult, Soldier, Lion, Persian, Sun, Father! Raven, Occult, Soldier, Lion, Persian, Sun, Father!" We three sisters, astonished and terrified, kept calling Mehrab, who was staring at the statue like someone metamorphosed, repeating those words deliriously, and we shook him so that he would come to his senses, but he wriggled out of our grip and, throwing himself on the statue, wept and yelled, "Where's the ladder, then? Where's the ladder? The first rung, Saturn. The second, Venus. The third, Jupiter. The fourth, Mars. The fifth, Mercury. The sixth, the Moon. The seventh, the Sun. The seventh, the Sun. The seventh, the Sun . . ."

Not so long before, we had thought that Leyla was the inheritor of the family madness, but when Mehrab set eyes on the statue in the temple, I changed my mind and realized that Mehrab was heir to that accursed madness. I believe those three days and nights in the temple are what later made Mehrab go to war and come back insane and made what happened, happen. Because it was after the discovery of the temple that, when we went back to the mansion, he stood in front of the full-length mirror in his room, touched his face and body in amazement, and said, "I didn't look like this on Venus! Who is this in the mirror?"

As far as I am concerned, everything in Mehrab's life began with that temple, from the very moment he caught sight of Mithra, because even at the war's front, a few years later, he kept wagging his finger threateningly and asking, "What's the latest with Mithra, hmm? What's the latest with Mithra?" What else did he mean by "Mithra," if not the statue of Mithra?

Right? But the Two Sisters would say, "No, that's not what he means!" They said he meant a woman called Mithra with whom he had fallen in love . . . But. Well. When did Mehrab even find the time to see such a woman and fall in love? He was always either in the mansion, or at the front, or living for forty days as a hermit in the Mithra temple . . .

Later, Khanom Joon told of how in the period after the war Mehrab came running home one day, more insane than before, and said that he had seen with his own eyes that some Revolutionary Guards and Basijis had dragged Mithra and the Bull out into the middle of the forest and buried them alive. It was at that time that he used to wake up screaming and shouting and say that he could hear Mithra roaring furiously, and the bull bellowing from underground in the middle of the jungle, asking for help, after which in the obscurity of the night he would rush out to that same spot and keep digging the earth with his bare hands . . . keep digging the earth . . . keep digging the earth . . . But on the day, we discovered the Mithra temple, Mina and Mandana wouldn't accept what I had to say; so be it. Years afterwards, during the war, when Mehrab hit his head so hard against the wall that blood started flowing down his face, and said, "You idiots, haven't you considered the number twelve at all? You idiots, haven't you considered the number twelve at all?" Only then did they say, "Aha! This is the Madness!"

But these two sisters of mine, Mina and Mandana, didn't realize that the symptoms of the Madness revealed themselves mysteriously, surreptitiously, and slowly. It is true that for a while after the discovery of the temple, Mehrab attended to his daily tasks and came with us to school, but there's no reason for a person who has been driven mad to start doing mad things right away. It's possible that the madness shows itself later, so that no one catches even the faintest whiff of it until years later. Hadn't that been the case with Mom's grandfather's grandfather? The one auntie Narges said had been a lamplighter in Qajar times. So often had he gone out punctually each night, sticking a long pole into the gas holes that he ended up obsessed with his work. For forty whole years that was his job, every night at the same time, until electricity arrived in our neighborhood. He was then retired from service, but he would still go out at precisely the same time every night carrying the same pole with its flaming end looking for those same gas lamps, which were now electric. According to auntie Narges, the poor lamplighter used to stick his pole with its flame into the electric lights at the appointed hour. As soon as the electric lights turned on, he felt happy and proud, standing up straight and smiling proudly at the passers-by, a smile that meant, "Look, I've lit the lamps for you . . . Look, it's me who's responsible for lighting up your city." Yes, the Madness is this sort of thing. Sometimes it happens gradually and insidiously, so that you don't realize exactly at what hour and second on a thoroughly normal day of your life it has laid you low.

That night we discovered the temple and Mehrab was distorted by the statue, recalling memories of his ancient life, we had no choice but to tell Mom and Dad that we wanted to sleep in the forest the following night. They weren't particularly surprised, since we had put up a tent in the forest several times before, but, as always, they wanted to send Nader and Shafiqeh with us to prepare our tent and bedding and food; we wouldn't accept, on the pretext that we wanted to be on our own in the forest and seek adventure, a bit like Tarzan or Tintin. That night, Mom was eventually persuaded to let Shafiqeh put some food in a basket for us, and she was reassured that we were taking the tent and sleeping bags, mosquito nets and mats with us. I also took a book: Ahmad Hami's *Mithra the Divinity*. We lit a fire in the temple and threw a blanket over Mehrab, who was still on both knees staring at the statue and muttering invocations under his breath. That night, the ancient statue visible through the flames cast us into a mysterious silence, whilst I tried to recreate in my mind the feelings of the last person who had, thousands of years before, left this temple for the last time and set down the last stone slab over the temple ceiling. Did they know? Or did they not?

Chapter Five

Just when I thought I understood life and its secrets better than someone of my age usually would, something happened that made me realize I knew nothing about it. That day, as I paused briefly while reading the letter and, letter in hand, stood at the top of the slope in our garden watching Mr. Peyk, the Zorvan postman, recede into the distance on the road leading from the mansion to the village, I realized that until now I had only been capable of looking at the garden of life, full of secrets, through a tiny window set in the massive wall of time and place, and perhaps would always only be able to do so. That day I realized that the location of the window might change, but that its size would always stay the same: small . . . small . . . very small. Through that tiny, that very tiny window, each time I could only catch a glimpse of a fraction of the vast garden of life; a fraction of the eternity of a tree . . . A part of the limpidity of a spring . . . A trace of the reverie of a butterfly's wing . . . A shard of the anxiety of a crow's shadow falling on a yellow dragonfly; a tiny corner of life. Almost nothing. However hard I try, however much I see and understand, this life does not afford me the possibility of seeing anything in its entirety. I understood this limited truth that day when, only a little while after the story of the temple and Mehrab's metamorphosis, after having heard nothing from Behnam, Mr. Peyk, the only postman in Zorvan, pedaling hard and dripping sweat, came up the garden hill to flaunt another unknown fragment of the mysterious garden of life, before me. To slap me in the face. To spit on me . . . With a letter in Bahman's crabby, froggy hand.

Shokoof, I wanna tell you stuff I never told no one before . . . I dont feel well and I started to feel even worse after I left your mansion . . . Im gonna take a risk and tell you this stuff cos otherwise Im gonna curl up and die . . . Tho I dont know why Im telling you this. I know when I smaked my old man in the gob it mustve come as a shock, yeah??? God knows what horible things your Mom, auntie Jarireh must think about me . . . Im not like you Shokoof cos I grew up in a difrend way with a difrend old lady and old man in a difrend part of town . . . My old man only knows how to insult peeple and belch and shout and get drunk on cheep booze and once hes off his face to get under peeples cars and fix em. He says if hes not pissed he cant fix cars so once I told him I must take after him cos I got shit for brains The basterd prick grabbed hold of me and wacked me so hard I chucked up blood I cant stand him and I cant stand my old lady too even tho shes your auntie Narges . . . Have you seen when she comes to your house how proper she talks? Thats all just empty showing off. She doesnt speack this stupid way at home. Shes a bloody spy that woman, I move and she reports it to my old man so he can wack me. And I never told you this stuff Shokoof, whenever I come to your house and to that garden and huge freaking mansion and the servants and all those posh people for a while after Im all down, like . . . Dont think Im jelous . . . The question is, how can two sisters be so difrend!!! Ones your Mom, ones my old lady!!! My old lady spends all day taking pills and kipping and defending my old man, she walks up and down and says her head hurts and walks a bit more and says shes depressed then throws down a pill . . . He can do whatever he damn well likes, she always defends him, she dont care at all she just says itll help me grow up as if someone hitting you helps you grow up??? do you remember once my arm was broken? They pretended to everyone Id fallen off my bike . . . Bullshit . . . fuck them . . . My old man broke it Yeah that's the stupid prick of an uncle you got there Shokoof. I know you must be wondering what the bloody ells going on . . . Shokoof Shokoof Im going mad in this house.

I wanna get the hell out of here but I dunno when or where exactly . . . And my God I dunno why you need to know Im getting out of here or why you should even care?

You know I say if we wanna grow up quicker and get out of here what should I do? You wont believe it, often I stuff my face on the sly so that Ill grow faster, so Ill get big and escape from this hell. Maybe this way my old man ll be afraid of me and stop hitting me Screw him the bastard piece of shit He was still hitting me even with me the size I am until that day in your house when I smaked him good and proper . . . That made me feel good I can tell you if I dared Idve punched him some more so much that he chuked up blood That day I rekoned if I did that in front of all of you he wouldnt dare lift a finger on me . . . I was right . . . He hasnt laid a finger on me since but I know hes counting down the seconds till I give him an excuse again . . . Sometimes my old man when hes gotten up write side of bed he picks on me, tells me to come and learn how to fix cars with im but then as soon as were under the car and I ask him a question he swears at me tells me Im a idiot and I dont understand nothing. Actually I really like fixing cars and Im really good at it but the old man swears so much at me and shouts at me I cant even be with him for a minute. Listen Shokoof I think thats why Im writing to you actually cos I wanted to ask what do you think I should fucking do. I know your proper, like, always with your head in a book and studying and all and that you grew up in a proper family so maybe you now what someone with no luck like me should do after running away? Yeah?

Even though I like fixing cars I know every time I go under one I get reminded of the old man and that really gets to me . . . Itd be better if I give it up, dont you think? What if I did my militry service? Or go to clergy school? The lads at school say these are the only places you can go and do nothing and kip and get paid for it even tho the clergy men live worse than tramps so theres no bloody future in that . . . But I herd that if after militry service I join the army then there is a future, like You have to learn fighting with enemys . . . I'm not afraid of thumping or getting thumped and Id be happy to get rid of all my rage like that . . . So maybe Ill join the army then, right???? Tho the clergy men kill people a difrend way let me tell you they kill you softly a few times my old lady made me go to the bleedin mosk to hear their bleeding wining I now what those good for nothings go on about. They kill your hart and soul they kill your thinking, dont you agree? This bloke, this clergy man was saying if you kill your own kid but you make sure you never miss your night prayers then you go to heaven cos the kid is part of your propety like and you can do what the hell you like with your propety can you beleive that??? It means heven is full of murderering motherfukers? We didnt wanna do you remember a few years ago suddenly our Mahsa got a fever and died? . . . You wanna now what really happened? Shokoof if I dont tell nobody this stuff Im gonna go out of my mind fall down and die. Poor Mahsa my four year old inocent sister the poor kid didnt die of a fever. My old lady killed her. Yeah, your dear auntie. Yeah your dear auntie Narges took her to the bathroom with her own hands and stuck her head in the basin full of water and killed her and then with her wet hands came into the living room where I was doing my homework and said very carmly and just like that "go and tell your dad I killed Mahsa cos she was making a racket. Yeah . . . it was that easy . . . then what happened? Nothing . . . they took her to the loony bin and made her stay there a little wile then the doctors said you can go home know back to your normal life so it meens if your strong enogh you can kill your other kid too. My old man was struck dumb and didnt say a thing to my old lady but he was getting the booze down more and more every day . . . And me after that every night I was terified my old lady come and kill me in the night so night after night I kept my eyes open like a dog . . . Your the first person Ive told any of this too . . . And then my old lady is always doing her prayers and saying honoring your father and mother and your teacher is the highest of duties . . . yeah . . . praying and the Quran . . . honoring your father and mother . . . respect your teacher . . . The teacher in our school is even nastier than my old lady and Im supposed to respect him? I saw with my own eyes our religion teacher take the kids into the lav at brake time I cant get the sound of that kid moning out of my ears when they came outta the lav the teacher wipes away the kids tears and says go back to your classrom like a good lad that same day when it was brake time I went up to that lad and told him Ab, mate, dont be scared, Im gonna go up to that teacher and stick a nife into him he didnt say nothing. I says lets go an tell your old lady an old man but he didnt say nothing again so I says lets go an see the deputy and the head but he didnt wanna he was scared the poor kid hed gone dumb you no what happened next? The next morning when I went to school I saw Ab d hung himself from the bar what holds up the voleyball net Just like that . . . over . . . No doubt his old lady an old man are peices of shitttt just like mine Since then you dont now how crap I feel whenever I see that bar or that teacher my brain freezes my eyes fill with blood do you now that day when I saw Abs body hanging from the bar of the voleyball net I promissed myself one day Ill kill that teacher . . . and then youll read about it in the news . . . The teachers called Saeed Tousi Im telling you this cos if one day you red about him being killed in the news paper then youll now no doubt its me what killed him.

You now write know when Im righting all this stuff for you in my own mind Im wandering why Im righting this stuff too you in the first place and why dont I right it for Mahin and Mozhgan insted or for Iraj? When we came to your garden for the holidays I thought Id tell you all of this stuff but there was no time was there There was all the stuff with us getting lost and that palice and that woman and Leyla . . . there was no time for us to talk

Listen let me tell you something promise me you wont get upset . . . swear by Bahmans life an soul you wont get upset . . . That night when you were galloping off on that horse I notised that pritty boy Behnam couldnt take his eyes off of you In that room with all those mirrors to I notised when everyone was dancing he was wispering something in your ear and I saw you turn white and after that you was stearing clear of him but truth be told I didnt dare come an ask you what hed said to you to make you upset? I dont like that little showoff prick Behnam with his funny forenn accent and his prancing around . . . just you say the word and Ill sort him out . . . put a few slashes on him . . . Just saying . . .

By the way Ill tell you something elsell make you go what the hell from the time when I came back home till now Ive dreamed of that woman loads a times shes always in the same house on the top story of the palace . . . in my dream she always says the same thing to me: Bahman in this world evryone gets to see what they wanna see so what do you wanna see?

What does this mean Shokoof? What? What did that woman mean? Tell me why Leyla went? Has she come back?

I gotta go but dont you go sending me no letters for know, O.K.? I gotta go somewhere new so when I got a new address Ill right to you myself.

Shokoof, fuck, I still dunno why Im righting you all this stuff you now? Damn.

Yours always your sacrifice Bahman

Tears in my eyes, I asked myself if it wasn't the same Bahman who, that night in the palace, picked up the tombak and in protest at the mournful melody coming from Mahin's tar, beat out a danceable tune in 6/8 time and got everyone to jig and laugh? Wasn't it him who in the mirrored room put on a flowery shirt and shaliteh-skirt and did an impression of a woman and made everyone burst with laughter? So, were the people of old right when they said that the more someone laughs, the sadder they are? From now on I must remember . . . must remember . . . must remember not to trust in lips and not to take my eyes off other people's eyes, because whatever happens, eyes never lie. From now on I must remember . . . must remember . . . must remember that beneath every rough and rugged exterior there certainly lies a warm and innocent heart suffering and weeping.

Bahman himself knows that there's no secret in our mothers' family that stays hidden for very long . . . Although they themselves, Aziz, for example, that the Quran says backbiting is like eating the flesh of your dead brother, it seems like this flesh tastes good in their mouths, because they never hold back from gossiping and spreading rumors . . . Each maternal aunt and uncle is worse than the next, but fortunately Mom is different . . . So does this mean that Mom and Dad were in on the secret of little Mahsa's being killed? Don't say Mehrab knows too and that's why he made us spit on the palms of our hands that day in the temple and swear on Khanom Joon's life and soul not to reveal our secret? Although these Two Sisters . . . ugh, these Two Sisters . . . that's why I have to practice keeping quiet, practice keeping secrets, practice being alone.

As I expected, a little while afterwards news of Bahman's running away from home reached us, but not in the way I expected, and the whole thing was so weird that we were left with our mouths agape in astonishment. At first, everyone said it wasn't true, then some said he'd been bewitched, and the servants and maternal uncles and aunts performed their prayers in dread and said that the apocalypse had started. I knew the truth about Bahman running away from home, but they, my maternal relatives, said that auntie Narges had sworn that the truth was that Bahman used to lay an egg every day. They said that amidst the news of national progress and development, the government's multimillion-dollar contracts with Western oil companies, the Red Prayer strike at Saint Mary's Church in Paris, the inauguration of this project and that factory, scattered reports of labor committee protests across the country, and the release of Dariush and Googoosh's new cassette in the newspapers, this incident didn't cause much of a stir, but in any case, they say the news was leaked and spread; The day his parents took him to the local hospital, doubled up in pain from stomach aches, he laid a sizeable egg in front of the disbelieving eyes of the doctors and nurses, while his father turned crimson and then purple in anger and disbelief and clipped him firmly on the back of the neck and—it's not clear why—shouted, "You shameless, dishonorable so-and-so!" It was his bad luck that the first egg had not yet been laid when the journalists who had come to the hospital to photograph a successful heart transplant rushed out of the operating theatre to take photos of the wretched Bahman from behind and print it in the newspapers. They showed the newspaper to me too. They had blurred out the face of a young man in the photo, and instead of his full name had put simply "B, 17, from Tehran."

The way that the rumor wound its way to the mansion servants, taking on ever more lurid details, was that Bahman, although in certain regards rather ill-starred, since he was nonetheless very tall and rather attractive, was not so unfortunate when it came to finding girlfriends. The servants said that his first girlfriend, who was, moreover, three years older than him, broke up with him appalled and vomiting as soon as she discovered he laid an egg a day and that his mother made omelets and kuku with the eggs, and didn't for a second think of getting back together with him, whereas the second girlfriend did exactly the opposite. She accepted everything quite calmly and easily. Everything was going well until poor Bahman realized that not only was his girlfriend writing a book about him on the sly, "Memoirs of Me and My Chicken-Bum Boyfriend," but that in gatherings of friends where he hadn't the slightest expectation of it, she suddenly let the secret out and got everyone to lay bets, and Bahman out of embarrassment to lay an egg there and then in front of everybody's gaze. The servants say that worse than all this was the fact that Bahman found out that the girl was secretly saving up the money from the bets to pay for a one-way ticket to Sweden. As a result, according to what the family said, one day poor Bahman, who just couldn't catch a break, jumped over the wall into the courtyard of the neighboring house, went into the cupboard where the neighbor kept bedding for guests, and started to cry. The way that Shafiqeh and Shahnaz muttered about it, my uncle and auntie didn't think his crying was at all important. In an alcoholic and poor family like Bahman's, the last thing anyone cared about was the feelings of a child. Who could be bothered to go into mourning on account of an insignificant little egg emerging from the behind of a seventeen-year-old boy? In this way, it was easily overlooked until sunset when his mother casually dropped in at the neighbor's house and declared in a loud voice, so that her son in the wall cupboard could hear, that if people chose to make fun of him that was their business, but if he had a brain in his head he could make a bit of money from it and help his father out. And he'd get out of military service too. What could be better? As for Bahman, however, it seemed a much better idea had occurred to him, since he sprang out of the cupboard, his face wet with tears and red with rage and embarrassment, went home, threw a few clothes in a small bag, and went straight to the nearby base to sign up as a soldier and thus wipe himself from the locals' stubborn memories before the news could reach his classmates. He took so long to come back from military service that two years later, when first the revolution happened, then the war started, his corpse returned to his neighborhood along with the first caravan of martyrs; with pride and honor, an unrequited martyr. They prepared hejlehs[16] for him, and girls and boys wore black for him, and his family finally proudly acceded to a fashionable and pleasing moniker: the Martyr's Family. Whatever it was, it was a better name than the one the mischievous boys of the neighborhood had given them: the Chicken-Bum Family. Despite all this, I would continue to get letters from him regularly for years afterward. In

[16] Hejleh is a symbolic small room resembling the bridal chamber, decorated and displayed during religious mourning ceremonies and memorial services for youth who became martyrs before marriage.

the same crabby, froggy hand, with the same spelling mistakes and insults and signature at the bottom:

Yours always your sacrifice Bahman

After reading Bahman's letter, with tears drying on my cheeks, I sat down under a tree in the garden for a while, thinking about those around me. How well did I know them? Did I know them at all? I knew almost nothing about Mina and Mandana, and I had always considered them very close to one another and very distant from me and Mehrab. What did I know about Mom and Dad? About their lives before they married? About the people of Zorvan? Perhaps I only know each member of the family, close or distant, based on a single characteristic, on a single insignificant attribute. For instance, in my mind, I always say, "Auntie Touran the Voracious," or my maternal grandmother "Aziz the Timid," or for example "Auntie Malek the Melancholic," and "Khanom Joon the Sage." Without knowing it themselves, some of them are affected by something I have named "the lock." They have locked on to something and their entire life revolves around that habit, that lock, and naturally I only know about that lock and nothing more.

That day, Bahman's letter in my hands, as I looked around at the farthest reaches of the garden from underneath the great Caucasian elm tree, I itemized the following types of lock as known to me in the family: the "fear of God" lock; the "work" lock; the "money" lock; the "chatterbox" lock; the "stuffing yourself" lock; the "popping out babies" lock; the "old days were better" lock; the "whatever will become of us?" lock. For example, Touran Khanom and her six badly-behaved children, the paternal aunt of the maternal uncle of some distant or close relative or other, are afflicted by the "stuffing yourself" lock. Nothing in life is as important to them as eating. She organizes her relationships with people based on the food she can or cannot eat with them. For example, she will become the best of friends with someone who eats mostly kebab and rice or lamb shank and rice, but if she once eats rice with lentils with someone, then she doesn't bother to meet up with them again. Or she'll classify people based on the kind of food they eat and make up her own vocabulary for them. For example, she'll say that "Such and such are pumpkin rice eaters." In other words, they are poor and of no use to her. Or she'll say, "So-and-so are lamb kebab eaters." This means that they are very wealthy and therefore good and proper people. Or for instance when she wants to say, "I swear it's true," she says, "by the life and soul of Mirza Qasemi." Once I heard her tell someone in a serious tone, "Just think, I once passed on Ghormeh Sabzi, twice on crispy bottom of macaroni, and once on broad bean rice with lamb shank, and what are you compared to them!" As close and distant family later told us, Touran Khanom, who was known to everyone in the family, close and distant, as Auntie Touran, out of love of food and living at others' expense eventually took herself and her six mischievous greedy guts children off to the house of one of our relatives in a mysterious and remote village called Razan in Mazandaran, where they were turned by magic into a group of jinnis and disappeared for ever from our family.

Or the cousin of Mom or Dad's paternal aunt who pops out child after child, her face paler every time we see her and her stomach more swollen than before. She doesn't even have the strength to walk or talk. And if she does ever open her mouth in front of the reproachful gaze of the family, she smiles lifelessly and says, "What do you want me to do? I love kids." Yet we know she's lying. Her thoughts are *locked* on popping out babies.

In the eyes of the entire family, Bahman had run away from home, but in reality he had been affected by the "writing letters to me" lock, and although I was awake, I had been affected by the sleeping lock. Mom said it was because of all the hormones released during puberty. I knew it was because a long time had passed without me hearing from him. For a long time after I got my first period, Mom connected everything I did to my periods, thinking that it was because of my period that I was listless, because of my period that I was so quiet, because of my period that I slept so much, and because of my period that I ate so little. Although I was the one who had just started to get her period, it was Mom who was suffering from the period lock.

That day I had stood behind the door of my bedroom and whispered to Mina and Mandana that my underwear was bloody, and trembling with fear I asked them, "Does this mean I'm going to die soon?" Maryam, who was, as she was most mornings, busy changing the bedsheets, happened to be passing by and heard what I was saying, upon which she ran and reported everything to Mom. There is an unwritten rule in the mansion, namely that the cooks and servants have the duty to report whatever happens in it promptly to Mom and Dad. That said, Mehrab believes that important reports are first delivered to Khanom Joon. As Mandana later related to me, as soon as she heard the news, Mom ordered Maryam to tell Mandana to give me a couple of juicy slaps on my cheeks. I had absolutely no idea what was going on and, expecting the others' sympathy, was struck dumb in astonishment as Mandana casually slapped me, but she swiftly hugged me and said, "I'm sorry, I'm sorry, the order came from the top. I got a couple of slaps too the first time I got my period." Mom came in and said, with a triumphant smile, "Congratulations. You got your period. You got slapped so that from now on your cheeks will be ruddy and beautiful and so that you don't forget you've grown up!'

Yes indeed! Mom is that kind of woman; on the one hand, she is the manager of the provincial branch of the Organization for Children's and Adolescents' Intellectual Development and personally received an official letter of commendation from Her Majesty the Empress Consort for her efforts in expanding the Organization's civic and educational activities, and on the other she loves preserving ancient traditions even at the risk of her colleagues accusing her of being backwards. In these cases,

Mom usually replies to her colleagues that, given the speed with which this country is progressing and modernizing, not one of these beliefs and customs will be around in ten or twenty years. "So, for as long as we're alive," she says, "Let us gladden the souls of our ancestors with what's left of them and make some memories for our children."

Yes, for Mom that slap, rather than being a genuine and serious belief, was more of a modest effort to make a tradition memorable for me, yet at the same time she told me I should remember that getting my period meant I had grown up! Does it mean that I have now grown up? That easily? Does someone grow up with a drop of blood on their underwear?

I must remember to write in my notebook of memories that age fifteen, after getting a period, tastes of a pair of sharp slaps and a dragging, tedious, motionless summer. I must remember that fifteen is an age when the older members of the family, especially the Two Sisters, gradually expect that you should make judgements about them and give your opinion in favor of one or other of them in their quarrels. It's a cursed age when everybody expects that you start talking. Talking. Talking. It's an age when the Two Sisters stare you shamelessly in the face and exclaim, "How don't you know that? Aren't you fifteen now?" It's an age when early one morning you wake up to a *sedreh* and a *kosti* and arrangements for the *navjote* initiation ceremony, where Jamshid Khan and Khanom Joon, seated and leaning on a cane, surrounded by relatives and the Jaamasp the Magus, even as they stare at you with serious eyes, ask you smiling: "Is it your intention to follow the Zoroastrian religion and customs? Is it your intention to follow the path of our good ancestors?" You ask yourself, taken aback and terrified, "Is it really my intention?" In a sleepy voice and with frowning eyebrows, I answered, "No." And faced with Khanom Joon and Jamshid Khan's astonished and disapproving looks, I left the room, and in my pajamas jumped on Shabro and galloped to the forest where I could scream a little distance away from everyone.

I must remember that fifteen is an age when, even though you've fallen in love, kissed and been kissed, at the bottom of your heart you sometimes want to put your doll Talkhun in Shabro's saddlebag and, deep in the jungle, far from others' gaze, play with it. Fifteen is an age when you like to have secrets for yourself, and without knowing which of these secrets you want to think about on your own, close the door of your room on others. You don't know exactly what you should hide from whom, and for that reason you like to hide everything from everyone. The first thing is your own romantic adventure. Then the adventure of the palace. Of the temple. Of Eblis. Of Leyla. The secrets want to burst out of every pore of your skin. That's why you are in constant struggle with your own skin and soul. Fifteen is the age when, from others' perspective, you become mysterious. You turn silent. Whereas from your perspective, you are merely protecting your skin and soul, your secrets. You are protecting your being yourself. Against the outside. Against whatever is outside you and trying to break into or invade what is within you and turn you into somebody you don't want to be. You build a strong, invisible wall around yourself. You let your hair flop down in front of your eyes so you cannot be seen. You vanish. Even at home you don't let anyone, especially not the Two Sisters, touch your bedding. Or your wardrobe. Or your desk drawer where you've hidden that handwritten manuscript of the *Shahnameh* as a memento of the mysterious palace, the notebook with your memoirs in, and the two notebooks on love. You don't even like anyone to take a photo of you. You keep frowning and you don't know why. Fifteen, after getting your period, is the year of stubborn opposition to growing up. Your entire being is striving to resist growing up. Perhaps without you even knowing, something inside you is protesting. Something in your being wants to say "No!" Fifteen is the age when childhood is assassinated; either you surrender and kill the child in you, or others assassinate it for you. The result is the same. Exactly what the adults all want, the sacrifice of childhood innocence and excitement under the feet of ill-tempered and monotonous adulthood.

Therefore, after reading Bahman's letter, not hearing from Behnam, getting my period, resisting donning the *sedreh* and succumbing to my family's irritation, first silence overcame me, then the desire to be alone . . . and, eventually, I started sleeping for longer. At first it was eight hours, ten, then twelve, and after that, whenever I came to, I would notice that I had fallen asleep and had been dreaming in some corner of the fields or house or forest or temple. My dreams, at first short and simple, little by little became long and complicated. My dreams plunged so deep into the stream of rebellious hormones, of carefree, show-off hormones, that one day I went to sleep and only woke up three days later to ask, terrified, "Where's Behnam?" When I was fully awake and realized that I had been asleep three whole days and had completely forgotten that Behnam had abandoned me a while ago, I was afraid. After I fell asleep again, I woke up a month later and when I did, once more asked, terrified, "So where's Behnam?" This time, when I realized that I had been sleeping for an entire month and my memory of the past was confused, I began to be so afraid of sleep that I cut my finger with a knife and sprinkled salt in my eyes every night so that I wouldn't fall asleep. Yet in the end, after several days in a half-waking, half-sleeping state, I succumbed and didn't wake up again for months, before eventually asking, the moment I woke up, terrified, "So where's Behnam?"

The prayer-writers' prayers and amulets had no effect, nor did the consultations with specialists and their tests. In the end everyone reached a simple conclusion: I needed sleep. Just that.

Once, in one of those half-waking, half-sleeping states where I used to walk eyes closed and sleep eyes open, I did some calculations and realized that from childhood to that present moment I had met twelve prophets in my dreams. I had seen the face of one of these twelve with such clarity that if I were to encounter him in real life, I would immediately be able to recognize him; he was an old Indian man who had appeared in my dreams six or seven months before the whole adventure of the tree and the palace and Behnam and Eblis. He was the twelfth prophet.

Half-awake, half-asleep, I saw him, short and bent, come toward me as I lay on the bed, and as I watched him, he bent over me and with two fingers pulled out something like a little tack from between my eyebrows, then walked backwards away from me, the tack between his fingers, before disappearing into a luminous crack in the wall. I felt a light tingling between my eyebrows and touched the spot with my hand. I wouldn't see him again in any dream until many years later, long after the revolution and the end of the war and my and your return, when I saw him on the road behind the mansion, with the same dog, the little brown dog that had woken me up from the long sleep, heading away from me toward the forest. I immediately recognized him from behind. It was the same short, bent Indian prophet I had dreamt of, the same dhoti around his waist and legs and the same thin, white scarf wrapped around his upper body, covering half of his wrinkled, sun-beaten body. What was he doing appearing in my waking state? And in Zorvan, too? After all those years? I went hesitatingly towards him, as he moved away from me with calm, uniform steps. What should I say to him anyway? I walked faster, drawing closer to him, and took a long look at him before, without realizing it, the words sprang out of my mouth. "There's hardly any doubt." The little brown dog stood between the two of us, sometimes looking at me, sometimes at the old man. The dog's face had not changed one bit after all those years. With an inner calm and without turning to face me at all, the old man repeated to me, as he continued to walk, "No. There's hardly any doubt."

Was it him? Did he know me? Hesitatingly, I asked him, "Why did you visit me in my dream years ago? How did you know me?"

His head bowed, walking slowly and with uniform steps, he

cast a fleeting glance at me out of the corner of his eye. "I don't know anyone," he said.

"You mean you enter the dreams of people you don't know, for no reason, and do things for them?"

The old man stood still. He looked at me carefully with his black kohl-lined eyes, and with an Indo-Persian accent, said, "Your life was transformed after I removed that tack from between your eyebrows, was it not?"

I was rooted to the spot. So, he knew exactly who I was. Then he turned slowly away from me and resumed walking in the direction of the forest. Sinking down into thought, I set off behind him, following him as he went into the forest and reached a wooden hut which he then entered. I had never seen that hut there before. I sat on a tree stump outside it, waiting for something unknown. The dog too sat down by my feet and did not take its eyes off me. To remember the past, I played with it a little. Then I sat waiting again. I wanted to say something to the old man, but didn't know what it was. An hour later he came out of the hut. He handed me a bowl of masala chai and said, "Don't wait here. There is nothing further I can do for you."

I drank the chai to the last dregs and suddenly remembered what I wanted to ask him. "Can Kay-Khosro handle it?"

"Like you," he said. "In due time, people will visit him in his dreams. So go now. Go. Go."

He took the bowl from my hand, turned his back on me and went back into the hut. The dog went with him too, turning back to me every now and then, looking at me and wagging its tail.

Thus, the days passed with me in a half-waking, half-sleeping state and pining at my separation from Behnam, while I had come to realize that when he left he always took a little bit of us with him and left a little bit of himself behind with us. That is why I am suspicious of all beginnings and endings. Because I have realized that whatever has ended, continues its life quietly and insidiously. Just like him in my heart.

Weeks passed . . . Months passed. There was never any word from Behnam, until one day Mehrab came and stood over me while I was half-awake, half-asleep and gave me the news: "Behnam's gone to America." The sentence was short and simple. Half-awake, half-asleep I felt Mehrab's hand calmly brush away a teardrop rolling down my right cheek. Is what happens in life not sometimes less believable than what happens in our dreams? That night, after that long kiss, had he not said, as we wished each other goodbye, "I shall see you soon right here once more"? Though months had gone by since then, the word "soon" helped retain a thousand hopes in my heart. It could mean the days and weeks ahead. Somewhere around here. One day, from among these same days . . . Don't say abandonment is the custom in romance? To hell with literature lessons, the ghazals, the qasidahs, the poems which, whatever they are, speak of separation from the beloved. That night I dreamt of Leyla. She was sitting on the swing in the middle of the kitchen, with her long, white hair and childlike, innocent face, sucking on a tart medlar as the wind tossed her long hair up and down. We had a good long chat, but when I came to, I had forgotten everything except one thing. She had said to me, "Move away from yourself. Call yourself by your own name. Don't say 'me.' Say 'Shokoofeh.'[17] So that Shokoofeh turns into a tree. Into spring. So that Shokoofeh turns into somebody who cannot be abandoned so easily."

Leyla was right, that's exactly what I should have done, but could I ever get the better of this whole half-waking, half-sleeping thing? I was angry with him, with my own feebleness, but he was locked inside me. In the old days they used to say people's names are sacred, and that when you call someone

[17] Translator's Note: the given name "Shokoofeh" means "blossom."

by their name, you take over a piece of their soul. Each time he'd uttered my name, he had made a piece of my soul his. With every time he'd said "Shokoofeh," he had summoned me and the trees and the spring. Now that he had left and I would never hear my name from his mouth again, it was as if he had stolen my soul, the trees and the spring from me. All the same, a little later I wondered, stupidly and hopefully, whether life and time did not follow a circular course? Saturday, after passing through several Saturdays, returns again to Saturday. Spring, after passing through several seasons, returns to spring. Sunrise, after passing through several hours, returns to sunrise. So won't Behnam return to me? But then I admonished myself, "No . . . no . . . he won't return to me!" Just as no spring water returns to its source. Just as no book returns to its beginning. I was angry. I was seething with rage. I had to do something. I had to change. I had to make myself feel better. So much for the tree and the temple, and so much for him . . . Everything dissolves me into myself. Why does everything suck me down into myself? I have to come out. I have to breathe. If it's that easy to leave, if abandoning, if being abandoned is that haphazard, why should I pass my life in sorrow at being far from him, half-waking, half-sleeping . . . So it was that one day, half-awake, half-asleep, I decided to wake myself up, in whatever way possible, and keep myself awake. An inner rage urged me to lift myself up and get me to react. So it was that one midnight I was woken up by a dog barking. My eyes opened suddenly, though I was not asleep. In the half-light of the room, I gazed at the ceiling. Then at the window. Outside the window, the crescent moon was staring at me. I heard the barking again. It didn't sound like Paapi, our dog. I got out of bed. After God knows how many months, I put my foot on the ground fully conscious. My legs tingling, I went towards the main door of the mansion. The mansion was dark, and it looked like everyone else was in their own rooms dreaming deeply. As soon as I opened the main door, a little brown dog came inside and circled me once, before heading upstairs. Our own, old dog Paapi, stood further off in the courtyard, watching us. The brown dog moved about as if this were its own house, and it knew exactly where to go. I followed it upstairs. It went into my room, lay down on my bed, and started licking itself. Comfortable and confident. As if this had been its room to begin with, this bed its bed. And so it was that after months of sleep, I set foot in the waking world, and the dog did not stir from my side until, a little while afterwards, it left as unexpectedly as it had come. Without me even having had time to give it a name.

The following morning, everyone was happy to see me sitting at the breakfast table. They all made some comment, and with glee and enthusiasm reminded me of the bizarre things I'd done; I hadn't gone to school. I was behind with my studies. I had missed my birthday and many other things besides. That very instant at the breakfast table, as everyone was looking at me happily and chattering all at once, I understood that being forgotten is one of life's blessings. Someone who has been forgotten by those around them is like a freed slave. Free from being told what and what not to do. Free from the good and the bad. Free from too much attention. Free from too little attention. Uncalled for attention. Ill-timed attention. Free from expectation. The expectation that you talk. The expectation that you judge. The expectation that you grow up. The expectation that you tie the kosti around your waist. The expectation that you have opinions on politics. And at a time when suddenly everyone had turned political. During my half-waking, half-sleeping period I had come to notice that Mom and Dad's friends, from this party and that group and such-and-such a political faction constantly got together in our house, smoking cigarette after cigarette, drinking alcohol one glass after another, and setting forth political theories.

So it was that the following day, as I was sitting next to my bedroom window, looking at light and shadow passing over the forest foliage and the village of Zorvan beneath me, I remembered what Leyla had said. It occurred to me that before people got too used to my wakefulness, I could get away with doing things I hadn't been allowed to before. Wasn't I supposed to change, after all? Although I had no idea why I should change, or what I should change about me, an energy or an uncontrollable rage seethed within me, wanting to transform me into somebody that nobody, that he, could ignore so easily. I wanted to turn into what lay beyond me. To reach what lay beyond me.

Usually none of us children went to the surrounding villages on our own. Apparently, this rule had been established in the mansion decades before we were born, after Auntie Malek's romantic failure. As we later learned from the whispered rumors of the mansion, as soon as that nobleman, who lived in Zorvan, had spurned Auntie Malek's love, she had returned to the mansion, shut the windows and drawn the curtains in her room, and for seven months didn't allow anyone to enter. Apparently, it was only Khanom Joon who, night after night, when Auntie Malek was asleep, used to go into her room with the help of the Ball of Light, leave her water and food, and wipe the tears from her cheeks. The Ball of Light had explained matters to Khanom Joon and had even told her that it wanted to go and avenge the nobleman traveler's betrayal, and as the people of the house relate it, Khanom Joon did not stand in its way. It was after this affair that Khanom Joon ordered that henceforth the young women and men of the mansion not be allowed to set foot in Zorvan alone, or still worse, that they not be allowed to engage in romantic relationships with the villagers. Khanom Joon was that kind of woman. For all her enlightened and forward-thinking qualities, she could be as severe and vengeful as any shaman or chief of a primitive tribe.

That was also the reason we didn't attend the local village schools. We all went to the best school in the city. We used to come and go with a car and driver, as Dad worked in Tehran, and because of her own work Mom took a lot of trips to other cities and provinces. So it was that early in the morning that day, after a cursory wash of my hands and face, together with the nameless dog, I set out and after making my way through paddy fields and tea plantations far from the gaze of the mansion's residents for the first time set foot in Zorvan, the nearest village to our mansion and fields. The dog did not leave me at any point. He would go ahead so that I would be able to navigate Zorvan's backstreets and reach the paddy fields. Or he would sit down next to a house and get me to understand that I might knock on its door and find a friend within. It didn't take me long to become friends with village girls my age, and they took me with them to the paddy fields and tea plantations and the buildings where silkworms were raised. From the outset, my new friends were in unspoken agreement about my silence, and they were so kind that they ran ahead to show me how to plant or harvest rice, pick tea leaves, or separate the threads of silk from the cocoon in great cauldrons of boiling water. Or to invite me for dinner or lunch in their smoky houses. They taught me how to toss the tea leaves, knead them, roll them, and finally dry them out. They taught me how to eat food with my hand, without a spoon and fork. To milk cows and sheep, and chop firewood with an axe, or to make fences out of long, slender pieces of wood. I worked every bit as hard as everyone else, so that they soon considered me one of them, and I even heard the women whispering jokingly amongst themselves that they had picked one of their own people to be my future husband.

Headscarves knotted behind the neck, bending from the waist, skirts tucked under the elastic of the waistband, the hems of their trousers rolled up to the knees, the Gilak women and girls all sang together. In unison:

One foot forward, three seedlings in the mud: *I'm planting Mowlayi rice.*

One foot back, one step right, one foot forward, three seedlings in the mud: *I have set my hopes on Karbalaee's house.* One foot back, one step right, one foot forward, three seedlings in the mud: *if I get to marry Karbalaee's lass.*

One foot back, one step right, one foot forward, three seedlings in the mud: *It'll feel like I have the whole world.*[18]

Finally, a straight back. A deeeep breath. A smile at the neighboring rice planter. A long gaze at the horizon. A new bunch of seedlings in the left hand and again one step right, one step forward, the seedling in the mud . . .

There where the women planting rice straightened their backs and stood staring at the horizon, did they think of their husbands and loves and fiancés sighing lengthy, languorous sighs? Were their thoughts also locked on a single sentence? The same sentence . . . the same single sentence . . . that same single sentence again? Instead of locking on to why Behnam had abandoned me or why I love him, my mind had got locked on to this single sentence, this single question, like a key stuck in the lock, neither able to withdraw nor open the door: "Does he love me? Does he love me? Does he love me?"

Once, when we were sitting together for a mid-morning light meal, I looked at the simple, noble faces of every one of the women and girls and in a split second the key turned in the lock and the door opened. I broke my lengthy silence with this question: "In your opinion, what is the meaning of love?" Mouthfuls of bread and cheese were stuck in some mouths, tea spurted out of others, and the roar of laughter passed from above the women working in the paddy fields to reach the women working in the tea fields, before passing over them to reach the women of the forests and mountains. The simple village women . . . Oh, these beautiful simple village women . . .

One of them, while roaring with laughter, said, "So that's what

[18] TN: Pilgrims to the Shiite holy city of Karbala in Iraq, referred to as "Karbalaee" upon their returns, were afforded great respect.

was wrong with you that you'd been struck dumb?" . . . Then she puckered her lips and said: "The meaning of love's kiss, kiss, kiss . . . " An old woman sitting there spread her legs in the air, and as she pointed to the middle of her baggy trousers, gave a brazen laugh from her toothless mouth and said, "It means this . . . it means this. . . . " A newlywed, her cheeks turning as bright red with embarrassment as the soles of her galoshes, her head down and her gaze focused on her tea glass, said, "It means that you take your heart out of your own body and put it in your husband's chest. When your husband's not there, your heart's not there either." Another, who seemed to have a lump in her throat, said, "It means you see he doesn't want you, but you still want him." Another one said in an angry tone, "It means that he deliberately breaks the bowl of milk you've given him but you want him even more. It means he flings the socks, whose wool you sheared yourself, carded yourself, knitted yourself so you could give them to him, into the fire right in front of you but you still want him more. You just cannot not want him." An old woman said, "It means when he's dead you cannot drink gunpowder tea anymore because he loved gunpowder tea. You cannot even cheerfully puff on Borazjani tobacco before going to bed, because he loved to smoke it before going to bed."

I should remember to write in my second notebook, then, that love means watching out. That it means putting up with separation. Forgiving mistakes. That you cannot not love him. It means being alone.

That day at twilight, after working in the paddy field for hours, when I paid a visit to the temple in the forest so that I could be alone for a while, I saw, from behind it, a ghost leaning against a tree. I don't know why for a second I thought it was Behnam. I wanted to call him; Behnam! But in that very instant it turned to face me and I saw Eblis the Beautiful looking at me with sorrowful eyes. She drew near and said, "You were right. I am Eblis."

How limpid her eyes were. How heavenly her voice. When she spoke, it was as if streams were murmuring and leaves rustling in the breeze. I wanted to ask, "Why do you come here? Why are your eyes so full of sorrow?" Yet I remained silent. I sat on the ground next to the brown dog and, as I always did, made a little pile of wood and dried leaves and lit a fire. Eblis came and sat down beside us. The colorful peacock was still in her arms and the snake on her left shoulder threaded itself through her long locks of hair.

"Just like you," Eblis said, "we like secrets and beauty. Just like you, we have been abandoned."

Chapter Six

Who knew that a handmade butterfly net, bouncing up and down in the half light of dusk, hunting for fireflies in the meadows of Zorvan, would lead to Jamshid Khan, Fereydoun Taban's grandfather, to his ideal wife—Khanom Joon, Faranak? In the family's tellings of it, at considerable remove, and in mad Auntie Malek's telling of it, closer to events—since she always had her head in the papers handed down from earlier generations—it was said that once upon a time in the olden days, Jamshid Khan, whose sword-stroke was so strong that they called him "Ali the Striker," was the most celebrated pirate in the Persian Gulf. One stormy night, as his ship with its three hundred Zanzibari slaves on board lurched and rolled, his head spun so much that he fell asleep and dreamt that a handsome young man clad in a white cloak and trousers, a cape, the crimson hat of the Magi on his head, holding a sword, a bow and arrow, a crow perched on his left shoulder and a dog by his right leg, entered his cabin and in an ill-humored voice said, "O vile man! If you do not change your manner of life in this very breath, and if from this very moment, you do not begin worshiping Mithra, as I command, and do not strive to be faithful and committed to compassion and the freedom of the people and the prosperity of the earth, then I shall, by Divine order, turn you into a solitary Scops Owl, and you will cry 'O God, O God' so much you will start to hack and cough and blood shall drip from your larynx and after a thousand years of having to suffer the wound in your larynx, you shall die even as you are hacking away and crying 'O God!'"

The way that Auntie Malek recounted it, with great relish,

she said that Jamshid Khan, whom everyone feared, was himself afraid for the first time in his turbulent and adventurous life, and in his dream asked of that imposing man, "But what should I do?" The young man, who, though he was not standing in a halo of light, yet shone with it, replied, "Start with your name. By Divine command I name you Jamshid: he who brings prosperity to the earth." The wretched Jamshid Khan, terrified, asked, "So, from now on what path should I take in life?" "The path," he replied, "that is pure, forgiving, courageous, and true to its promises." After saying this, he gave Ali the Striker a book bound in gold-inlaid Khotanese deerskin and written in gold with a silver margin before disappearing into the swirling dust of the cabin. In his half-waking, half-sleeping state, although Ali the Striker thought long and hard about which one of the Imams or their descendants this handsome man, who resembled a noble knight, might be, it certainly did not occur to him—indeed he was not even capable of imagining,—that when he awoke, he would actually see the handwritten, gold-encrusted book in his own hands. There was nothing to do but prevent himself from turning into the blood-dripping Scops Owl as soon as possible. Cold sweat still clinging to his damp and salty body, he took up the book, and without daring to open it, placed it in the sideboard and vowed to read and learn it by heart as quickly as possible so he might uncover the book's secret. So it was that, still barely awake, he gave the order to change course. He who had intended to sell three hundred Zangi slaves on the coast of Oman, to steal copper from Omani ships and sell it in India, to steal spices from Indian ships and sell them in Bandar Abbas, instead gave the order to set sail for Zanzibar again. When a month later they had reached their destination, he lined up all the slaves in front of the disbelieving eyes of the port workers and his comrades, and after ordering their collars and chains be taken off, stood on a wine barrel and said, "You are all freed. I repent of my sins. Forgive me!" And to each one he gave three gold pieces. His speech barely concluded, he gave the order to hoist the sails and set course for Bandar Abbas. Four months after that dream, he set out for the Spring of Ali in Rey, where he underwent the sacred ablution in its blessed waters, poured the water of repentance over his head, and took the name Jamshid. And to this day, some hundred and forty years later, he has never once strayed from the path of friendship, loyalty, truthfulness, and righteousness, though even now, when he reflects on the imposing figure of that noble man, bow and arrow in hand, a shiver runs through him, and he wonders: "Have I, at last, become the righteous man he expected me to be? Yet the adventures of Jamshid Khan's life are more than this; the adventures of his long life did not come to an end with Naser al-Din Shah's coronation and Amir Kabir's murder, the assassination of the martyr king, the Constitutional Revolution, the First and Second World Wars, the occupation of Iran by the great powers, Britain, Russia, and Germany, from the year of the Great Famine to the coronations of Reza Shah and Mohammad Reza Shah and the Islamic Revolution. No; rather, according to the narrators of the deeds of the dynasty, especially Khanoom Joon and Auntie Malek, the deeds also included the strange orders he carried out after receiving them in his dreams, and his self-sacrifice in conserving the sacred fire, and his secret archaeological excavations.

The water of repentance that he had poured over his head at the Spring of Ali had not yet dried when one moonlit night, as he was sleeping in a caravanserai, still betwixt and between and hemming and hawing as to how he might turn himself from Ali the Striker—thief, womanizer, and slave-trader—into a pure, forgiving, kindly believer, or harder still, how he could figure out how to perform and say his prayers in such a way that they would be acceptable to that bow-and-arrow wielding, red-hatted prophet, he dreamt again that that beautiful young man entered his cell in the caravanserai, came towards him, shook his shoulders firmly and said: "Why are you asleep? Get up, get up, get up, quick, pick up the book, put on your boots, get on your horse, head in the direction of the first dandelion clock you see blown by the wind, and ride until you reach the princess. Remember, when you marry her, wheat must grow from your boots." In his sleep, confused and bewildered, Jamshid Khan asked, "How might I know who she is?"

"The princess will shine forth from a halo of light," the tall and graceful man replied.

The narrators of the family tales, Auntie Malek at their head, relate that Jamshid Khan started from his sleep dazed and amazed, asking himself what it meant for her to be shining forth from a halo of light. And what on earth it meant that wheat must grow from his boots. His head spinning from these questions without answers, he took the mysterious book with its ancient writing out of the treaure chest, donned his leather boots, and mounted his horse, and from Rey set off on the road along which dandelion seeds were being blown away, and so astonished and stupefied was he at his recent dreams that he forgot night and day, or even to trim his hair and beard and take off his boots, which was why by the time, at sunset, he reached the rolling hills around the village of Zorvan and saw the girl catching fireflies from the air with a little handmade net, the wheat from the fields he had passed through had sprouted from the top of his boots and its ears had formed. He stretched out his arm, picked a few grains of wheat from his boots, and put them in his mouth. "As he rode closer and closer to the young girl, a sudden, profound, and exhilarating love overtook his heart, so overwhelming that it made him forget entirely the words of the prophet with the hat. His despair over finding the princess, and the image of the girl with her insect-catching net, with the fireflies flickering on and off in the air and within her net, had such an instantaneous effect on his fatigue, hopelessness, and confusion that it prevented him from even for a moment wondering, what about the princess, for whom I have traveled six months, from city to city, from village to village?" He wouldn't allow affairs to take their course until the following night, or even the following morning. Without any preliminaries, he lay the gorgeous girl, shining like some magical spirit in the glow of the fireflies, down on the ground in the meadow, for a few minutes entirely forgetting about repentance and the prophet and reverting to the Ali the Striker that he was. He pressed the girl's slight body firmly into his embrace, like the rudder of a ship in a stormy sea, drowned it with kisses and did with her what any man does with a beautiful woman. Yet just before getting started, he came to his senses for a moment and was full of pity for the girl whose heart was beating rapidly like a trapped sparrow's. He sat the wisp of a fourteen- or fifteen-year-old girl down, she whose body had contracted in dread and fury, her face turning crimson from shame, kissed her, and whispered in her ear, "Tonight I will make you my bride. To hell with the hatted prophet. But I will solemnly swear that for my entire life I shall remain your obedient, loving and faithful servant." Whereupon he screwed the girl, as her frightened eyes, a tear freshly appearing on her left cheek, stared at a spot in the air and, for the entire time that the bulky man whose heavy breath smelt of the salt and seaweed of distant seas, was crouched over her, thought of how to keep alive the frail firefly flashing on and off in her little fist.

An hour later, Jamshid, who had seated the frightened and distraught girl on his horse beside him, passed through the crowd that had appeared, lanterns in hand, having spread the news of the meadow incident from mouth to mouth sooner than he had expected, thereby alerting the girl's family, and stood in front of the mansion, the girl's house. Where five stout men, clad after the local manner, with drooping moustaches and daggers drawn, stood waiting for him. Had it not been for Jamshid Khan's sharpness of spirit and his ill-gotten gains, things would have certainly ended in those first five minutes once and for all, and they would have hung his head, detached from his body, on the Zorvan village gates as a lesson to others. In less than five minutes, all the important information was exchanged between them: Jamshid said that he was under the Lord's protection and a leading merchant from Rey who had come here for the sake of proposing marriage, while the brothers said that spilling his blood was permitted, since he had raped their sister, a descendant of Shah Ismail the Safavid. Jamshid, who could not believe fate had been so kind to him as to bring him unwittingly straight to the door of a princess, said, "If you justly shed my blood, not a speck of the love and respect I have for the princess and her glorious family will be diminished, not at all—I consider myself a sacrifice for her pure soul." Then he took the gold-encrusted holy book out of his saddle bag and said, "I swear by this holy book, which a beautiful prophet gave to me in a dream, ordering me to come in this direction to seek my bride. To find her I searched so long and hard that I did not take my boots off even once." And it was then that everyone's eyes alighted on his boots with their ears of golden wheat, and before he had finished speaking, he, who was well acquainted with the weak spots of the people of his land, put his hand under his cloak and opened the coin bags and poured gold coins and jewels over the head of his future bride, who was sitting in his arms on the horse. The people, who until then had never seen gleaming, plump gold coins, rushed to his horse's side and scrambled over one another to snatch them up from wherever they were to be found. A few minutes later Jamshid Khan passed, head held high, between Faranak's five brothers—the Khanom Joon of the Taban dynasty—and without fuss entered through the mansion's centuries-old gate that they had opened for him. He held his bride's hands with deep love and respect and took her inside. That very night the village mobad who had received his fee of a handful of gold coins in advance, solemnized their marriage contract, which contained the stipulations on the part of the bride's family that Jamshid Khan should never abandon this property or mansion and take up residence in another location or city, that he was not allowed to sell the mansion, nor knock it down, and most importantly of all, that he must henceforth follow and protect the Zoroastrian religion and the ancient sacred fire. They explained that while they were descended from Shah Ismail the Safavid, on the mother's side they were Zoroastrian. Moreover, according to the documents, they had never abandoned the Zoroastrian religion, not once, but in fact had been the secret revivers of this religion in the Safavid era.

The following morning, there commenced in Zorvan seven days and nights of splendid wedding celebrations, but Jamshid, who was under the impression that everything had been carried out according to his will, did not know that, even as the first rays of the new dawn shone on him as he woke a new groom and son-in-law, he would not see his new bride, Faranak, in bed beside him. When he started from sleep that first morning, the full moon was setting and it was still dark, and yet Faranak was not in the bedroom. Nor was she in her own room. She was not in the storeroom or the kitchen, and just as Jamshid was getting frustrated and worried, he saw her out of one of the mansion windows running at the foot of the rolling hills under the last silver light of the moon, as the fireflies and the dandelion seeds dancing in the air surrounded her body like a white and shining halo. For a while he was all eyes, astounded by such beauty. At length, Faranak noticed her husband, and stared at him nonchalantly from the midst of the moonlike and blinking halo, he who was watching her from the window in disbelief. Then she shrugged, turned her back on him, and resumed her nocturnal hunt.

Jamshid's heart swelled to bursting, and he felt that once again he had fallen in love with her, unable to quell the rapid beating of his heart. He left the room, descended the mansion stairs, and ran through the grasses, and when he had brought his body to Faranak's, hot and aroused, he understood that this was his destiny: to fall in love with his wife at least three times a day, his heart swelling with joy, and make love with her amidst her playful dances in the meadows and forests, surrounded by dandelions and fireflies. For all that, Jamshid did not yet know that Faranak was first and foremost the bride of the moon, and only secondly his bride. He realized this at that very moment, in the middle of the meadows, as he caught sight of a ball of light coming down from the moon toward Faranak, circling her and leaping up and down and making a sound that resembled tittering. Jamshid did not dare ask what this was and where it had come from. What Jamshid did know was that he was in love with Faranak and that unconditional love meant unconditional trust. He knew that his questions would be answered one by one as time went by, although it took a hundred years for him to find the answer to this particular question.

Six months after the hectic and time-consuming ceremonies for the wedding and the preparation of the bride's trousseau, when everyone was sure that the new bride was pregnant, when Jamshid had bound himself in love to Faranak with all his being, a miracle took place; for the first time, Jamshid glimpsed a fleeting smile on his spouse's prominent red lips—a smile that from Jamshid's point of view could only have one meaning: that his lady bride had little by little forgiven him for his first savage act in the meadow. Faranak, of course, never forgot that dismal sunset when Jamshid Khan had done what he did to her and thus caused a single, perpetual teardrop to appear on her left cheek, yet that night for the first time she looked into Jamshid's eyes from up close, a faint smile appeared on her rosy lips, and with her own hands she untied the knot of her silk sleeping gown so that she might give Jamshid Khan, tall and graceful and good-looking and more than twenty years her senior, a taste of the pleasures of true love with the firm pomegranates of her breasts. It was as if that night Faranak had suddenly come to feel that life had other agreeable pastimes to offer besides playing with dandelions and fireflies; making love was one of them. The madness of collecting and scattering dandelions and fireflies inside the mansion was another. Yet more important than anything else was to read and understand the secrets of the gold-encrusted holy book. That night Faranak found the ancient book, far from Jamshid's gaze, and was surprised to discover that she could read it, word by word and line by line. It was the word of the ancient religion of Mehr,[19] Mitrā, known as Mithras, a religion based on the influence of the stars and planets on humans, whose moral principles were compassion, loyalty, just action, keeping secrets, and skill in the martial arts. Once she had finished reading the book, Faranak realized that her marriage with Jamshid was not merely based on his mannish desire and fancy, but that it was her destiny, too.

Now that after all these years Faranak has become the Khanom Joon of the Taban dynasty, Malekdokht, Khanom Joon's eldest daughter, whom everyone calls Auntie Malek, faced with countless questions about the Ball of Light that always hovers behind her mother, replies that on moonlit nights her mother, Khanom Joon, stands under the moonlight and waits for the Ball of Light to bring her a message from the moon, whereas Jarireh, who is married to Khanom Joon's grandson, claims to have more accurate information and says that Khanom Joon travels to the moon and back in person, since as a young girl, she became the bride of the moon and all the women had gone to a secluded place and in mysterious ceremonies with only women present, asked her to take their requests to the moon and transmit the moon's message to them in return. The way Jarireh relates matters, the women, according to a tradition dating back millennia, threw their rings and earrings and even gold teeth into a bowl full of the water of the Spring of Revelation and confided them to the daughter of the moon, as beautiful as the moon of the fourteenth day, so that, alone, she could take them to the meadow and vanish there for a time. When she returned a few hours later, beneath her long silk scarf, she would put her hand, eyes closed, into

[19] Mehr, the first element in Mehrab's name, means "kindness, affection, and sun."

the bowl and delivered the message to the owner of the gold. When three messages had thrice been given to three women, it was Khanom Joon, Faranak, daughter of the moon, who had to take the bowl of the Spring of Revelation, which was for the women of the village consecrated to the messages of the moon, and pour it over the head of the oldest sleeping Zoroastrian woman in Zorvan, sitting beside her till the morning to watch the expressions on her face attentively, so that she could be the first person to ask the woman, the moment she woke, what she had dreamt of. The old woman had certainly had dreams, and it was Khanom Joon who had to interpret the dream for the locals. Her interpretation determined the fate of the harvest, contagious diseases, weather, natural disasters, deaths and births and marriages, or the prosperity and happiness of the villagers for the coming year. Even now, after so many years had passed, and despite the fact that not one of the villagers is a Zoroastrian anymore, they continue to practice this custom, and during the last full moon of the year, just before the Nowrouz festival, the Taban mansion is filled with women clutching gold and heading to Khanom Joon's room to ask her to transmit the moon's message to them.

Although they say that during the hundred or so years of Khanom Joon and Jamshid Khan's life in common, there has been no keeping of secrets or deception, the matter of Khanom Joon and the Ball of Light remained for everyone, until the end of her life, like some secret unrevealed, even for Jamshid, her husband. Then, one year and two months after Khanom Joon's eldest grandchildren, Bijan and Azar, were respectively assassinated and executed, in sorrow and pain she felt that her death was upon her. For that reason, she ordered everyone to come so that she could tell them. Jarireh and Malekdokht sent everyone in the family the message to get themselves to the mansion as soon as possible. Khanom Joon and Jamshid Khan's seven daughters and sons and all their grandchildren and great-grandchildren rapidly made their way there from all around the country. The death of Khanom Joon, with that mysterious teardrop on her left cheek and her Ball of Light full of secrets, was hardly a small thing. For more than one hundred years she had been the senior member of the dynasty and custodian of the secrets of the mansion and its people and its holy fire. The Ball of Light was still rolling on the floor from one side to the other next to her. Her children, grandchildren, and great-grandchildren came to her and, with great respect, knelt around her. And she began the longest speech of her life, all in one breath, having first established with everyone that they had no right to interrupt her.

As she looked into the eyes of every one of them with that beautiful, proud face and toothless, trembling mouth of hers, Khanom Joon said, "To start, I have to say that my will was written years ago and is in a small wooden chest in the keeping of the mobad Jamasp. After my death, you may open it in the mobad's presence. The inheritor of this mansion and the ancient tradition and the holy fire will be my grandson, Fereydoun Taban. It will be his duty to choose his own heir."

Without realizing it, they all turned their eyes turned to Fereydoun Tabaan and bowed their heads in respect to him, and some even got up and embraced him and congratulated him. Then Khanom Joon sighed and said, "But I wanted all of you to come here so I could tell you something else. The secret that I have kept close to my heart ever since I was fifteen."

Everyone's gaze was fixed on her, excited and silent. "I was only fifteen years old," Khanom Joon began, "when they gave me to Jamshid Khan, and I cried tremendously when people were not looking, because rather than bother myself with a husband, I preferred to spend my time playing with dandelions and fireflies in the meadow or transmitting the moon's messages to the locals. That first night when I saw my husband . . . " Here Khanom Joon paused and scowled meaningfully at Jamshid Khan, and Jamshid Khan, turning red and black from shame, looked at the ground. Not realizing that all forty-seven of their children, grandchildren, and great-grandchildren knew everything about the scandal of their first meeting. Eventually Khanom Joon stopped scowling at him and fixed her eyes on her children. "That night of our first meeting, they put bridal clothes on me and sat me down by the wedding spread. But what kind of bridal clothes? Everything had happened in such a rush that my mother was forced to bring out her own dusty wedding dress from her youth from the chest and make it fit me using safety pins and needles. At that time, everyone believed that if a bride did not wear bridal clothes, then her future was doomed. Once everyone could breathe a sigh of relief that my ill-fitting clothes were ready, I went up and hid myself in the attic of this very mansion, away from everyone's gaze, locking the door behind me so that nobody could find me, and promising myself that if they did, I would hang myself there and then, or escape by the window and go and get myself lost in the forest."

Just then sighs and *oh nos* went up from the breasts of all the children, *may disaster not strike, Khanom Joon*s and *God what would we have done ifs* could be heard from various corners of the room. But Khanom Joon continued regardless. "It is not hidden from Pure Ahura, and may it not be hidden from you, that I could not stand Jamshid Khan, and if afterwards he hadn't sought to win my heart by a thousand methods, it would've been impossible for me to have adjusted to life with him." Here Khanom Joon drew a deep breath and again stared at Jamshid Khan with narrowed eyes. When a few long minutes had passed and no sound passed Khanom Joon's lips, everyone started sighing and moaning, because they thought that, woe is us, Khanom Joon's life was over. That was why they all spoke to her with one voice and terrified, "Khanom Joon . . . Khanom Joon . . . are you still alive?" But suddenly, in her typically commanding tone, she said, "Ahhhh! Quiet! I'm thinking!"

Jamshid Khan was still looking at the ground, sometimes shaking his head in regret or shame. Eventually Khanom Joon stopped staring at Jamshid Khan and resumed. "As I was in the attic, crying, I saw that seven dwarves had come out of a slit in the wall, each one of them carrying something: spools of thread, and needles, and thimbles, and shovels, and picks and this sort of thing. Five of them were men and two of them women. I couldn't believe what I was seeing. I was scared and leapt behind the chest of winter clothes to hide, or so I imagined, but they had seen me, and they froze where they were. They were only as tall as my finger. Eventually one of them, who was carrying a needle on his shoulders, stepped forward and said, "We have seen you and you have seen us, so now according to the custom of generation after generation there are only two paths we may take, the first being that if until the end of your life you tell nobody about having seen us, then we will be your obedient servants, whereas if you reveal this secret to anyone, we will come to you every day and torment you so much with these here needles and picks that you will die young.'"

Khanom Joon fell silent again, staring at the ceiling, and this time everybody waited for her to resume speaking. "There was no choice," she continued. "I came out from behind the chest and gave them my promise. Then they sat down beside me and told me about themselves. They said, 'Do not look at our tiny height and build, we have powers that you big folk do not. We know all the places treasure lies underground, and we can fulfill all wishes. We know the secrets of all ancient languages, and the locations of all underground springs.' I suddenly acquired inner courage, and my fear of the disaster of marriage vanished. I felt that with their assistance I had the strength to do anything, and that nobody could trap me any longer. So it was I gave them my promise and quit them, my mind at ease, to go sit by the marriage spread, leaving everyone surprised and staring at me open-mouthed; I sat down there, but not in that baggy ill-fitting dress, rather in a beautiful, golden, jewel-encrusted dress, so suited to the occasion, and so heavy and striking that everyone was struck dumb in astonishment. That's how the Ball of Light came to be with me until today, carrying out my wishes, whether big or small. It also helped me read Jamshid Khan's ancient holy book and live according to its commandments." Then she turned with longing to the Ball of Light, which until then had been still and resting, as if it too had been listening to what she had been saying, and said, "May Pure Ahura bring you good. You have made me happy . . . Now you are free . . . You may go now that I have revealed this secret of a hundred and more years and am breathing my last."

At this time, a great sorrow had come to sit on Khanom Joon's eyes, or so it seemed. She turned once more to her children and grandchildren and great-grandchildren and said, "Of course, before I told you all this, I got permission from the seven dwarves and thanked them for the life of service and kindness they had devoted to me, so now leave the room, because I want to die alone." Astonished and weeping, everyone kissed Khanom Joon's hand in a respectful manner and left the room, standing behind the door, either silent or whispering, awaiting death's entry. But a night passed, and death did not come. A day passed too, and still death did not come; not only did Khanom Joon not die but the Ball of Light continued to loyally serve her and the Taban family. All the same, from that day on, Jamshid Khan changed. He became sorrowful and did not part lip from lip for some time.

After that day Jarireh would walk up and down, saying, "Is there any woman in the world stranger than this one?" Yet many in this dynasty believe that, however strange Khanom Joon's story with the Ball of Light and the seven dwarves and her secretive visits to the moon, Malekdokht's story is just as strange, if not stranger, but at least no less strange. She who, on the night of the full moon, walks by the banks of the River of Astonishment and murmurs secrets to it and to and the moonlight while wearing her shabby and faded wedding dress, died one night on account of a love affair that ended disastrously, and yet nobody realized she had died. Nobody held a funeral or five-day mourning ceremony for Malekdokht—but she had really died, even though she is still alive.

There are numerous tales and rumors about Malekdokht and her love and the talisman and the rug and the River of Astonishment and the mirror and her ruinous beauty. Everyone has something to say. One of these tales says that Malekdokht, Khanom Joon's eldest daughter, lived in her youth in her own mansion, part of the extensive Taban estate, and people called it the Mansion of Astonishment, since it was the only mansion to have been built beside the River of Astonishment. They say that one moonlit night as Malekdokht was singing in her bewitching voice, a voice which struck the owls dumb and rooted the foxes to the spot, the Ahriman of Jealousy, who happened to be wandering around nearby, fell in love with her. The Ahriman of Jealousy, foul-faced and foul-tempered and foul-mouthed, turned so fervent and ardent that he had no choice but to transform himself into a handsome young man in order to attract Malekdokht to him. The way the narrators of the family's deeds relate it, Malekdokht was not averse to the young man, but was nonetheless not in love with him. They had a relationship for a while and each time the Ahriman of Jealousy saw her he wanted to take matters a step further, but Malekdokht did not allow him to, pushing him away in embarrassment and shame, until one cold winter's night when the moon was hidden behind black clouds, a noble traveler arrived from far away, passing by the river and the little mansion, knocked on the door and sought permission to spend the night there. Malekdokht accepted cheerfully, and the man slept that night in one of the mansion's tens of rooms, before he left in the morning giving Malekdokht a small but valuable present. A gold brooch in the form of a butterfly. Malekdokht did not want to accept the present, since she had given the young stranger a place to stay simply out of humanity and kindness, but the young man insisted. Just as the two of them were passing the brooch box back and forth between them, for a moment the young man took Malekdokht's hands in his in a gesture of gratitude, and suddenly her body shook so severely with love that she passed out in the traveler's arms. The young man, terribly upset at this turn of events, called the servants to come and help, and had no choice but to stay and look after her. For three days and nights he sat beside Malekdokht's bed, she whose ruinous beauty made the flowers wither, and before he even knew it, was trapped: he fell hopelessly in love with her. On the third night, as the light of the full moon shone through the window onto Malekdokht's bed and magnified the beauty of her face a hundred-fold, he bent over her to pin the brooch onto her clothes. As he gazed at her, Malekdokht suddenly came to. As soon as he sat down on the bed, the noble young man said, "I swear by this moon of the fourteenth night that I am caught hopelessly in love with you and that so long as I live I shall remain faithful to your love." The words had not yet completely escaped his mouth when the Ahriman of Jealousy turned up, and when he saw Malekdokht enraptured in the man's gaze, he writhed in anger and jealousy before he turned into smoke, with a mad gesture afflicted the young man with amnesia and placed a curse on the wretched Malekdokht. The curse he placed on her meant that Malekdokht could from now on look at no person and no thing directly. She was only allowed to look at people and things in a mirror, nor was she permitted to step outside of her room in the mansion, on pain of death. The amorous young man, rendered mad by the Ahriman's act, ran out of the Mansion of Astonishment shouting crazily, and no one saw him after that until the day of his return, when he ended up getting Malekdokht killed. After the curse, Malekdokht stayed imprisoned in the mansion, the only thing she could do was to have a giant mirror made and brought to her room, having it installed opposite the River of Astonishment in the hope that the Noble Traveler would one day cross the bank of the river and she might catch sight of him in it.

Years passed in this manner, and Malekdokht had nothing to do save weep over the golden butterfly on her breast, weave rugs, and gaze into the mirror, until one day, as she was staring into it, all of a sudden she caught sight of the Noble Traveler crossing the river bank, singing to himself. Malekdokht was so happy to see him again that for a few moments she forgot about the curse. That said, certain of the narrators of the family's deeds maintain that she did not forget about the curse in that moment, but rather that she no longer gave it any importance. Thus, for the first time after the curse had been placed on her, the amorous Malekdokht turned away from the mirror and ran to the window and lovingly and joyfully uttered the young man's name: "Vafaa!"[20]

The moment the young man turned his head toward the sound of her voice, everything turned dark, the clouds clashed, the sky bellowed, the mansion shook, and the mirror broke. Terrified, Malekdokht ran out of the room and the mansion, but however much she looked, the man was nowhere to be found. Nor was anyone else there. She saw a wooden boat by the riverbank, three half-consumed candles at the front of it and a paintbrush beside it. Without having any idea why, she wrote her own name on the side of the boat: the Lady of the Mansion of Astonishment. And sat in the boat. The boat disappeared into the roaring river, and only reappeared three days later, when the children of Zorvan found it on the shore, smashed up, together with the corpse. They say that Malekdokht resembled some magnificent painting, her long, date-colored locks flowing around her and her hands crossed on her breast, as she lay there in the boat, the three candles still burning at the front of the craft. The handsome nobleman afflicted by amnesia was drawn there by the hubbub people were making. He knelt by the broken boat. He gazed at Malekdokht's pallid

[20] Meaning faithfulness and loyalty.

face and said, "Alas. What a beautiful woman," and at this ruined beauty he shed a tear which fell on the golden butterfly on Malekdokht's heart. The Noble Man moved away from the boat, weeping, and singing of the faithlessness of the world, unaware of the fact that a few hours later, under the effect of his pure tears, the golden butterfly that he had himself once pinned to Malekdokht's breast, would come to life and, with a sigh, leap out of death's trap.

This tale ends here, but there is another among the many tales of Malekdokht's mysterious life. They say that the night the broken boat was found, the full moon was gleaming in the sky and at midnight was shining upon her grave through a window in the family mausoleum when Malekdokht, in a white gown and with long date-colored hair, came out of her stone coffin as the wolves howled, the snakes mated, and the owls hooted, and set foot in the main mansion. The first person to see her was her mother, Khanom Joon. On the spot she said, "Tell the truth! Is it really you, or your ghost?"

Malekdokht said, "I swear by love that this is me. His teardrop brought me back to life and now I must find him."

So it was that Khanom Joon allowed her to quietly gather provisions and set off in search for the man she loved. However, the man in question was not far away. He was in Zorvan. He had become a shepherd and lived far off in the forest. The two of them lived for years in poverty together, but joyfully and happily, until the middle of the night when they were found by the Ahriman of Jealousy, whose spell woke the man up terrified from a nightmare, whereupon he suddenly remembered everything . . . including the fact that he had been traveling and that years ago he was supposed to have brought back a particular medicine for his aged mother.

When in the morning the wretched Malekdokht realized the man had abandoned her, she did not part her lips. The narrators of the deeds of the Taban dynasty relate that she wanted to scream with grief, or smash the dishes, but instead she took up a broom and started sweeping the room. She dragged the broom made of wheat and barley stalks, swoosh, swoosh, swoosh, over the carpet: once, twice, three times, a hundred times. This was the same carpet that she had woven during the years when the Ahriman of Jealousy had placed a curse on her and she was able to view the world only in a mirror. It is said that the images appearing in the carpet were echoes of the things she had seen in the mirror, which is why she had woven the River of Astonishment into the middle of it, and the mirror and the Noble Traveler in a corner. Some people say this carpet is still spread on the floor of Malekdokht's room. That same room which even Khanom Joon and her Ball of Light never enter.

That day Malekdokht felt that the more she swept, the more she felt seeds on the rug beneath her. Perhaps they were the last remaining seeds from the broom's dried wheat and barley stalks. She sat down in the half-darkness so that she could pick up the seeds from the carpet, but it looked like they were stuck to it, and their number increased by the moment. She took a step back. She shuddered. She suppressed the lump in her throat and calmly lit the lamp so she could see better. She held the lamp close to the carpet and saw that the flowers in the carpet's design had started to move; they were creeping and growing and sending out shoots. Wild vines and climbers, yellow and red tulips, Shiraz narcissus, and branches of both weeping and pussy willow were slowly moving upwards, turning toward the only source of light, the smoking lamp. Malekdokht sat down and stared at the mysterious growth of the patterns on the carpet. When all the humble items in the room, the mattress, the sheets, the double-wicked Aladdin lamp, the mirror on the wall, the copper samovar and the broom, and finally the lamp were covered by roots and branches and flowers, she was about to stand up when she saw that a wild vine had reached the knee of her left leg. She stood and watched; once the honeysuckle creeper had reached her thigh, it turned and with a gentle sigh blossomed when it reached her pubic triangle. At that very moment, Malekdokht, in all her ruinous beauty, amid all the vines and flowers and stems issuing from the carpet, died of the sorrow of being separated in love from the Noble Traveler, and what a shame it was that nobody knew it. She died, and as a sign, at the moment of her death, all the blossoms and flowers growing from the rug, as well as those in the courtyard and garden and Zorvan, withered and dried up, and for three years not a single tree blossomed or bore fruit, even though, despite having died, Malekdokht stood up and continued with the rest of her life; yet no one, save herself, the four walls of the hut in the middle of the forest, the lamp and the mirror on the wall, and the flowers of the rug, realized she had died at the very moment she had heard the gentle sigh of the honeysuckle blossom in the triangle between her legs.

Chapter Seven

In wild medlar season, peacock molting time, well after the pelicans, storks, and flamingos have migrated from the cold lands of the Soviet Union to the Anzali Lagoon, when the snakes and bears are not quite ready for their hibernation, when they the coffins have not yet been loosed on the River of Farewell, a year before the revolution, one night a hand gently shook my shoulder and in my half-sleeping, half-waking world the sound of a kiss placed at the end of a lock of my long hair left me transfixed. Then a warm, familiar voice whispered in my ear: "I told you I'd see you here again!" In the gap between reality and dream, as it strove to recognize this voice, my mind asked, "Who is this? Is it him?"

It was him.

It was him.

It was him.

I leapt up. I could make out Behnam's silhouette in the half-light, gently tugging at my hand. Confused and stumbling, I stood up, my hand in his, followed him out of the bedroom, went down the spiral staircase, and stepped through the door of the mansion into the courtyard of night. My heart was beating fiercely, and after this long wait, just as I felt like I was expecting a kiss or a hug or kind words from him, the sight of two strange men in the courtyard froze me in my tracks. I stared at them sleepily, as Behnam murmured in my ear, "They have to cross the border. Do you know anyone who can help them?"

I looked at the sky. I had to stop myself shedding hopeless tears. I turned my back on him so I could still my thumping heart and put my tears back in their place before he realized what was going on. I took some deep breaths in the hope of coming to my senses and returning to reality. Wake up. The nameless brown dog had awoken along with me and was now sitting beside me and staring at me, confused. I looked at the sky again. It was still a few hours until the first light of dawn. Enough to get them as far away as possible from the surrounding pastures and their shepherds. I turned to face him so that I could show him I was alright, but without wanting to, I said to him, a sour expression on my face, "I'll take them." As my gaze fell on Behnam for a moment, I saw his eyes looking at me inquisitively. As if he could not make out why my expression was sour. I quickly turned my back on him and went to my room. There is nothing better when it comes to hiding feelings than turning your back. I needed to turn my back on him. On expectations. On unexpected feelings. I was confused and amazed, in body and mind, and I wasn't sure whether I was awake or only dreaming that I was. In a daze, I threw what I needed into a knapsack and, stumbling all the way, got myself to the kitchen. I splashed water on my face and downed a glass of water in one go. The cool flow of the water in my mouth and throat and esophagus helped me come to. I felt better. Now I could face him again. I took my hair down and brushed it with my fingers, before tying it up tightly again on top of my head. With a spirit I had not expected from myself, without hesitating, I went into the courtyard, accompanied by the dog, which did not leave me for a moment, and in a voice loud enough to prove to myself that I was feeling well, said, "We've got to get going quickly." We set out, with Shabro and Afsun, from behind the mansion on a wooded road that I knew would take us to the Soviet border in eight hours. To the River of Farewell. All the while in my heart I cursed myself for having all this time missed this emotionless being.

As were sat on Shabro, from time-to-time Behnam looked at me through the darkness and the falling autumn leaves, while I was caught up in a loop of contradictory thoughts. Eventually, without me asking, he explained concisely that his father had enrolled him at Harvard against his will, and that he had gone to study there for a few months but couldn't stand it and came back to Iran, telling his family that he couldn't bring himself to accept studying in imperialist, world-devouring America while at the same time defending the Communist Soviet Union. His father, a former member of the National Front and a follower of Dr. Mosaddeq, was upset by this decision and called him a green and obstinate young man. After that, Behnam spent most of his time in safe houses with his comrades and at the end of each week visited south Tehran and taught the children working in the brick factories for free, bringing them food and books. Now he was taking these two comrades of his, party members, who had fled from a street fight with the Shah's secret police, the SAVAK, to cross the border. Then he brought his head calmly toward me and kissed the corner of my lips. I was a bundle of nerves and against my will I stopped scowling. Despite all this, in my heart I continued to stubbornly think, "He is so selfish. I cannot stand him. Not one bit." But he took a deep breath next to my ear that broke the strings holding my heart. I felt the skin on the back of my neck prickle and my heart started beating so furiously that I was afraid he might hear it. I was still frowning, and I didn't see any reason why I should appear more cheerful to him. Had he thought of me at all during all this time? Now that he had come, it wasn't even for me, but for his political work.

As if he had read my mind, he said, "I've been thinking about you a lot, but did you know there's going to be a revolution soon? The people are angry. They don't trust the Shah and his corrupt court anymore." A thought went through my mind: "Oh, not you . . . Not you too . . . Please . . . " My head was full of the political talk that friends near and far had unleashed in the house and about which they shouted at one another. He resumed: "Poverty and injustice must be abolished. The oil wealth must be fairly divided among the people."

In the months of half-sleeping, half-waking, I heard them constantly, walking around the mansion, cigarettes and drinks in hand, coughing and defending their political and economic theories with excitement and shouting. Our mansion had become the favorite haunt of Mom's and Dad's friends, of Uncle's and Auntie's, every one of whom variously advocated for the Communist Tudeh Party, the National Party, the Mojahedin-e Khalq, the Fedaiyan-e Khalq, the Aksariyat . . . Sometimes when their voices didn't reach my room, Mehrab appeared standing over me and repeated what they had been saying as if he were a tape recording. Because it was only he who knew that when I was asleep, I was awake, and when awake, asleep. I had heard Mom saying that all the parties had come into being on the same night and had common demands—the just division of wealth and for foreigners to leave the country—but that none of them could sit around the same table and engage in discussions with the others for even an hour without quarreling, or reach a mutual understanding on their demands. I had heard Dad, even as he delighted in the discussions, directing a sarcastic remark at the supporters of this party or that group, to the effect that in this country there is one political party for every two people, and that as soon as a third turns up, they set up a branch.

Seeing my silence, Behnam continued. "The experts in our country are all American, German, or British. Although on the surface we're not colonized, practically speaking we are. They've taken over our oil and economy and politics and they're plundering this country." I recalled mentioning that Mom had given the following response to a similar point: "The reason is that they conquered our country in a single night during the Second World War and we were not yet powerful enough to be able to get their hands off our resources without shedding blood. But that doesn't mean we're happy with the state of affairs. For the time being, though, we don't have enough experts of our own. More than half the population of this country is illiterate."

I looked up at the dark sky. I had no interest in these discussions. Couldn't Behnam talk of love and the moon? Tell me how much he had missed me? Ask me how much I had missed him? Or recite a love poem by Forough for me? Or how about not saying anything at all? And just taking me gently in his arms and letting Shabro follow his path and the two of us listening to the crunching of the autumn leaves beneath his feet? My attention wandered to the cooing I could hear in the distance, *coo, coo . . . coo, coo . . . coo, coo*. Behnam was still talking. "In your opinion, is it fair and just for rich people—for example, take your father and mine—to live in vast houses and mansions, with furniture and carpets and paintings worth millions of tomans, or to own multiple estates, when people living on the outskirts of cities have to make do with battered shacks and struggle to put together their evening meal?" I thought that it wasn't just, but I remembered that Khanom Joon always talked of the unstinting will and efforts of our ancestors, who had striven heart and soul to preserve the sacred fire and suffered so much to stay alive surrounded by so many enemies, or of what great and painful lengths they had gone to acquire every single one of the items in the house, each one a symbol of the culture and art of the different ethnicities of Iran, from here and there, from Balkh and Samarqand, from Isfahan and Shiraz to Kerman and Ctesiphon and Kashgar, and of how they had fought tooth and nail to preserve them through the long centuries, even in times of war and poverty and general catastrophe, as if they were their own life and soul. I had never thought of our mansion as a symbol of wealth. On the contrary, I thought that every corner of this mansion was the symbol of the culture of this land.

I turned round in surprise and looked at him. No doubt he knew all this. Didn't he? There was no need to say it. "I know our country has only recently started developing," he said. "But right now as we are talking, a great many people are hungry, and we need to find a fast solution to poverty. Haven't you read Samad Behrangi's books, or Ali Darvishian's? They're right.

Poverty and injustice do their work, and we need to solve these problems as soon as possible. In my view, the quickest way to solve this crisis is to take wealth from the wealthy and give it to the poor."

I, who hadn't uttered a word to him this whole time, suddenly found speech leaping unawares from my mouth: "Do you mean, for example, that they should take gold away from the gold dealers and hand it over to the poor, or that they should sell the ancient works of art from the museums and divide the proceeds among the poor?" He said, seriously, "Yes! Yes! In my belief, private property is meaningless. Or what value does cultural heritage have when the people go hungry? Does capitalism even have a nation? Since the capitalist nation is international, and capitalists invest their capital wherever they can, the proletariat is international to the same extent and likewise has no nation. That's why the cultural heritage of a single country is meaningless. Wherever the proletariat is, that's where culture is too."

Shocked, I asked, "The proletariat has no nation, so does that mean our capital is Moscow, for example, not Tehran, and our poet is Pushkin, not Hafez?"

"Yes," he replied, passionately. "Exactly!"

Shocked, without reflecting I cried "whoa," and Shabro stopped. With a whistle I made Afsun stop too. Angrily, I said, "Get off." I told his comrades to dismount, too. They did so in surprise. I leaned over towards Behnam who was now standing on the ground, and said to him, furiously, "But my poet is Hafez, not Pushkin, and my capital is Tehran, not Moscow. And the cultural heritage of my country is not the cultural heritage of the Soviet Union."

I had never known myself so angry. I geed up Shabro, grabbed Afsun's reins, and as I set off, still accompanied by the dog, I said, "It would be better for you and your proletarian friends to walk a little, since these horses you were riding are both private property and Iranian Turcoman horses, each of them worth more than two thousand tomans."

Behnam's two comrades looked at us in disbelief and confusion and, along with him, set out after me. Behnam, who had not expected anything like this reaction from me, had turned purple with anger and took rapid strides to catch up with me and repeat his slogans—the same ones that had made me lose my patience. "You are a smug bourgeoise, well-off and without pain, a silly, spoiled girl who understands nothing of the pain of the poor and the proletariat. You live like the child of aristocrats and know nothing of the peasant's miserable life."

Even as I maneuvered beneath the sharp and passionate hail of words, I occasionally stole a glance at Behnam's beautiful, black, aquiline eyes, red with anger, and delighted in them. Why was I not afraid of him? Why, when I could not stand what he said, did his angry black eyes thrill me so much? Why, while I wished he were dead, did those glistening beads of sweat on his temples set my heart racing? I couldn't figure it out at all. Finally, after an hour of walking filled with talk and revolutionary slogans, Behnam picked up his pace, grabbed Shabro's bridle, and said, "Fine . . . I'm an extreme Communist. That's exactly what my father says. That's exactly what my university professors say, whether in Iran or in America. But you should know that it's not only me who is like that. We are a movement. A massive communist-socialist movement. A movement that believes that all the people should do equal work for equal pay. A movement that believes that private property should be abolished and be replaced by collective and state property. Maybe I'm mistaken, but what about the rest of them?"

He was sweating profusely all over and a clump of his gorgeous, long, black hair was stuck to his white forehead, making him more gorgeous still. Without thinking, I spurred Shabro on and went on my way. After talking so much, he fell silent, and I could finally hear the starlings, the kingfishers, the pheasants, and the scarlet rosefinches emerging from between the horse's footsteps, singing for the colors of the autumn trees, far from the revolution and politics and the Shah and Lenin and Marx.

A woodpecker was drumming in my ears: "*Tak tak . . . tak tak.* Forget all this talk. Listen to me . . . *tak tak.*"

Ah! Silence at last. Gorgeous silence has arrived. An hour passed in silence and gradually everyone's nerves settled. I halted Shabro and Afsun so that we could all rest. Behnam's eyes were calm and kind once more. I shared a little fruit with the others. When we had sat down, he took my hand and said, "I shouldn't have said all that to you. Forgive me." I said nothing and took a bite of my apple. "But remember," he said, "that our lives are short, and practical and rapid solutions for eradicating poverty and injustice must be found." A cool breeze was blowing, soothing our hot bodies. I took my hand out of his and lay down on the grasses behind me, gazing up at the sky and the trees as I took bites from my apple. It was starting to get light, and we still had a long way in front of us. The dog was lying on the ground beside me, gnawing on a piece of bone I had given him. When I turned back to face Behnam, I had the feeling he was waiting for me to say something. I didn't. As I gazed into his black eyes, I began to wonder why I loved him when I absolutely could not stand him. Don't say that, as some believe, we know one another from our past lives and that we are now involved in completing or correcting those lives.

He lay down next to me and gazed at the sky. I thought how everyone wanted to first of all kill and take revenge and smash and overthrow, so that they might be able to build afterwards. One person, like him, wants to plunder people's museums and houses and shops and offer the soil of the land to the Soviets with both hands, and someone else wants to destroy the monarchy because they cannot bear to see a royal family scrounging and living for nothing even as they themselves must work like a dog to earn their daily crust. This was what I was thinking when he took my hand. Ah, so nice! Perhaps he finally wanted to leave the world of politics behind and after this long vacuum, this year-long vacuum, say something romantic. He smiled. I offered him a faint smile in return. Looking at me kindly, he squeezed my hand and said, "But tell me, what reward do traitors deserve? Shouldn't they be executed?" Appalled, I pulled my hand from his and leapt up. What fresh madness is this? I looked at him, red with rage. He looked at me hopelessly. He bowed his head and said, "I will walk to the border and then back to your mansion, but I want you to know that despite all these things, I really love you and I love you even more every time I see you." He shook his head in sorrow and longing and said, "If only you were a Communist too." Enraged, I smiled mockingly and said, "Fortunately I have made a better decision for my life." Even though at that moment I didn't know what.

The two men mounted the horses, and we set off for the border on foot. We were silent for an hour before Behnam finally started talking about Bahman. "Mehrab told me," he said, "that Bahman had run away from home, and asked me to use the Party's networks to find him. He said some people thought he had gone to do military service, but we found him in the Nezamabad suburb. He was working as a mechanic. I went to see him on the pretext of getting a car fixed. He stopped dead in his tracks when he saw me. I asked him to change the oil and the clutch pad, and as he was doing that talked to him about school and family so I could figure out what the problem was or what I could do to help, but he kept interrupting me and switching the topic of conversation to you. I think he's in love with you."

He looked at me inquiringly and said, "Isn't he?" His expression was serious. I think mine was too. For me, after reading his letter, Bahman had turned into a psychological question, a sociological problem. He was like a tangled thread I wanted to unwind, even as I could not figure out where it started. Behnam continued. "We exchanged strange words, words whose meaning I'm not sure about exactly, even now, or why we even exchanged them at all. That day, as Bahman was talking to me, he took off his shirt as if wanting to show me something and threw it on the chair next to me before going under the car.

I noticed a tattoo of the Shah's imperial crown on his muscular chest. I asked him with a laugh, 'You're a Shah supporter, then?' With a serious expression he replied, 'I like how genuine he is.' He said that, then went into the pit under the car. 'So now the Shah stands for being genuine?' I asked. From down there he said, 'You asked your question, and you got your answer.' I realized he must've gotten out of the wrong side of bed. I wanted to change the subject, but then he said, 'You posh little Mojaheds and Communists don't know a thing about running the country.' This really got to me. I said, 'You're right that I come from a well-off family, but I believe in class equality and social justice.' His head popped out from underneath the car, blew a raspberry, looked at me up and down like a wise man beholding a fool, and said, 'When your belly's full you can talk a load of old crap.' I was preparing to reply when one of his colleagues, whose engagement celebration it had been the night before, came in with a box of sweets and pastries. Without even coming out from underneath, Bahman congratulated him. His colleague put the pastries on a table and disappeared somewhere into the nooks and crannies of the garage. Bahman stole a glance at the pastries from down in the pit, and then looked at me, said, 'Whenever I see sweet pastries, I start thinking about doomed fate.' I was taken aback. 'Why?' I asked. He disappeared under the car again, but I could hear him saying, 'If I tell you, you won't like it.' My curiosity was aroused further. 'Tell me,' I said. 'Back in the old days,' he said, 'the khans of two tribes had been enemies for years till one day the eldest son of one of them who was called Mammad Gol sees the two daughters of the other khan at the spring and right on the spot falls in love with the older one whose name was Mahshab. But Mammad Gol, who knows the khans of the two tribes won't agree to this union, goes to the elders and says there's no other way for the tribes to make peace apart from marriage. But Mammad Gol doesn't say he's in love with Mahshab. When the khans of the two tribes hear about all this from the elders, they think, "what a great idea," and Mammad Gol's father goes off to seek Mahshab's hand in marriage. Mahshab's father accepts and explains everything to his daughter, but guess what, the girl's in love with someone else. In love with the handsomest and best mannered boy in the tribe, called Bahador.' Just then, Bahman's head popped out from under the car again and looked at me in a meaningful way, and even though, Shokoofeh, I didn't get what it meant, it gave me the feeling that he was trying to convey something specific by telling me this story. To cut a long story short, Bahman disappeared back under the car, and then resumed: 'When Mahshab's father hears this, he gets upset and says to his daughter, "Do you mean to say that the people's welfare is worth so little to you? Do you mean you're prepared to let the fighting and bloodshed continue between the two tribes just because of your heart?" The girl simply replies, "The hostility between the two tribes has to end the same way it started. It didn't start with me for it to end with me." And she just won't agree to the marriage. The news is passed around until eventually it reaches Bahador, and together with his father and the senior members of his family, he comes to seek Mahshab's hand in marriage. Bahador says that if you force Mahshab to marry, she'll kill herself and I'll kill myself too. Since Mahshab's father loves her dearly, he's got no choice but to accept and long story short they sort everything out for the wedding and send someone with sweets and pastries to Mammad Gol's tribe to apologize on their behalf and also to explain what happened and invite them to Mahshab and Bahador's wedding and tell them that Mammad Gol can marry Mahmonir, Mahshab's younger sister. Over there, when Mammad Gol sees the messenger carrying the sweets and pastries, he's happy because he thinks that Mahshab's accepted his proposal, but the messenger says, no, sorry, these are the sweets for Mahshab's wedding to Bahador, and then explains the story of Bahador and Mahshab's love with all sorts of details, before saying, but you can marry Mahmonir, Mahshab's younger sister, who is both prettier and a better hostess. When Mammad Gol hears this, blood gathers at the front of his eyes and, slashing his own hand with a knife, he lets the blood drip on the pastries and says, "Tell Mahshab that I swear by this blood and pastries that I will be honored to attend the wedding." Long story short, the wedding night comes round and Mammad Gol and some of the young men of the tribe make a surprise attack on the ceremonies and kill Mahshab's and Bahador's parents. As soon as Bahador arrives at the gathering he sees what's happened and together with his companions he speeds off in pursuit of Mammad Gol and they kill Mammad Gol and his companions, but Bahador is wounded too and a little afterwards dies next to Mahshab's tent. When Mahshab sees Bahador's been killed, she takes off her wedding clothes, wails in mourning, scratches her face, and plunges a dagger into her heart, dying next to Bahador. Then when Mahshab's tribe hears what Mammad Gol has done, they attack his tribe and kill his parents and sister and brothers. This is how dozens of people are killed because of the love of just two people and the bloody pastries become a sign of that unrequited love and doomed destiny, and the war between the two tribes which'd started years before because of an unrequited love affair, continues and is still going on because of another unrequited love.'

"Just then, Bahman emerged from under the car, the palm of his hand bleeding, trying to clean it with a greasy and dirty rag. Horrified, I stood up and grabbed his hand so I could see how I might help him, but he snatched his hand away, and as he did a few drops of blood fell onto the pastries. We both stared at each other as we saw this happen. I'm not a superstitious person at all, but suddenly I sensed that there was a bitter fate in store for the both of us. After that we didn't say anything of consequence to one another. I asked whether the work on the car was finished. He nodded his head in confirmation, and then I asked him how much it was. He didn't answer and turned his back on me, so I put 50 tomans on the table, got in the car and drove off. Ever since, I remember that strange meeting from time to time, and I don't get what was wrong with Bahman that day at all, or what he was trying to make me understand. Why did he keep mentioning you, and why did he tell me the story of the bloody pastries? And why was his hand bleeding?"

Behnam paused. He sighed and then asked me, "Did anything occur to you?" I shook my head to say no. But something had occurred to me. That Bahman was not in a good way. Quite the opposite, in fact. I remembered the blood-dripping eyes of love from an old tale that one day Hasrat, our elderly gardener, had related, telling us that in the old days, in the very, very old days, when the love of the angels, of Eblis and Gabriel, had been enough for God, and he had not yet created man out of boredom created humanity, the earth was the dwelling-place of the Virtues and Vices. One day, when the Virtues and Vices had gathered, Madness suggested that to kill time they might play hide and seek with one another. Madness closed his eyes and started counting, "One, two, three, four, five, Ready or not, here I come!" As he was doing this, Grace hid herself inside a drop of morning dew, and Treachery went into a foul-smelling bog. Authenticity hid inside an ancient forest, Caprice among playful clouds, and Jealousy in a volcano. Dishonesty told his neighbor he would hide in the mountains, but instead took himself to the depths of the sea, while Greed went into a bag he had himself sewn. Only Love stood hesitating, unable to decide where to conceal herself. At that moment, Madness finished counting and said, "Ready of not, here I come," and Love, panicking, leapt into a nearby rose bush, but the thorns pierced her eyes, blinding them. She wept from the pain, but did not make a sound. The first person Madness found was Laziness, too slothful to stir from where she was, then Grace, followed by Jealousy and Dishonesty and everyone else apart from Love. Madness was seeking high and low for Love when Jealousy and Treachery gave them away, saying that Love was inside the rose bush. Eventually Madness found Love. Love, covering her bloody face with her hands, tears and blood dripping through her fingers, moaned, "I've gone blind . . . I've gone blind . . ." Madness said, "Forgive me, forgive me. It's my fault this happened to you . . . If only I hadn't suggested this game. Now how can I heal you? How can I help you?" Love replied, "Nobody can heal me, but if you want to help me you can take my hand and be my guide from now on." And so it came about that ever since, Love has been blind, and Madness her guide. Just like in Bahman's case.

Thus we both continued in silence until we reached the river that marked the border, the river that the locals called the River of Farewell, so much were they used to bidding farewell to their relatives, close and distant, by its banks as they sneaked across the border. We had to wait among the trees for night to fall again, so that the border police would not see us as they passed by in their boat. At sunset, a Soviet patrol vehicle passed on the other side of the river and we withdrew further into the trees. During the hours that followed, when the forest had become a waiting room for us, the two men went into a corner and soon fell asleep, but he was not tired, and softly read poetry to himself—"The Tulips' Blood" by Khosrow Golsorkhi and "Winter's Over at Last" by Saeed Soltanpour—even as he whittled away at a dry branch with his knife to make two rings. We sat in deep silence as a weak moon shone through the trees, passed over us and the river, and went to the other side: the Soviet Union.

Gradually, it grew dark. We still had to wait a little to be sure that the blackness of night would swallow us up entirely. I looked at the river. In the mist and the darkness, something was moving on the water. I looked more carefully . . . I remembered Jamshid Khan's riddles. In gatherings, he was always either asking riddles or suggesting they play *moshâ'ereh*, the game in which one person recites a line of poetry starting with the same letter that ended the line before. "What is it," I said to Behnam, "what is not needed by the one who makes it, is not used by the one who buys it, and is used by one who has no idea he's doing so?"

He looked at me in surprise. A lack of interest was visible in his eyes. As if I had dragged him from the valuable window of a far-off thought to stand beside the worthless little opening of dull riddles. "I don't know," he said, still busy whittling away at the wooden rings. I took his hand. He stood up and followed me in the direction of the river. Coffins made of cheap wood, all the same shape, were moving along it. Forty . . . seventy . . . one hundred. The coffins calmly and noiselessly cleaved through the mist, the darkness, and the silence of the night as they moved downstream. Behnam froze. I moved along with the coffins. He followed me hesitantly. We walked for a while until we saw them. They were on both banks of the river, in local costume, silently pulling the coffins toward them using fishing nets and gaff. Several women and men and children on this side of the river . . . several more on that side. From above, the night sky watched them, from below the cold ground; in the mist . . . in the darkness . . . in the silence . . . they were completely absorbed in their work: they were hunting coffins. The coffins of their sons and daughters . . . their husbands and brothers and fathers . . . their loved ones who had fled to this or the other side of the river in hope—in hope of reaching the developing and free world on this side, or the classless and equal world on the other side. Among the men and women who, nets and gaffs in hand, were up to their knees and chests in the water to pull the coffins toward the banks, we walked, he and I, staring, lumps in our throats.

Some had already pulled the coffins to the bank and stood weeping in anxious silence, striking themselves on the head while simultaneously taking out the nails from the coffins. As soon as they saw their loved ones, they flung themselves on their half-frigid corpses, tore at their own hair and faces with their fingernails, screaming noiselessly and weeping. By the time Behnam and I had come to our senses, it was completely dark, and the blackness of night passed through the living and the dead, the coffins and the river, the trees and the fog, and plunged into the mouths of the silent mourners, never to come out again.

I started to talk hesitatingly. I wasn't sure whether he wanted to know about realities like these. "These are the lucky ones," I said. "So many of them die so far away that the news of their death doesn't even reach this side." Astonished, Behnam asked, "What are you talking about?" I said, "About the Communists who flee to Uncle Joe's house in the hope of living in a classless society." He looked at me with furrowed brows and questioning eyes. I continued: "They all give up the ghost from hunger or cold or crushing work in Siberian labor camps, or Ukrainian gold mines, or elsewhere, without ever having the opportunity to come back to Iran." Suddenly, he put his hand over my lips. "That's enough," he said. "Don't talk nonsense. This is all impossible." I calmly pushed his hand away and said, "These are things only people living near the border get to hear about. The rest of the country knows nothing about it. The Shah and the government are so terrified of Communism that they don't even want things like this to be published."

He said nothing. As if the breath were trapped in his chest. I continued: "But you have to know. These things are as real as these coffins." He was staring at the coffins with desperation and with eyes welling with disbelieving tears. I said, "Although the Shah knows what disaster befalls them in the Soviet Union, he doesn't give them permission to return because he considers them traitors. We only hear about all this occasionally from the villagers who live along the border. Every few years or so only two or three people from the hundreds who have fled ever manage to get back to their country alive and tell about the appalling things that have happened to them."

Behnam said in disbelief, "It's not possible. It's a lie . . . We are at the center of the Tudeh Party's organization. If things like this were happening, we would be the first to know. Why would the Soviet Union do such a thing to its own supporters anyway?"

"I don't know," I said. "I'm only telling you what you can see and what I've heard from people. The villagers on this side are often related to the ones on the other. The village on the other side is even called Zorvan and they even share a common local language. What's said on this side reaches the other. What's said on the other side makes it here . . . The people on both sides come and go at night by boat, making night visits, for parties, weddings, or mourning. Their children secretly marry one another. They even organize joint mourning ceremonies. According to Dad, the people on both sides have set up a secret organization linking the local and border police forces, the SAVAK, and the KGB. They steal the bodies of their executed relatives from their graves and hide them in a cold room. A lot of them do this for money. According to the locals, most of those who escape to the Soviet Union are killed as spies. When the number of bodies has grown too high, officials discreetly tell people on both sides to come and pick up their loved ones' coffins. The names of those killed are written on the coffins. People identify them when they open the coffins, so if a coffin doesn't belong on this side, they send it to the other using ropes attached to trees on both sides of the river . . . or they send it from the other side to this. Just like what they're doing—look."

On the other side of the river, the Soviet side, a group of people were busy pulling a coffin toward them. I resumed: "It even happens that people occasionally come from far-off cities to these border villages in the hope of obtaining information about their loved ones. Often the coffins get to the lower reaches of the river without anyone having pulled them out of the water. The people living downstream take the unclaimed coffins out of the water, bury the bodies and hold suitable mourning ceremonies for them."

I who was always silent had suddenly become talkative. I don't know, perhaps this was my last attempt to bring him to his senses. I said, "The locals believe that if a body is unburied, or is buried without being claimed, then its ghost will wander forever in a dark and cold underground maze, or along the riverbank searching for its body. That's why the people bury the unclaimed bodies of their own accord, and an elderly man and woman, as part of custom, play the roles of the corpse's parents and hold mourning ceremonies as if for their own child, weeping respectfully. Dad and I have attended these secret ceremonies once or twice. How often the people on this side have recited the first surah of the Quran, the Fatiha, for the Russian dead, or those on the other have made the sign of the cross for the Iranian dead."

At last, a sound like moaning came from the depths of his throat. "It's not possible . . . It can't be . . . It can't be."

I let go of him. He would have to bear the heavy load of the truth alone. I went to help a woman who was struggling to pull a coffin out of the water on her own. As we tugged it out, several people came to help and took out the nails with steel crowbars. On the coffin, in Russian letters, was written: Ахмад Бабаи. A man read it slowly: Ahmad Babaee In hushed voices, people passed on the news to their neighbours: Ahmad Babaee . . . Several at a time, they whispered to one another, "Ahmad Babaee . . . " An old man who was, with the assistance of several others, in the middle of pulling a coffin out of the water, let that coffin go as soon as he heard this name, ran over to us, pressed the young man's body into his arms, and started to howl with an open mouth and yet in silence . . .

Howling . . .
Howling . . .
In silence,
without disturbing the sleep
of a single bird.

We remained there for a while, until, after so much crying and sighing, people eventually settled down and the coffin pullers moved off into the darkness of the forest before the border patrols on both sides could reappear.

When we came back, I no longer had the energy to do

anything. I wanted to sit in silence for a while and stare at the emptiness of the night, but I saw that Behnam's two comrades had stood up to perform their prayers. I had no idea that Communists also prayed. As soon as they had finished, they said they should set off. It was time. We went towards a tree to which I knew a boat rope was attached. The last time we had sent anybody to the other side, a small group of Auntie Azar's friends, had been a few weeks before my waking-sleeping period. I found the rope and together we pulled the boat from that bank, which was hidden under foliage, to this side. Several boxes of Russian mulberry brandy were hidden in the boat. They belonged to smugglers. As we pulled the boat across, his cold hand was atop mine, shivering . . . I said, "You must tell your comrades what we saw. Perhaps they'll give up on going."

The river was about ten or fifteen meters wide. In that autumn of falling leaves, the river calmly followed its course, heedless of what was happening on either bank. Heedless of our sorrow. Of the silent howl of those who had vanished into the darkness, coffins on their shoulders. The two men quickly sat in the boat. They seemed very determined and cheerful. Behnam also sat in the boat and began talking to them. I suspected they wouldn't believe him. Auntie Azar's friends hadn't believed either. Their voices, threatening, gradually grew louder. Behnam stood up and said, "I've told you what I saw with my own eyes." "Then why didn't you call us over?" one of them said. The other replied, "Did your Shah-supporting girlfriend make something up?" "I'm shocked too," Behnam said. "I still don't want to believe it, though what I told you is exactly what I saw and heard, but the choice is yours." One of them looked at me, frowning, and then, turning to Behnam, said, "Whatever the case is, the other side can't be worse than this." "Well, I'm going," said the other. "The SAVAK is after us here. Over there we'll be with our own people. We have a letter from the Tudeh Party. They'll understand that we're not spies." The two men stood up and coldly embraced Behnam. After saying goodbye, Behnam came over to me and we stood under the tree together and watched them move away from us in the darkness.

We made the long journey back in silence, and he went straight back to Tehran without resting, but before he went, we did dismount from Shabro and Afsun and rest a little next to the spring, underneath the ancient maple tree that people called "Mr. Tree," lighting candles in the hole of its trunk and tying colored string around its millennia-old branches in order to make vows and wishes. Right next to the Seven Sisters Spring, where locals said that at the time of the Mongol invasion seven sisters had fled from the Mongol soldiers and disappeared into a spring at that very same spot, he took my hand and said, "There are so many things I cannot find any explanation for. Like the whole story with the coffins. With the palace. Like the feelings I have for you. But I want to have this spring and this tree as my witnesses and tell you that I want to stay faithful to you and of the love I have for you. I don't know what life has in store for me and you. We're still very young . . . But . . . " Then he unfastened both our necklaces and put one of the wooden rings he had carved on each, before putting them both around our respective necks and saying, "But these wooden rings will remind us of each other. Of the secrets and mysteries we have shared until now." He wrapped his arms around me and said, "With all my being I want you to believe that whatever happens between us, my love and respect for you will not diminish one bit." Then he pressed me fiercely to himself and kissed me.

As I watched him move away, I ran a finger over my lips and thought how much that had been like a kiss of farewell.

Chapter Eight

As fate would have it, the following winter, amid the bleating of frightened sheep, the jangling of Turkmen tribal women's bangles, and the chirping of the vast meadows' sorrowful sparrows, the first bullet of the revolution was destined for my poor fifty-seven-year-old Uncle Bijan's heart, so that Leyla's prediction of two years earlier, delivered from the swing under the Gowkaran tree in the middle of our kitchen, might come true. The Shah went, Khomeini came. The crown went, the turban came. The Iranian lion and sun emblem went from the flag and the Arabic "Allah" emblem came, and had it not been for Mobed Rostam Shahrzadi's standing firm in the parliament, the three colors of red, white, and green on the flag would have forever given way to the Shi'ites' favored green. The people called all this going and coming "the revolution," and sat and watched the hasty serial trials and assassinations and revolutionary executions of the country's leaders and ministers and managers and major investors, some frightened, some confident in their hearts that the leaders of the revolution knew what they were doing. In the middle of all this, there was no news of Behnam again, and I couldn't imagine that he too was mixed up with revolutionaries and involved in or at least a contented witness of all these revolutionary assassinations and executions. I fingered the wooden ring on my necklace uneasily and thought, *If he is, then what?* Every day on the television that was now in the service of thin, bearded, frowning revolutionaries could be seen the cheerful and excited people's demonstrations against the Shah's regime. Unaware that forty years later, not only themselves, now in the streets chanting the slogan "God, the Quran, Khomeini" and pulling down the statues of Reza Shah and Mohammad Reza Shah, but their children and grandchildren, too, who had not even been born in the Pahlavi era, would fish those names out from the storage box of history and shout them pleadingly in the streets: "Shah, come back, Shah, come back, Shah, come back," or "Reza Shah, apologies . . . Reza Shah, apologies . . . " And that only a fortnight later Reza Shah would respond to their appeal when his seventy-four-year-old mummified body was exposed in the historic cemetery of Shah Abd-ol-Azim. No . . . When we were sitting in front of the Panasonic color television watching the demonstrations against the Shah, we had no idea that years later those same grandchildren of the revolutionaries would come up with the following joke: "For two weeks we called on Reza Shah and he showed us his mummy, but we've been saying 'Mahdi,[21] come, Mahdi, come' for forty years and there's still no sign of him!"[22]

They say that the bullet issued from the revolver of a lowly employee of the Mazandaran Province Registry of Titles, Deeds, and Documents who had been on his way on his 1958 Vespa to the pastures of the Yomut nomads in the west of Gonbad-e Kavus to seek the hand of their Khan's daughter, all in order that the pose of an idealistic young revolutionary would be engraved on the fifteen-year-old Khan's daughter's heart. According to what was later written in the newspapers, the Registry of Titles, Deeds, and Documents employee, emerging from the Khan's tent, happened to notice Uncle Bijan, clad in local dress and wearing a Turkmen wool hat, busy attending to his sheep, and though at first the employee doubted his eyes, once he asked around and it became clear that this person was

[21] The twelfth and absent Imam of the Shiites.

[22] A reference to the slogan, compulsory in schools, universities, and government offices, calling for the return of the Imam Mahdi, the twelfth and hidden imam of the Shi'ites.

a stranger who had only been with the nomads for a few weeks, he was sure that this was none other than the fugitive First Deputy Prime Minister from the Shah's regime, the one who was always talked about on the television. The employee, who had the gun with him in his belt in order to show off in front of the girl's family, having gotten his hands on it in the clashes and occupations of police stations and bases during the demonstrations, started for Uncle Bijan without warning, in front of the eighteen men and women gathered for the marriage proposal ceremonies, and in a loud voice, hands trembling, said, "First Deputy Prime Minister, hands up!" When my uncle heard this, amid all the bleating of the sheep, he remained where he was, leaning on his shepherd's crook, and said, "You're right, I am the First Deputy Prime Minister of the sheep." And along with eighteen nomads he started guffawing, but the lowly official, feeling he had been humiliated in front of the girl and her family, shouted, in a Turkmen accent which he tried his best to turn into a correct and eloquent Persian, "I am talking to you! Hands up, or else I fire." Uncle Bijan, standing casually and lighting his Oval Oshnoo cigarette with a match, said, "First let me smoke this cigarette, and then kill me."

According to what they later wrote on the front page of the *Keyhan* newspaper, all eighteen of them, as well as the young man, gun in hand, stood and watched as my uncle calmly smoked his cigarette, stubbed it out under his foot, turned to them and said, "Bury me under that tree over there." And he gestured toward the only tree, far off in the middle of the meadow, with his crook. Those present moved their heads respectfully and kindly to say, "Of course." Then my uncle turned to the Registry employee, weapon in hand, and said something that he could never have imagined would, years later, turn that insignificant young man into the president of Iran. Or perhaps he did know, because my uncle continued by saying to him, "Before you kill me, I want to do something so that you make something of yourself later." The weapon shook in the hand of this opportunistic man, stammering in excitement and disbelief. "H-h-h-h-how come?" "What's your name?" my uncle asked. The man, short, thin, small, with squinting eyes, said, "Mahmoud . . . Mahmoud Sabbaghian. Why do you ask?" My uncle said, in a commanding tone, "Mahmoud, quickly, go and find a tape recorder and a cassette and bring them here." The man, with his shoddily assembled face and eyes that were close together, still holding the weapon with both hands and aiming it at my uncle, turned to the eighteen people behind him and said in the local dialect, "Move it . . . move it . . . Get me a tape recorder . . . Didn't you hear me? . . . Quick . . . quick." The men turned enquiringly to the women, and the women to the children, and eventually a boy of ten or twelve said that there was an old Sony tape recorder in so-and-so's tent but apparently its battery was flat. The man, gun in hand, shouted at the boy to run and get it. Half an hour later my uncle was recording his last address to the noble nation of Iran over an old cassette of "Cheerful Songs by Soussan," facing the crackling Sony tape recorder whose battery had been coaxed into one last burst of life by the application of spit to its terminals, in the khan of the tribe's black tent, where the marriage proposal ceremonies were supposed to have taken place an hour earlier, surrounded by the cigarette smoke and aroma of the sweat of the locals, now thirty-nine in number, before heading for the tree he had indicated, accompanied by a group of people and sheep. Then he stood there so that he could, with a single lead bullet to the heart, register his name in post-revolutionary history as the first victim of revolutionary terror.

As soon as he had executed my uncle in the meadow, the killer came to his senses, and gun and cassette in hand, started striking his head and yelling, "Dirt on my head, what the hell! What have I done?" After which he ran to his clunky Vespa, jumped on it and sped off to the nearest public telephone, three villages away, where he rang the first person he could think of in the Mazandaran Province Registry of Titles, Deeds, and Documents whose number he had memorized, and informed them that he had carried out the revolutionary execution of the fugitive Deputy Prime Minister. The person he spoke to then called someone else, and that person in turn informed a cleric to whom he was related, whereupon the cleric and a bearded Revolutionary Guard toting a Heckler & Koch G-3 arrived at full speed in a jeep in those hills where until then had never echoed the sound of a bullet being fired. They retrieved my uncle's body from among the sheep and took it to the provincial capital, and thence to Tehran.

In the interval between transferring the body from the tents of the Yomut nomads to the provincial capital, and then to the Evin Prison morgue in Tehran, the lowly Mazandaran Province Registry of Titles, Deeds, and Documents employee had been turned into a hero, into a shining example of the golden revolutionary opportunities available in service of the downtrodden hut-dwellers, someone who with a cassette in his left hand and a weapon in his right thrust the power of the oppressed into the faces of the world of capitalist imperialism and the Taghuti[23] regime, until, just as Uncle Bijan had predicted, he found overnight renown, and would afterwards even turn into the most hated president in the history of Iran, someone who people would, on account of his resemblance to the monkey on a packet of chips, come to call "Cheetos." On the Sony cassette in his left hand the legend "Cheerful Songs from Soussan" had been crossed out, and underneath it, Mahmoud Sabbaghian, whose destiny would later be to change his surname to Ahmadi-Nejad, had written in a crabby-froggy hand "the Last Message of the Cursed Deputy Prime Minister of the Cursed Taghuti Regime. February 14, 1979."[24] On the weapon

[23] TN: *ṭāghūt* is a word occurring in the Quran and adapted by the revolutionaries to describe the Shah's regime and the lifestyle of people they considered close to it, meaning something like impious and corrupt. The original meaning refers to anything worshipped other than God: an idol, false god, demon.

[24] Three days after the date which would become enshrined in the Islamic Republic of Iran's public memory as "the Victory of the Revolution."

in his right hand was engraved "Webley," which only those who knew about such things would realize stood for "the Webley Premier. Made in England."

A few weeks later we were yet to have gotten used to mourning Uncle Bijan when we learned that Auntie Azar had been arrested, to be rapidly executed a few weeks later for having participated in the demonstration against compulsory hijab and worked with Queen Farah's Special Office. My uncle and aunt were buried at the end of the mansion courtyard, at the edge of the forest, in the pouring rain with the voices of the wet crows echoing around, and at Khanom Joon's order the mansion doors, which had prior to that been decorated every day with branches of cypress and thyme in accordance with a centuries-old tradition so that they would be open to any passerby, were now locked to all strangers. Mom crossed out from the telephone book the names of all her siblings who had become revolutionaries overnight, while Dad buried himself under the heavy quilt of silence and depression, surrounded by the black and white photographs of his childhood, his index cards and books and journals.

The sorrow and shock of unexpectedly losing our Uncle and Auntie was hardly small, but it was the reaction of our relatives, near and far, of our friends and friends of friends, that pushed us further than before under the shell of depression. Many of them, until the previous summer constant guests of ours in the mansion, cut off their relations with us out of fear, did not attend Auntie and Uncle's funeral, or even took our photographs out of their family albums, to be torn up and thrown out. Some of them fell over themselves to escape from Iran as soon as possible. Most of Mom's family members who had turned revolutionary overnight took the pictures of the Shah and Farah off of their walls and burned them in secret, removed the photographs of themselves in mini-skirts or shirts and ties from their family albums and cut them up with scissors, emptied out their bottles of alcohol into the toilet bowl, smashed their wine and whisky glasses, either threw their ties away or sewed them into pleated skirts, and framed Khomeini's photo and put it up on the living room wall where the Shah's had been. Those who had tattooed an image of the Shah or the crown on their back or chest either burnt their skin or told the tattooist to turn the crowns into turbans. The others phoned constantly and, shouting with great passion or moaning and crying, told of this or that person's fleeing the country and emigrating, wanting us to advise them on what they should do. So much did they call them, as the senior members of the family, that the telephone receiver was hot in Khanom Joon and Jamshid Khan's hands, everyone asking whether they should leave or stay. Whether we would leave or stay. Whether they should send the children ahead, or all leave at once. Should they leave via the Turkish border, via Pakistan, or Iraq? Should they go to their co-religionists, the Parsis of India, or go to Europe and America?

Anxiety hit our house like the thick curtains of our reception room billowing in the stormy winds that snowy night long ago when half the mansion's roof was ripped off, yet Mom and Dad did not bat an eyelid. They did not have the slightest intention of quitting the country, even though Khanom Joon's sensitive and unerring instinct for sensing historical dangers had compelled her, months before the flames of revolution erupted, to once again—God knows for how many times in the dynasty's history—conceal the sacred fire, now 4,585 years old, along with the family's rare and irreplaceable relics, in a place known only to her and Mobad Jamasp. Such was the situation until we realized one night that the revolution might also bring good things, when we children for the first time met with our distant ancestors, at the same time unexpectedly encountering Uncle Bijan and Auntie Azar. What's more, this happened right there in the heart of the mansion, at the table around the Gowkaran tree in the middle of our very own kitchen.

What happened was that a few weeks after Uncle and Auntie

had been buried in the garden, the two of them, surrounded by our ancestors, both contented and discontented, made a surprise entry into the mansion through its back door to give us all collective advice and persuade us to flee the country as soon as possible with a view to saving our lives. This was the moment I realized that "to leave or not to leave" could be as big a question as "to be or not to be." In the middle of all the greetings and kissing with the ghosts of distant ancestors, amid all the expressions of love and undying devotion and sacrifice, Uncle Bijan and Auntie Azar had scarcely arrived when they told us to quickly pack our suitcases and, indicating the ghosts of distant family, continued by saying, "We brought these to you as historical evidence to persuade you that now is the time to migrate . . . take your lives and souls and go . . . like these . . . like them . . . those ones. The revolutionaries will raid here today or tomorrow and arrest you all, and you will be wiped out just like us." We were, however, so excited by and pleased at seeing both their ghosts and our ancestors' that we weren't listening to them at all as they ran frustrated and agitated through the rooms pulling our suitcases from under the beds and out of the closets, shouting, "Quick . . . quick . . . right now . . . get moving . . . get moving," but Dad, who had found a few ghosts who thought like he did and was standing in the living room hand on waist and cigarette in hand, said, "No, we're not going anywhere."

One of the distantly-related happy ghosts, whom we understood to be an ancestor ten generations removed, said, "I agree. Don't go. Don't go. Nowhere is like one's homeland." But another, an unsatisfied ghost, whom we understood to be fifteen generations removed, replied angrily, "You have to go, and take the sacred fire with you, just as our own ancestors were obliged to migrate to India with the sacred fire." As all of this was going on, Khanom Joon had managed to make her way through the dead and the living and, rapping the ground with her cane, turned to the ancestor fifteen generations removed and said,

"It's obvious you've never seen an airport, because otherwise you'd realize what a lot of hassle it is to cross the border, especially with a sacred fire. Do you think it's still as it was five hundred years ago when they moved the sacred fire about over mountains and through tunnels using carts and mules? And in any case, most of the tunnels have been blocked and can no longer be used."

Mom, who had been chatting away with one of the mothers-in-law from six or seven generations past, said, "Perhaps it'd be a good idea for us to do what the rest of the family's done and send the kids out of the country for a while until things have settled down. Right?" But Dad, shouting so that Mom would hear him, said, "A *dehqan*[25] is never separated from his land." When some of the ghosts heard the word *dehqan*, with knitted brows they asked, "Do you mean to say that we were not *dehqan* enough because we had no choice but to flee?" In the middle of all the din of the dead and the living, the argument had reached a point where Uncle Bijan and Auntie Azar, besieged by a number of ghosts, began suddenly to fling the suitcases from the top of the stairs into the middle of the living room, and, turning to the servants, who were flabbergasted by watching the debate of the living and the dead, yelled, "Hurry up and put the suitcases in the cars! The Revolutionary Guards will get here any moment! We've thrown whatever you need in them . . . Take your documents and leave . . . Quickly, quickly. You have to cross the border with Azerbaijan. We've arranged everything. The smugglers are waiting for you there."

When Uncle Bijan and Auntie Azar shouted, for a moment the hubbub in the house ceased, and everyone's eyes, whether living or dead, fell in astonishment on the two of them, who seemed to have come from another world; and yet no one

[25] Originally meaning farmer, the word was later was applied to the class of large landowners whose function was to watch over and pass on ancient culture and traditions, including the Zoroastrian religion, to succeeding generations after the Arab invasion.

budged an inch. A few moments later, everybody was busy chatting and arguing about history and family and politics and religion once more. As for me, I had quietly followed a group of wandering ghosts through the living rooms and the library to the kitchen, and from the sleeping porch to the closet, and, all the while, listening to what they were saying, it seemed to me that all Uncle Bijan and Auntie Azar's apprehensions were meaningless and greatly exaggerated amid these animated and nostalgic ghosts.

As I reached the reception room, following one of these jesting ghosts, an old woman with gold teeth, a white headscarf and a flowery shirt, picked up a historic earthenware bowl engraved with an image of a lion biting the hind flank of a bull, turning it over with great care before handing it to the ghost standing next to her, one who had been born five or six generations after her, and with a sweet sorrow spoke of the day she had purchased it in the bazaar in Samarqand for only a single silver coin. Further on in the same direction, an old man in Indian clothes and a turban was talking to those around him in Persian and Sanskrit about the *Story of Sanjan*, saying, "I was dead by then, but I was witness to the fact that in the Safavid period Zoroastrians didn't have the right to build houses that were more than even a single story high, because having a two story house was a sign that one occupied a high position. What's more, the Zoroastrians had to tie a little bell to their feet so that the Muslims could keep away from them. Worst of all, they had declared that the wealth of a dead Zoroastrian should be inherited by his Muslim family, and this was how crores and crores of avaricious Zoroastrians became Muslims, and that was when we emigrated to India. But what a journey it was . . ." And he turned to another ghost and shook his head sorrowfully as he recalled these distant, painful memories.

The other ghost, middle-aged and upright, said, "That actually was quite better than our situation . . . We fought with the Arabs face to face, but after we were defeated, we had no choice but to emigrate to Moghestan Island, although after a while the Arabs attacked us there too and killed a great number of us . . . After that we had no alternative other than to launch our ships and set sail towards India . . . But may your eyes not see a bad day . . . We were caught up in a storm and so much did we pray to the sacred fire of Bahram that we had brought with us that after forty days our wandering ship reached dry land. This was one of the miracles of the sacred fire, for otherwise not a single one of us would have made it to India. And many died in that very ship. I myself died of a fever onboard."

That day when some time before sunrise the mansion was finally emptied of the debates and discussions of the cheerful and playful ghosts, and of the handful of them who had been frowning and depressed, as well as Uncle Bijan and Auntie Azar who had given up hope in us, we all sat round the kitchen table and talked by and by of the likeable and strange family ghosts, some of whom had been born in this very mansion, and had once been just as alive as we were, and passed around Mom's large black-and-white photograph. Before the ghosts left, Mom had gathered all the dead and the living around the Gowkaran tree in the kitchen and taken a photograph with the studio camera mounted on a wooden tripod she had bought from one of the inheritors of Naser al-Din Shah Qajar. An hour later we all stood around her in the dark room and with amazed eyes saw how the faces and eyes of the dead and the living appeared through the photographic developing fluid and smiled at us.

Auntie and Uncle had been correct. They really did turn up early the following morning and had barely parked their green Nissan Patrols when they poured into the mansion. Their boss was none other than Mash Mammad, our very own shepherd, whom we had seen much less of since the revolution, his parents leading the sheep to pasture in his stead. Khanom Joon had a particular affection for his mother, Reyhaneh, and twenty-five years earlier had taken her at her own expense to

Mashhad so that she could give birth to the very same beloved pearl of an only child now standing before us in revolutionary pose, weapon in hand. So that he could be called "Mashdi" right from the moment he was born![26] Mash Mammad, twenty-five years old, had now grown a beard, and he knitted his brows so severely that he did not give us permission for a second to say, "Mash Mammad, is that you?"

He did not look us in the eye or give any sign of recognition. As he stood in the drawing room and held up his large gun in the direction of the dancing Qajar woman on the ceiling, it crossed my mind that it was right now that the wine the Qajar woman was holding would spill down on to his head . . . It did not, but how our hearts plunged when he lowered his gun and leaned on it in a roguish pose and glared at us. Then he turned his head to look around the house and like a man given to ogling, stared at every one of the items in it in turn. At length he said to Dad, "You are Taghuti, all the property in this house will be confiscated on behalf of the Mostazafan Foundation of Islamic Revolution." My heart sank. What he said sounded so familiar. Wasn't what this what Behnam had wanted too? The confiscation of the property of the rich on behalf of the poor? Before Dad could open his mouth, Mash Mammad gestured to the historic paintings on the ceiling, doors and walls, and continued, "These paintings are Taghuti too. The faces of all the women must be removed and their legs and breasts must be either painted over, or if you like I can remove them for you right now," and without a moment's delay he raised his gun and fired at the uncovered breast of one of the laughing Qajar women. No blood was spilt but our hearts all sank when a piece of the tile from the woman's white breast came off and fell to the living room floor, right in front of Khanom Joon's foot. A sigh rose up from all our hearts, but Khanom Joon did not bat

[26] TN: "Mashdi," a contraction of "Mashhadi" which may be further shortened to "Mash," refers to someone who has made a pilgrimage to the city of Mashhad in north-eastern Iran, burial place of the seventh Shia Imam, Muhammad al-Rida.

an eyelid; rather with total surety of purpose, as if she had seen such scenes before in her long life, leaning on her cane, she took a step in his direction and asked, "Mash Mammad, is your mother feeling better?" Mash Mammad, whose revolutionary enthusiasm was wounded by this question, pointed his gun in her direction. We all screamed, but Khanom Joon took another step forward, so that the weapon was now pressing into her chest. Jamshid Khan came to his senses and went to stand beside Khanom Joon. "This is the property of our forefathers and ancestors," Jamshid Khan said, "and nobody has the right to lay a finger on the doors and walls of this house or the objects within it." Mash Mammad, who was on the verge of seeing his authority damaged in front of his comrades, raised his gun again, took direct aim at the heart of the miniature rose on the middle of the Afsharid vase, and fired. Bang! "I have the right!" he said, and the Afsharid vase shattered and its pieces fell on the floor. This time Khanom Joon spoke in a louder voice. "It looks like you've become hard of hearing, so I'll have to shout. I asked whether your mom, Reyhaneh, was feeling better. It seems she had caught a cold." This time Mash Mammad said, frowning, "We're here to confiscate property, not to ask after the family's health." Khanom Joon said menacingly, "To whom will you give our ancestral property when you confiscate it? To your mother Reyhaneh who steals a sheep from us every month without us saying a thing? Or will you give it to your opium addict father?" This time Mash Mammad stuck the gun into Khanom Joon's chest. Pressing it in, he shouted, "If you open your mouth once more, I'll fire." Furious, Jamshid Khan thrust himself between the gun and Khanom Joon and said, "Where are the papers authorizing the confiscation? Which court has ruled that we are Taghuti without even a hearing?" One of those accompanying Mash Mammad, who was much older, pushed himself forward. "We don't need court papers. We are the law." The words had not yet escaped his mouth when suddenly Mash Reyhaneh came through the door striking herself on the head and crying, "Dirt on my head, what the hell are you doing . . . what the hell," ran into the middle and, pushing Mash Mammad's gun up, shouted, "What the hell are you doing, Mammad!" And she struck him firmly on the head with both hands.

It was only once Mash Mammad and his comrades had sped away in their Patrols that we realized Khanom Joon had taken Uncle and Auntie's warning from the previous night seriously, guessing that if the Guards were going to come, they would certainly use local forces who knew us well. Early in the morning, therefore, after the ancestral ghosts and Uncle and Auntie had vanished, she had confided a packet of hundred-toman notes to Shafiqeh, along with a letter, telling her to run and take them to Mash Reyhaneh's house and inform her that Khanom Joon had known that for thirty years that she had been stealing a sheep a month from them and although she was very upset with her, she was prepared to forgive her, and even make a present of this money to her. All she had to do was to sign this letter and promise to stop stealing. Once Mash Reyhaneh and her opium-addicted husband set eyes on the packet of hundred-toman notes, they did not even ask what the letter contained, and given their modest literacy, they signed it by dipping their thumbs in ink and pressing them on the bottom of the letter, before tossing the money in the air. In the letter it was written that: *We confess our fault and acknowledge that for the thirty years now that we have been shepherds to the Tabaan family, we have stolen a sheep from them every month, and that they have the right to make a complaint against us in court whenever they so desire.* And just as Shafiqeh was about to return to the mansion, letter in hand, she noticed the Patrols making their way up the road on the hill leading to the house. Quickly, she went back to Mash Reyhaneh and her husband and asked them to come with her and, if Mash Mammad was among the Guards, to stop him. So, they came running.

Thus, we realized that Uncle Bijan and Auntie Azar's worries were not without cause. When the Guards finally left off their sinister activities, at Khanom Joon's behest we all took ourselves to Uncle and Auntie's graves and prayed for them and made food for the sake of charity and handed it out in the Zorvan mosque. After that night we wouldn't see them again for years, not until my marriage to Behnam. The will Uncle Bijan had made in the presence of thirty-nine Turkmen nomad men and women and his revolutionary killer was never executed, but as fate would have it, years afterward, when Azadeh, his only daughter, had grown up and become an old hand as a newspaper journalist, the Ball of Light stealthily brought the old Sony cassette tape with the words *Cheerful Songs by Soussan* scratched out on it, after it had already passed through a thousand hands, to her, sitting behind her desk at the offices of the *Sarmayeh* newspaper, at the end of the East Dead-End Golriz St., Jordan Avenue, Tehran. Azadeh made three copies of the cassette and sent them to exiled colleagues in Germany, Britain, and France as evidence of the crimes carried out by this regime, in the hope that one day an international court would condemn them.

So things went on until one snowy night Dad, in the midst of a long episode of depression, was abruptly woken up by a brief phone call, after which he assembled several sets of sheets and blankets and without explanation rushed outside, got into his black Cadillac, and shot off toward Tehran, to the old Shah Reza Avenue, the University of Tehran, the Faculty of Literature. It was snowing the entire way, and in the silence he fell to thinking about the word "republic." When, at three in the morning, Dad arrived at the University of Tehran, Mr. Janfadaee, caretaker of the Faculty of Literature, was waiting for him behind the great gate so that with tears in his eyes he could show him the library books the revolutionary students had piled up in the courtyard to burn in a revolutionary spectacle the following day. Dad immediately lit a cigarette and telephoned his two colleagues in the Ancient Culture and Languages Group, the two women Professors, Parvardegar and Gharib, for them to come and help him stow all the important books in locked cupboards in their offices, or if they had no other choice, to take them home with them. Then he stood under the softly falling snow surrounded by white Oriental plane trees until his cigarette was finished, and with a lump in his throat watched as the snowflakes settled on the history of the fire temples and inscriptions, on the Iranian garden and the Arch of Chosroes in Ctesiphon, on Persepolis and the Temple of Anahita, on the history of Iranshahr, and steadily buried them.

A year later, when Professor Parvardegar came to our house in order to shake Dad out of his long depression and isolation, and to obtain his assistance in combatting those who intended to eliminate the subject of Ancient Iranian Culture and Languages from the universities, she told Mom that in the middle of that snowy night that Dad, weeping, having gathered up the wet and snowy books and placed them lovingly between the sheets and blankets in the boot of his car, had said to her, "The revolution that begins with book burning and assassinations does not end in a republic."

During the months of isolation at home after the revolution, when Dad, unshaven and eyes hollow from lack of sleep, crept out of his room but once or twice a day like some aged and solitary lizard to eat a little something, before silently and slowly creeping back among his books and index cards for a book of his own, *A Pahlavi Lexicon*, was consumed by word obsession: he used to pick up the magazines and newspapers and take them to his room and spend hours circling words with a red pen and writing word lists in the margins. One day at the dinner table, as he set down a pile of magazines and newspapers, he said: "They have brought new words with them. It's possible to follow the shifts in political power in the vocabulary of these newspapers. You don't even need to read the news.

You just need to follow the words." Then he turned to Mom and to us and said, "These are publications from the first six months of the revolution." As I was sitting next to him, I picked up a magazine and inspected the list of words Dad had circled in red: comrade, the People, enemy of the People, Leninism, socialism, the Red Army, revolutionary terror, the dictatorship of the proletariat, firing squad, cultural hegemony, proletarian internationalism, the enemy of the worker, religion the opium of the masses, the Communist Workers Party, the Proletarian International, Workers Unity, the liberation of the toiling class, the overthrow of neoliberalism, Maoism, well-off and without pain, the uprising of the hungry and the toilers, revolutionary revenge, revolutionary execution, symposium, imperialism, America the world-devourer, the Phalange, Stalinism, fascist, Bolshevism, Uncle Joe, Comrade Lenin, syndicate, militia, and West-struckness.

Then Dad pushed another pile of magazines and papers towards us and said, "These are publications from ten months after the revolution. After the fall of the Provisional Government. After the occupation of the American embassy." I perused the wordlists written in the margins of these publications: the Downtrodden; the Foundation of the Oppressed; Corrupt on the Earth; Sharia obligation; Sharia judge; Sharia rulings; hypocrite; fealty to the Imam; the Imam's line; hijab; the Islamic Guardian-Jurist; against the Guardianship of the Islamic Jurist; the nest of spies; Taghut; the Islamic umma; Ali's umma.

We had not yet gotten used to these Arabic and Islamic words when soon afterward the war broke out, bringing with it a flood of other new words and compounds into the vocabulary of our daily life, ones we had never previously heard: Allah's vengeance, combatant, self-sacrificing, jihad, martyrdom, the road to Karbala,[27] the road to al-Quds,[28] martyr, the martyr's

[27] During the Iran-Iraq war, one of the principal slogans of the revolutionaries was that they would conquer Karbala, the Shiite holy city in Iraq.

[28] Jerusalem. *Al-Quds* is one of the Arabic and Islamic names for the city, usually pronounced *Ghods*, meaning "the holy."

blood, Komayl's Prayer, the Martyrs' Sepulcher, the Martyrs Foundation, the Martyrs' Caravan, hidden holy helpers, the Imam-e Zaman's[29] horse, and the untraceable.

As a result, we too, like Dad, became afflicted by the mania of words and began paying attention to the names and new words appearing in the newspapers. Affairs got to a point where even the names we heard were no longer the usual old Iranian names like Iraj and Manouchehr and Minoo and Touraj and Behrooz and Fereshteh and Mahtab; rather whatever we heard, it was Mohammad and Mohammad and Mohammad and Mohammad, then Hasan and Hoseyn, and Ali and Ali and Ali and Ali and Ali, and Fatemeh and Fatemeh and Fatemeh and Zahra. As if people were no longer the same people of two or three years ago. Worse than all of these were Khomeini's own words and phrases. It wasn't clear which language's grammatical rules his sentence structure followed. It drove Dad crazy with frustration, and each morning at the breakfast table he read what Khomeini had said aloud to us from the newspapers, sarcastically and between gritted teeth: "If today it should explosion, neither I nor you nor anybody, neither the clergy nor Islam will be able to prevent it." And I turned the Moin, Dehkhoda, and Hayim dictionaries upside down to figure out what sort of verb "to explosion" was. His face inflamed, Dad laughed, irritated, as he repeated this sentence of Khomeini's: "Don't make something happen that something happens that makes people think something's happened." Or, "If it is the case that instead of making the people's economy, you see where it is that is ruined and people are deprived of everything, you sit by the seat of power and by cursing and abusing one another, neglect matters in that regard, this is none other than what the Great Powers want!"

[29] *Zaman* means "the time, the age." Muhammad ibn Hasan al-Mahdi is believed by the Twelver Shia to be the last of the Twelve Imams and to have been in hiding since the end of the ninth century. He is the eschatological Mahdi, who will emerge at the apocalypse to establish peace and justice and redeem Islam.

We didn't know whether to laugh at this mangled and mistaken phrasing or cry. Was Khomeini Iranian and Persian-speaking at all? Dad used to shake his head in frustration and remark that their PhD students, their colleagues, doctors and professors, had taken this illiterate little man as their inspiration and launched a revolution behind him. But the truth of the matter was that it was not so much Khomeini's literary skills as his way of thinking that drove Dad into a rage. He would circle snippets and read them aloud: "The economy is for donkeys," or "If you care about Islam, you should know that the universities are more dangerous than cluster bombs." Or this: "Break all the pens . . . if you want your country to be a proper place, get rid of music, and do not be afraid if they tell you that you have become backward. Victory will come when all of Islam's rulings are in force in Iran." Or: "This revolution must stay alive. Shed blood! It stays alive with this shedding of blood."

Although we children, like Dad, had been consumed by word obsession, we nonetheless tried to refrain from reading the news so that we would worry less. All the same, every morning great big headlines in 74-point font and grim black-and-white photographs of those executed plunged into our eyes and souls and hearts like arrows and shrapnel: *Deposed Shah's Collaborators Killed . . . Firing Squad for Eleven Major Former Regime Traitors . . . Firing Squad for Hated Shah's Regime Leaders . . . Assassination of Deposed Shah, Farah, Ashraf Declared Permissible* . . . Many cheered and applauded the execution of the leaders and officials of the Pahlavi state, like Mom's newly prosperous family, who had begun with great alacrity to get their hands on lucrative posts and positions—head of the Office of the Basij in Shilat; Basij Commander, Sagharisazan District. Many others kept quiet, either not knowing what to do or out of an abundance of caution, like most people, while others had no choice but to keep quiet, because they were in a mere minority, like us or our close friends.

Amid all this chaos, I wondered constantly which group

Behnam was part of. I no longer had any hope of hearing from him. At our last meeting and during our last kiss, the way he looked and spoke smelt of farewell. That whole epoch of depression and sleeping-waking was enough for me. I didn't want to be caught up in that uncontrollable situation again. I had to learn to take hold of the reins of my feelings. After Dad had stepped back from the university, he no longer had any contact with Behnam's father, or at least not that I was aware of. Yet despite the distance, it did once occur to me that I should write him a letter. I sneaked into Dad's study and found the address and telephone number for his house in Dad's address book, but the moment I came to write something, I reproached myself for it and flung the pen into the desk drawer. At the mere thought of writing to him my heart trembled, but my intellect, my seventeen- or eighteen-year-old intellect told me forcefully that we were moving on two contradictory paths and to "be there for those who are there for you." This was how I began to wonder what path I was on anyway. Day after day Mandana, Mina, Mehrab, and I sat around the Gowkaran tree in the middle of the kitchen, and while eating fruit wondered what we wanted to do. Mina and Mandana, who had obtained their high school diplomas in the thick of the revolution, both wanted to become dentists. Mehrab, who after the discovery of the temple, had changed his mind set and aims entirely, wanted to follow in Dad's footsteps and study ancient Iranian history, whereas the harder I thought about it, the less I knew what I wanted to do. The problem was not that I didn't know what things I liked to do. The problem was that I had realized that, more than anything else, I liked living in the mansion. I didn't want to be far away from it. It was as if everything began with the mansion and led back to it. A great deal of work and responsibility lay in wait here—I loved literature, and works of literature were all around me. There was no need for me to go to university on account of it. I loved writing memoirs, and notebooks and paper were all around me, besides the 1,700 or so unread notebooks of memoirs in the rusty trunk in the corner of the attic. I loved ancient heritage, and the mansion was full of old objects. I loved nature, and here I was surrounded by forest and rivers and hills. And then of course there was the question of deciphering the Gowkaran tree in the middle of the kitchen. There was no need then for me to go to university. Whatever I desired to obtain, had been collecting for me for generations in this very mansion and garden. I had to spend time getting to understand it. I didn't want anything else. Right here was enough for me. Much more than enough, even.

Mandana and Mina said with one voice: "This means you're just a layabout." They were right. I looked at my three siblings and said: "If only there were something outside of this mansion that I really desired." Mehrab stared into my eyes and asked, "Are you sure there isn't anything?" It crossed my mind that perhaps he knew.

So it was that I completed my final years of high school without feeling the slightest sense of rivalry with my classmates, finishing as quickly as possible so that I could shut myself up in the beautiful, safe mansion forever. Devote myself to taking care of it. It had crossed my mind that it wouldn't be a bad idea to take a course in the restoration of historic buildings. Whatever happened, we had to restore the white breast of the Qajar woman on the ceiling. In this way my life would not be pointless—to look after the mansion would be my life and objective.

Unlike in the past when the mansion, far from the city and our capital, had been the resort of guests and the place for the celebrations and meetings of Mom and Dad's and Uncle and Auntie's friends and likeminded acquaintances, with Uncle and Auntie no longer there and relatives emigrating and the Guards raiding and Dad retreating into isolation and Mom being purged from the Organization for Children and Adolescents' Intellectual Development, the house had come to smell of inertia and stagnation and death. It had become silent and empty. Furthermore, by Khanom Joon's order Uncle and Auntie's graves had been placed where they could easily be seen from the mansion's balcony and from Khanom Joon's room. As if Khanom Joon wanted to remind both herself and us that dying young was an event that repeated itself throughout the history of this land.

The mass executions and assassinations of the leaders of the Shah's regime commenced only three days after the victory of the revolution on February 11, 1979. As it happened, it was the same day that they had killed Uncle Bijan. The condemned received death sentences after summary court hearings of a few minutes. Some of them were killed by firing squad on the roof of the Refah School where Mehdi Bazargan had his offices; others they killed unawares with two bullets to the neck in the corridors of the courts, and still others in prison courtyards or here and there in the streets. There were no tribunals or lawyers, since the revolutionaries—and particularly a fresh and eager cleric called Khalkhali, the very mention of whose name was enough to bring us out in blisters, and who had become a sharia judge overnight—believed that no one living needed a lawyer. Khalkhali used to say, "Either the accused is telling the truth or lying, and it is the sharia judge who determines what is truth and what is lies, and not anyone else!" They termed these hasty revolutionary executions "divine justice," and in their honor fired shots in the air in certain city squares, announced them proudly by bellowing into the city loudspeakers, and quietly swiping their property.

And so it was that we who had been consumed by word obsession saw on television that they had sat the handcuffed, compassionate, successful and educated managers of the Pahlavi state down under the Arabic slogan that they had written in a rush with a marker pen on a wall: *wa-lakum fī'l-qiṣāṣi ḥayātun yā 'ūlī 'l-albābi la'allakum tataqūna*. Although when I looked at the old Quran in our library, I understood that the meaning of this verse was "O people of reason, there is life for you in retribution so that you may incline towards piety," I knew that besides its illusory meaning that life could be granted through killing, it contained another hidden meaning, one that I would only gradually come to understand. Namely, "O people of Iran, know and be ready that the Persian language and culture, that once before Yaqub ibn Layth-e Saffar and Rudaki and the Samanid kings and Ferdowsi saved with devotion and self-sacrifice and great effort from the invading Arabic language, will once more be crushed under the gibbet of that language so that they may endorse the saying of Muhammad, the Prophet of Islam, that "for God the most repugnant language is Persian, and the language of Khuzestan is the language of Satan, and the language of hell is the Bukharan language, the language of the dwellers in heaven Arabic."[30]

And so it was that Jamshid Khan's words became a catch-phrase for us. Once, when he was sitting in front of the television listening to a young, black-bearded cleric talking, someone who at the time had no idea he would become the country's seventh president, he heard it said that conspirators should be hanged in front of the people during Friday prayers for greater effect. At that very moment Jamshid Khan shook his head and, appalled, said, "People thought that the revolution would liberate the forces of good. This revolution has liberated the forces of evil."

[30] Source: Muḥammad ibn Aḥmad al-Muqaddasī, *Aḥsan al-Taqāsīm fī Ma'rifat al-Aqālīm*, "the Best Division for Knowledge of the Regions."

Chapter Nine

When I woke up that morning, it was as if they had poured lead into my body; I couldn't haul myself out of bed. My body felt like a hot kiln as I yelled, "Mehhhhhrab! *Mom*!" It was Khanom Joon who got to me before anyone else, however. She looked at me to see what was going on. Putting one hand on my forehead and the other on my wrist to take my pulse, she said, "It's not your body that's gone heavy. It's your heart. It's the heart that pulls people this way and that." And she ordered that a preparation be made from the Problem-Solving Tree[31] that grew beside the ancient ruins of the Aspi Mazgat fire temple, and that I should both inhale its vapors and that its incense should be burnt. They did, but it was no use. Then Jamshid Khan sat beside me and read me Samad Behrangi's book *The Legend of Tenderness*, so that if it was because of my love for someone that my heart had grown heavy it might be lightened again and I might start talking, but my heart didn't lighten up, nor did I start talking, although it did cross my mind, "What if Jamshid Khan knows?" I knew that I was locked onto thinking about him. That I had fallen under his spell. I, who not long before had secretly made fun of the rest of the family for their mental and psychic locks, realized that however much reason forbade it, my heart was locked onto him, onto his young, manly voice, onto his black eyes and his milky skin. My heart was locked onto his strong embrace, his beautiful human ideals, however much my reason said his embrace

[31] Moshgel-Gosha Tree. A legendary sacred tree people believed would solve their problems if they burned the incense from its leaves or ate its fruit.

was fleeting and his thinking dangerous. Despite all that, I knew that the matter didn't end with him. Scattered thoughts whirled in my head, whirled and whirled, before being brought up into the copper bowl next to my bed: *I miss him . . . blechhhh . . . ah my poor uncle and auntie . . . blechhhh . . . what happens if I never see Behnam again? Blechhhh . . . this war . . . what is this disaster that has befallen us? Blechhhh . . . how I hate the long black manteau and maqnaeh we have to wear at school . . . blechhhh . . . Fereshteh . . . Fereshteh . . . oh, Fariborz . . . blechhhh . . . what if Behnam's joined the Revolutionary Guards? Blechhhh . . . what if . . . what if . . . oh no, what if he falls in love with a different girl? Blechhhhhhhh.*

For three nights and days I was unable to get out of bed, until at last, on the fourth day of fever and shivering and lead in my body, the excited voice of the television reporter, talking, like every day, of war and executions and arrests of Taghutis and counter-revolutionaries, twisted and turned in my ears until I started screaming and scratching my face and hitting myself, suddenly and without warning. My whole body was gripped by convulsions. Appalled, everyone rushed to my bed and grabbed my arms and legs so that I wouldn't injure myself. My teeth were locked, and my fingers were all contorted and twisted together . . . However hard they tried, they could not get anything past my locked teeth, or prise apart my rigid fingers. My body shifted from this side to that, the vein in my neck was bulging, and then as the reporter's howls twisted and turned in my ears, my locked mouth suddenly opened. Words flew out of my mouth like flames from a volcano and sparks from damp wood: "Shut this stupid filthy radio up will you . . . turn off the damn TV . . . I don't want to know anything else . . . I don't want to hear anything else!" And I kept pounding the bed with my body. Was this outpouring of everything not actually the consequence of Behnam's absence, but spat out of my mouth in the name of the revolution and executions? It was. It wasn't. It wasn't. It was. As Maryam and Shahnaz sprinted to turn off the radio and television, everyone else, rooted to the spot and in shock, watched me pouring everything out in my convulsions, while Shafiqeh ran to fetch an egg to break over my head so that it would become clear whether anybody had injured me with the evil eye.

The egg certainly didn't break, but a week later, once the television reporter's voice had been shut up, the spell on my body did gradually break and my body felt lighter. Bit by bit, it warmed up again, started moving, and managed to get itself out of bed, until a few days later, once again the long manteau . . . once again the maqnaeh wrapped under the chin . . . once again the black socks . . . until once again it donned the black chador and goes to school. A school where Fereshteh no longer was. Where Fariborz was not even a pistachio shell. My body got ready to once more head to school, where every Saturday the principal and the supervisor, after half an hour of slogans and "Allah is Greatest" and blessings upon the Prophet and his family and insulting America and Britain and the USSR and Israel, stood at the head of the morning line-up and with the patience of Job measured the turn-ups of the trousers of every one of us 250 female pupils to make sure they weren't tighter than 35 cm, to make sure that the back of our long manteaus did not stick to our behinds, that they didn't have slits, that our hair wasn't spilling out of the corners or sides of our maqnaehs, and that the bulge created by our tying back our hair could not be seen from up the maqnaeh. Every morning grim-faced, sycophantic religious girls volunteered to inspect the bags of all 250 pupils for books other than textbooks, for music cassettes, romantic novels, mirrors, and hairbrushes. Woe betide the pupil who brought lipstick or perfume with her. If she wasn't expelled, she would at least have to spend two weeks at home and her parents would have to sign a Moral Commitment Sheet. If a love letter were found in a girl's bag, then they would hand over her file to her, with no recourse. Expulsion. Finished. But worse than all this was if they found pamphlets or cassettes of speeches from political parties. This was something that could easily lead to any pupil ending up in jail or being executed.

That day I plucked Fereshteh's blue Bic biro from the air, did I imagine at all that one day I would see her mournful black-and-white picture in the *Keyhan* newspaper? That blue biro in the penholder on my desk would remind me of her until the end of my life, and not just her, but Fariborz and the pistachio shell, too. Remind me of the incompleteness of this life, and of our suspended lives; the biro that was flung into the air and plucked from the air . . . a friendship that had formed in the air . . . a life that had come to an end in the air, only half done . . . that had fallen to the ground, where nobody picked it up again. That biro hanging in the air was her. It was her suspended life, which fell to the ground without settling in anyone's safe hands.

That day I had gotten to school late, because on the way the car had acquired a puncture. She and one of her friends were sitting in the school security guard's little booth talking, and as soon as I arrived I flung my bag hurriedly into a corner of the yard so I could run to my exam, before remembering that I hadn't taken my pen out. Just as I was about to rush back to where my bag was, she realized what was going on and asked, "Do you want a pen?" And before I could answer, she half got up, laughed, and threw her blue Bic biro toward me; I plucked it from the air, laughed, and ran off to my exam. That biro suspended in the air was the beginning of our friendship. We both liked our literature and art lessons, and before the revolution we used to swap romantic novels with one another at school. We were always on the same volleyball and table tennis teams, and once a month we went to one of the cinemas: the Soheila or the Abshar, the Kurosh or the Moulin Rouge. We saw *Gone with the Wind*, *Casablanca*, *Désirée*, *Doctor Zhivago*, *Tears and Smiles*, and *The Wizard of Oz* together, and many others besides. Sometimes Mina and Mandana and Mehrab and

Fereshteh's brother Fariborz would come with us and we used to wander all night in the streets of Rasht talking about the films and of how once we had gotten our high school diplomas we would go to bars and discos together after the cinema, and dance and drink away from our elders' gaze. We used to emerge from the cinema and it would be merely the beginning of our fun. First, we would pay a visit to Akbar the grilled liver seller, who used to set up shop with his brazier near the cinema and was in our view the best grilled liver seller in the whole of Rasht. Then we would take ourselves to Café Noushin in Shah Avenue to eat ice cream, before walking to the Mohtasham Garden. Sometimes we had dinner, either at 444 Kabab and Pilau on Bisotun Avenue, or in the Iran Hotel. Best of all was when Nader took us to the beach in Anzali after the cinema. We would light a fire and swim until the middle of the night, or sit around the fire and sing along to Fariborz's guitar. When Fariborz played the guitar like that for us with such passion and feeling, did we imagine that in all the fever and confusion of the revolution he would end up being shrunk into a pistachio shell at the bottom of Fereshteh's bag? The street clashes of the revolution turned Fariborz into a pistachio shell. A pistachio shell which one day, as Fereshteh and I were sat next to each other in Nader's car and, as was our habit, turning each other's bags inside out, I would throw out of the window unawares, before asking laughingly, "Why don't you clean your bag?" And she, her face frozen and drained of color, would reply, "That pistachio shell was the only thing we found in Fariborz's pockets after they returned his body to us." Fariborz had been killed during clashes in the revolution. By an army bullet to his left breast, and now the only memento of him was being trampled by unknown passersby.

That day when they took Fereshteh away, her arms pinned, I was standing by the blackboard reciting our lesson about geographical determinism—how geography was the source of history, civilization, politics, and culture. Suddenly, I saw her through the open window of the second-floor classroom, leaving the yard, three or four armed Revolutionary Guards around her, and without realizing what I was doing, I ran to the window and shouted, "Fereshteh!" My classmates and the teacher likewise rushed to the window. From between the bearded, frowning, armed men who held her upper arms in a tight grip, Fereshteh turned toward me, towards all our classmates and the geography teacher, her face drained of color and fearful, and took one step . . . two steps . . . three steps, and with the fourth grinned and shook her handcuffed hands in my direction and in a loud voice said, "Don't worry, one day we'll finally go to the disco together and drink *araqh sagi* till morning and dance," even as she was being pushed out of the school by the Guards' hands and weapons. I never saw Fereshteh again, not until Mehrab showed me her photograph in the newspaper: her photo alongside those of nine others. Next to her photograph was written: "Parents and guardians of those executed should present themselves to Rasht Central Prison together with identity documents including photographs of themselves and of their children appearing in this image in order to receive the bodies. It should be noted that bodies will not be returned without payment of the appropriate sum." Besides the photo of Fereshteh, whose headscarf they had forcibly pulled down on to her forehead, was written, "Fereshteh Mowlayi. 17. Rasht."

It was then that I thought to myself, "If only I never had to go back to school. If only I were brave like Monireh." Monireh, the only Baha'i girl in the school, who, after the headteacher and the girls had so often scowled at her, and even on occasion spat on the floor whenever they saw her, had broken free from the school altogether. The principal had issued a firm order that nobody was to shake Monireh's hand, play with her, or talk to her, because she was unclean. I however granted no importance to this order, and under the headteacher's contemptuous gaze from her large office window, as the only Zoroastrian in the school, continued to talk to her and play with her and shake her hand, but this wasn't enough for Monireh. 248 other pupils either looked at her through narrowed eyes, or didn't look into her eyes at all. Now that Fereshteh and Fariborz had been cruelly killed in this way, I could better understand how Monireh felt. How she probably felt in the morning when she woke up and once more put on her long manteau, once more her maqnaeh, once more her black chador so that she could put up with the menacing eyes of her classmates, the principal and the teachers. But she didn't put up with them. That morning when she decided never to come back to school, she must have felt such a tremendous sense of relief.

For some time, I had been experiencing an emotion that was novel to me. The ten-day-long nervous madness had abated but had given way to something more deadly: disgust. Disgust for school. Disgust for my classmates. Disgust for the streets. Disgust for Behnam. Disgust for the television, the radio, the newspapers. Age eighteen would have passed me by in disgust for the headteacher and the school counsellor, the television reporter, the black-and-white photographs in the newspapers, and the morning slogans in school, had I not stopped myself in time.

Age eighteen was when I realized I had an illness by the name of depression: I was scowling. I was listless and confused. I was afraid. I was quiet. Quieter than before. And after the long half-sleeping, half-waking period, I was now in the grip of chronic insomnia. As if my body, mind, and psyche were retaliating for all that over-sleeping. I had woken up. A revolution had taken place in my half-sleeping, half-waking state and no doubt I now had to suffer reprisals for my negligence. Age eighteen was an age when I was able to follow the phases of the moon, from crescent to full, from full back again to crescent, for an entire month. I saw how once the moon rose in the west at the same time as the sun set, and when at night I saw the crescent moon in the sky, I fell to thinking about the earth's casting a shadow on it, and all of a sudden I felt my own shadow in it; I was part of the darkness of the moon.

At night I would move from my bedroom window to sit beside the turquoise pool and then under the trees so that I could, head in the air, follow the course of the moon. On moonlight nights something in me cracked open, blossomed, shed its skin, and reached its climax . . . Something bubbled up within me, made me melancholic, made me restless. It was during these night wakings that occasionally Mehrab and Dad joined me, and we drank the finest freshly-brewed tea together. It was at the age of eighteen that I realized I did not understand dynamics of the relations between people in school, and society. The revolution had brought with it a whole host of new unstated rules that eluded me. Even had they wanted to get me to understand those rules, I would have put off hearing, understanding, accepting them. Eighteen was an age when I hated any kind of rule. I wanted to be alone. I would have liked to have run away from school. From the religion lesson, the Quran lesson, the school counselor. Even from the history lesson or for recess without Fereshteh . . . without Monireh.

I wanted to drift into a state of reverie, completely lost in thought. I didn't even feel like reading books anymore. Or listening to music. Talking. Uncovering the secrets of the Mithraic Temple and the mysterious palace in the middle of the forest. Even when I thought about it carefully, I no longer felt like thinking about Leyla and Behnam. For me, the age of eighteen was like a long menstruation. It was an age when the headteacher and the supervisor and the school counselor and the Guards and even the grocer at the end of the street wanted to teach everyone Islamic morality. I wanted to be on my own and think about Fereshteh and Fariborz. About the Bic biro and the pistachio shell . . . I wanted to conceal myself in my room in the mansion, far from the city, even as I knew that in that same mansion's other rooms, the others and especially Dad were not really doing any better than I was. I wanted to escape to somewhere far away. Somewhere where I'd no longer have to go to school: the long manteau again . . . the *maqnaeh* wrapped under the chin again . . . the black socks again . . . morning slogans in the line-up again. Seeing the security guard's little booth again, without Fereshteh half rising to toss her blue biro in the air in my direction, laughing and inquiring, "Do you need a pen?" At age eighteen, in my last year of school, I was thinking of quitting education for good.

Our family, living far from the capital, was still not sure how to deal with so many events in quick succession, when I quite unexpectedly figured out my path and started feeling better. And that too was thanks to one of those dreadful television programs; one afternoon I came out of my room, went downstairs and saw that the television was in the living room, its volume very low, and that Mom, Dad, Khanom Joon, and Jamshid Khan were glued to it, the colors drained from their faces, listening carefully.

As soon as they saw me, Mom said they should turn it off, but I told her not to. I would have to get used to it in the end. I sat down next to them. It had been a while since I'd watched television. A cleric, whose name they said was Hoseyni, was standing next to a blackboard in a loose brown cloak and large black turban and teaching family morality to an informal group of young people who, backs to the camera and facing him, every now and then endorsed what he was saying with loud voices. "Sometimes," he was saying, "you see someone who's tall but short on endeavor. Sometimes you see someone whose head is small, but whose thoughts are vast. The rules of the Islamic sharia are just like that. You shouldn't judge them using rules that have been determined in advance. In the Islamic sharia it's not like two times two is four. Three times ten is thirty. No! Sometimes you'll see that four times ten is a melon tree." The audience laughed. The five of us looked at one another wide-eyed. The cleric, pleased with his witty remark, resumed, laughing, "The Quran says, 'و ما جعلنا القبله التی,' We who used to perform our prayers facing this way, all of a sudden We said, 'do it this way.'" And he turned to face the blackboard before turning back to the class and the camera and continuing, "And We did not give the command 'الا لنعم من يتبع الرسول ممن ينقلب على عقبيه و ان كانت لكبيره الا على الذين هدى الله,' that means 'We wanted to see who is a follower and who isn't.'" The class audience repeated after him with one voice, "And who isn't . . ."

I looked at Mom and Dad. Khanom Joon, frowning, struck her cane on the floor and said: "And these are the people who are now in charge of the country's culture."

Excited by the audience's endorsement, the cleric scratched his head under his turban, set it at a jaunty angle like the roguish characters from pre-revolutionary popular movies, and continued addressing the students: "Or for example the Quran says, 'عليها تسعه عشر,' We have established nineteen officers responsible for torture in hell." He pulled a face, smirked and said, "Nineteen? Well, He could've added one more and that would've made twenty!" The students, thick stubble on their faces and wearing gray- or cream-colored shirts with clerical collars, giggled. The cleric continued: "But God deliberately said nineteen to see who would protest by saying, 'Where's the other one?'" Once again the class laughed with a single voice. Then he continued addressing the students with the same smile. "'و ما جعلنا عدتهم,' We did not appoint these nineteen except to see who whines and who says, 'this is great.' Sir, hell belongs to Him and so the selection of its officials is also up to Him. What does it matter to you?" The students shook their heads and with one voice repeated, parrot-fashion, "The selection of its officials is also up to Him," and giggled away; hahaha.

That day, as I gaped at the figure of the crooked-hatted family morality cleric, I genuinely saw sincerity in his idiotic eyes. He wasn't duping anybody. He didn't want superstition and ignorance and fanaticism to replace science and knowledge. His science and knowledge were these thoroughly idiotic and nonsensical words, and the television of the revolution had given him the opportunity to display and multiply his ignorance most sincerely.

That was when I stood up, and as I was leaving the room I commented, "Have you noticed how ugly everything's become? How everything's turned black and white? How all the cheerful colors, cheerful songs, cheerful programs have been removed from life, magazines, radio, and television?"

They looked at me in silence.

Then all of a sudden, with a joy that I had not known within myself, I said: "If you want to spend the rest of your life listening and watching this nonsense, that's up to you, but just now I've realized I want to spend my life doing something beautiful."

Mehrab, who at that very moment had been coming down the stairs, asked, "That means doing what?"

"I want to seek out beauty," I said.

"You mean you want to become a makeup artist?" Mom asked, startled.

"Not at all!" I said. "I want to pursue whatever is intrinsically beautiful. Like painting. Like sculpture. Like singing. Music. Calligraphy. Poetry. I don't know. I want to devote my life to love, or gardening. Maybe nature photography. Maybe I'll go and learn pottery, or collect local stories and songs and proverbs. Or for instance learn rug and carpet weaving."

Dad was enthusiastic in his endorsement. "Well done, well done. What beautiful ideas."

"But unrealistic," said Mom.

"So will you go to the Faculty of Fine Arts?" asked Mehrab.

"No," I said. "I want to stay right here. In this mansion. As far as possible, I don't want to set foot outside the garden and the mansion and Zorvan. Perhaps at most I might go and take a few courses in the city."

"You can go and pick tea or spin silk with the Zorvan women," Mehrab said.

"Or work in the paddies," I said.

Mom and Dad exchanged glances, and Mom said, "We have

to think of a solution too. Since I've lost my job, I have to find something else for myself to do." And so it was that that day in my mind I clarified what I was going to do for the rest of my life. I went to my room cheerful and laughing, and as I lay on my bed, I thought of our family and of the mansion and the sacred fire. Of the historic paintings on the walls, of the objects and the handwoven carpets. I thought of how in this family we had always been collectors of beauty. Our ancestors had always retained anything that was original and beautiful in their collection, in the mansion, on behalf of future generations so that it would not be crushed under the mass of all that was ugly. For no doubt their society too was steeped in ugliness.

I thought of recent years. Of how collecting the hideous had become a prosperous affair for many; purchasing and wearing manteaus and *maqnaehs* and black chadors. Collecting and spreading news of the war, executions and assassinations, the nonsense in Arabic that came jabbering from the clerics' mouths. I remembered how several people at school collected empty firearms cartridges, or combatants' headbands with slogans like[32] فَتحُ القَريب نِصرُ مِنَ الله و or يا زهرا اَدرکِنی.[33] Some assembled collections of green plastic grenade-shaped money boxes which they would send to the front at the end of each trimester. Others used to collect magazines with black-and-white photographs of the war and heroic, pious combat poetry. Others collected stamps of Khomeini, of the Takeover of the US Spy Den, and of martyrs, while others still had more profitable collections: veritable hoards. They collected different kinds of foodstuff and hygiene supplies so they could sell them at a dearer price when the time came.

I imagined everyone was up to this, because they had been

[32] TN: Arabic: "A victory from God and an imminent conquest," Quran 61:13.

[33] TN: "O Zahra, come to my aid!" (Arabic, a prayer addressed to Fatimah, known as al-Zahra, "the resplendent," a revered figure for Shiites especially, daughter of the Prophet Muhammad and wife of the first Shiah Imam and fourth Muslim caliph Ali ibn Abi Talib).

drowned in reality. There were lots of them, but we were on our own. They collect the realities of Iran, whereas I want to . . . I want to collect the *dreams* of Iran. I was over the moon at this idea. I rolled over in bed and looked at the tiles on my bedroom wall: Bijan being hauled out of Afrasiyab's well, helped by Rostam. Manizheh is stood on one side, in tattered clothes, observing. I got out of bed and ran my hands across the tiles. Hundreds of years must have elapsed since these tiles were made. Beaming from ear to ear, I went toward the bedroom window and gazed at the blue sky and the forest. I took a deep breath and thought that they were collectors of history, collectors of wishes. They were collectors of scowling judges, sharia rulers, vendors of religion, politicians, and the Fatemeh-commandos of the Revolutionary Guards.[34] We were collectors of poetry and harps. Collectors of the Lut Desert, the forests of the North, the mountains of Kurdistan, the wine of Shiraz and the watermills of Shush. We were the collectors of the legends of Mounts Alborz and Damavand, the carpets of Kerman, Bakhtiari gelims and Qashqai gabbehs. Wasn't it in the Avesta that humanity had been created to aid Ahura Mazda in making the world more beautiful and better? For the betterment of the world, I had to concentrate on beautiful things. I would have to become the collector of the bashful Iranian kiss. Collector of Iranian poise, *taarof,*[35] and manners. Collector of conscience, morality, and dignity. Collector of the songs of the Maestro Seyyed Javad Zabihi whose larynx Muslim fanatics had ripped out. Or the songs of Maestros Banan, Badizadeh, Daadbeh, Delkash, and Maestra Qamar-ol-Moluk Vaziri, or the hopes and bravery of Bibi Khanom-e Astarabadi. I and we would have to become

[34] A sobriquet people applied to those women who swiftly became devoted supporters of the Islamic Republic, took up arms, donned black chadors, and joined the Islamic Revolutionary Guard Corps or Basij.

[35] Reciprocal politeness and kindness, a word describing a form of civility or art of etiquette that emphasizes both deference and social rank. Taarof between friends, or a host and guest, emphasizes the primacy of friendship.

collectors of handwoven Baluch cloths and Bushehr straw mats and Khorasani saffron and the pottery of Hamedan and Kurdish dancing. Gatherers of Abu Rayhan-e Biruni's manuscripts and those of Zakariya Razi, of Omar Khayyam and Avicenna, Hallaj and Bayezid Bistami.

I thought I wanted to become the collector of ideals and dreams and the utopia of Jamshid Shah. What was wrong with that? Let the rest of them say I was an idiot or crazy. Let them say I am running after the wind. What does it matter. I wanted to be the collector of flowers: flowers on rugs. Let other people be collectors of reality. I would collect the scallops of the Caspian Sea and the Persian Gulf and the ancient potsherds of the Falak-ol-Aflak Castle and the citadel of Bam. Let others bother with the war and Friday prayers at the University of Tehran and executing political prisoners. Let others make fun of me. I, however, want to be the steward of the legacy of the Way of the Simorgh or Mithra that Mehrab had told me about. Actually, I want to be the collector of Behnam's wishes and ideals. My very own Behnam . . . Behnams. Of course I know now that assembling such a collection is a very difficult task. Because many of these things will have to be extracted from the bog of party or religious or ideological thinking. That is my task, then: finding and gathering beautiful thoughts and ideals.

Then I thought how it wouldn't be possible to make money and earn a living doing this, but maybe alongside collecting I could build a greenhouse for roses and irises and sell flowers. I wondered who would buy flowers in this time of war and misery and weddings in mosques and tekiyehs.[36] Yet it would be better than sitting and doing nothing. Dad, thanks to all the efforts and insistence of Doctors Parvardegar and Gharib, had just gone back to work, where he had learned of the murder of his dear colleague Dr. Ahmad Tafazzoli by agents of the regime.

[36] A structure used for the performance of passion plays about the martyrdom of the Imam Hoseyn during the Islamic month of Muharram, as well as other forms of pious ritual mourning.

Although Dr. Tafazzoli was the same age as him, he had years before chosen him as a model for his own work: determined and focused on discovering unknown dimensions of the culture and civilization of ancient Iran. That was exactly why they had killed him. His very existence was a denial of Islamic civilization in Iran. Nor was it obvious how long the new regime in the universities would put up with Dad. Mom too had been kicked out of her job in the Organization for Children's and Adolescents' Intellectual Development. Had been "purged," as the revolutionaries put it. From the window I caught sight of Hasrat, who was busy in the garden as usual. Full of enthusiasm, I went outside and called him and shared my idea about the greenhouse with him. It was obvious that in his view it was all a bit too optimistic, naive even, but he couldn't bring himself to say so, instead telling me he liked it. He didn't say "no." That he hadn't said "no" was already good. We set off walking around the garden to find an appropriate place for the greenhouse, me with no idea where I would find the funding for it nor learn what I had to do for it.

It was by thinking about flowers and the greenhouse and collecting beauty that I gradually began to feel better. Depression and stagnation gradually gave way to animation and elation. Perhaps it was a hollow cheerfulness, but that was what saved me at this time of depression. As I walked past people in the street, I wondered, "Is everyone else depressed like me?" In my opinion it was more like they were in shock. They would have to spend decades in cultural shock until gradually they could suffer from depression and despair. National depression. Social despair. The cultural shock that swept people up in those early years was produced hastily assembled culture of the barefooted revolutionaries and cell-dwelling, grasping mullahs who had reached the zenith of power and wealth overnight. Most of the major revolutionaries came from poor families who considered us, the middle class, alien and hopelessly West-struck. We, like most people, were unable in the first years of the revolution to easily reconcile what we had accepted as our lifestyle during the Pahlavi era with what they named "Islamic culture." On the way to school I walked among people and looked at their clothes. Dad always said, "The revolution is hurriedly throwing together a culture for itself—a makeshift, distorted, unwritten culture with no historical or even religious underpinnings." They turned clothes, the way people shaved, attire for special occasions, and even colors into a political and religious code; as quickly as that, dark colors and black became symbols of the humble and simple revolutionaries, while joyful and bright colors became symbols of luxury, fit for non-revolutionaries and West-struck people. Men were forbidden from entering government offices in short sleeves, and women without *maqnaehs*, and even sunglasses, belts and wristbands and headbands were presumed symbols of luxury and counter-revolution, but as Dad put it, ties were always in the front row of the accused. From the revolutionaries' point of view, ties meant a deliberate display of West-struckness and even Satan-worship. Something that was not removed from Dad's neck until the last day.

I spent my time wandering through the trees in the garden and staring fixedly for hours at the movement of butterflies and the spinning of leaves in freefall, contemplating their beauty and variety. I bought books about flower arranging and cultivation from the bookstores in town and flicked through them, but it did not take long for my attention to wander. I used to stare at the forget-me-nots that grew of their own accord and plunge deep into thought. It was as if I was waiting for something. I was thinking of Behnam again. Not angrily or with pique. Rather fondly once more and missing him. I thought once more of that wet kiss in the forest. Sometimes when somebody, Mina or Mandana or Hasrat caught me off guard in some corner of the garden and asked me what I was doing, I would reply that I was busy. Of course, they didn't get that staring at flowers is a form of being busy. That watching the flow of the clouds is an important activity. That in a period of depression and fear, to think about beautiful things, your dreams and wishes, and to smile is highly, highly important, a vital task.

In the damp, cool, dark haven of the trees, in a place where light reached the ground with difficulty, I began to imagine gradually bolder activities; I was undoing his buttons. He was undoing mine. I undressed him. I kissed the tops of his shoulders, and so much did he kiss my neck that it bruised. Did I think that he, Behnam, imagined me in the same way? Did he imagine undressing me? Did he take my breasts and squeeze them? I rubbed the wooden ring he had fixed to my necklace with my hand and looked at the movement of the wispy white clouds above me with a smile that seemed to signify that some happy event would rain down on me. I held up a dandelion clock, rubbed it on my lips, kissed it and blew it into the air, awaiting some inspiring and happy news. Something that would light up my life beyond school and religion, war and politics and executions, and make it blossom.

Whether I imagined it or really said it, I'm not sure, but I said to Behnam, "How much do you love me?"

"This much," he said, and started kissing the tops of my shoulders. But then disconcerting thoughts occurred to me between the hugging and kissing, and I found myself saying, "In any case, Tehran is my capital, not Moscow, and my poet is Hafez, not Pushkin."

He laughed and ran his fingers down from the top of my breasts to the skin of my stomach and my navel and on in a straight line to the dark and humid cavity between my legs, making me gasp, before saying, "If love is a world feeling, if freedom is a world feeling, then one's homeland can be the world too."

I pushed his hand back suddenly and with a serious expression said, "We have not yet become enough of a homeland. We have not yet learned to love ourselves, keep love of the world for yourself."

Standing up, he pressed his lips firmly on mine, drew his

thumb over my frowning forehead so that it would relax, and said, "I learned love from you, I expanded it to the homeland, then the world. Any lover can love the world."

I answered his kisses with burning kisses of my own. I liked his utopia. Where loving humanity meant loving the world. But don't say that I had fallen in love with his utopian ideals, rather than with his actual self. Yet even so I didn't understand why, if we were supposed to love not only our own homeland but the whole world too, then why all this talk of the Soviet Union and Moscow and Lenin and Stalin? Why no mention of Nigeria, or Fiji, for example, Addis Ababa and Tokyo, Paris and New York? Amid all this hugging and kissing, I said, "Your ideals are beautiful. I will put them in my Collection of the Beautiful."

Sometimes, far from the gaze of the house's other residents, I visited the spot where I first kissed Behnam and first saw Eblis. Perhaps Eblis should have come to see me again and shown me a way forward. So why was there no news of him? Didn't they say all the time on the radio and the television that Eblis invited human beings to follow their own worldly whims and desires so that they would stray from the path of God and Islam and the Prophet? I wanted nothing else. If the Eblis that I knew was kind and beautiful, then whims and desires were beautiful. If kissing is beautiful, then making love must be too. And thus I gave myself over to dreaming of Behnam until that day when I couldn't figure out whether I had made love with him himself in the Mithra Temple, or with an imaginary him.

The two of us were in the Temple of Mithras and the bull was standing over us. The sun shone through the opening that served as an entrance, bestowing on the dark and damp temple a dreamlike and poetic quality. He pressed me against the cool wall and said, "It's not clear at all whether we'll get out of all this war and killing alive, so let's kiss each other as much as we can. Come on, let's make love." And without a word, I grabbed his hand and slid it under my skirt. “So where did all that shame and shyness and silence of yours go?” I asked myself. His long, slender, cool fingers slid gently into my body and were swallowed up in its warmth. And thus it was that our love-making began, and each time he plunged his burning manhood into me, he found me a virgin, and the blood of virginity trickled down my narrow thighs onto the ground of the temple, and every time he came, he sprinkled his primeval life-bestowing water on my body and on the ground so that our bodies would once more separate virgin from each other . . .

I would walk in the forest and repeat to myself, “I am only eighteen. I am only eighteen and I want to live happy and free. That’s it. I shouldn’t have to feel guilty without reason. I shouldn’t let the laws of the Sharia that are served up to me and us all day and night on radio and TV penetrate my body and soul and thought. My body depends on me. I organize my own thoughts.” My basic task was this: caring for myself, myself. Caring for my body confronted with the onslaught of dos and don’ts. Caring for the untouched character of my thoughts, my feelings and natural instincts amid the onslaught of sins and traditions. I must not surrender to the uglinesses and narrow-minded laws and bad news. I promised myself that I would not allow fear and sorrow and despair—in short, the common culture of those days—to penetrate me. All of a sudden I would shout in a loud voice, “My duty is to be joyful.” And raise my head and laugh to the sky. To the trees. To the dandelions. To the light.

Chapter Ten

The days were passing happily by in this manner when some news came, but not the inspiring news I had been awaiting; one day Maryam, our cook, whispered in Mom's ear, "They say your sister's child . . . Mr. Bahman . . . in the war . . . in Khorramshahr . . . he's been martyred." The word "martyr" was not yet part of our oral culture in the mansion. It would be a while yet before the war matured and launched its unprecedented terminology into our midst. For that reason, in our view Bahman had been killed. Not martyred!

With the sound of the mourning march and the intoning of Perso-Arabic laments falling like a rain of grief from the loud-speakers onto our heads, the crows jumped, and the sparrows scattered throughout the Syrian ash trees fell mute, whilst we shed silent tears for Bahman without me yet knowing that in a month's time I would receive a letter from him in that same crabby-froggy handwriting full of spelling mistakes, signed as always "Your sacrifice Yours always Bahman."

Women and men, clad in black and beating their chests, proceeded slowly alongside the caravan of the martyrs, moaning and crying out the names of those killed as they struck their own heads and faces and wept. My aunt and her husband, Bahman's mother and father, beat their chests at the front of the ranks of black-clad mourners without sighs or tears, and murmured, "Our son has become a martyr in the path of Islam. We did not deserve to be martyrs. He did." Some people wrote messages of love and mourning on the flags draped over the coffins, their

"Allah" visible, so that they would be buried with their beloved sons. A father wrote on his son's coffin, "My son we are proud of you." Another wrote, "In hope of martyrdom and of seeing you again, brother." A young woman who had suddenly let go of her black chador, so that her white wedding dress stood out amid all the black of mourning, threw herself on a coffin and cried out, "Hossein darling, I'm here at your tomb in my wedding dress so that you'll know I'm faithful to your love."

Some while later, when we were still wearing our mourning black for Bahman's untimely death, Mr. Peyk, sweating and pedaling as always, got himself to the mansion and handed the following letter to me:

"Yo Shokoof . . . Its me. From the other world . . . Probably youve still got your black clothes on. Youve seen my coffin, aint you. So now Im a coffin an a little memoriel at the end of the street. Were my mom an dad there to? I bet if they came they dint even cry a drop. May I be your sacrifice I wrote you a letter soon as I could so you woudnt get all upset . . . You see Im alive. I aint died. I dont wanna give up the gost to the fuckin Angel of Deth right now. Ha ha ha . . ."

Shocked at reading these lines, I raised my head and stared into space for a few moments. Mr. Peyk's bicycle moved off down the hill, with him sitting bolt upright in the saddle, both hands on his waist and not pedaling. Why was it I always liked to see the mailman leave? I looked at the letter again. Was Bahman really alive?

"I heard my mom and dad have gone all revulutionary guardy and basijy and gone to the Mehran front . . . haha a drunk an a mad kid murderer woulda gone all guardy . . . Ive shat in there throats. Ive shat in the throat of there revulution. How are you any ways Shokoof my dear? God forbid youve gone and become

part of all them revlutionries . . . Yeah? Have you? No way hun no chance you would . . . Bet your studyin aint you? You done the college entrance exam? I heard about your Uncle Bijan and Auntie Azar. I was really gutted. My condolences God willin itll be your last sorrow and youll never see another one . . . What your Uncle said on that tape was right . . . I read bits of it in the papers . . . Well later theyll see what he said turns out to be true . . . Whats new with that commie comrade of yours? Behnam? He dropped in on me once . . . Maybe he told you about it himself . . . It was a long time ago. There was something about that pretty boy what made me real angry . . . Head always either in the clouds or in his books . . . It was like he didnt understand nothin about real life . . . I dunno maybe it was other stuff ment I coudnt stand him."

Suddenly, I was struck by a question: why had he written of Benham using the part tense? I resumed reading.

"Whatever . . . Whats new with you? Do you wanna go to college? Obviously you do . . . If you dont who will? Ive written my adress at the front on the envelop. You can rite me a letter. Will you? Please write. I was in Khoramshahr till three months ago but know Im in Ahvaz. You must definitely know Khoramshahr has fallen . . . What terribel days an nights Ive seen death with my own eyes . . . Me and a few of the boys got the hell out of this slawterhouse an me for one for now I aint got no intension of dying an drinking the snake poison martyrs nectar . . . tho its a bad war here . . . frickin awful . . . the people of Khoramshahr fout with there bear hands . . . Iraqis armed to the teeth . . . they dont give our peeple safe conduct . . . I seen stuff with my own eyes you woudnt beleive . . . but this peeples frickin amazin . . . they fout street by street . . . district by district . . . defended themselves . . . with petrol bombs . . . with their granpas wepons from world war 2 . . . with shovels an axes . . . hand to hand . . . house to house . . . I seen them with my own eyes fitin

even with vegtable knifes an forks . . . one night I had to hide in a ruined house from fear of the Iraqis. In that house their were the bodies of a granpa an granma an a woman an a bunch of kids big and small . . . Their were 2 babies among them kids two. One of them had a blue pacifier in its mouth an the other a red one. She was sleeping like our Mahsa too . . . You feel damn rotten when you see the bodies of a poor woman and kids. The old mans false teethd landed in the dirt a meter away.

"Thats how life is here in the middle of war . . . Hard . . . Shit. Its bullshit what they say on the radio and TV the sacred defense the sacred defense . . . Nothings sacred in war . . . In war everythings filthy. You kill its filthy . . . You get killed its filthy . . . would you beleive it I got promoted. Seargent-major. But its a load of old crap. Most of the time when we were fighting street by street next to the empty handed people against the wife pimping Iraqis, when I set my rifle sites on the forhead of an Iraqi Id think how this Iraqi is no dout someones loved one . . . hes got a mom an a dad, a fiance an a kid . . . But there was nothing to be done I squeezed the triger . . . I dont kill him he kills me . . . But I dream of the picture of the forhead or the heart of that Iraqi soldier in the circle of my rifle site every night . . . Lifes shit . . . crap . . .

Right let me tell you before I forget why I wasnt in that horribel coffin you was cryin over . . . To be honest Ill tell you the truth Shokoof but only you . . . I didn't tell noone else and I'm not gonna neither . . . An after youve read this letter burn it so it dont cause no problems for me later. Before the war I happened to be in Khoramshahr anyways . . . When the Iraqis started atacking the army an the soldiers an schoolkids an bakers an grocers all joined together an we all fout side by side against the wife pimping Iraqis. Every where was full of trenches. In the streets . . . In houses . . . In offices an schools . . . In the hospitel . . . Every where you could see bits of blown up palm trees . . . Once I was caught in a trench outside of the town for three days an nights . . . Their were little brown hills all round me an a bit further on you could see peoples homes . . . Us Iranians was on this side of the hill an the Iraqis on the other side . . . We were so close to one another we could here each other talking. The Iranians who knew Arabic sometimes used to talk to them in loud voices . . . Or give them funny answers . . . Sometimes when there was a sease fire for a few minutes we used to toss a few bits of food for each other. Once I saw an Iraqi toss an appel for one of the lads an they said somethin to each other in Arabic an chucled . . . Imagine . . . A few minutes later they were gonna riddel one other with bullets . . . Thats exactly what they did three days later when Id been saved I saw theyd both bin killed . . . I knew the Iraqi cos he had a bunch of apples in his backpack.

It was right at dawn when I noticed the nearby earth work. I walked forwad an saw a conscript with his face blown off I felt so bad I looked in his pockets an found his service card an a letter an his ID tag I think if he hadnt killed hisself hedve bin a writer one day cos his letter was properly nice . . . Not like me with all the wrong stuff I write he he . . . The letter was in is pocket an was actually his will when I red it I decided to swap my identity with his. Ill put the will in the envelop with this letter so you can read it. Theres something in the letter too I think has to do with you Maybe itll matter to you I think it will I dont now if its true or not but maybe it is maybe it's not I know youll be upset God forbid you are Dont be sad Lifes shit really."

I raised my head again. What did it mean that there could be something in an unknown dead soldier's letter that might have to do with me? I resumed reading:

"So in short I dont want my mom an dad to presume Im still alive. Its better if they think Im dead. You know what my name is now? I mean do you know what the name of the soldier what killed hisself was? Omid Raisi. Youre the only one in the world what knows this and thats it I now youre mouth is locked an I can trust you.

Ive jabered on so much for you Shokoof my dear for know Im staying at the front I got nowhere to go. Here when there isn't so much fiting Im busy doing mechanic stuff The armys my life an home now I fix cars for fun an all I imagine an dream of is you Ill write to you again You write to me to Will you? Write! Any news of Leyla yet?

Your sacrifice Yours always Bahman"

I thought of Bahman, and all his surprise attacks. Of fate, and its unforeseen games. Both of them struck me each time I encountered them like an avalanche. I opened Omid Raisi the unknown soldier's crumpled will, my hand trembling from contact with the dried blood on it, and I could hear the sound of my anxious heart beating.

"Comrade Yashar, I am writing this letter for you and you alone, because, the mumps we both got at the same time years ago at school be my witness, I know that you alone feel my pain. So for that reason I am now writing you a letter, to tell you that my heart is heavy and swollen and painful, just like our faces and throats on that cold winter's day, and with each whistling bullet that passes by my head and ears and cheeks from out of the darkness opposite, it grows heavier, more swollen and more painful.

"I will write the address at the foot of this letter so that they can get it to you once I'm dead, although on this accursed frontline all sorts of people can be found. It's not at all unlikely that some shady person turns up and deliberately sends this letter to my parents. I don't want them to realize what is really going on at all. From the revolution until now, stuck in the middle of this killing field, I have never felt this stupid or afraid. I have the feeling that I've never understood what is right and what wrong, even in the thick of the revolution when you and I were together in the streets and chanting slogans . . . These days I'm always thinking about what the criterion for distinguishing right

and wrong might actually be. Were we right to have made the revolution? Didn't we want equality and social justice? Have you seen justice in these last years? I can't sleep at night because these questions keep repeating in my mind. Only you and I know what happened to us and our comrades during the interrogations. If only we hadn't succumbed to our fears in jail and we'd let them execute us like our comrades Manouchehr and Behrooz and Parvin. If only we hadn't been such cowards and hadn't given Ataa and Bijan and Parvaneh away.

"I want only you to know that after I've finished writing this letter, I intend to put an end to myself. I will try to do it in such a way that the others will think an enemy bullet hit me from in front. I hope I have the skill to do this one thing. This way is better for everybody—I don't want to be like Sasan. Sasan was one of my fellow conscripts who was about to run away on the day of our operations, but several traitors gave him away to the commander. The commander gave the order to halt three times, but Sasan went crazy from fear and ran off towards the desert, behind the frontline. The commander shot him personally. Me and two of the guys ran over to him. There were tears in his eyes. He grinned at me and said, 'I wanted to eat my Mom's ghormeh sabzi.'

"The same day he killed Sasan, the commander did something else really rotten, immediately writing to his parents that Sasan had been killed running away and in contravention of orders from above and cursed him forever. After the affair with Sasan, no one else wants to die like that. And if someone did, you can be certain that he wanted to take revenge on himself, on his fate, his family, the war, the revolution. He wanted quite deliberately to smear mud on the reputation of life.

"Now that I'm getting everything off my chest before I die, let me clarify that what bothers me is not just the war and the sound of bullets and the travails of conscience that claw at your heart. It's not just seeing so many bodies of women and children and old and young in the streets and houses that gnaws away at

you . . . It has to do with other things that cannot be explained. Sadeq Hedayat was right when he said, 'In life there are wounds that slowly consume and scrape the soul in solitude like a canker. It isn't possible to reveal these pains to anyone, because in general people are accustomed to regarding these unbelievable pains as belonging to the category of rare and strange events and happenings.'

"Be that as it may, perhaps there are things that I can write about a little for you, but I cannot give you reasons or evidence for. Believe them if you like, or don't.

"What's going on is that I have seen black shadows arriving at night and dragging the bodies away with them from the back streets and main avenues and earthworks, taking them and eating them. I ask myself, could it be that Sasan and Ahmad had seen these shadows as well? Isn't that obvious? Once I even came face to face with one of these shadows and fired on it, because it was trying to wrench my friend Hadi's body from my arms, the same Hadi who had until a few minutes before been singing like a lunatic behind the trench. We had been under siege for five days and nights and the Iraqis didn't hold fire for a minute. We had all officially gone crazy, but Hadi was in a worse state than any of us. That last day he was singing a Lori song at full volume: 'Wet Nurse, Wet Nurse, it's wartime, you see /It's full of cartridges, the ammo belt above me.' And what a plaintive voice he had . . . However much everyone said to him, 'By doing this you're giving away our position to the enemy,' he wouldn't care at all. It seemed like he had gone crazy. He had become shell-shocked. He made up silly songs and sang them as loud as he could. 'Our position's been given away. Hurray, hurray, hurray.' As if he were drunk or had smoked hashish or something. In the middle of a heart-rending Lori tune, he'd burst into tears and then all of a sudden he'd start laughing and couldn't stop. He would laugh at the sound of the bullets passing right by his ears and neck, at the maneuvers, at the shells, at the RPGs. He even laughed at the fact that in the middle of laughing he had wet himself in fright

at the sound of an explosion. For five days and nights nobody moved an inch . . . many were killed . . . only a few of us stayed alive . . . That night Hadi laughed so much that when the enemy for once stopped firing for a moment, his voice could be heard in the Iraqi earthworks. The Iraqis thought we were making fun of them. They got even more worked up. They started swearing at us and increased their rate of fire so much that we couldn't even breathe any longer, yet Hadi didn't stop laughing until suddenly he moved a little and died from a bullet shot straight to the back of his neck. When his laughter was cut off, the Iraqis started chanting loudly, whistled and clapped, and we got so worked up that we increased our own rate of fire multiple times. Just then, my eyes alighted on that black shadow. It was like the shadow had come out of the middle of the earth or from some corner of the night. I was holding Hadi's arms in my hands, but suddenly the shadow yanked Hadi towards itself. It was so strong that Hadi's arms easily came unclasped from my hands. I started shouting and yelling and clutching at Hadi's clothing so that the monster would be frightened and go away, but it wasn't frightened and wouldn't let go, nor did my fellow soldiers even turn around and look at me. I shouted their names . . . 'Asghar . . . H amid . . . Yaser . . .' But it was like they had all gone deaf. They'd all gone blind. Hadi was being dragged toward the darkness and the only thing left in my hand was the button from his shirt. I've put the button inside this letter. I know it's a meaningless thing to ask, but sew this button onto one of your own pieces of clothing . . . That way at least I'll feel that something will be left in this world to remember him by, him with his black hair and one meter seventy, who'd done all his growing up in an orphanage."

I shook the envelope and a small green metal button fell out. I squeezed it in my fist. I remembered the blue Bic biro and the pistachio shell. I felt like I knew Hadi. I felt like it was my responsibility for him not to be forgotten, even if only by means of this button. I ran to my room and took out my little sewing box and carefully attached the green button to my left sleeve. This button would bear with it the memory of the writer of this will, Hadi, Bahman, the war, the corpse-eating monster, and even Fereshteh and Fariborz. I returned to the courtyard, found a quiet corner, and resumed reading:

"Right now, the light from the maneuvers and explosions is so bright I can write to you. Imagine, you can write by the light of explosions and maneuvers. A few nights back, a kind of unprecedented courage sought me out that means that now I couldn't care less about the explosions going off around me.

"I've realized people are scared just to resemble themselves. In childhood and adolescence, we resembled ourselves a lot. Do you remember, Yashar? Each one of us . . . me, Parvaneh, you, Bijan, Akbar, Parvin, Manouchehr . . . We didn't resemble one another, but we were all friends. We all had a unique perspective on life, on good, on evil, love, family. I liked these differences, but little by little as we grew up, in certain ways certain things made us come to resemble one another. Made us resemble everyone else. In my opinion, fear made us resemble one another. I've realized that growing up means succumbing to fear. Fear of the future, unemployment, poverty, reputation . . . these fears paralyze you. These fears meant that we came to resemble the grown-ups we used to detest.

"For instance, when I think of that night . . . The night of me and Hadi and the corpse-eating monster . . . If that night one of the three or four of them in the neighboring trench had overcome their fear and turned toward me, he would have no longer resembled the two or three people next to him. I mean, perhaps he didn't lift his head because he was afraid the other two or three might make fun of him or reprimand him afterwards. Before I came to understand these things, I too used to try to be like everyone else. Do you remember in prison when Reza Abdollahi gave in under torture and betrayed his brother-in-law and sister, he came crying into the ward and confessed to us that he had

broken down. He said, 'If only I hadn't broken down, but I did.' Then we all looked at him with contempt and turned our backs on him. We reviled him. I even remember that Farshid Hasanlou spat at him and Ahmad Abbasi punched and kicked him. Do you remember? Then all of a sudden Behnam Rostami got up and hugged Reza Abdollahi and said, 'We're all human . . . it's so difficult to resist torture. I understand.'"

My breath was caught in my chest. Behnam? Behnam Rostami? I read on anxiously:

"After Behnam had spoken, a sudden wave of sympathy flooded through the ward. A warm, human wave. Then little by little we and everyone else got up and consoled Reza Abdollahi and apologized to him. Now that I think about it, even then it was only Behnam Rostami who resembled himself—we didn't. At first we were like Farshid Hasanlou, and then we wanted to be like Behnam Rostami.

"It was after this that our resistance broke and we started giving in and giving away, because we felt we had permission to be like Reza Abdollahi. To be real and normal like him. Not be heroes. To be honest, maybe I'm wrong . . . Perhaps even before Reza Abdollahi's honest confession everybody would've given people away under torture, but in front of each other they would've played at being heroes! If that wasn't the case, then how come safe house after safe house was given away and comrades were arrested right and left? In any case, I'm sure that before him, none of us would have had the courage to be normal. Let's just say how impossible it is to endure the pain of the thin whip on the underside of and in between the toes, or how the pain of batons and thick cables in the beating tunnel smash your bones to smithereens. At the time of the revolution and playing the hero, did anyone dare to talk of defeat and tortured confessions? Yes, I've realized that fear makes people come to resemble one another . . . It makes them contemptible, liars, selfish. Now

that I'm writing this, I should also say that, if you remember, the only person in that ward at the time who didn't give in and didn't break was Behnam Rostami himself. That's why they executed him."

What? Behnam? They executed Behnam? As I resumed reading, the letter was trembling in my hand from fear and doubt.

"But they released all of us sooner or later. All of us traitors and 'penitents' who, resembling one another, spied on each other and sold each other, were released, but Behnam who resembled himself was executed. Do you remember what the poem was Behnam recited for us before being executed? I've memorized it:

If you've survived,
If you've resisted
Sing. Dream. Get drunk.
It is the age of bitter cold.
Fall in love. Make haste.
The wind of the hours
Is sweeping the streets,
The alleys . . .
The trees are waiting
But you, do not wait."[37]

Behnam? My Behnam? Teardrops spilt on to the blood-stained paper . . . Why had Mehrab, who was so close to him, or Dad, who was an old friend of his father's, not told me? Did they even know themselves? Yet I consoled myself immediately that it was hardly possible there could only be one Communist called Behnam Rostami in the country. Perhaps a hundred people had the same name. I consoled myself by

[37] Jaime Sabines. Persian translation by Mohsen Emadi.

asking myself whether I had forgotten the list published in the newspapers of those accepted in the university entrance examination. There were a hundred people called Maryam Ahmadi. Or fifty whose name was Akbar Abdollahi . . . I would have to ask Dad to write to Behnam's father or give him a call and ask after his son. I would have to talk to Mehrab. Perhaps he knew something. It was totally impossible for this Behnam to be my Behnam . . . and yet the Behnam Rostami I knew had the same characteristics. He did resemble himself, and recited these kinds of poem, and spoke in this way . . . The letter fell from my hand and I wept . . . I wept . . . I wept . . . I cried so much that the teardrops made my face and clothes wet as if they were rain. For a moment so great a grief sat on my body and heart and soul that speech began to stutter . . .

It fell silent . . .

It went dark . . .

And I understood nothing more. Then gradually, between the sobbing, I heard a melody being hummed . . .

A sorrowful melody . . .

Tremendously sorrowful . . .

And the world spun and spun about my head.

Eventually, my wet eyelids opened, but feebly; the mansion . . . the garden . . . the sky . . . the ground . . . the trees . . . the trees . . . the trees . . . all were spinning and I saw that I had stood up amid a whirlwind of tears and sighs and the sorrowful melody and was suspended in the sad air, still shedding tears . . . The melody, which appeared to reach my ears from somewhere roundabout, somewhere close by, filled my entire body. So deep and plaintive was the melody that it appeared to hail from some other world . . . As if it was a song performed by gods mourning us ill-fated humans. The melody belonged to that world, and yet was close by . . . as if it came from within me. From my body. I ran my hands eagerly over my upper arms and torso. Over my ears . . . The music was not coming from outside. It really was coming from my body . . . from beneath my skin . . . from the center of my heart. Then everything became still. I remember nothing more.

I had fallen on the floor and it surrounded me, without me realizing that this melody would not stop until the end of my life. Afterwards, when the sound did not stop even during sleep, laughter, travel, wartime, lovemaking, and even prison and torture and death, I realized that once somebody has caught the bitter regret of love, that sadness will never release them. This sorrowful music will never separate from their being, even when they laugh. Even when they become a bride.

Hasrat our gardener stood and looked at me with his tired seventy-year-old eyes. "Love is full of sorrow," he said.

He helped me sit. It was night and the mansion and garden lights were on. I sat on the ground, miserable and unsure what to do. Hasrat patiently gathered up the pages of the letter from the ground and placed them in my hand. Then he sat down beside me and without warning said, "Love is a curse."

I said nothing. I didn't know how he'd figured it out. "How should I live from now on?" I asked him. He shook his head and said, "You'll work out how to keep on living with what's left of your heart."

Then he helped me get up and slowly led me via the back gate of the courtyard up to my room where he put me in bed. Mehrab saw us on the staircase, however, and came along. When Hasrat had left, I told him everything. I told him I was in love with Behnam and that now he had been executed in prison and this sorrowful melody remained trapped inside my body. I wanted to say too that Bahman was alive, but I remembered Bahman had insisted I tell no one. I said nothing. I placed Omid Raisi's letter in his hand and told him that one of Behnam's cellmates had sent it to me. Shocked by this news, Mehrab started pacing up and down in the room and saying that for this and that reason it was impossible that Behnam had been executed. Then he said that just a year ago a letter from Behnam had arrived in which he said his parents were planning to go to America and were insisting he go with them. Then he ran to Dad's study, and although it was late enough, rang Behnam's house. And I feebly followed him. Nobody picked up. Then he called the house of a mutual friend to ask after Behnam. They said they knew Behnam was in prison but did not know he had been executed. Then they said that these things shouldn't be discussed on the phone, since someone might be listening, and promptly hung up. Mehrab finally surrendered. He took me in his arms and we cried together for some long minutes. I threw myself on the bed and hid my head under the pillow. If only it were possible not to exist for a few days. To take a break from life. If only it were possible to tell life, "Leave me alone for a few days at least."

"Out of our group of twelve people, two now have died," Mehrab said. "We haven't heard anything from Iraj and Mozhdeh who ran away to the Soviet Union. Even their families don't know anything. We haven't heard anything from Leyla. Mahsa the innocent was dead from the very beginning. That means right now six of us are no longer here or have disappeared." I had nothing to say. "The question is," he said. "Why are they dead and we alive?"

The sun had not yet risen when I suddenly woke up. Mehrab wasn't next to me. The melody was still trapped in my body. Just as gentle. Just as sorrowful. Just as insistent. I got up and in the hope of finding out more about Behnam, picked up the papers from beside the bed and continued reading:

"A few weeks ago, in the middle of the night when just like now I was sitting behind a stone slab and just like now I had crumpled myself up so much that even in my mother's womb I had not been so tightly knotted, suddenly, without thinking it out, I started sliding along the ground, heading behind the frontline. Bullets were hitting things all around me. Hamid saw what was going on and shouted, 'Omid, where are you going?' But I didn't answer, and I slid along the ground so much that my clothes were completely frayed and torn, my body injured, and the sound of the bullets

farther and farther away. Some of them had hit my upper arms and the blood had made all my clothes wet. Still holding my gun, I went for a walk through the waterless and plantless desert. Like someone metamorphosed. Like an errant ghost . . . I remember that I kept muttering a sentence to myself like lunatics do. 'Who told you that you have to be somewhere you don't want to? Who told you that you have to be somewhere you don't want to?' I spent two days walking aimlessly. I buried my gun somewhere in the middle of the desert, before passing out from weakness and tiredness and hunger at the first nomad tent I reached. When I recovered consciousness, I saw they had cauterized and bandaged my wound, and people were sitting around me drinking tea and chatting. They told me they knew I was a runaway soldier because other runaway soldiers had come to their tribe in the past. They spoke Persian with difficulty. Arabic was their language, and their clothes were in the Arab style, too. I saw no menace in their sunburnt faces. I didn't feel like they wanted to turn me in or bother or hurt me in any way, but after a night I realized they expected something of me. In their broken Persian, they got me to understand that in exchange for marrying one of the tribe's girls and working for her father for two years for free, I could stay there in complete safety until the end of my life and that they would protect me from the war and the revolution. If you think about it, all in all it wasn't a bad proposal. Whatever it was, it was better than killing and being killed, or being devoured by that corpse-eating monster. It might even be said that it was very good. Especially once I looked at the innocent and beautiful faces of the girls and saw that some of them were prettier than our own Tehrani girls. As it happened, two other runaway soldiers were there. They had accepted the proposal and had gotten married and were living there without any headaches. Several days went by and those good people treated me and my wounds very well, and put the local costume on me, too. Then they left me free to think carefully. I saw them every day going to the mountains and the meadows with their sheep and buffalo, returning in the evening. Their women and girls sat under the tents weaving gelims and jajims and baskets and making yoghurt drink and whey, as well as food and medicine from the herbs growing in the mountains and meadows. However much I thought about it, I couldn't see anything wrong with that way of life. It's true that I hoped to be a literature teacher, but I could stay there and teach their children to read and write. Like Samad Behrangi. If you want to know the truth, one of the girls had even caught my eye. She was very beautiful and tall and she walked so casually that it was as if the ground itself should be proud she was walking on it. I liked their language and I even gradually learned to speak a few simple sentences. Everything was going well. I was getting on well with the two ex-soldiers and the locals and I used to help the men pasture the sheep and the women draw water from the well. I even made a water channel for them so that they could have water right at the door of their tents. For that reason they called me 'the Engineer.' Finally one day I began a conversation with the girl I mentioned. She didn't answer. So it was that I went to the same old man who had told me of the conditions that first day. We talked a little of this and that, but as I was about to open my mouth to say that I liked that girl and wanted to marry her and stay, he said, 'I told you, if you want to stay you have to marry one of our girls. So are you going to stay, or go back to the war?'

"There was no menace in his tone. I can't even say there was any ill-will or pride in his tone. No! Not at all. It was just that when I heard from his own mouth what I already knew, it was if someone had given me a fillip and said: 'Yet again somebody else is deciding what you should do, you fool. Yet again you're going to be like everyone else.' Everything collapsed on my head. To be honest, now that a few days have gone by and I look back at what happened, I see how stupid it is that because I heard something I desired myself but heard it from the mouth of another I became disillusioned and despairing.

"That very night I ran away from there and didn't look back once, and tonight I'm back right here so I can kill myself with my fellow soldier's weapon, the one I buried. Nobody's seen me yet. When I've died here and they see my body, they'll be astonished

for sure and will attribute the whole affair to one of the Hidden Holy Helpers or the Divine Secrets. Do you know why I've come here, to the middle of the war, to kill myself? Of course, I know you think it's stupid, because all I have to do is to half stand up for the enemy's bullets to hit me and, as my fellow soldiers say, to get martyred. But I want to prove to myself at least that my death was my own choice. That I have chosen something for myself in this life. I want my death at least to resemble myself.

"The only thing that makes me upset at this last moment is that I don't have a mirror near me. I wanted to wish my face goodbye in this half-light, illuminated by the light from the maneuvers. However much I think about it, I cannot remember when I last saw my face in a mirror. What do I even look like?

"Once me and Shahram, my fellow soldier, were on watch duty together. 'Your shoelace is untied,' Shahram said to me. As I bent down to tie my laces, a bullet passed over my body and killed him. After that I became obsessed by asking myself whether he knew that one day he would be killed by my shoelaces? Did he actually look at his face in the mirror that day, and why should I be the last person in this world to see his face before death?

"To be honest, now that I've written this for you, I realize what a load of nonsense it is. I could've not written this and died. It's all a bunch of meaningless words, but now that I've got this far let me write this for you too: it was my father and mother who made me come to the front because they were worried that I'd continue with my political activities and get arrested again. They were the ones who kept complaining that because I'd gone to jail they'd lost their reputation with the neighbors and our family and so on and that nobody wants to socialize with them anymore and our relatives have even removed our pictures from their photo albums and thrown them away. They told me that if I went to the front, I'd restore their lost reputation! It's very rude of me to say so, but I've pissed down the throat of the good reputation they would've acquired by my getting killed . . . by being martyred . . . Let me tell you this, then I'll finish myself off: my mother dobbed in her

brother and my father his brother-in-law, and both of them, after a few months in prison, were executed as counterrevolutionaries. Then my parents gobbled up their land and inheritance. To be honest, I sometimes think that if I hadn't gone and volunteered, they would've quite likely dobbed me in too . . . I'll never forget the night my parents invited my maternal uncle and my paternal aunt's husband for dinner; that was the same night the Guards raided the house, after arranging it with my parents, arrested them for being supporters of the People's Mujahidin, and took them away. I'll never forget my uncle's face as he turned to his sister, my mother, in disbelief and spat on the floor. Whereas my aunt's husband didn't even look at them. He just stared at me. Perhaps at that very moment he was wondering, with these bastards for parents, what kind of pimp would I turn out to be. To be honest he wasn't exactly wrong. I would demonstrate this in prison not long after . . . I am a villainous traitor like my father and mother. A bastard pimp in all meanings of the terms . . . I've jabbered on way too much. I feel sick just thinking about myself. Goodbye."

Chapter Eleven

The following day, confronted with Mehrab's empty place and everyone else's tearful eyes, my breakfast table "good morning" turned into a cry in my throat. All the same, everybody stared in astonishment at me and the sorrowful melody which persisted in issuing from my body and heart, withering the flowers in the vases and rendering the house birds silent and sad. It fell to Mina and Mandana to read out Mehrab's note: "Don't be upset with me. I'm going to war. Not for this revolution and Islam. I'm going to find myself while taking back my country's soil. To find humanity. Dead or alive, I'll send you letters."

I don't recall a great deal after that, except that the weeks and months succeeded one another with a monotonous and enervating movement, and that in Mehrab's absence Shahnaz, our middle-aged servant, who had loved Mehrab ever since his childhood like the precious darling child she had never had, suddenly became listless and silent. She wouldn't lift a finger around the house. She would just sit in a corner of the kitchen by the window, stare out of it and cry without making a sound. Once when I saw her like this, I thought the poet was right: the one who is absent brings down the one who is present.

Someone who didn't know better would've thought Shahnaz was Mehrab's mother. It was she who had washed and dried Mehrab ever since infancy, burped him, cooked his favorite foods, tied prayers against the evil eye around his neck, put sugar-coated nuts and seeds and raisins in his pockets, taken responsibility when he did something wrong, and even on the night of the palace it was her, and only her, who set off for the forest, torch in hand, without anyone else knowing, so she could find us, find Mehrab. And she was indeed successful, since the following day as we were walking along the path from the mysterious palace to the house, it was she who suddenly appeared in front of us in the middle of the forest: tired and muddy, but as fearless and determined as a lioness. That day, once she had spotted Mehrab, she did not stir from her spot. She stood and, her eyes flashing with joy, looked Mehrab up and down, before turning to all of us and saying, "Come this way. This is the way back home." And then she set off in front of us.

That was how Shahnaz was. Rather than expressing her motherly love for Mehrab through her words, she did it through her actions. Perhaps because she knew her place. She knew that a servant cannot show herself to be more loving than a mother. And for me and Mehrab, this was sad.

On the other hand, during Mehrab's absence, Mom would take herself to his room constantly, on whatever pretext, at night, in the middle of the night, sit on his bed, smell his clothes, and silently sing lullabies and cry:

"La la, the world is a passing place / A passing place that's short
Someone's gone and someone stays / Someone else is on their way
La la la la pennyroyal / That the world is a road
Someone's gone and someone came / Why doesn't anyone stay?"[38]

Gradually a state of mind appeared in Mom which we accepted was a kind of melancholia, without being able to give it a name—a sort of inertia combined with movement. A sort of unconsciousness combined with alertness. A sort of absence combined with

[38] Nizami Ganjavi, Haft Peykar, 12th Century.

presence. Mom was living in a vague, poetic state . . . Once, very early in the morning, before even first light, Mom came and knocked on each of our doors to wake us up. It was still completely dark. We all started walking behind her out of the mansion into the courtyard, from there into the garden and onto the slope where we stood next to the spring, at the foot of the walnut tree. This was the same spot where, they said, one summer when he was only five years old, Mehrab had climbed the tree and then refused to come down. According to what they told me later, when Mehrab was up there they all thought he had gotten stuck, but then they were surprised to see that he was sat on the uppermost branch, cheerful and comfortable, and it appeared that he was talking to the sun. They say that when Mom climbed up and sat next to him, Mehrab said something that nobody understood. He said, "After the last supper, he went up there." "Who?" Mom asked. "Mithra," he replied. "Who's Mithra?" asked Mom. He merely smiled and continued staring at the sun.

Mom stood on the slope somewhere around there. Everyone in their own place. Far apart. It was chilly and my sleepy body was shivering. We pulled our scarves tight around us and waited for something without knowing what. No one asked anything. We all watched to see what state Mom was in. We stood aimlessly like this as a pale light gradually emerged and we could see that the mist was slowly making its way towards us from the forest to embrace us. A cuckoo sang in the distance. A sparrow nearby. My body's sorrowful music drifted out into the mist, mingling with the gentle murmur of the brook and the meadow. The breeze blowing on the grasses brushed them against our calves, and the skin on my upper arms was prickly with cold and the feeling of a strange grief in the air. Shabro and Afsun made their way slowly over to us through the mist. Occasionally we turned and looked at one another. Sometimes inquiringly, sometimes kindly, sometimes transformed . . .

What if Mehrab suddenly emerged from the mist, I thought. I looked at Khanom Joon; she was leaning on her cane, breathing deeply, her head aloft and her eyes shut. As if she wanted to be sure that little bits of the fog would be sucked inside her. Jamshid Khan was standing further away in a black waistcoat and a camel-colored wool cloak, facing Zorvan, who every now and then took out his gold pocket watch from his waistcoat and looked at it. Dad was standing a couple of paces away from Mom, while Auntie Malek was further away, behind Mina and Mandana. As the mist crept forward, every now and then Shahnaz, Reza, Nader, Shafiqeh and Maryam appeared and disappeared.

The mist got thicker and thicker, and the daylight stronger and stronger, until Mom turned round to face the east and stared at the sky. We followed suit. The pale figure of the sun slowly rose above the Zorvan mountains into a cloudy sky, gray and dark. Mom finally parted her lips. "Out of respect for those who are living their final day of life today," she said, "Greet the sun. Maybe my Mehrab will be one of them."

The war we'd thought would be over in a few months was now two years old and drawing more and more young people into its trap. Whenever the television showed the sad, heart-rending funerals of the war martyrs, one of us got up and turned it off, because Mom had gone to a corner and was sitting, hugging her knees close to her chest, her gaze fixed on the screen like someone metamorphosed, singing, "For each corpse that lies under the earth / There is a mother of soil and a mother of blood. / The mother of blood nurtures with caresses / But the mother of soil takes him back."[39]

Some kind of silence and firm and unbreakable waiting had taken hold of the house, the street, the village, and the town. Nobody spoke in a loud voice in the house. Nobody laughed. Nobody uttered the words "war," "Mehrab," or "Leyla." We

[39] Nizami Ganjavi, Haft Peykar, 12th Century.

were waiting just like everybody else. Waiting for the war to end. For the young folk to come home. For news of Mehrab. For news of Bahman. For political prisoners to be freed. To hear that the Sisters had succeeded at the university entrance exam. Or even for news of Leyla? Behnam? Why was there no news of Leyla? She'd said she would climb the tree. That was all. Doesn't someone who leaves come back? Wasn't the verb "to come back" invented to go with the verb "to leave?" Otherwise Leyla, in her childish manner, could have made clear what she was going to do: "I want to live up the tree." Or, "I want to live with the palace woman, or the Simorgh." That way it would've been clear what we ought to have expected—that there was no possibility of her coming back. But instead, she had said she wanted to climb the tree. Had she even got to the top of it? How had she climbed it? How could we be so thoughtless that we had not said a thing to Mom and Dad about the palace and the top of the tree and Leyla's leaving? Why had we let them think that she had gotten lost or died? Should we say something now? Say something, expecting what to happen? Now I was gradually growing up and looked at matters from new and more realistic angles, I felt the weight of a great irresponsibility on my shoulders . . . So many things had happened one after the other in the mansion that I hadn't thought of Leyla for a while. In my heart I was confident that she was up there living with the palace woman learning the secrets and path of life. Perhaps this is a feature of childhood that you trust what you feel so much. Whereas to be grown up means to hesitate . . . Means to tell yourself not to be so sure in what you feel . . . Means to doubt anything related to people . . . suddenly Mehrab's departure had emptied my heart. What if Leyla had wandered off into the forest and become food for wolves and jackals? What if she hadn't even found her way to the palace and the top of the tree? Anxiety and a guilty conscience had started to gnaw away at what was left of my feelings of trust and security. Oh . . . if only Mehrab were here and I could talk about this anxiety with him.

What if Behnam were still alive? I had rung the only number listed under "Dr. Rostami" in Dad's telephone book several times, but nobody had ever answered. Had they really gone to America, then? What if he had really been executed? Sometimes when no one else was watching, I would sit on the chair in Dad's study, receiver in hand, and listen to the sound of the phone ringing for minutes, imagining it ringing in a house void of its inhabitants, its sound winding its way through empty rooms—through all the crevices of the house . . . through the cracks in the walls . . . through the holes the termites had left behind . . . in his room I had never seen. Sometimes I dreamt of him approaching my bed, kissing a tress of my hair and saying, "I told you that I would see you again, right here," . . . but a little later I dreamt of his dead body on my bed, bruised around the neck, while the wooden ring had sprouted on the ring finger of his left hand. Once I dreamt that Mehrab, Bahman, Behnam and Leyla were galloping around the garden on horseback, talking and laughing in loud voices and playing tricks on one another. When the next day, remembering this dream, I went to the same spot in the garden where they had been riding, I saw the hoofprints of four horses. I asked Hasrat whether anybody had come riding here recently, but he said not so far as he was aware. I thought to myself, "What if the four of them are all dead?" A little while after that I dreamt that the Gowkaran tree was not in the kitchen but in the garden, and that all twelve of us were sitting in its shade, happy and without a care in the world, passing time and talking and laughing, as we had used to do in the mansion every summer in the old days. What a beautiful sight . . . a wave of security and joy rolled through . . . the blue sky . . . the scattered fragments of white cloud and the dappled light of the sun reached the ground through the dense foliage . . . A mat was spread on the grass under the tree, a bowl of fruit on it. Bahman was walking around the tree with measured steps, and little Azadeh was running around him, every now and then picking a flower and giving it to Mahsa, who had, as always, made a place for herself on Bahman's shoulders. Then Bahman asked Mahsa in a lively and joyful tone, "Can you guess how old you would be now if you were still alive?" And Mahsa's sides split with laughter as if she had heard the funniest joke in the world. Mehrab and Behnam were leaning on the tree's mighty trunk reading a book together, sometimes raising their heads to talk. Further off, Mina and Mandana and Mahin were walking arm in arm and whispering and sometimes giggling, like those times when they girl-talked together and told each other about their crushes at school. Iraj and Mozhgan were sitting on the mat and had put their faces into the path of a cooling breeze and smiling. Then Mozghan stretched out and, as she put her head on Iraj's legs, took out a yellow-pink peach from the bowl and bit it firmly, before the two of them turned their eyes to the sky, smiling. As they did so, Leyla and the woman from up the tree came down from up there. I, who had simply been observing events up to that point, was thrilled to see Leyla and ran towards her to hug her, but she did not see me at all. It was if no one could see me. Leyla, who in my dream had turned into a gorgeous adolescent girl whose long white locks reached her waist, took the book from Mehrab and Behnam, passed by me without paying the slightest attention to me, sat on the mat next to Iraj and Mozhgan, and gestured to everyone else that they should join her and the woman from up the tree. They all moved to be next to this woman, surrounding her on both sides. I went too. Then the woman from up the tree, a goblet of wine in her hand, looked around her to make sure no stranger was present, as if she wanted to share a secret with them. Then she whispered in a low voice, "Can you guess how old you would all be now if you were still alive?"

For some time things went on in this manner; the no-news-manner. Months had gone by since Mehrab's departure and there was no trace of him. When all of Dad and Mom's telephone calls and letter-writing to the War Office and the Ministry of Defense and soldiers returning from the war yielded no results, when we found out that Shahnaz had gone to Tehran, alone and without telling anyone, had visited the War Office and had come back empty handed, when no further letters had reached me from Bahman, when no further trace or news of Behnam, living or dead, was forthcoming, one day I finally took the plunge and went to Dad's study and told him, my breath turning in my throat and in a tone that I tried too hard to make sound natural, that if he saw fit to ring Behnam's father and ask him whether he had any news of Mehrab, perhaps that would not be such a bad idea. This way I thought that I might both hear something about Behnam, living or dead, and if I was lucky, about Mehrab, too.

I don't know whether I was obviously blushing, or whether it was because my stammering and straightening my chest gave me away, that Dad stared at me with a startled gaze. Had he figured out what was going on in my heart? Because he picked up the receiver without asking why and dialed a number that wasn't at all the one I had previously called myself. The whole time that the receiver was pressed to Dad's ear, he didn't take his eyes off me. Did this mean I was supposed to leave the room, or that I had permission to stay and listen to their conversation? What if Behnam were alive? Was it possible for me to accept so easily that he had died? I was shifting from one foot to the other, hesitating between leaving and staying, when someone picked up the receiver at the other end. My heart sank. I took a step back to be nearer the door, but I still didn't want to leave the room. Dad greeted them and enquired after their health, listened carefully for a few seconds, then said a few things before without warning saying into the receiver: "I'll say goodbye then. Speak to Shokoofeh." He handed me the receiver.

My eyes almost burst out of my head in astonishment. I had nothing to say to Behnam's father. Frowning, I gestured with my hand to indicate that I would not speak. Dad was still holding the receiver up and offering it to me. I had no idea what was going on.

A moment later, a voice came down the line: "Hello Shokoofeh." My knees went weak and hot blood rushed to my ears. I turned to stone. With no explanation, Dad put the receiver on the desk, coughed once, and said, "I'll go drink some water."

As Dad left the room, I was still rooted to the spot staring at the receiver on the desk. A familiar voice could be heard coming from it. "Shokoofeh . . ."

Was that his voice? Behnam? Was he really alive?

Again, the voice said, "Shokoofeh . . . Shokoofeh . . ."

At last, I was able to stir myself. I took two large strides forward. I grabbed the receiver and pressed it to my ear. Probably hearing the sound of my breathing, he said, "I've missed you so much."

I didn't say anything. Was I even able to say how terrible his absence had been for me, all these years without news of him, the news of his death?

"What beautiful music I can hear," he said.

Again, I said nothing. Why was he so at ease and calm? Didn't he realize that four years . . . four whole years had passed since we'd last spoken?

"These are difficult times," he said. "We've all been deceived."

It was if my tongue was stuck to the roof of my mouth. The receiver was so hot on my ear that it might catch fire any moment. I couldn't stand him . . . For the love of God he was alive and yet had sent no news of himself all these years?

He took a deep breath and said, "I was in prison for three years. Six times in prison I was taken to be executed. Six times they carried out a mock execution."

Oh how much did I love him! He was alive and nothing in the world mattered more than that.

"Please, talk," he said.

I came to my senses. I cleared my throat and said, "Hello."

"I thought of you a lot in prison," he said, his voice more energetic. "And not just because I love you . . . But because I realized you were right."

He loved me . . . he loved me . . . I tried to control myself. With a voice that seemed to be tying itself in knots in my throat, I asked, "Right about what?"

"When the rope was around my neck, and even when for a few seconds I was being hanged from it, I was thinking that the biggest mistake I've made in my life was to participate in this revolution. Too late and at far too great a price, I realized that our ideals would not be realized by this revolution."

He sighed and continued. "No! It would be more accurate to say that they would not be realized by any revolution."

Ah, O God, it was really Behnam speaking to me. I wanted to scream from happiness. Cry. Laugh. Swear at him. But I cleared my throat and asked in a monotonous voice, "How did you come to that conclusion?"

"You don't have to be too bright to figure out what a disaster has happened to this country," he said.

He coughed once and then said, "*We* brought it about for this country."

I wanted to shout, "You cursed idiot you're alive . . . you're alive, my love . . . that's all that matters," but I cleared my throat again and said, pitilessly, "Now that the revolution has trampled on you too, you cannot just disclaim responsibility for it with a simple confession."

Gently, but without energy, he said, "You're right. Every time I see the photos of people executed in the papers, I cannot shut my eyes for several nights. We, myself included, are their killers. Because of our naivety. Because of our zealous extremism and our stupidity."

We both fell silent.

Eventually, he said, "I'm sick of myself."

"Saying that won't help the country feel better!" I said.

"That's right," he said. "But at least to make up for my mistake I want to go to the front."

It just jumped right out of my mouth. "Oh, not you, too."

"But who else has gone to the front?" he asked.

"Everyone," I said. "Do you see any young people in the streets? Mehrab. Bahman. Reza and Maryam's grown and half-grown sons. And recently even Reza himself went. Our old classmates . . . Who else do you want me to tell you about? Auntie Narges and her husband, both my maternal uncles. Apart from a whole bunch of more distant friends and relatives. The teachers from school. The Zorvan baker and his four sons . . . Everybody."

He sighed and said, "I've shut myself up at home, but the news gets to me. I know about Mehrab. I heard about Bahman's being martyred, too. I am so sorry. My condolences."

He paused. He sighed and said, "Everyone has their own reason for going to war. I'm going to settle my guilty conscience."

"How did you know Mehrab's gone?" I asked.

"I spoke to your father."

I was astonished. "When?"

"Two or three times," he said, unruffled. "Ever since I was released, we've been talking every now and then about the state of the country."

It sprang angrily from my mouth: "You've spoken to my father but not to me?"

"He knows about us," he said.

I was apoplectic. "Us? Which us?"

"He knows I love you," he said. "He knows that if we make it through this revolution and war and what follows alive, then we'll get married."

I jumped up, appalled. "Married? Me and you?"

"But isn't that what's going to happen?" he said.

For a moment I was so sick of him that I shouted, "Four years . . . do you understand? For four whole years I had no news from you. Not one letter. Not one phone call. Nothing. The entire country's been turned upside down, there's been a revolution, Uncle Bijan was assassinated. Auntie Azar was executed. The war started. Mehrab went to war. Bahman got killed but I had no news from you, so I didn't even know whether you were dead or alive or had left the country . . . in fact I was certain that you had died. And now you're telling me you've been talking to my father for three months? About us getting married? Did you think you're somebody who could decide for himself whether I get married?"

I slammed the receiver down in disgust. I stared at it for a moment. Then I picked it up again and once, twice, three times slammed it down, and as soon as I went to the door to leave, Dad opened it, astonished, a glass of tea in hand.

A little while afterwards, during the hottest days of summer, just two months after the liberation of Khorramshahr, a city that had been occupied by Iraqi forces for 576 days, the weather hot and humid, I saddled Shabro after saying my goodbyes to the mansion, the tree, the temple, the forest and the greenhouse, kissed the residents of the house, and set off at a gentle pace, unenthused, doubtful, and overflowing with disgust for Behnam. I was not leaving of my own accord. Khanom Joon had officially forced me to do it. I wanted to stay and pursue my destiny within the confines of the forest, the temple, the greenhouse and the mansion. I wanted to become a collector of beauty, just like the forebears of this dynasty. I didn't want to set foot outside of the mansion except to complete my collection. I wanted to ignore all the bitter and ugly things that lay outside this mansion. I wanted to forget about him entirely. If I didn't see him, the war, and the miseries outside the mansion, they would disappear. Wouldn't they?

It had already been some time that the rose greenhouse had been established and was progressing well, with the help of Hasrat and Dad and with Khanom Joon's encouragement. My customers sometimes ordered them for weddings and birthdays, but most often for martyrs' mourning ceremonies. Mina and Mandana neither helped in the greenhouse nor learned anything new. They longed bitterly for college and were waiting for the Cultural Revolution to end, the purges to cease, and the doors of the universities to open. Every year they said that if the universities did not open this year, they would leave the country. Yet they were neither prepared to leave, nor felt like staying and putting down roots. They remained suspended between hopes and bitter regrets and realities. At night, like most of the young people among our relatives and friends and acquaintances, they wove dreams of America and England, and in the morning around the Gowkaran tree, as the family chatted away, they would unpick the threads again. This continued until one night the two of them fell in love, both of them celebrating their engagements shortly afterwards on the same night. Without actually being twins, Mina and Mandana had, ever since childhood, acted as if they were without realizing it, and they had fallen in love with two brothers from among the descendants of Khanom Joon's sister who had been invited to our mansion for a few days. Both young Zoroastrians had completed their military service before the outbreak of war. They were well-mannered and appeared intelligent. Each was the type of person of whom it could be predicted that a glittering future lay in store for them: high-ranking managers, faithful husbands, and fiercely devoted fathers. Just like their own father. Both were top-ranked students in Technical Engineering from the Aryamehr Technical University, and their studies would have been completed a year earlier, had it not been for the closure of the universities with the Cultural Revolution. Although they were upset by the course of the revolution, they did not get involved with it, and intended to get to America however possible—something that did not sit well with our family's taste, but which Mina and Mandana did not greatly object to.

In this way, with Leyla and Mehrab gone, and with Mina and Mandana's romantic absences, the house was emptier and more silent than before, until one night Mom left, eyes closed, and came back, eyes cried open.

It all began when one night Dad saw Mom get out of bed, eyes shut, go downstairs, pass through the hallways and living room, open the mansion door, pass through the courtyard and head into the forest; Dad followed her shadow by shadow, torch in hand, all the while calling her: "Jarireh . . . Jarireh," yet Mom didn't hear a thing. The way Dad later told us about it, Mom, eyes shut, walked as if in bright daylight with her eyes wide open. In this way they went on and on until they reached a grave which could be identified by the pieces of stone on top of it, and on a piece of wood at its head "Mehrab Taban" was written in charcoal. Dad froze where he stood. He watched Mom, who was sitting at the head of the grave, pick up one of the stones and cradle it in her arms, weeping and crying out, "Mehrab . . . Mehrab." She caressed the stone in her arms and shed tears for it. Dad told us that Mom was saying, "Mehrab my dear, why have you left us like this? Why have you brought this disaster on yourself?" Dad, appalled, thought, "Don't say this really is Mehrab's grave and I didn't know." Fearful, he started picking up the rubble and digging the ground with pieces of wood. Yet however much he dug, he found nothing underneath, except some of Mehrab's clothes from when he was one and his pacifier in a nylon bag. Dad, crying and frantic and afraid, woke Mom up with a slap to her ear. When she saw herself and Dad in the forest in the middle of the night, Mom froze in shock, but as soon as she noticed the disturbed grave and the bag of clothes and the pacifier, she started clawing at them, and yelled at Dad: "Why have you wrecked Mehrab's grave?"

It was already early morning when Dad brought Mom, feverish, home, surrounded by mist and rain and the songs of early-rising birds, she repeatedly clawing at her face and head and moaning and crying. An hour later, after a hot bath and several strong sedatives, she finally went to bed. On the phone with Dad, the family doctor said that Mom's depression was becoming excessively severe, and that if it wasn't brought under control, it was possible matters would become dangerous.

To stop this happening, after a general discussion it was decided that the only solution would be for someone to go to the front to look for Mehrab, to bring back either him or news of him, so that everyone, but above all Mom, could emerge from this depressed and uncertain state. But who? We were sitting around the Gowkaran tree and thinking of how Dad was practically the house's only breadwinner, without whose daily management the family's only inherited income—from the rice paddies and the sheep—would disappear. And in any case Mom was more dependent on him than anyone. If anything were to happen to Dad, then there would be no hope for her. The young of the family were either already at the front or had left the country. Uncle and Auntie had been killed. Mom had completely cut off relations with her sisters and brothers. Mina and Mandana and I were not at all up to this kind of job. Their fiancés were not suited to the task at all. We had no one else. This was what I was thinking when my eyes met Khanom Joon's, sitting next to mad Auntie Malek. She was sitting on that side of the table, me on this. She gazed at me so persistently that all of a sudden I read her mind and my eyes rounded in surprise. What? Me? No way!

Mom and Dad and Auntie Malek, who was only sane when she wanted to be, were quick to show firm resistance to this idea of Khanom Joon's—wasn't it enough that two of our children have already disappeared? And now we want to send this one to war of our own accord? To the killing fields? Don't even talk about it. When did anyone ever send a girl off to war all alone? What? With a horse? Khanom Joon, with all due respect, but, God forbid, it's as if something's hit you on the head . . . Auntie Malek said bluntly, "I'm crazy, but what's your excuse?" Mom and Dad went off in a huff to their bedroom, while Auntie Malek sat there waiting to see who would emerge victorious. Although with that fantastical mind of hers she already knew. In truth, she was sure because Khanom Joon's decision was always the final one. Not only because she was the senior family member and the inheritor of the sacred fire, respect for her a duty, but above all because it had been proven to everyone that in practice, she was wiser and shrewder than anyone else and that behind her every opinion lay some wisdom, the correctness of which would later be demonstrated to everybody else. And it was just this that broke my spine out in a cold sweat. But why should Khanom Joon, wise and shrewd, who knew so much about affairs both concealed and revealed, expect something so impossible from me? Why me, really? What about Mina and Mandana? Or their fiancés? Why shouldn't Nader go looking for Mehrab? Whatever happened, he was a man, and he could sleep wherever he needed to, and go wherever he wanted.

"Don't even mention it, Khanom Joon," I said firmly. "You know that I don't set foot outside the mansion except to complete my collection." And as she was wont to do, Khanom Joon raised her cane once, thumped it on the ground, and with a broad smile said, "That is exactly why I want you to go." And she said "you" with such emphasis that not a shred of doubt remained that she had made up her mind and would insist upon it. "When you return," she said, "You will bring something with you that cannot be found in any beauty collection in the world."

So it was that I, who had wanted to spend my life in devotion to flowers and collecting beauty and the secrets of the mansion and the palace and the temple and the Gowkaran tree in the middle of the kitchen, headed for the field of war and blood.

Before my departure, everyone stood in the courtyard next to the turquoise pool and watched Shabro and me in silence. Apart from Khanom Joon, it was if everyone was already burying my body, staring at me fixedly in a mournful silence. Auntie Malek was standing behind Khanom Joon and Jamshid Khan and in a loud voice uttering incantations over her inherited jade stone and blowing on it: "Calm in the storm . . . love in hatred . . . health in sickness . . . ffffffff." When she had done this three times, she came toward me and hung the jade stone, God knows how many centuries old and suspended from a leather strap, around my neck. Dad, who looked like he had been hauled here from another world, sighed and muttered, "O night, thy bounds your foreshores are distant and unseen / Yet thou art my brother in sorrow and pain."[40]

Then he opened the car door and took a wallet containing the last notes from his savings out of the glove compartment and put it in my pocket, before saying, in a voice shining with contrived hope, "You are my Gordafarid!"[41] We both knew that I could neither be Gordafarid, nor did I want to. Yet I didn't know that this would be the last time we saw each other, and that a few years later he would be abducted in that very car by plainclothes security police who would leave his body next to it in the Pounak desert near Tehran, his blood spurting onto the rear wheel on the driver's side . . . and meanwhile they would steal the only manuscript of his last book, *A Pahlavi Lexicon*, from the very same glove compartment and take it away with them. Mom, her eyes tearful and bewildered, said, "Ring whenever you get the chance. Write. I entrust you to God so that you do not go and get lost like Mehrab. Don't vanish like Leyla." She wiped away her tears and gave one of the several cameras she had kept since her youth to me, without either her or me knowing that a few years later, at the height of her depression, she would set fire to the mansion and that she would cut herself to pieces using the dagger that Jamshid Khan had kept as a memento of his unruly years. To my and everyone else's utter astonishment, Khanom Joon gave me her Ball of Light and murmured in my ear, "It will show you the way, and will be more useful to you than a hundred men and bodyguards. But don't forget, it cannot prevent you from learning the lessons you need to in this life." Jamshid Khan gave me two mementos, one from his youth and another from his unruly days: a cashmere shawl which he said no wind or rain could

[40] Aghaji of Bokhara, a poet of the tenth century.

[41] Gordafarid: A beautiful and highly resourceful woman warrior who appears in Ferdowsi's *Shahnameh*.

penetrate, and a vz. 24 bolt-action carbine rifle left over from World War Two. Without either of them knowing—or perhaps they did—that years later the two of them would be the last remaining source of support for us children. As I took the gun from him, I looked at Jamshid Khan with furrowed brow and said, "I don't know how to use it. And I don't want to." And he answered, curtly and practically, "You must learn. You will." Mina and Mandana, who were standing next to their two fiancés, pressed a package into my hand containing two maps of the country, a compass, binoculars, and a pocket edition of the Gathas. And the servants, who even in these times of hardship had not deserted us, bound an amulet against the evil eye to my arm and muttered لا حولَ و لا قُوَّةَ إلّا بِاللّهِ العَلي العَظيم[42] in my face, blew on my face and sprinked water behind me. Last of all, Shahnaz came close to me and placed a large man's ring on my thumb, and whispered in my ear, "Put this on Mehrab's finger. He'll come back safely. I know." I looked at the ring. It was an agate Sharaf-e Shams ring[43] with the letters of the alphabet in abjad order and numbers and shapes engraved on it. I held her against me and said, "I know too. I'll make sure I return your Mehrab to you."

We made our arrangements: Mina and Mandana would not marry until my return and would in the meantime take care of the mansion and of Mom, Dad would as usual deal with things relating to the land, while Hasrat would manage the greenhouse until I came back. I had to come back. And soon. Would I come back?

[42] There is no strength and no power save in God the Most High, the Mighty.

[43] A ring with a yellow agate stone on which prayers with special and often esoteric significations are written.

Book Two
The Ordeal of Liberty

Chapter Twelve

I murmured into Shabro's ear: "This is what's going to happen. We will go as quickly as we can so that we can get to the front and to Mehrab and Bahman as soon as possible." The fact of the matter was that even if Khanom Joon had not insisted that I go by horse, I apparently could not have gone by train or by coach or plane anyway. Before my journey, we had done our research and discovered that on the roads between the cities, and even in the city centers, they had sent out stop-and-search patrols of Basij and Revolutionary Committees and Guards and that the officers would not accept that a twenty-year-old girl, not even a university student, could travel unaccompanied by her father and brother or husband between a city and another where she had neither a house nor family nor even any kind of friend or relative. Besides this, they suspected single women and men travelling on the roads of being members of counter-revolutionary groups like the People's Mujahidin or the Minority or Majority Factions and would arrest them. Moreover, hotels would not provide rooms to women or girls traveling alone and looked on them as if they were women of ill repute.

I looked at Shabro's legs moving beneath me, and then behind me: at the four-columned, five-hundred year-old mansion, and at them. My dear family, from whom I had never been separated even for a night, was still standing strangely and helplessly in the mansion courtyard, waving goodbye to me. Dad had put his right arm around Mom, and she was crying in his embrace. Dad's left arm was still moving in the air. Auntie Malek, who it seemed had once again decided to be mad, had raised her arms aloft and with her long white locks flowing was dancing and chanting incantations like some ancient shaman. Khanom Joon was leaning firmly on her cane as always, and stood next to Jamshid Khan, their gazes fixed on me. With a sure smile which, to be honest, I understood nothing of and which in fact irritated me. Mina and Mandana blew kisses at me, and from far away I could see that the servants had placed their right hands over their chests and that, frowning and tears in their eyes, they were moving their lips in prayer for me. Our dog Paapi ran behind me wagging its tail. As I turned round to look at them, a voice inside me told me to imprint this image forever in my mind, for I might never see them next to one another like this again. A lump barred my throat. I turned to face forward again and geed Shabro up . . . "Come on, Shabro, come on."

For days Shabro and I, enveloped in my body's sorrowful melody, passed through forests and over hills and rivers, filling our lungs with the breath of dew and trees and rain and moss, sleeping by the fire underneath the ceiling of sky and foliage. Even though my body was soon covered in mosquito bites, and every night, before I slept, I looked around me ten times for fear that some wild animal would seek me out, the forest and I had been partners since childhood. I understood its workings, to a point, and in return it did not treat me too harshly. At least, that's how I hoped it would be. The forest was generous, its skirts full of fruit and food and water and medicine. From age five or six, I had come to know its edible mushrooms and greens with the help of Khanom Joon, Hasrat, Shahnaz, Shafiqeh, and Maryam. I knew where to eat the stalks of raspberry bushes or bulrushes so they would be juicy and tasty, or I knew where, if I didn't have water, to find and eat the crunchy and sour clovers which grew everywhere. For example, I could tell the difference between the edible ewe and morel mushrooms and the poisonous ones, or

I knew that pheasants laid their eggs under raspberry bushes and broad-leaved deciduous trees, or how it was possible to make the world's most delicious omelet from the eggs of wild ducks, burnet-saxifrage, and morels. I knew that if I pounded wild medlar leaves and applied the result to my wounds, the bleeding would soon stop, but if on the other hand I boiled them then drank the liquid, it would soothe sore throat and toothache.

Until I put myself to the test, I had imagined that I was a brave person, but on the journey, as soon as sunset's sorrowful silence took hold of the meadows and forests, it would set my heart beating in trepidation, pain would shoot down my spine in fear and I would scramble about to find a safe spot as soon as I could and light a fire. To light or not light a fire was itself a troublesome question: if I did light one, it was possible I would attract the attention of troublesome people from miles away, but if I did not, then I could neither warm myself nor make food. Worse than all that, if a wild animal attacked, how could I defend myself without fire? Though I had been born into a family that was Zoroastrian to the roots of its teeth, and fire and the sacred fire had always been the center of our attention and respect and life, it was only on this journey that I came to understand practically its importance for soul and psyche. At night as I gazed on the fire, I recalled my ancestors who believed in different types of Ahriman and to whom only fire in the darkness of night gave a feeling of security and saved them from biting cold and killing fear. I would think of Houshang and the Sadeh Festival.[44] I would think of the mansion and the days when the doors of the garden were open to all visitors, strange or familiar, to participate in the Sadeh Festivals, Chaharshanbeh Suri,[45] and

[44] The celebration of the discovery of fire by Houshang Shah according to Iranian legend.

[45] Chaharshanbeh Suri is the festival of fire celebrated on the eve of the last Wednesday of the year, of ancient Zoroastrian origin. It is the first festival of Nauroz, the Iranian New Year.

Nowsareh,[46] and of the sacred fire and of those days which, just like that, now seemed so far away.

The first days of my journey were the most difficult. Every day I uttered all sorts of dire words about Mehrab and Khanom Joon and my own miserable fate, even as I also considered Mehrab's going to the front to be my own fault, and that I was indeed responsible to Mom and to Shahnaz. If I had told Mehrab that Bahman was still alive, and hadn't told him about Behnam's death, would he have gone to war all excited in this way? However much I was angry at him and at this forced journey, my conscience obliged me to seek him out. And yet I was still not convinced as to why I should have to take this path on my own and by horse. Had Khanom Joon not insisted so much, it would have eventually been possible to find a way for me to go by bus and plane. I mean, I could have gone with Nader. Couldn't I? I was angry, and yet I tried to think more about Mehrab than about myself. All of us except for Mom were sure, in our own way, that he had not been killed; one of us had dreamt of him, another had seen him in the coffee grains or in a tarot reading, and still another was convinced inwardly that he was alive. Several times Shahnaz had started doing the housework, cheerful and laughing, and when we had asked her what had happened for her to be in a good mood after so long, she had replied that she had seen Mehrab the night before. That he was well. That she knew he would come back.

But what if he had been taken prisoner? What if he had gotten shell shock? Don't say he was missing in action. *Mafqud-ol-asar*, "trace missing": this was one of these hastily assembled Arabic expressions that had become fashionable once the war started. It meant that a combatant had disappeared in war: that there was no news of his having been taking prisoner, but also

[46] The ancient fire festival, held five days before the great celebration of the Sadeh Festival.

no trace of him being either dead or alive. I remembered Omid Raisi's letter. Were the missing-in-action not the very same people whom the Monster of Darkness had taken with it? I was angry and frustrated, and all manner of things occurred to me. What if he had abandoned the front and gone in search of the Third Step of the Mithraic Cult. In this country who had ever seen a woman, a young woman, go to the front on her own? On television they always showed women behind the front, ardent in their devotion, clad in chador and maqnaeh, either sewing men's underwear with floral patterns for the combatants, or preparing parcels of nuts and dried fruit and placing passionate mystical love letters inside them, or as nurses in desert hospitals hooking the wounded up to intravenous drips. How could I be sure that they wouldn't just arrest me at the front? It's easy to say that a girl of my age can venture alone into the mountains and forest, and to the front. What is this, the Michael Strogoff TV series? I'm not Oriana Fallacci or Joan of Arc!

This was how for days on end, grappling with such complicated emotions, I kept following the Ball of Light the least recollection that Khanom Joon had murmured various orders into its ear and that it must be carrying these out along the way without me knowing what they were. Gradually, my fear subsided; I didn't die of hunger and thirst, although most of the time I procured just enough food to eat and not starve, and what was funny was that until the Night of Eblis it did not occur to me that I could ask the Ball of Light for whatever I wanted. During all this time, no savage wild animal had attacked me, nor had any man assaulted me, for me to seek help from the Ball of Light. It was my guide, showing me the safest and shortest route. What could be more important than that? In any case, contrary to my expectation, the first person I encountered on this journey was neither a shepherd nor a villager, but Eblis.

One warm and orange sunset, Eblis was sitting under an ancient walnut tree, one among the many trees scattered across a vast mountain landscape, her usual snake on her shoulder and peacock by her side, watching the sun go down. I scrutinized her from afar. She was dressed as she always was, in a cream cape with a decorative green sash on its sides. She had tied up a part of her hair, the rest flowing free over her shoulders. She had wound a gold cloth around her forehead and tied it behind her head, which bestowed her with an aristocratic appearance. As soon as I saw her, I dismounted from Shabro. The tree above her was laden with ripe walnuts. I was hungry. I took out some leftover Khiki cheese, almonds, bulrush hearts, and sour, juicy clover stalks from my saddle bag. I was about to climb the tree and pick a few walnuts when I remembered that Hasrat always used to say that the walnut tree was very proud and you shouldn't climb it unless strictly necessary. It wouldn't like it and would throw you to the ground. For that reason, I found a long stick and shook the upper branches of the tree with it. Eblis did not stir from her spot. I gathered the walnuts in silence, made a fire, and sat cracking open the walnut shells and eating the fresh nuts. Eventually Eblis stood up, came over and sat next to me, and started cracking the walnuts. Our hands turned green from opening the nuts, and then quickly turned completely black. Eblis showed her black hands to me, before breaking the silence. "I have done a thousand things with human beings before, but not cracked walnuts." We both laughed.

"Hasrat says that the memory of what happens around a walnut tree gets recorded in its trunk and bark," I said.

As she put a walnut into her mouth, she stretched out her arm to touch the trunk and said, "So remember then that Eblis came here to see her."

I was hungry and didn't feel much like talking. She looked at me carefully and said, "You've gotten thinner, but more beautiful too." I looked at her in surprise. She continued. "This is the music of your soul that is dripping out."

So constantly did the mournful music sound in my ears, day and night, that sometimes I completely forgot about it. "Grief makes one useless and weak," I said.

She said, "And of course burnishes the soul."

I kept myself busy with the fire. "I can answer all the questions you have in your mind right now," Eblis said. "I can tell you right now where Behnam is, what disaster has struck Mehrab, and what Bahman is doing."

I looked at her from across the fire and the night. I didn't want to think about Behnam at all. Didn't I, really? Why then did my heart start beating furiously the moment I heard his name? But what disaster had struck Mehrab? What was Bahman up to?

"I have another question," I said. "When will I get to the front?"

Eblis smiled and said, "The way is reached by taking it."[47]

I looked at her meaningfully. I realized that she wouldn't just answer any question easily and straightforwardly. I was contemplating this when suddenly a spread of food appeared before us. I was so hungry that I didn't even ask where all this had come from. I stretched to pick up the first piece of chicken and ate it, before allowing the scent of the saffron and the rice to make me drunk. It had been a while since I had eaten warm, delicious food. Barberry rice with chicken, ghormeh sabzi stew, and fesenjaan stew, too! When I was full to satisfaction, I finally looked at her. She had placed her hands on the ground and, prostrating herself on the soil, was saying, "I pray to the pure life-giving earth."

I laughed and said, "Everyone else prays to heaven."

She said, "This is one of their idiocies. On the day of creation, the angels prostrated themselves on the earth on which humanity came into being. The qibla of the angels is the Earth, not the sky."

I was contemplating her words when a chalice of wine and three earthenware bowls appeared before us. I wanted to ask why there were three bowls. But before I could open my lips,

[47] 'Ayn al-Qożżāt-e Hamedāni.

Eblis poured the wine, and without raising her head, said in a commanding tone, "Come out of your skin and wet your lips with us."

All of a sudden I saw the Ball of Light rise up and turn into a young man. Dressed in traditional Zoroastrian costume, he turned to Eblis and bowed deeply. Eblis gestured that he should sit and eat something. The young man sat silently and respectfully beside us, dipped a piece of bread in the fesenjaan stew, and put it in his mouth. Eblis passed him a bowl of wine. The young man took it with the utmost respect, with two hands, and took a draught. Then Eblis commanded: "Leave now and carry out the order, but be back here before sunrise."

The young man stood up and in the blink of an eye turned back into the Ball of Light before vanishing into the darkness.

"I had no idea the Ball of Light was a young man," I said.

"Its skills are without number," said Eblis. "For this task, it had to be a young man."

"What task?" I asked.

"He had to deliver a piece of the sacred fire to a mobad in a temple hidden in the surrounding mountains," she said.

"Why?" I asked, surprised.

"Because your Khanom Joon is a shrewd woman," she said, "and knows that the only way to save anything is to multiply it."

I thought a little, before asking angrily, "So isn't it capable of getting me to the front in the blink of an eye? Couldn't it have prepared some food for me all this time? Why didn't it go looking for Mehrab anyway?"

Eblis shrugged and said, "There is a wisdom in everything."

My blood was boiling. What on earth did Khanom Joon . . . "Let us seek refuge from this Khanom Joon." It struck me that perhaps Eblis and Khanom Joon knew each other. Eblis poured another bowl for me, and moved her head with a smile to indicate that they did indeed . . . And even though I was angry with Khanom Joon, at Eblis's suggestion, I drank to her health and her long life, a little after which, out of drunkenness, and the feeling of security brought by Eblis's presence, the warmth of the fire and the delicious food, I lay down and my eyes became heavy. I was drunk and couldn't figure out if a lot of time had passed or just the blink of an eye. I came to my senses when I caught the smell of a gold Captain Black cigarette, the same kind my Dad smoked. Could it be that Dad was here? I jumped up. No. There was no sign of him. When I sat down, some of my drunkenness left me. There was a mattress underneath me and a clean, soft, warm cover over me. The fire was burning fiercely, as before, even though not a great deal of wood was left in it. She lit a cigarette using her own and handed it to me. We looked at the starry sky in silence and smoked American cigarettes.

Without warning, I said, "I cannot stand him."

She smiled. "I too at the height of love could not stand him."

She could not be talking about Behnam. No doubt she was talking about God, then.

"Was he really worth it?" I asked.

She moved her head and said, "Of course."

"Why?"

"The experience of love is worth everything. The beloved is an excuse."

I took a drag on my cigarette as I played with the wooden ring on my necklace and said, "How is it possible to stay in love with such people? They have betrayed us."

"They haven't betrayed us," she said. "Lying is betrayal. He wanted to test my love, and I came out of that test head held high, even though I have been cursed for all eternity. 'He concealed the trap of his trickery in my path / Adam was a grain in the loops of that trap.'"[48]

"Is it true that you claimed to be God?" I asked.

"Of course," she said. "I am God. Just as you and anybody else can one day become God. I am a courageous lover accepting

[48] Sanai of Ghazni, a mystical poet of the early twelfth century.

of changes. During the course of love's changes I reached a point where there was no more me and Him. Whatever there was, was love. Love without ifs and buts. I fell in love and attained the position of God . . . but He was already God and never abandoned His traditional role. That's the difference between me and Him. I can change and improve myself. He doesn't."

I thought about what she had said. When I got back to the mansion, I would have to write it down in my notebook on love. "What kind of love is the purest love?" I asked.

"The true lover," she said, "turns from a being into a quality: if the lover is the sun, then they turn into shining; if a blossom, then into blossoming; if a spring, then flowing. At the height of love, the lover becomes a part of nature: simple, easy, yet impossible."

I was utterly caught up in what she was saying. How many things there were in life that I still had to learn.

I was silent. After a while, she continued. "They say I have a single beautiful face and ninety-eight ugly ones. Ninety-eight of my faces are Ahrimans, whereas He, unlike me, has one ugly face and ninety-eight beautiful ones. His ugly face is wrath. My beautiful one is love."

"What is the point of everyone else seeing your ugly faces?" I asked.

"It is the false lovers, the ambitious, the wicked who see my Ahrimanish faces," she said. "Countless people. In the old portrayals, I am depicted as a sifter. I draw people into my trap by tempting them and in this way separate the just from the unjust."

"But how do you know true lovers won't be tempted?" I asked.

"Love was from the first rebel and bloody / so that whoever was outsider to it should fail.'"[49]

I stared at the blue-orange flames of the fire. I felt a great disappointment wash over me; what am I compared to such a

[49] Mowlana Jalal od-Din-e Balkhi, usually known in the West as 'Rumi'.

quality? "How alone we are," I said. "He is alone. I am alone. God is alone. You are alone as well."

"We are all as alone as everyone else," she said, "but still dependent on one another in some mysterious way. Even God after a while came to comprehend that we mean nothing without each other, or to put it more precisely, His being means nothing without mine."

It struck me that this was rather a bold claim. As ever, she read my thoughts. "But it's the truth," she said. "Beauty acquires meaning when opposed to ugliness, good when opposed to evil. I give him the possibility of being seen."

"Then Behnam is more independent than God," I thought, "if he can keep going so easily without me. He and I are neither good nor evil. In that case naturally we don't need one another."

"He will come back to you," she said, "just as any original thing returns to its origin. Like the season of spring which returns to spring, the sunrise which returns to the sunrise, like the Lord who returned to me."

"So," I asked. "After the whole business with the curse, you saw Him again?"

She laughed and said, "A great deal . . . having said that, a lot of the time He didn't know it . . . or He realized it very late." Her eyes flashed with a devilish light, and she laughed playfully. She went into thought for a little, before resuming. "The two of us have similar habits. For instance, we are both creative. And we both like to seek adventure. We both support the people we care about; He supports the wise, and I support the lovers. Or we both like to transform into different beings and individuals and experience what it is to live like them."

She paused, then said thoughtfully, "And what's strange is that the same story often repeats itself. I am overcome by Him . . . I fall in love with Him . . . or even fall victim to Him. Even when I had become a wagtail and He was no more than a hungry little innocent girl."

I looked at her inquiringly. She continued. "He was a little, lonely girl, poor and living in a miserable little house where nobody took care of her. It had been days since she'd eaten anything. Sometimes she was so hungry that she ate seeds and wild plants. One day she was sitting on a rickety little chair in the porch of the house. She was so weak that she just kept staring motionlessly at a single spot on the floor of the porch where a playful wagtail had settled. The wagtail kept hopping towards her on its slender feet. It viewed her as merely a harmless tree or a simple bush. Eventually the bird jumped onto her left leg, and as it innocently tilted its head, it gazed with its tiny, black, glinting eyes into her sad and motionless ones. It shook its tail feathers and sang a brief song. It wanted to cheer the girl up by singing. But the girl, with unexpected speed, grabbed the wagtail in her fist, wrenched its head from its body and flung it into the corner of the porch. The bird's beak was still opening and shutting and saying something, the wings and feathers on its body still moving in the girl's hand.

"That day the hungry girl plucked the bird's feathers with a still trembling hand and eyes full of tears, before throwing it into boiling water. As she ate, she did not pass up even on the little bird's head. She was hungry and this paltry piece of meat could only keep her alive for another day."

Eblis sighed. She turned to the fire and rearranged the pieces of wood a little. Then she resumed. "I was that wagtail, and that day God was that poor, hungry little girl . . . Days and months went by and gradually the condition of the little girl's family improved. Now there was food in abundance in the house, but she, recalling those tiny, black, glinting eyes, went off her food. She would sit for days on end on that same rickety chair gazing at the wagtail's empty spot in the porch and contemplated the word "trust." She felt no sense of regret. Hunger justified killing the bird, but what had become of trust? This question drove her to frustration . . . until one day she fell asleep on the chair. When she opened her eyes again, she saw that she was now looking at the little girl, at herself, sitting on the chair with motionless, sad eyes, from the perspective of the little wagtail. She tilted her head a little and looked at the little girl on the chair out of the corner of her eye. The little girl's eyes appeared sad and bewildered. For that reason, she wagged her tail a few times and sang a brief song for her. When she looked closely, she could make out a smile, faint but warm and kindly, on her face. Perhaps the girl was harmless, just like herself. Didn't they resemble one another? Once more she looked the girl on the chair up and down with her tiny glinting eyes. What harm could possibly befall her? None of the people she had seen up to now had ever hunted wagtails. Larger birds, certainly. But a wagtail? No! That was why she quickly hopped onto the girl's left leg so that she might sing more for her . . . so that girl's eyes would not look quite so sad. But right when she was cheerfully singing for her, in the blink of an eye she saw her own body, wings beating, far away in the little girl's hand, blood spurting over her feathers. Her head had been ripped off and flung into the corner of the porch. Her little beak was opening and shutting and was still singing a song for the little girl on the chair:

"A lover is someone
Who chooses
Who
May sacrifice them."

Eblis sighed . . . then she smiled and stroked the peacock. I looked at her bashfully and thought, "How adorable this woman is. How is it possible not to fall in love with her? I must remember to make space for her beautiful ideas in my Collection of the Beautiful." Shortly afterwards, Eblis opened her arms and the peacock came quietly out and sat in my arms. One of its tail feathers, an eye among its thousand eyes, was left behind in Eblis's arms. The snake too, a little later, slowly crawled onto my shoulders and found a nice spot for itself. It hissed in my ear. I smiled and looked into its golden eyes.

I saw myself, without shoes, my clothes tattered and dirty, my body mixed with a foul-smelling oil, guided by Eblis's snake, passing underground through the opening of a tight hole and searching for Dad in long, dark passageways. As I walked, I bumped against this side and that and fell down and got up again and continued on my way. Where was this? Somewhere far, far underground I reached a large plain lit by a mysterious and vague light. The ghosts of women and men emerged from the ground and mingled and made frightening and eerie noises.

Terrified, I cried, "I have come to find my father. I must take him home."[50]

I was astonished to hear something like this come out of my mouth. As if the words had emerged of their own accord and without me willing it. A tall ghost, aged yet taut, took form amid the mass of naked ghosts and came forward. He was holding a long cane.

In a resonant and deep voice, he said, "Why are your cheeks emaciated, your expression desolate?

"Why is your heart so wretched, your features so haggard?

"Why is there such sadness deep within you?

"Why do you look like one who has been traveling a long distance?"

I answered: "Should not my cheeks be emaciated? Should my heart not be wretched, my features not haggard? Should there not be sadness deep within me? Should I not look like one who has been traveling a long distance, and should I have hastened here from so far away, from the wilderness? My father, whom I love deeply, who went through every hardship with

[50] TN: the dialogue of this section was originally adapted from Davoud Monshizadeh's Persian translation, *Afsâne-ye Gilgamesh*, of the *Epic of Gilgamesh*, but since this was itself a translation of a translation of a translation, namely of Georg Burckhardt's German translation of George Smith's English translation of the Sumerian tablets, the text has been reworked using the English translations, direct from the Sumerian, by N.J. Sandars (Penguin Classics) for Tablet XI, and by John Gardner and John Maier (New York: Knopf, 1984) for Tablet XII, which is a later text and therefore not included in most English translations. The Persian text was then rewritten by the author to correspond more closely to the English.

me, has been overtaken by the fate of mankind. Seven days and seven nights his lifeless corpse lay there till maggots came forth from it. I mourned him grievously and did not bury him. How can I stay silent, how can I be still? My father has turned to dust and to clay."

The lofty statured ghost said, "You should not have come here. No one has summoned you here."

I said, "Give him to me so that I may bear him back to my home."

He said, "Whoever comes here may never again walk on the earth."

I said, "At least raise his spirit up from the ground that I might bid him farewell."

He said, "Open up now a hole to the underworld that his ghost may issue from the darkness."

At that very moment, Eblis's snake dug a hole in the ground and Dad's ghost came out of it. He was frail and dark and downcast.

"Tell me, father," I said. "Tell me the ways of the underworld that you have seen."

"I will not tell you, my daughter," he said. "I will not tell you. If I must tell you the ways of the underworld that I have seen, you will sit down and sorely weep."

"I will sit down," I said. "I will sorely weep."

"Then look," he said, and extended his hand toward me. I gladly took his hand in mine, but it swiftly turned to dust and shadow and disintegrated. Then he took a step forward and pulled me into his arms. I embraced him too, gladly, but his frail and dark body swiftly turned to dust and shadow and disintegrated.

CHAPTER THIRTEEN

Through the rolling hills and across a vast plain, the wind brought the far-off sound of women and men wailing to us. However hard I looked, there was nobody in that direction. With every step we took through the wheat fields, hundreds of sparrows leapt into the sky and settled down again a little way off amid the golden wheat. One step, hundreds of sparrows in the air . . . once more on the ground. Another step, hundreds of sparrows in the air . . . once more on the ground, and so we went on and on until we arrived at a modest mausoleum atop the verdant hills. Once we had reached the top of the hill, we saw a crowd on the large plain on the other side clinging to stone pillars, both large and small, weeping pitifully. A spring bubbled away beside an ancient stone shrine. I dismounted from Shabro, drank from the spring water, and sat down on the spot. The men were clutching small, ancient stone images resembling clover to their chests, or sitting on them, while the women were cradling longer, larger ones in their arms, rubbing themselves against them, weeping and crying in anguish. Here and there mats were spread over the wide grass meadows, covered with cloths and food. Crows fluttered and jumped around the mats and cloths, yet did not steal from the feast. On every mat there was a large plate of food, but we could not figure out what it was.

I rested there for an hour. The weather slowly got cooler. I stood up, collected dry wood from around about, and set a fire going. I thought how these people had cried so much that they could not have any energy left, meaning it would be better for me to make a bigger fire for them to warm themselves by. I collected more wood and piled it up to make the fire bigger and bigger. The people's weeping and wailing gradually subsided and they came toward the spring, the shrine, and us, warming themselves by the fire. No one paid any attention to me. As if the fire and I were supposed to be there.

A young woman wearing a black chador came and sat next to me. To start a conversation, I pointed and asked, "What kind of food is that?"

"Talkhun," she said. "Sacred food. The Prophet Khezr likes talkhun."

I wanted to ask, "Who is Khezr anyway?" but instead I asked, "What are these stones and why were you all weeping and lamenting over them?"

"We were weeping and lamenting for our own sakes," the woman said in surprise. "This is a cemetery. It dates back thousands of years. We have come here after a year of abstinence to beseech the occupants of these graves to make us pregnant and give us children."

"But is it in their power to do so?" I asked.

"I myself was born with their help," the woman said confidently. "As we are weeping and lamenting, we make a covenant with God to be righteous people."

"What kind of person is a righteous person?" I asked.

"The righteous person," she said swiftly and surely, "is a kind person, faithful to promises and covenants, serving people, pure in action, truthful in speech, a keeper of secrets. When we are like this, the Lord gives us the gift of children by way of these great ones. Meaning He considers us worthy of bringing up a human being."

I thought how this resembled our own belief: Good Thoughts, Good Actions, Good Speech.

The woman extended her arm in the direction of the gravestones and said, "Do you see these stones, big and small? The long ones like dicks and the short ones like cunts?"

When I heard these bold words I almost had a heart attack.

Although I had encountered them in Moin's Dictionary or had pictured them in my sexual dreams involving Behnam, I had never gotten to hear them in an ordinary conversation.

"So do you see that big dick?" the woman asked.

My body tingled at hearing that word again. I nodded my head. "Yes."

"When my mother couldn't get pregnant, she came here, after a year of self-denial, at the same time of year, on the same day, and tied pieces of cloth and prayed to that stone for a night and a day until she got pregnant with me. And now I have also made a covenant with him that I will be a righteous person until the end of my life, so that I will be worthy of having children."

All of a sudden, a man looking in amazement at the sky shouted, "Come on . . . come on . . . it's time!"

All of the men and women ran frantically from wherever they had been standing and assembled together, before sitting down in ordered rows by the spring and gazing into the waters.

Everyone was still looking at the water when, just as Shabro was beginning to paw restlessly at the ground and neigh, it stopped; the flowing water ceased moving, struck dumb, and the people stared at the motionless water, their breath trapped in their chests. Only the sound of the gentle breeze in the meadows could be heard. Even the sparrows were dumbstruck.

A few moments later the water started flowing once again. It started speaking. Once again, the sparrows began to bustle about. A woman shouted, "The Prophet Khezr's hand has alighted on my talkhun! Look." And we all looked. Something looking like the five fingers of the hand had fallen on one of the plates of talkhun. To me, something that looked like burst bubbles. The people shouted with joy, intoned blessings on the Prophet Muhammad and his Family, and started praying and shedding tears of excitement. For a moment my gaze and that of the woman to whom the sacred plate belonged became entangled. All of a sudden, I saw her face grow old and young again and, why I know not, I had the feeling she wanted me to pick up the plate and offer the food to everyone else. I got up, lifted the plate from in front of her and held it in front of everyone in turn. Each one of them, as they tasted a piece of the sanctified talkhun, directed their gaze towards somewhere in the vicinity of the spring and shrine and prayed: "O Prophet Khezr . . . deprive us not of your grace. O Prophet Khezr, grace our lives with children and wheat and cattle."

Shabro was calmly grazing once more. When everyone had eaten a piece of the sanctified talkhun, I placed the plate back on the same woman's cloth. At that very moment the woman grabbed me by the wrist. I was taken aback. She put her other hand in her pocket and brought out a coin. A lead coin. Then, without looking at me, she pressed it into my palm and said, "Keep it." I looked at the coin in surprise. It didn't resemble any of the coins in circulation. I put it in my pocket and went back over to the young woman with whom I had been conversing. She opened her handkerchief, which contained bread, cheese, and fresh herbs. She wrapped the cheese and herbs in a large piece of bread and handed it to me. I thanked her and took it. "How come the water suddenly stopped?" I asked.

As she pointed to the shrine, the woman said, with a cheerful expression, "This is the tomb of the Prophet Khezr. It was the Prophet Khezr who came and dipped his foot in the water for a moment and left. This year will be a good one for everybody. It means he has accepted our covenant." Whereupon she raised the palms of her two hands to the sky, muttered a half Persian, half Arabic prayer under her breath and then rubbed her two palms on her face. Next she raised her head and, as she was rolling the bread, said in a loud voice, "Give blessings to the Prophet and his Family for the health of the Green Master." Everyone, in whatever position they were in, sitting, rising, standing, or walking, suddenly stood stock still like statues and said, with a single voice, اللهم صل على محمد و آل محمد[51] And then

[51] God bless Muhammad and his Family.

they immediately started bustling around, resuming whatever they had been doing.

"What's the connection between the Prophet Khezr and these gravestones?" I asked. "Nothing and everything," she said. "Think of it this way: either everything is connected to everything, or nothing is connected to anything. When like today we are lucky and the Green Master comes at the same time we're here, this means these things are connected and wishes will be fulfilled."

We ate our bread, cheese, and herbs. The woman was gathering up her belongings when I asked, "So what happens now?"

She explained: "The same stone I showed you will appear to me in a dream tomorrow night and make me pregnant."

"What if it doesn't come?" I said.

"It will come, it will," the woman said with confidence. "Tomorrow night I will sleep in my room alone. Without my husband. And I will wear my finest nightclothes and put on makeup and spray perfume on myself. He will appear in my dream at midnight." She directed a playful laugh at me, and resumed. "And he'll get me pregnant."

"He?" I asked in surprise. "Or it?"

"Him," she said, surprised. "Obviously him. That dick you see has a soul. It's alive. There's the soul of a young man of high rank from ancient times inside it. A nobleman or a prince. A vigorous and goodly young man from a great family."

"Won't your husband get upset at all this?" I asked.

The woman blushed a little and, laughing, said, "No. This is a sacred tradition. Everything happens during the dream. Why should he get upset?"

Then, as if she had suddenly seen me for the first time, "By the way, who are you? Where are you going? Why are you alone?"

"I'm going to the war to find my brother," I said. "It's been a while since there's been any news of him. We're worried."

Immediately the woman got up, took my hand and with great excitement brought me to one of the tallest gravestones and said, "Rub your hands on it. Implore from the bottom of your heart, pray that your brother is found. Make a covenant with God that you will be a faithful person, keeping secrets, doing good works, speaking truthfully . . . and your brother will be found. Have faith."

I didn't want to ignore what she was saying, even though I didn't believe in it. I closed my eyes, but did not pray. I couldn't believe that Mehrab's life depended on that long stone reproductive organ. When I opened my eyes, the woman was looking at me suspiciously. As if she had understood that I had not taken what she said seriously. "It's obvious you heard what I said with the ears on your head," she said. "Whenever you listen to me with the ears of your heart, you'll find faith and a miracle will take place."

I was embarrassed that I had given her cause for distress. I apologized. She said nothing and went back over to her belongings.

I slept there that night, and early in the morning, when everyone else was still asleep, I went on my way once more through the wheat fields, past the timid sparrows, though before I left I gathered a great deal of wood again and revived the mighty fire. I pulled the blankets back over people wherever they had slid down, and asked the Ball of Light to rustle up blankets for those who did not have them. In thanks, I placed a bouquet of wild flowers with a dizzying scent that I had picked nearby next to the young woman, and then, with Shabro, set off.

The weather had turned cold. With Jamshid Khan's memento Kashmir shawl wrapped around my body, I went on and on for days and nights, and although sometimes I visited towns and villages with the Ball of Light, it was some time before my lips parted in speech. The dreams I'd had, the things I'd heard, and the events I had gone through made me think. In silence. I went to the towns and villages to buy food and to see what sort of state they were in. Such scenes I saw, and yet I did not part lip from lip. I insisted so much on my own silence that after a while my lips stuck together and dried up. Sometimes it occurred to me that all this silence could make me forget how to speak. That was why I would sometimes, somewhere between the mountains and the gorges, shout in a loud voice "Hellllooooo liiiiife!" so that I could hear my own voice and be sure that I could still speak. During this period of silence, I thought of what Eblis had said, and of the woman from up the tree, and of the young woman in the ancient cemetery, and of the events I had witnessed on my journey and in the towns along the way. I would have to include many of them in my Collection of the Beautiful. It was during those days that, because of the torrential rain that caught me unawares, I was forced to seek shelter in a cave for three nights and days. It was a small cave and five people might have been able to squeeze in next to one another with great difficulty. Its mouth was very small, and had Shabro not brought me there, there would have been no way I would have spotted it. I threw my sleeping bag and other gear down and managed three nights and days on minimal food. On the fourth day, when the shining sun emerged from behind the clouds and I wanted to continue on my way, Shabro struck the ground several times with his muzzle. I pushed the earth aside and pulled an old metal spoon from underneath it. It seemed to be made of zinc. I placed the spoon in my rucksack next to the lead coin as a souvenir of the cave and those days of extended silence, and went on my way.

Thus we proceeded for weeks through mountainous country in silence until, in the twilight of one autumn evening, as a chilly wind blew and the lights in the village ahead came on here and there and the last crows headed cawing back to their nests, I arrived at a settlement. I wanted to mingle with the people a little, talk to them, and break the fast of my long silence. At the entrance to the village a handful of young people were sitting or standing on a large stone slab next to the road and talking together. Each of them was holding a large torch. The light of the flames fell on the golden handles, making them shine. The torches themselves weren't made of gold. They appeared to be made of brass. A spring bubbled away beside the slab. As soon as I drew near them, one of them, his clothes strikingly cleaner and neater than the rest, came toward me and Shabro, and with a curious and polite expression asked, "Hello, are you a traveler or a guest?"

"A traveler," I said.

"Alone?" he asked with surprise. "Without a man?"

I shrugged. He glanced at his comrades, and as soon as he had turned back to face me, I saw that his expression had changed. A momentary spark flashed in his eyes. Abruptly, he said, "All strange women and girls passing through here have to put out for me once."

They all laughed in unison and a young man handed his torch to one of the others and took Shabro's bridle in one hand and put the other on my thigh. Afraid and angry I struck Shabro with my heels and geed him up. Everything happened very quickly and unexpectedly. Shabro neighed and reared up on his hind legs, but they just pulled Shabro's bridle and neck harder and the young man wrenched me off the horse in a rapid movement that took me by surprise, and dragged me behind the stone slab. He slapped me a few times and pulled my pants down and thrust that large, frightening thing that until then I had not seen with my own eyes inside me. I screamed from the pain and the terror. My voice echoed and woke up the sleeping crows. Yet it seemed that the more I screamed and asked for help, the deafer the villagers became. Was there really no one in the village? The man put one of his hands over my mouth and as he pounded his waist into me and then circled, before again pounding and then circling, while with his other hand he punched my mouth and head hard several times. I passed out.

When I came to, the taste and smell of blood in my mouth and nose, another of the young people had pounced on me and was thrusting his waist back and forth, while two more of them, torches in hand, were standing over him facing me. I moved lifelessly along with his movements and kept staring through my blood-stained eyelashes at the torch behind him. When he got up and casually pulled up his pants, he aimed a kick at me and departed along with the two others. I heard the noise of whispering from behind the slab and then nothing. There was darkness and silence. The crows were sleeping and the breeze had subsided. When I came to properly, I could hear the sound of pipes and drums in the distance. The village lay in a gorge between two mountains and there was no way of escaping. I would either have to pass through the village and continue on my way, or go back the way had I come. I was afraid and wanted to go back. Beaten, raped, and wounded, with shaking hands and a face sticky with blood and dried tears, I straightened up my clothes. There was a spring there. I washed my hands and face and between my legs, and, why I know not, for the first time in my life I wanted to pray. To beseech the great Ahura Mazda that those filthy cruel people would get their just deserts. I wanted to pray and, like those women and men from the ancient cemetery, implore of a sacred personage that He save me from this horror and humiliation and protect me throughout my journey. But it wasn't that I wanted . . . no . . . I needed to pray with all my being . . . to implore . . . to cry and to seek aid from Ahura Mazda and the seven Amesha Spentas . . . I remembered the Prophet Khezr and his spring. Jamshid Khan, who each morning before sunrise went to the chamber of the sacred fire of Borzin Mehr and put wood on the fire and prayed with all his being. Khanom Joon, who sat on the mansion balcony facing the sunrise and murmuring words from the gold inlaid book that years before the unknown prophet had given to Jamshid Khan in a dream. As I splashed cold water on my face and my wounds, I howled . . .

And howled . . .

And howled . . .

I cried so loudly that once more I disturbed the crows' sleep. It was at that moment that I understood why those women and men from beside the ancient stones howled and cried like that, from the bottoms of their hearts. Each one of them cried on account of their own pain. On account of their misfortunes, their deep regrets . . . on account of their suffering and their dreams vanished on the wind.

Such was my state when a hand placed itself on my shoulder. Terrified, I threw myself backwards. No doubt it was another man. But no. It was a beautiful young woman in colorful, sequined local costume carrying a lantern. She knelt down beside me and asked, "Sister, why are you injured like this? How come your clothes are torn? Who did this terrible thing to you?" I don't know why but when I heard the word "sister" all of a sudden such a stream of security and confidence flooded through my veins that I threw myself into her embrace and once again started weeping profusely. She held me tight in her arms, kind and compassionate, and consoled me: "Don't worry. Are you a traveler? There's no man with you? We village women will take care of you." Gradually, other lantern-bearing women gathered around us. A little later I learned that they were all on their way to a wedding and that the woman who had consoled me was the bride herself.

The bride took my hand and pulled me up. Addressing herself to the other women in the local language, which to me sounded like Kurdish, she said something that she translated for me afterwards: "They'll give you a bath, put clean clothes on you, and bring you to the wedding."

The bathhouse was a small mud room in the house of one of the village women, with a zinc bowl and a barrel of warm water and pleasantly-scented bentonite clay for washing your head. The towel was a clean red and black wrap made of cotton and hemp. Under the lantern light I looked at my face in a little mirror set into the mud wall. My left cheek was bruised and the bone above my right brow was broken. They brought me a colorful local dress and shawl. They were so beautiful that for a moment I forgot about my pains. Then suddenly, angrily, I remembered the Ball of Light. I took it out of my knapsack and put it to rest in a corner of the bathroom where it could hear me say all sorts of unpleasant things: "Why didn't you come to help me? Didn't Khanom Joon send you along to look after me? Idiot . . . Clumsy oaf . . . Useless thing . . ." Eventually it responded. "Khanom Joon did warn you," it said. "I cannot stop you learning life lessons." Ahhhhh, curses on this life . . . Curses on Khanom Joon and her lessons . . . I clutched my knees and wept bitterly.

An hour later as I entered the room clad in local dress, the women young and old were sat around, their expressions saddened and concerned, whispering in the local language about me to one another. One of them translated for me and said that they were all worried about me and wanted to know who had done this terrible thing to me. They asked about his clothes and general appearance. When I provided indications, they looked at each other in astonishment and turned purple and after that no one asked anything else. Then I lay down in a corner and in order to calm my spirit it occurred to me I might read the Gathas. I opened a page for divination at random. Ushtavaiti Gatha, Yasna 43. Happy is the person who attends to the happiness of others. O Ahura Mazda, bestow the best of rewards on that person who taught us the truth and to live well . . . O Good Thought always respond to our questions . . .

An hour later, the villagers were standing hand in hand around a great fire in a circle in the village center, dancing like some connected and organized chain. Amid the hubbub of the music and light and color and laughing faces and long plaited hair, the wounds of my body and soul howled noiselessly. I went into the wedding gathering to see if, with the bride's help, I could find the men who'd attacked me and dishonor them in the village. Perhaps if I were lucky and someone helped me, I might be able to bring them to justice. The beautiful bride and her friends were standing in a corner, and as soon as she saw me, she motioned to me to join her. I had not yet made it over to her when the groom arrived and the bride introduced me to him. As soon as he raised his head, I recognized him. It was him. Horrified, I took myself to one side. The bride realized what was going on. She scowled. As soon as the groom saw me, he turned his back and hurried away. Enraged and agitated, I said to the bride, "It was him. That was him." I had to dishonor him in front of everybody. The bride's friends looked at me in shock. The bride's eyes and cheeks turned red and she said, "That's impossible." I said I was certain. That was him. Suddenly, the bride turned her back on me and left.

I had no idea what was going on. I told her that the groom, her future husband, had raped me . . . but she had turned her back on me so she could continue celebrating her wedding to that same man? Did that mean it didn't matter to her at all? A little while after I went up to her again. I found her behind a tent where the banquet had been laid out, muttering softly with a young man and woman, who left as soon as they noticed me. I said angrily to the bride, "Why don't you believe what I'm saying? If you don't believe it, then I'm going to start shouting right here and tell everyone that he and his friends raped me." She angrily gestured to all the lights and hubbub in the tent and said, "Do you see these people? They are all related to one another. They have come together here from five clans. For just this one night we have spent a fortune. Everyone is happy. Look at them. If I don't marry him, both me and my family will lose our reputation, and blood will flow. The young folk from the five clans will be set at each other's throats pointlessly, for no reason, and get themselves killed. What did you think would happen anyway if you shouted and told everyone? They'll all say that you're a debauched woman wandering around on your own in the mountains and the desert."

I could feel my blood boil and suddenly I yelled, "Pointlessly and for no reason? Hey everyone, the groom is debauched. The groom—"

Sharp slaps struck my face. The bride yelled, "Who are you to talk about my husband like this?" Once more I yelled: "Help! The groom raped—" The bride grabbed my hair, took a dagger from her waist and dragged me under the trees lying further off in the darkness, and said with rage, "If you've had your fill of life, then raise your voice once more. I swear by my mother's hair, I'll kill you. Who are you to know what life is like here? The wife's duty is to obey her husband and her husband's family. I am going to do my duty. What will you do? You don't know your own country if you've set out on the road on your own. You are debauched. Everyone should rape you. If you stay here one minute more I'll set all the men on you myself."

Shocked, terrified, crying, I ran off toward the house of the woman who had been my host. What sort of people were these? What sort of land is this where they treat a girl on her own like this? I quickly changed my clothes and mounted Shabro and in the darkness passed through the deserted lanes and alleys of the village and headed for the heart of the mountains.

Shabro and I went along, me moaning with repulsion and rage, crying and abusing everything and everyone—including Behnam and Mehrab and Khanom Joon and the Ball of Light. So much did I scream and roar at this injustice that my voice grew hoarse. Eventually tired, dejected, and caught up in all sorts of complicated feelings mingled with hate and loathing and range, I spread my sleeping bag in the shelter of a large slab of stone and cried myself to sleep.

I started awake early as Shabro neighed and pawed at the ground. I looked around me. I was in a mountain pass and Shabro was neighing at the mountain wall and lifting up his forelegs and pounding the ground with them. I looked. A colossal stone horse was watching us through the foliage. As soon as I tried to pass through the trees and bushes, I found myself surrounded by scorpions. Was Shabro neighing because of these scorpions or because of the colossal horse on the wall?

The scorpions were dotted here and there, moving around with their fearsome tails held high. I flicked them this way and that with a piece of wood and made my way through them with great difficulty, before coming face to face with a massive ancient inscription. It was so magnificent that it took my breath away and all thought of the scorpions completely vanished. Opposite me, above the inscription, there stood a king with the clothes and imposing aspect of those whose pictures I had seen in history books and in the films of the Celebration of the 2,500th Anniversary of the Founding of the Persian Empire.[52] The king's imposing gaze took my breath away. He, a crown on his head and a great sphere on top of that, was mounted on a splendid horse, while opposite him knelt two men, wearing the Roman dress I had seen in the film *Julius Caesar* with Marlon Brando.

My body still hurt from the catastrophe of the previous night. Despite that, I piled several flat stones on top of one another so I could reach the relief. I ran my hand over the half-erased image on the stone wall and I felt the vastness and mystery and secret of history fall on me and my misfortune like rain and light. It was as if the powerful muscles of the horse's calf, the sword and the folds of the trousers and the shirt and the bag hanging from the king's waist had come alive for a moment under my hands and swayed with the blowing of the breeze. From up there, I gazed around me, and it looked like there were other inscriptions and reliefs on both sides of the pass. I wondered whether there wasn't a time when this would have been a place where kings and soldiers and dignitaries passed through, or indeed ordinary people like me. My forebears. Despite the hatred and rage that had dwelt within my being since the previous night, my body tingled with an unfamiliar and mysterious excitement and for a moment made me forget the pain of rape, injustice, and humiliation.

[52] The Celebration of the 2,500th Anniversary of the Founding of the Persian Empire was a national event that took place in October 1971, involving elaborate and grandiose festivities commemorating the founding of the Achaemenid Empire by Cyrus the Great.

I moved forward and tried not to think about the catastrophe of the previous night and this morning's scorpions. I thought how I had no choice but to move forward. I had to move forward as much as I could so that I might have a chance of forgetting the past. Shabro followed me. There was another relief further on. Dozens of men in sumptuous clothes stood arranged in two rows, facing one another. In the lower row a man standing farther forward than the rest was holding a horse's bridle. In both rows the men were holding various items. Items such as coins, chalices, batons, and swords. These items were made not of stone but of brass.

I rubbed my hand on a stone slab. In some places there were the outlines of images, faded and worn away. How many stories lay behind these reliefs of which I knew nothing? Further on there were things written in an ancient script I could not read. I cursed myself for having paid so little attention to the history teacher Mr. Julaee's lessons. Why had I never learnt the script of our ancient ancestors? I got out my camera, Mom's present to me, and took a few photos. Then I sat and wrote down my memories of the past few days in my notebook of memoirs. I remembered a phrase I had read somewhere: "History is written by the victors and art is made by the vanquished." Which one of these groups did I belong to? If I was writing down my appalling memories of the previous night, then to art, but if I was writing about today and these magnificent ancient passageways, then history? So it was that I sat, notebook in hand, stupefied by history, listening to the sorrowful music that emanated from my body, as all the while the trees cast their shadow on me and on the inscriptions and the sparrows and starlings and filled the silence between us, the silence between me and history, me and my ancestors.

I don't know whether it was because of warrior emotions induced by the statues of Achaemenid, Arsacid, and Sasanid kings and soldiers, or the excruciating events of the previous night, but I took Jamshid Khan's gun and knife out of Shabro's saddle bag, put a lump of earth on a stone slab, and tried to shoot at it. Then I tried to throw the knife so that its sharp point would penetrate a tree trunk. The wounds on my body and in my psyche hurt from the night before. I wanted to say horrible things about everyone, even the Twelfth Prophet and the Gowkaran tree in the middle of our kitchen. After all, hadn't everything started with him or with that accursed tree, the Tree of the Incident? Why on earth had it grown right there in the middle of our kitchen anyway? What was the meaning of the adventure in that ridiculous palace anyhow? What did all of these things have to do with each other? I was confused and frustrated and angry. Scatterbrained and unfocused . . . overflowing with feelings of rage and hatred and rancor . . . All of a sudden I started yelling. Despite my sore throat, I screamed. From the bottom of my heart. From the bottom of my throat. With all my might.

The sound of my scream wound its way through the pass and struck the kings and heroes and soldiers and splendid horses in the face before returning through the autumnal trees to me . . . to frail and fragile me. To humiliated and raped me. I screamed and cried so much that my tears dried up and my sore throat became so severe that I couldn't even breathe comfortably. After that I spent several hours shooting and knife throwing, in rage and indignation. The feeling of being disgusted with everything had come to find me, and now I was so disgusted I wanted to fight like a soldier. Not to defend! To fight. I wanted to hit. Kill. Attack. Spill blood. Die. I looked at the massive-bodied heroes and soldiers of the surrounding mountains and said to myself, "You are a soldier . . . soldier . . . " and fired some more at the lump of earth until at last I managed to hit it three times. And once I got the tip of the knife to penetrate the tree trunk.

At that very moment a man and a woman with large guns on their backs and daggers at their waists came out from behind a stone slab. Without a moment's hesitation I pointed my gun at them and said, "If you come any closer I'll kill you." The woman said, "I'm one of those women who saw you last night next to the spring and took you home." The man calmly took a step toward me and said, "Not all of us men are like those four, trash and rapists. We have families, too, sisters and mothers and daughters we love and respect."

My arm relaxed a little. Did this mean they could be trusted? The two of them came a little further forward and said, "We've come to help you get your revenge."

I gripped the gun tightly once more. "Why?" I said.

"Because it is proper and correct," the woman said, "for the oppressor to receive his just desserts, because otherwise the world would be full of oppression."

"Last night," I said, "when the bride was slapping me and telling me I was lying, where were you?"

The woman gestured to the man standing beside her and said, "We are the same two people who were talking with the bride last night behind the tent. We are her sister and brother. She was doing her best to stop bloodshed and clan warfare. From our generation alone ten of our cousins were killed in these clan wars before they were even thirty years old. And a great many have been killed on the groom's side too. His father was killed by ours. That is why the elders agreed my sister should be the Bride of the Blood-Truce.[53] In order to keep the peace and prevent further bloodletting."

"All the same, how could the bride get married to a man who just an hour before the wedding had raped me?" I asked angrily. "What did she tell me all that for anyway?"

At that moment, the bride emerged from behind a stone slab. Her head was bowed and her expression shamefaced. With hatred, I pointed the gun at her. "Get the hell out of

[53] The Bride of the Blood-Truce is a custom practiced by members of certain tribes in order to prevent feuds becoming prolonged and bloody by creating additional kinship relations between the warring parties. If a man with a son is killed, the killer's daughter must become the son's wife. The presence and approval of the graybeards of both parties (clans, tribes) is necessary for the practice to be effective.

here," I yelled. "You're a new bride and I don't want to spill your blood. Get lost."

The bride, a guilty and downcast look on her face, took a step forward and in a gentle voice said, "Last night I wanted to save your life, as well as my own and everyone else's. If you had cried out last night, and even a witness had spoken up, nobody would have defended you. And it would have been even worse for some people to have defended you and then there would've been enmity and bloodletting between the clans again."

She took a step forward. In hatred I fired a single bullet at the ground. As fate would have it, it landed near her feet. Inwardly I thanked God that with my bad aim the bullet had not actually hit her feet. All the same, I shouted, "Get lost. I don't want to see you."

"You're right," the new bride said. "If I was in your place, I'd feel that way too. That's why I came with my siblings to help you."

I spent four whole weeks examining the inscriptions and the reliefs of the warriors of history, and from the three siblings learned how to shoot as well as to throw a knife. I gradually grew to trust them and told them about my journey, but when they asked me about the Ball of Light and my body's mournful music, I gave no answer. At sunset they would head back to their village, returning to see me again the following morning. The two sisters taught me how to shoot with both a gun and bow and arrow on horseback, while from their brother I learned how to wrestle and win. For the first two weeks, the only feeling that calmed me down was the thrill of revenge. However possible, though I didn't know how, I wanted . . . even with the aid of the Ball of Light, to make them suffer the same awful things I had suffered. Or at least for them to get so badly beaten up that they wouldn't be able to get out of bed for months. But then the brother asked, "If you answer violence with violence, won't you just be like them?"

How then must justice be established? And in any case how could we know that they wouldn't assault other women afterwards? During the third week I sought the siblings' advice so that I could hear all ideas, while at the end of the fourth week, we all came to an agreement on the punishment we had envisioned. The new bride seemed happier than all of us.

At last, we were ready. On the day of revenge, I wanted to say goodbye to the siblings. Nobody should know that they had worked with me on this, but all three of them disagreed. "It looks like we've also changed during this time," the new bride said. "We're not afraid of them anymore." Then twelve middle-aged and elderly women and men arrived and joined us. A woman and a man stepped forward and said, "Those of us who have come here are among the notables of both clans, of the bride and the groom. We all want this violence to come to an end and for you to get your revenge." Their expressions were noble and had seen much suffering; in those faces, so genuine, could be seen a whole history of love and hate.

We then divided up the tasks. I would have to use all the techniques I had learned in those weeks so I could prove to myself I had become capable. The following day, we arrested the four men and brought them there. By the time the four of them had finally been gathered together, hands tied behind their backs, it was already evening. They were dazed and confused on account of how many times we had struck them on their heads and necks. I had arrested the groom. After that I had beaten him to my heart's content. The three siblings stood behind them, swords in hand. The twelve clan elders stood around, holding their guns. Then the four rapists came round, and as soon as they noticed me and the three siblings, they were struck with terror. The groom, however, half stood up and shouted at his bride, who was standing over him wielding a dagger. "What the hell are you doing here? Do you want me to kill your father and only brother as well? The same way I killed your cousins?" The new bride pressed the dagger on her husband's neck hard enough for blood to come out. "You tell me why you raped her, you shameless man."

The elders took a step in our direction. The groom had just noticed them. He was surprised to see a number of his own people. "Uncle . . . Mother . . . why you?"

An old woman came forward and said, "We don't want any more blood and fighting," and spat on the ground in the direction of the four young men. Then the mother of the groom stepped forward from out of the crowd, went towards her son, slapped him fiercely, and said, "If you look at a woman or a girl the wrong way even once more, I will expel you from the clan."

I said to the four men, "The punishment which we have in mind for you should solve your problem and perhaps even your clan warfare once and for all. From now on, if you injure anyone, that injury will be visited on your body and soul too. From now on, you will be the first victims of your own violence."

"And how the hell do you want to do something like that?" the groom asked, smirking.

I brought the Ball of Light out of my pocket. It spun rapidly over to the four men and touched each of their foreheads. A few moments later, the rope no longer bound their hands and arms. As soon as the groom found he was free, he took two giant strides toward me and punched me hard in the face, but at that very moment he was thrown onto the ground as if his own face had been punched as hard.

He was still on the ground feeling the effects of his own punch as I mounted Shabro and addressed myself to the siblings and to the twelve elders: "I am grateful to you. This whole affair has taught me an important lesson." The siblings stepped forward and said, "It was an important lesson for us too." Then the bride unclasped a brass necklace with traditional designs on it from around her neck, placed it around mine and said: "White road."[54]

[54] Meaning "safe travels."

Chapter Fourteen

Sister?
Dear sister?
Who is this?
She's come from a long way away.
Brother?
Dear brother?
What's she doing here?
She's traveling a long way.
But doesn't she know this is the end of the road?
She'll figure it out. Little by little, she'll figure it out.

I heard their voices in a half-waking, half-sleeping state. Weeks had gone by since the whole business of the rape and my revenge, yet it crossed my mind that maybe these people wanted to molest me too. With a fierce grip on the knife at my side, I opened my eyes. But the eyes and expressions looking down on me were not threatening. Quite the contrary. How bright and kind their faces were! And there was a glint in their eyes—the glint of innocence. The glint of joy. As I was about to get up, a young woman wearing a simple cotton tunic and a silk shawl, a crown of wildflowers in her hair, split from the crowd, smiling at me so that I drew nearer. It struck me that her face was like the daughter of the King of the Peris, kind and beautiful . . . What if I had died and this was paradise?

The young woman took my hand affectionately, and, running playfully, took me to the middle of the cave. She spun round and said, "Isn't it beautiful here? It's beautiful . . . It's amazing . . . Look. Look."

I looked around me for the first time. The cave had been decorated all over, was spotlessly clean, and, it might even be said, beautiful. The first thing to attract my attention was the fire in the middle. The light that it shone on its surroundings seemed greater than what might be deemed natural. Next to catch my gaze were the iron pans around the fire, followed by the wooden chairs and beds covered with colorful, handwoven gelims and jajims. The plants were climbing up the walls, here and there rugs were spread on the ground, the gorgeously colored cushions resting on them, the lanterns lit in various corners, and the great wooden table bore earthenware and metal dishes full of fruit and wine and delightfully colored foods. Although the table was laden with food, it looked more like a council table. Chairs were arranged around it, and books, notebooks, and pens had been placed in front of each chair. In the center of the table, there was a large footed bowl made of brass, in which colors and images appeared and disappeared in the water inside. Around the outer rim of the large bowl, seven parallel lines were drawn. There was a large, exquisite harp in one corner of the cave and a woman was busy playing it. A little farther off, in the middle of the cave, was the trunk of a big tree, its crown poking through large opening in the cave roof, while light splashed into the cave through its foliage as well as through the opening. In one corner were several large bookcases with books bound in thick leather. What lay before me in the light and shadows was like a dream or the land of the King of the Peris.

"Where is this? Who are you?" I asked.

They all looked at one another in surprise, except the Peri-like Young Woman. At last a handsome young man said kindly, "First you tell us who you are? How did you end up here?"

"A traveler," I said. "I'm going to the front to find my brother."

An elderly man holding a bowl of wine, clad in robe and turban and resembling the statue of Ferdowsi in Ferdowsi Square in Tehran, came forward and said, "The front? Has a war started? Don't say the Arabs have invaded again. So who is your Rostam?"

Astonished, I said, "It's been a long time. The Iran-Iraq war."

The young woman who resembled a peri spun round, lighthearted and carefree, so that her long, white and blue cotton shirt would turn around her in a circle. "What could be better than this?" she said. "We know nothing about the world, the world nothing about us. You're the first person to have come here for decades."

I gestured in surprise in the direction of the last village I had passed through and said, "A few days that way is a large village. My map shows that there is another village four days away to the west. How is it that haven't seen anybody around here until now?"

They all looked at one another. Nobody said anything. To change the subject, I asked, "What is this large bowl in the middle of the table?"

A middle-aged man, whose face, clothes, beard and hair resembled the paladins of the Shahnameh, said, "It is Kay-Khosro's Cup. Nobody touches it apart from him."

"Who is Kay-Khosro?" I asked.

"Is there anyone else apart from Kay-Khosro," the paladin replied in surprise, "the living king, who possesses the World-Displaying bowl?"

A middle-aged man wearing a different robe and turban, perhaps resembling the Shirazis of old, came toward me and said, "You said you have a map. Show it to me."

I went outside to Shabro, who was busy grazing, and took the map out of the saddle bag. As I went back into the cave, I stood and looked over everything once more. The fire's soft smoke and the light of the sun pouring through the hole in the ceiling gave the cave a spiritual quality. A large image of an imposing and splendid lion with a sun above his back that I hadn't noticed before had been hewed into the cave wall. I was still sunk in contemplation when the same man came up to me and took the map from my hand with great excitement. As he opened it up, the others gathered around us out of curiosity to look at it. A young woman with an ill-assembled face, dressed like an Arab tribeswoman and with an Arabic accent, took a sip of wine from the bowl she was holding and said, "These roads, towns and villages . . . where are they? There are no such places around where we are."

"There are," I said. "Right now, we're here." And I placed my finger on the map. "I have been moving ahead using this map for months now. According to my plan, I should reach Khorramshahr in about another two months."

As he inspected the details of the map with a magnifying glass, the man who had first taken it from me exclaimed: "Map-making has developed so much! Back in the day, I drew up the first administrative and commercial map in the world. From the far side of India to the far side of Spain, with all the details of the cities and the Silk Road and post stations and caravanserais. I even wrote a travel guide for those going by land and by sea from the Tigris to the Persian Gulf and India and China. My book's over there, go see for yourself." And he gestured with his hand in the direction of the bookcases.

I was still searching for the man's name in the recesses of my mind when one of the young men, one with a handsome, kingly face and who with his imposing height, ancient clothes and sword hanging from his waist resembled the princes and paladins of the Shahnameh, shrugged and, walking away, said, "We've been here for years. We've explored everywhere around us too. We've seen nobody, no villages, no towns."

"How many years have you been here?" I asked.

A young woman whose face was as gorgeous as the full moon and who was promenading, clad in royal attire, between the lace and brocades, said, "We've lost count. It's been a long time." She turned to the young man and said, "Isn't that right, Bijan?"

Another woman, enticing and drowning in gold jewelry, said, "A thousand years, or two?"

A middle-aged man with long, flowing hair and a simple woolen robe said, as he moved toward the woman with the ill-assembled face, "Seven or eight hundred years?"

I don't know why, but seeing the two of them side by side brought to mind the pictures of Leyli and Majnun in books.[55]

"No way," a young woman said, "We haven't been here more than a hundred and fifty, two hundred years."

I looked at them in bewilderment. They must be joking. "How many years have you been here, really?" I asked the geographer.

With a serious expression, he gestured with his hand at a number of elderly men, saying, "Basically, these people you see here ended up here both before and after the Arab invasion." He indicated a number of others with his hand and said, "Those ones came after the Mongol invasion. This young man and that young woman came much earlier." He gestured to the Peri-like Young Woman in the cotton dress. "They have been here from the beginning. Some of them came much later . . ." He indicated a number of people with his hand and said, "For instance they came after the First and Second World Wars."

At that moment, someone's silhouette appeared in the cave entrance. Everyone rushed happily over to them, meaning I could not see their face. Whoever it was gradually moved closer to me, surrounded by the laughing and cheerful group, until finally I was able to see them clearly through the crowd. It was Eblis. I hadn't imagined that she had so many fans. As she handed the peacock to a man with disheveled hair, from amid the enthusiastic greetings of those around her, she addressed herself to me, a smile on her lips: "You made it here at last, then."

Some of them turned towards her slightly. One asked, "So you know this young woman?"

[55] Two Arab lovers who entered the culture and literature of Iran and the wider world through the long twelfth-century Persian poem of that name by Nezami Ganjavi; Leyli or Layli is also known as Layla or Leyla.

"Don't say it's because of her that you've come back to us after all these years," said another.

Paying no heed to the others, who chattered or asked questions incessantly, Eblis came and sat down on a chair beside me. She picked up a piece of bread from the table, dipped it in a bowl of yoghurt and ate it. Then she poured a bowl of wine for herself and me and said, "Drink." I did so, as did she.

The rest of the group, excited by her presence, sat down around the table. She turned to face them and said, "You are all in good spirits. I am happy."

An old man holding a book and a compass said, "It was kind of you to come."

Everyone then filled their wine bowls. Another man, who happened to resemble Zakariyya Razi from our school textbooks, got up, held out his wine bowl towards everyone else, and said, "According to millennial custom, the first bowl is the share of the departed lovers and noble ones. To the health of their souls." Then he gathered the long, loose sleeve of his right arm with his left hand, and slowly and respectfully poured his wine on the ground in a narrow strip. The rest did likewise. Then they filled a second bowl, and the old man said, "We drink to joy, prosperity, and life."

Next another old man stood up and glanced at the woman playing the harp, whereupon she adjusted her playing to accompany the poetry he sang: "Khayyam, if thou art drunk from wine, then happy be / If thou sittest with a moon-faced beauty, then happy be / For the end of the world's affairs is naught / So long as thou art, as if thou wert naught, happy be."

Then the old man sat down and put his arm around a beautiful woman. They clinked their bowls together and drank and kissed one another on the lips. Everyone drank, including me.

Eblis turned to another old man and said: "Master, recite us something from one of your love poems. I've missed your poetry." The old man took a deep breath. He shut his eyes, and with great feeling and in a charming accent that I thought must be Khorasani, recited from memory: "Come back, come back, whatever ye are / Be ye unbeliever, pagan, or idolater, come back / Our court is not the court of despair / Though ye have failed in repentance a hundred times, come back."

At that moment a man with a light complexion and a salt-and-pepper beard pointed at the old poet and whispered in my ear: "Whatever I know, he sees."

Who was he? Who was this? I rummaged around in the deepest, darkest recesses of my mind to see if I couldn't remember my history, literature, and science lessons. Wasn't he Abu Said Abu'l-Kheyr?[56] And wasn't the one next to me Avicenna? I looked at the faces of the people around me again. Was this a gathering of the great figures of our history? At that moment, another old man smiled at the previous one and in a delightful Hamadani accent said, "I'll give an *I*," and recited: "If thy hat is of gold, yet thine end is nothing / if thou art the king himself, yet thine end is nothing / if they grant thee the wealth of Solomon, yet thine end is nothing / ultimately thou shalt be the dust of the road, for thine end is nothing."

They were engaged in moshaereh.[57] The same old man who had initiated the wine-drinking ritual said, "I'll give an *S:* Since none may count on the morrow / Cheer up this downcast heart right now / Drink wine in the moonlight O moon-face, that the moon / May shine bright and yet find us not."

An old man with a pleasant countenance holding a bowl of wine said, "I'll give a *W*." He recited: "We lost all our force once separation's sorrow came / In pain we perished once the remedy from us parted."

I looked at their faces more closely and with increased

[56] A famous Sufi and poet who contributed extensively to the evolution of Sufi tradition.

[57] A traditional poetic game. The first participant recites a poem, and the second participant must in turn recite a poem whose first line starts with the last letter of the previous poem, following which a third participant continues, and so on. The features of the game cannot be reproduced in translation.

respect. Did this mean Ferdowsi and Mowlavi and Rudaki and Suhrawardi were really here? Or Hallaj and Nezami and Saadi? Farabi and Razi and Biruni? Khwarizmi, the founder of algebra and trigonometry and the prime meridian? Jabir ibn Hayyan, the founder of the science of chemistry? That couple then must be Leyli and Majnun, and that young woman dressed in silk and the tall man with the regal expression holding one another in each other's arms in the corner and whispering in each other's ears, might that be Bijan and Manijeh?[58]

Were they alive, or I dead? Eblis and the others nodded their heads in approval at the poets' poetry. Eblis, seeing how dumbfounded I was, indicated two young people entwined in each other in a corner exchanging amorous caresses and said, "Those two are Zarer and Atousa."[59] Another couple: Shahrzad and Shahriyar.[60] And another: Vis and Ramin.[61]

"What is this?" I asked.

"The Assembly of the Favored. The pillars of culture and science of this land. The number of these individuals never diminishes; rather, in every century a modest number is added to them. When one of them dies, they come here, and centuries before someone like them is born again and takes on their responsibility."

"What sets them apart from others?" I asked.

"The love and responsibility they bear in their hearts," she said.

I was wondering about their thoughts when she answered: "The heart guides thought. If the heart is beautiful, then thought will also move along the right path."

"This cave is much bigger than what you see," she continued.

[58] Two lovers from ancient Iran whose story is found in Ferdowsi's Shahnameh.

[59] Two lovers from Achaemenid times.

[60] Two lovers, the main characters of the *Thousand and One Nights*. The original book is called the *One Thousand Legends* (in Persian, *Hezâr Afsân*).

[61] Two lovers from the Parthian period. Their story was versified by Asad Gorgani in the eleventh century.

"A great many live in the alcoves and shabestans[62] that lie further along that way. Can you see that man over there, writing something on paper? He is the one who calculated the value of *pi* for the first time and came up with decimals—even the four basic operations of arithmetic you learn at school, you owe to him."[63] I looked at him in surprise. I had never learned anything about him, whether in history or math lessons.

Eblis, who seemed to enjoy watching my astonished expression, continued. "Or that one, who not only proved that the world is round centuries before Galileo, as well as calculating its circumference, but even knew that it rotated on its own axis and around the sun."[64] As I looked at her in amazement, she smiled, indicated another man, and said, "You won't believe this one at all. Ten centuries ago he reported on the existence of the galaxy Andromeda."[65] She looked around with eyes from which rained flashes of joy, and said, "And that one there discovered the law of the refraction of light."[66]

I looked wide-eyed at the people around me, squirming from embarrassment. Why didn't I know all this? "I'll say this and then I'm done," Eblis said, wickedly. "Do you see that woman sitting by the water channel, writing?" I could see her. "She is busy noting down the sound of the stream. Your ancestors were such subtle thinkers that they invented a form of writing exclusively for recording the sounds of nature, animals, birds, rain and streams." I couldn't bear it any longer. Why had we been told none of this at school? What if she had made all this

[62] A shabestan is a large underground space with tall columns that is usually found in the traditional architecture of mosques, houses, palaces, and schools in Iran.

[63] Referring to Jamshid Kashani, a 14th-century Iranian scientist, known as Al-Kashi in the West.

[64] Referring to Abu Reyhan Biruni, an Iranian scholar and polymath of the 11th century.

[65] Referring to Abdulrahman Sufi Razi, scientist of the 10th century.

[66] Referring to Ibn Sahl, a physicist and optician of the 10th century.

up? "If our ancestors were this intelligent, how come we got our writing from the Arabs?" She chuckled. "Before they took over Iran, the Arabs had neither writing nor science, nor even architecture," she said. "Exactly the opposite of your ancestors. The ancient Iranians loved to invent scripts. Even Zoroaster invented one. In those times they even had a script used exclusively for correspondence between kings within the country. They had another script that was only for writing scientific and philosophical books, and yet another script only for religious texts. What's even more interesting is that they had mastered all languages and they were easy-going people who wrote letters to the king of every country in that country's language." I said, hopelessly, "So what happened then that we ended up in this dismal state?" "You have answered that yourself," she said. "You have become cut off from your past."

As I stared at the people around me, I thought of how, despite all these lost sources of pride, being Iranian was still a great reason to feel proud. As usual she read my mind, and said something that I have never forgotten. "All the same, bear in mind: you are Iranian with what you build, not with what you have lost." Then she turned back to the inhabitants of the cave and said, "Among these people there are a hundred with a heart like Jamshid's, eighty with a heart like Fereydoun's, forty with a heart like Rostam's, twelve resembling Faranak's, seven resembling Zoroaster's, five people with a heart like Kay-Khosro's, three like Mithra's, and only one with a heart like Cyrus's."

When I heard these great names, the hairs on my body stood on end. I wanted to kneel respectfully before them or kiss their hands and feet, but embarrassment held me back. There was fragrant, freshly brewed tea on the fire and its perfume had spread everywhere. It occurred to me that I might at least perform some service. I felt that I wanted to be their servant or even their maid; to sweep under their feet, make their beds, wash their clothes. To organize their books and tools for them. I wanted them to give me orders for an entire lifetime and for me to obey them unquestioningly. This feeling, with this intensity, was new to me, but I took great delight in experiencing it. I got up and took all the dirty dishes off the table, washing them in the spring in the corner of the cave before drying them and putting them back on the table. Then I poured tea into earthenware bowls for everyone and offered it to them one by one; they accepted. When they took the tea from me, I looked at the elements of their faces, at their eyes, at the wrinkles of their brows, at the shape of their noses and at their lips, and said to myself, "Am I really giving tea to Rudaki? Vameq and Azra? Suhrawardi and Eyn ol-Qozzat Hamadani? To Zakariya Razi and Sadee?" I wanted to burst from excitement. If I told all this even to Khanom Joon, she would not believe me. The moshaereh kept going even as they drank tea and until someone said: "It's time."

Immediately, each person got up and went into a corner. Two or three old men went over to the library and stood or sat there and started reading. Here and there a handful of couples were busy with amorous caresses. A few people stood all on their own facing the tree. It was like a scene from a play. Eblis and I were still at the table; she, looking cheerful, had put one hand under her chin and bit on an apple as she watched.

The Peri-like Young Woman with her crown of flowers and cotton shirt climbed a wooden ladder that had been leaning against the tree and perched on one of the upper branches. She was holding a bunch of flowers. She sat some six or seven meters above the ground. I realized that something resembling blood had congealed on the stone floor of the cave, underneath the tree. I was surprised. My food got stuck in my throat. There was silence. Breaths were trapped in chests. Somewhere water was dripping with a monotonous rhythm.

Drip . . .
Drip . . .
Drip, drip . . .
Drip . . .

Drip . . .

Drip, drip . . .

The Peri-like Young Woman turned to the Handsome Young Man and from up the tree said, "I am your restless lover and you still don't take any notice of me."

My heart plunged when I heard these words. I started thinking of Behnam and me. Despite how angry I was with him, I could feel just how much I missed him. The Young Man was sitting on a stone slab, his head down. Wasn't he another Behnam? Or a potential Behnam? "I can't bear it any longer," he said. And put his head in his hands.

"Answer me," the Girl said emphatically.

"I've always said it and I'll say it again," the Young Man replied. "I am suspicious of love. Love is an illusion. When all other feelings are fickle, why should love be different?"

The Girl said, in a baleful voice, "Still, after hundreds of years, after thousands of years, has my persistent love for you not been proven?"

The Young Man put his head in his hands once more and said helplessly, "No . . . no. My opinion hasn't changed."

"How is that possible?" the Girl asked. "After all these centuries you are still suspicious of love . . . of me?"

The Young Man lifted his head again and said mournfully, "My father, who had once loved my mother and us, abandoned all of us to leave Shiraz with another woman and go to Bukhara. And he never once looked back. We loved him and his abandonment killed us, although he never realized this. After that our mother, who loved us, took my two sisters and went off to Balkh, leaving me and my brother with our uncle. He was always kind to us, but a little while later he ended up poor and sent us to the governor of the city to become his servants. The governor, despite being famous for his kindness and care for the people, made us work like slaves, and at night took us to his bedroom. That is how we grew up little by little until my brother, who was my only confidant and knew the sorrow of my dark days and nights, left me for the love of a young woman and went off to Samarqand. A little after that the only young woman I liked left me for a merchant and became his wife. This was how that I realized that no love in life is enduring. I understood that lovers become haters; the joyful, sad. The just become oppressors; the kindly, jealous. Only loneliness endures."

The Young Man sighed and continued. "I have no trust in love. Even if you ask me the same thing in a thousand years' time, you'll hear the same reply. Done."

"What do you have trust in?" the Girl asked.

The Handsome Young Man raised his head. Looking at the walls and objects in the cave, he said, "I've told you a thousand times . . ."

In a tone like a judge's, the Girl urged, "Say it again."

Weary and helpless, the Young Man said, "I do know at least that caves last, roads last, rivers last. I know that my shoes will stay with me for years to come. I know that wine from Shiraz gets better the older it gets. I know that the trees never leave one another, the mountains remain where they are, and that horses never betray each other. I have trust in these things. I have trust in nature, death, loneliness, and in the transience of life."

The Girl, her head down, plucked the petals from the flowers in her hand and threw them down to the ground from up in the tree, singing as she did so:

"My wish was for you to make me moist like the rain
"And to take me in your arms like the mist
"My wish was for you to call me
"And tremble each time you murmured my name
"I will die without your love
"Every day
"Even though no one holds mourning ceremonies for me."

One of the old men next to the bookcases addressed the Girl enthusiastically, as if encouraging an actor in a theatre: "That was great. That was great."

Yet a tear welled up in the eye of the woman playing the harp and several men shook their heads in sorrow. There was a lump blocking my throat. I thought of myself and Behnam. Of how he had always made me certain of his love, and yet at the same time had abandoned me in a vacuum of doubt and silence. Was this Handsome Young Man right? Or was the peri-faced young woman? What would life mean, how could it be beautiful, without love, even of short duration? I thought that perhaps what mattered was to have felt love—to be capable of caring for someone unrelated to yourself more than you did for your own life, even if they were bound to leave.

Gesturing to the book he was holding, Hafez said, "Look . . . I'm of the belief that those who aren't actually in love are dead. And this is the verse that comes afterwards, as witness: 'For whomever in this circle lives not through love, / Though not dead, I rule thou shalt say the funeral prayers.'"

The Girl up the tree threw the plucked flowers she was holding down to the ground, waved at us with a kindly and yet melancholy smile, and then suddenly flung herself down.

Without knowing what I was doing, I leapt up and screamed: "No!"

Everyone was frozen where they were. Eblis, however, was still enjoying the spectacle and from time to time took a bite of the apple she was holding.

The young woman's head shook on the stone slab for a few moments, then she died.

Someone got up and wearily said, "Who's going to deal with the body?"

Several people casually shrugged and disappeared into the darkness of the cave. Several others stared at the body, lost in their sadness. The body lay on the floor and a narrow rivulet of blood ran down from the head. I was frozen, stupefied.

Meanwhile, her lover, the Handsome Young Man, was agitated. He sprang up, lifted his tense and wet face from between his two palms, ran over to the peri-faced young woman's corpse and cradled her head to his chest, roaring and crying: "No . . . no!"

Howling and weeping, he kissed the Young Woman's flowing, blood-soaked hair, then moaned: "No . . . that's enough . . . How many times have I said it, that's enough! I cannot bear it any longer. I *cannot* bear it any longer."

At last two young women got up from a corner, extracted the body from the Young Man's embrace, and dragged it to the back of the cave, somewhere in the darkness.

I got up to console the Young Man, but he ran out of the cave, sobbing.

Once he'd left, everybody gathered round the table and began talking about everyday matters. They spoke of food and poetry and philosophy and culture and stars and mathematics, as if a few moments before no such catastrophe had taken place before their very eyes.

Several hours went by. I was still confused and astounded by that scene and then by what had been said. An old man with a bent back and pale eyes came over to me. He was holding Mowlana's *Masnavi.*

"Are you still perplexed by what that young woman did?" he asked.

"Yes," I said. "What wisdom was at work in what happened? It seemed everyone knew but me."

"It's not only you who doesn't know," he said. "That young man, that lover, he doesn't know either," he said.

"How come?" I asked.

"Love's companion is nothingness / For as long as thou art, how should love appear?" he recited.

I looked at him. Realizing that I had not understood, he went on: "One day the lover went to the door of the beloved's house. From behind the door, the beloved asked, 'Who art thou?' The lover said, 'Me!' but the beloved did not open the door. Another day, the lover again knocked at the door of the beloved's house. Again the beloved asked, 'Who art thou?'

'Me!' the lover said, but again the door remained closed. On the third day, the lover, more in love than ever, went to the door of the beloved's house and knocked. 'Who art thou?' the beloved asked. 'It's me,' the lover said. 'There is in this dwelling but room for one,' the beloved said. The lover went away and for months pondered what this might mean, before eventually returning to the lover's house and knocking on the door. The beloved asked, 'Who art thou?' 'Thou,' said the lover. The beloved opened the door and the lover entered in."

Though I was still absorbed in what he'd said, he smiled and moved away from me. I fell asleep right there beside the fireplace. In the morning I woke up to the sound of a jolly voice. It was that very peri-faced Young Woman who the day before had thrown herself down to her death from the tree. I leapt up, horrified. Just like she had done the previous day, she came over to me, took my hand kindly, and playfully ran over to the middle of the cave, taking me with her. She whirled around and said, "Isn't it beautiful here? It's beautiful . . . it's amazing . . . Look. *Look.*"

The words sprang out of my mouth: "You're alive?"

"Was I supposed to have died?" she asked, laughing. "I have a thousand things I wish to accomplish while I'm still young."

Then just like the previous day she spun around playfully in the middle of the space of the cave so that her long, blue-white, cotton dress would turn in a circle around her. Holding a bunch of wild flowers, she passed by the various people there and bid them good morning.

Several hours elapsed before I fathomed the depth of this nightmare . . . Every day at exactly 5:13 P.M. everyone settled in their places for the Young Woman to once more ascend the tree and say to the Young Man, "I am your restless lover," and for the Young Man to once more reply, "I am suspicious of love." The Young Woman would once again say, "So in what do you trust?" and the Young Man would again answer, "In mountains and horses and trees," leading the Young Woman to once again sing hopelessly and throw herself down and for blood to flow from her head and for her to die and for the Young Man cry madly and shout that he could no longer put up with watching this catastrophe and that he did not know how he could rid himself of the evil of this recurring nightmare. Then a number of people would once more drag the body to the back of the cave until the day after, and the day after that, and the day after that. Until perhaps one day the Young Man might finally understand that if he wanted the Young Woman not to kill herself, if he no longer wanted to witness that catastrophe that had occurred for the first time two or three thousand years ago, then all he had to do was to understand the secret of love. To trust love and to give himself to it. Allow that feeling to be his guide in life. Yet he did not understand. He feared giving himself to this feeling and resisted it.

I was astonished by everything: the cave's mysteries and secrets, the people in it and the suicide scene that was repeated there each day at exactly 5:13 P.M., until one day a man whose job it was to buy tormented consciences appeared at the cave entrance, to free the Handsome Young Man from his suffering forever.

The Purchaser of Tormented Consciences asked for the Handsome Young Man as soon as he appeared at the cave entrance. They gestured with their hands to where he was sitting in a corner, deep in thought, with the Peri-faced Young Woman sitting next to him, casually braiding a crown of flowers around which bees were buzzing. Addressing the Young Man, the Purchaser of Tormented Consciences said, "I hear you want to be rid of this nightmare." The Young Man leapt up and replied, "Yes, I want to. Tell me . . . tell me what I should do."

"Come with me," the man said.

The man went ahead, and we followed him without question until, in the middle of the forest, he reached a moss-clad gravestone. The Peri-faced Young Woman, still twirling around in her long, blue-white, cotton dress and holding the crown of flowers, sat down laughing beside the grave and ran her hand over it, before turning to the Young Man cheerfully and saying, "My grave!"

With a sad and tormented expression, the Young Man said, "I know. I buried you myself."

The Purchaser of Tormented Consciences turned to the Young Man and said, "I will buy your tormented conscience for one gold coin. Are you selling?"

"Free me from this suffering," said the Young Man, "and I don't need anything from you." The man said, "To do this I'll have to kill you. Are you still selling?"

The Young Man was stunned. He stood, dumbfounded, not knowing what to say.

"You cannot put up with this tormented conscience anymore. And apart from me, there is nobody who can accomplish this."

We were standing in a ring around the two of them. The Young Woman got up from beside her own grave and went toward the Young Man, calmly took his hand and caressed him. She looked at his face, smiled, and said gently, "You absolutely don't have to . . . You shouldn't do something you don't want to do."

When the Purchaser of Tormented Consciences saw that the Young Man was unable to decide, he turned his back to go. But the Young Man ran over to the purchaser and together they went back to the grave.

"Kill me," the Young Man said. "But know that I am not in love and never wanted to be. I am sick and tired of love, but I didn't want her to kill herself because of me. I didn't want her to fall in love with me again in every lifetime and once again die of hopelessness."

The Purchaser shrugged his shoulders as if to say, "You know best." The Young Woman let go of the Young Man's hand and said, "So after death then you don't want to stay next to me?"

"No!" the Young Man said, infuriated. "I will neither stay next to you, nor anyone else! After death, I just want to sleep."

Tears welling up, the Young Woman sat down beside her own grave and wept bitterly. We all felt terrible for her, but was there actually anything anyone could do? Was it even possible to force someone to fall in love?

"We have to perform the correct sacrificial ceremonies," the Purchaser of Tormented Consciences said. "Meticulously." Then he took a gold coin out of his pocket and gave it to the Young Man. The Young Man said, "What good is this coin to me when I die?" The man said, "The tradition must be upheld."

He paused, then asked, "What am I being sacrificed for?"

"On account of your own ignorance," the purchaser said. "You are being sacrificed because year after year, in numerous lives, the opportunity was presented to you to trust in love, to accept love, yet selfishly and stubbornly you refused. All those centuries, all those years, every day the opportunity was presented to you, and yet you wasted each one."

"I just wanted to live," the Young Man shouted angrily. "That's all. Why couldn't I live like everyone else? Does everyone really fall in love?"

"No!" the man said. "That's why everyone dies and then it's done. But you can see that you're still alive. You must be worthy to live after death."

The Young Man lowered his head in surrender. The man took a white cloth out of his knapsack. He told the Young Man to strip and wrap the cloth around himself. The Young Man obeyed. When he had undressed, I saw a tattooed image of a bull and a lion tussling together on his back. I stared at that beautiful and noble body that would in a few minutes' time be buried underground and forever vanished from the world of being. I thought of Behnam. Of Mehrab. Bahman. Iraj. All the young innocents killed in the revolution or in this war. Tears filled my eyes.

Then the man took out a wooden-handled knife along with a whetstone and a pitcher of water. Next he turned to Majnun and said, "Go directly east. You'll reach your own tree.[67] Break a few large branches from it and bring them here." Majnun went off meekly to comply with the command, and a few minutes later, as the Purchaser of Tormented Consciences was sharpening his knife with the whetstone and the water, returned with a number of long, leafy branches. The Purchaser ordered the branches to be spread on the ground and the Young Man to sit on them cross-legged. Leyli and Majnun helped one another spread the branches. As the Young Man sat on them, my heart was beating furiously. I wanted to howl with grief. I don't know why I had a feeling that he was Behnam. That he was Mehrab. That he was Bahman. That he was Iraj. One of the Zorvan baker's boys. Or even one of Nader's or Reza's . . . or anyone's. What difference did it make? I wanted to grab the Purchaser's arm and tell him to let him go. Him with his gorgeous body . . . Forgive him, because of his youth. Forgive him, because of life . . . But I had lost control of my arms and legs and I didn't know what was right or wrong.

I looked at the rest of them. They were all just observing, in a state of surrender and calm. Occasionally they whispered to one another and sipped gently from their bowls of wine, watching the scene of sacrifice. They were so unperturbed that it was if they were just watching some performance. Shams and Mowlana were standing next to me. I wondered whether they wanted to do something. Even the Young Woman, the lover, was calm. But I wasn't. My heart was pounding furiously against my ribcage, so much so that I felt everyone must be able to hear it. Yet again I did nothing. I stood, my arms and legs shaking, and watched. Was I an observer once more? A good-for-nothing bystander? Wasn't it just like that time when I stood shoulder to shoulder with hundreds of others and watched as that rebellious young man was hanged right in front of us? What did they

67 The weeping willow. In Persian, it is called the Majnun Willow because its long, hanging branches resemble the head and hair of Majnun, who was always sad and crying for the love of Leyli.

say his name was? Majid? Which town had I seen him in? Now I could understand better. Majid wanted to plant a tree. That was why he laughed all the way to the gallows and waved at us, the good-for-nothing observers. It didn't matter to him that he couldn't sit under the tree he had planted.

The Purchaser of Tormented Consciences, who a few minutes earlier had kindled a fire in a corner, took a narrow stone slab out of his knapsack and found a place for it on the fire. Then he brought an earthenware vat and bowl. He poured a liquid from the vat into the bowl. Was it not haoma? In our mansion it was made from ephedra, but I knew that others made it from hemp seed or other things. Recalling the mansion my heart suddenly overflowed with warm and intimate memories of our house, family, garden and fields. How many months had I been away from them? How were Mom and Dad? What if something terrible had happened to Dad when I had had that nightmare? I needed to find a telephone in the first town I reached and call home. Where was Mehrab now? What were Mandana and Mina doing? What if Leyla had come back? In that, memories of home seemed unreal and far away. Even so, I missed everyone with great tenderness. The sounds of them talking in the rooms, of their laughter, of Khanom Joon's cane echoing in the hallways. The sound of Maryam and Shahnaz when they invited us to sit round the table to eat. The sound of the dishes of food and even the smells . . . the smell of Mom's darkroom . . . the smell of the flowers that Hasrat picked each day and put in vases in the house. The special smell Dad's room had: an old, deep scent mixed with cigarette smoke and incense and yellowing papers and ink. I even missed the smell of the room with the sacred fire. I wiped away my tears and thought that when I went back I would give permission for them to hold the Sedreh ceremonies for me—not simply for the sake of making Khanom Joon and Dad happy, but because now it seemed that I had a better grasp of the hidden meaning behind the sacred fire. I felt that I had to conserve history. I didn't understand why, but a sort of feeling of caretaking and belonging had come alive in me. I had to become the guardian. The guardian of all those modest but genuine things that had remained with us. All of a sudden the feeling that I might lose all those beauties, mysteries and secrets and sources of pride broke the lump in my throat and set my tears flowing so noisily that Eblis turned round to look at me.

I tried to wipe away my tears and turn my attention back to the Young Man. The Purchaser poured milk from a pitcher and mixed it with the drink. Then he stirred it with a barsam-stick.[68] After that, he scattered some seeds from a leather bag onto the heated stone slab. They were hemp seeds. Their pleasant scent spread through the air and I noticed that it gradually made everyone drunk and cheerful and laughing, although I continued to shed tears out of a deep pain. Even the Young Man's expression little by little became calm and resigned, and tension and unhappiness could no longer be seen in the lines on his face.

When everybody had gradually become cheerful and laughing and started bustling around, the Purchaser of Tormented Consciences knelt on both knees opposite the Young Man and handed him the bowl of electuary to drink of. He drained it obediently. A few moments later, a smile appeared on the corner of his lips. Little by little, I too came under the influence of the Shiraz wine and the hemp-seed fumes, beginning to feel drunk and high, but at the sight of that great, sharp knife in the man's hand, my heart began to pound again.

The purchaser addressed the Young Man. "Ready?"

The latter calmly nodded his head. I could see sorrow and fear in his eyes once more. His distressed face had turned red. The Purchaser stood up and walked behind him. He seized the Young Man's hair in one hand and pulled his head back, while with his other hand he raised the knife and placed it on

[68] A small branch cut from certain trees such as pomegranate, tamarisk, and haoma, and used in Zoroastrian prayer ceremonies.

his neck. I couldn't control myself any longer. I screamed and sprinted over to the Purchaser, clinging to his arms and yelling, "Please, I beg you, forgive him! Because of his youth. Have pity on his beauty. What sin has he committed by not falling in love? It's not his fault that the beloved killed herself. It's the lover who must be content with whatever comes their way from the beloved. The lover must be the beloved's follower. Let him go. Forgive him." I wept bitterly.

But the Purchaser would not relent. He untangled his arms from mine and once again brought the knife toward the Young Man's neck. I threw myself at the man's feet and pleaded: "Why don't you just kill me? If someone is supposed to die, let it be me. Whether I'm in this world or not doesn't make much difference, but this young man has suffered so much already. Let him go. Rid him of the evil of his tormented conscience but let him stay alive. Let him live his life. Attain his dreams."

I shed tears and pleaded. I caught sight of the others through my tears. They were all whispering to one another at once and observing us. I turned my head to look at that Young Woman, at the lover, and wailing and angry I said, "What kind of lover are you that you allow them to kill your beloved like this in front of you? Get up and save him."

Yet the Young Woman, not appearing to hear my voice at all, was stroking the moss on her own grave and mourning herself by intoning a plaintive elegy under her breath. The purchaser shook his legs free of my arms. But for a third time, I threw myself on the Young Man, distraught. I felt an unprecedented strength in myself, one whose source I was ignorant of. I felt that I and this Young Man, whose existence I had been entirely unaware of until a few days previously, were one and the same. I felt that to kill him was to kill me. I howled: "What point is there in killing him? Love just comes to you, it can't be learnt. It just has to happen to him. You cannot force someone to be in love. Leave him alone. Leave him alone!" And I hugged the Young Man tight.

Shedding tears with my eyes closed, I clung tightly to the Young Man. Then all of a sudden the sound of the spectators' whispering and the Young Woman's elegy broke off. Only the birds, the leaves rustling in the breeze, and the sorrowful music of my body could be heard. My eyes were still closed. When I opened them, I saw that everyone was standing around me, looking at me with joyful expressions. A few of them even clapped, as if they'd been watching a performance for pleasure. The Purchaser of Tormented Consciences and the lover were among them and stood staring at me. Why were they looking at me like that? A regal-looking man whom I had never seen before was also standing there in the middle. Next to Eblis. What if this were Kay-Khosro? I couldn't figure out what was going on. I looked up. The peacock was perched behind my head and had unfolded its magnificent canopy above me. The Young Man was still in my arms. I released him, dumbfounded. The Handsome Young Man smiled at me. His expression was joyful. His eyes looked like he had never witnessed any sorrow. He stood up next to me and then disappeared into the crowd.

Eblis took a step toward me and asked, "Are you in love with this young man?"

"No," I said, surprised. "No. Not at all."

"So why did you weep for him?" Eblis asked. "Why did you move heaven and earth to save him?"

"You don't have to be in love with someone to save them," I said.

"That's right," she said. "But you should be in love. Love's force makes a person brave and just."

"In that moment, I felt that to kill him would be like killing me," I said.

"And that's exactly what love means," replied Eblis.

Just then, I saw that the Peri-faced Young Woman and the Handsome Young Man had split from the crowd and were coming over to me. They looked at me, smiling, as if they had forgotten what a catastrophe had been on the verge of taking place just minutes ago. The Young Man sat down opposite me and, taking honey with his hand from the bowl that the Peri-faced Young Woman was holding, rubbed it on my lips and hands and said, "Blessings be upon you, lioness."

The Purchaser of Tormented Consciences took a step closer to me, inflicted a wound on my cheek with the sword he was holding, and said, "From the mansion, from the tree, from the palace and the temple to here, you have ascended four steps." Then he took my left hand in his and bound an iron band around my wrist. On it was written, "Mithra suffices me."

Eblis was standing facing me, looking at me with an approving smile. I was tired and confused, and as I licked off the honey from my lips, I suddenly felt extremely faint and wanted to go to sleep right there on the branches of the Majnun willow, amid the dizzying scents of the hemp seeds. And I did.

Chapter Fifteen

Shhhhh! . . . Quiet! . . . Listen . . . Now two hundred . . . Five hundred . . . Under the ground a thousand bodies have pressed their ears up against the asphalt upon which the demonstrators are tramping and are listening to them chanting slogans against them with a made-to-order, half-hearted anger. Against those two hundred, five hundred, one thousand bodies and millions of the living: Death to the Opponents of the Jurist's Rule! All of these two hundred, five hundred, one thousand bodies were against the Rule of the Jurist. Correct! But what about the nine-year-old Karoon?

It was one of the annual February 11 demonstrations. The anniversary of the victory of the 1979 revolution. It was taking place in the 1980s, 1990s, 2000s, or later. The government had spent hundreds of thousands of dollars on the demonstration so it could mount a spectacle in the streets, then film and photograph it for domestic and foreign television channels to show. It was one of those demonstrations where the participants—even those bent double by poverty and by the regime's injustice—constantly wanted to punch America and Israel hard in the mouth with their hijab. One of those demonstrations where they got unfortunate women, prostitutes or prisoners, with strange multi-colored clothes and heavy makeup, to poke the freedom of women into the eyes of the respectable viewers of state television, as well as to talk about revolutionary ideals and Islamic welfare so that in return they might accept a lighter sentence. It was one of those demonstrations whose participants were put on government buses in little villages before being brought to the main squares in cities where they were given a boxed drink and a sandwich, in return for which they would have to chant pre-arranged revolutionary slogans as part of the spectacle in the streets. "Our movement is an Islamic one / Following the Supreme Leader is a duty for everyone! Long may he be remembered, our Imam Khomeini / Long live our Leader Khamenei!"

Those made-to-order demonstrators stared into the government's television cameras so that they could read from a text that had been dictated to them: the duty of every Muslim Iranian is first and foremost to be faithful to the ideals of the Revolution and the blood of the martyrs, so that in this way they stand up to the Global Arrogance and above all to world-devouring America.

Even their clothes were strikingly different from ordinary people's, from those of the passers-by uninterested in the demonstration; as usual, at the front of their ranks were the clerics in their cloaks and turbans, as well as a few lowly government officials in the unironed jackets that were the hypocritical symbol of the humility and poverty of those responsible for the revolution. Behind them were the people, wearing black and gray. The female demonstrators were clad in chadors and maqnaehs and on the headbands around their foreheads were written Arabic words: [69]...مهدی ادرکنی, ...[70]...یوم الله. Even if it was in Persian, it was nothing better:جانم فدای رهبر.[71]

Mahin was one of the passersby. By the 1980s, or 1990s, or 2000s, or later, she had long put out of mind her love for Iraj and she was sure her sister Mojgan had died by Iraj's side. Because if not, why hadn't she gotten in touch with her? She hadn't called. Sent a letter. A message . . . Nothing. As she did every day, Mahin was going to the library. For a while to the

[69] Mahdi, aid me.

[70] God's day.

[71] My life is a sacrifice for the Leader.

Parliamentary Library, for a while to the National Library, for a while to Tehran University Library. Although she had succeeded in obtaining her doctorate from that very university in the field of Ancient Cultures and Languages, she had never been permitted to work, on account of her opinions and her sharp tongue, as well as because of the execution and assassination of her mother and her mother's two brothers, which was worse. What's more, she had been born in November, a Scorpio with a sting, vengeful and fiery, ready to participate in each and every anti-government demonstration, even at the cost of her own life, so that either the regime would fall in revenge for the blood of her mother and beloved uncles, or she would be killed, stinging herself.

She had thought a great deal about death. Time and time again she had seen herself in his eyes. Once, they had even made love. She had seen him on the eighty-seventh day of solitary confinement, looking like they did in Hollywood movies, standing in a corner of the cell, tall of stature, clad in black, grave, unflappable, and mysterious. She quickly recognized him. As if it were the fate of those who have looked into the eyes of death to identify him. "You've come at the right time," Mahin said. "My blood is on their hands." Death nodded gravely and pushed back the hood of his cloak. What a strangely good-looking, attractive man he was. Mahin had been on hunger strike for seven days. She wanted them to give her permission to call her father. She only drank two glasses of water a day, and for the rest of the time she lay in a corner half-awake, half-asleep, raved deliriously or muttered things to her mother, Azar, or waited for the door to open any moment and for them to drag her off, sit her in front of the camera, and force her to confess.

"Am I going to be in pain?" she asked.

In a deep, rasping, calm voice, Death said, "Not at all."

Mahin shook her head and all of a sudden started laughing at the thought that in her waking-sleeping state she was talking to Death, her laughter gradually increasing until she could not stop: *hahahaha . . . hohohoho.* She laughed so much that tears were flowing from her eyes and the warden opened the little window and snapped, "What the hell's wrong with you?" Mahin, however, did not answer, but instead with great difficulty tried to swallow her laughter, while the warden, muttering foul insults under his breath, went back to whatever he had been doing. "I'm officially going insane," Mahin said to herself, and burst out laughing again. She remembered the inherited family madness.

"You haven't gone mad," said Death. "It is me."

With her last remaining energy, Mahin suddenly sat up and stared at him.

"Does the other side look like the movies too?" she asked.

Death laughed and said, "Depends which movie."

"'What Dreams May Come?'" Mahin asked.

"It's more like 'Solaris,'" Death said.

This time Mahin put her hand on her belly and laughed louder. Death laughed too: *hahahahaha.* Mahin laughed still louder: *hahahahaha, hohohohoho.* She understood absolutely nothing of why she was laughing so much all of a sudden. At Death's laughter? At fear? Death can provoke strange reactions in people. This time the warden turned the latch roughly and kicked Mahin flush in the face the moment he entered the cell. She was in pain. Terrible pain. As blood flowed from the corner of her lip, she tried to control her laughter, but was unable to. She turned stubborn. She laughed louder and said to the warden, "Look . . . over there, in the corner . . . His Excellency Death has come personally to meet with me. Isn't that funny? *Hahahahaha . . . hohohohoho . . . hahahahaha . . . hohohohoho.*" She was truly laughing from the bottom of the heart. Like drunk people, or like someone who's smoked a joint. The warden, on edge, scowled at the dark corner of the cell, but of course saw nothing. This time he spat on the ground, and as he slammed shut the iron cell door said, "Crazy, good-for-nothing bitch." Once he was outside, he opened the little window and, with angry eyes scanning the little four-meter cell in its entirety, shouted, "If I hear your voice again I'll come fix you for good, you daughter of a whore." And he shut the window with a crash. When Mahin heard this insult a second time, she held her head in her hands and her laughter slowly turned into sobs. For some long minutes, her shoulders shook with the intensity of the crying. Eventually she lifted her head and addressed His Excellency Death. "So why are you just standing there? Finish it off." Death came calmly over, sat down next to Mahin, and placed her head on his chest. He took the scarf off her head and caressed her hair gently. The lump in Mahin's throat swelled further. Then she cried even more. Deeply and loudly . . . bitterly . . . so much that the front of His Excellency Death's black shirt was drenched with tears. Eventually, she lifted her nose, her eyes sparkling with the excitement of an idea that had occurred to her, a smile on her lips, and said, "Do you know what my last wish is?"

"Tell me," Death said, kindly.

"For aragh sagi and pepperoni pizza from Shams."

She had not even finished speaking when a shot glass and two liters of aragh sagi, fifty-five percent alcohol, made at the factory in Qazvin in the Shah's time, and a pepperoni pizza from the Shams pizza shop appeared in front of her. Mahin, tearful, laughed in disbelief and said, "I didn't know you could do these kinds of miracles." And she drank glass after glass without even offering one to Death. After drinking, she ate the pizza too, dead drunk and full up, and she belched, hiccupped, and eventually said, "I apologize." Then, casually, she said, "I was never able to fall in love, but it looks like I have fallen in love with you this very instant." Death looked at her in surprise.

Mahin continued. "Has anybody ever fallen in love with you before?"

Death shuddered, startled. He shook his head.

"You see," Mahin said. "In the end, everyone's life has its shortcomings. Even yours, Your Excellency Death." And she smiled.

"To be honest, I'd never thought about it," Death said.

"Maybe that's one of the blessings of your life," Mahin said. "When someone doesn't know about something, they don't wish for it. Like that homeless boy who didn't even know what a wish is, but as soon as he found out what it meant, yearned bitterly for it every day until one day he killed himself. Or me, who when I'd never eaten pizza, never felt like eating it, but who during these eighty-seven days in solitary have wanted to eat it every day." She hiccupped, and as her head sank onto Death's shoulder, she fell into a deep slumber.

A few hours later, in the middle of night, she started from sleep. Her head was still on Death's chest, and Death was calmly playing with her hair. Mahin did not stir. She calmly placed her hand on Death's chest. She wanted to kiss him so much. She had never felt such an uncontrollable desire in herself before. Death gently lifted her chin and kissed her on the lips. Mahin answered him with long kisses of her own, and in this way they made love three times before the sun rose, and each time Death plunged his manhood into her, he found her a virgin.

After they'd made love the first time, Death said, "Now that I think of it, it's strange that I've never made love before. I hadn't even though about it."

"So, let me give you the good news: from this point on, you'll never be free of desire," Mahin said.

And she once more plunged into Death's body and soul, and so pleasurably and subtly and creatively did she make love with him that after the second time they'd made love, Death said, "I've never felt pleasure as lovely as this in all my life."

And Mahin said, "Most likely you'll never experience it again, because I have never loved anyone this much."

And once more she dived into his body and soul in such a way that after they had made love a third time, Death said, "After this, my body no longer belongs to me. Without you, I will no longer have access to my body."

This time Mahin, tired and at the height of pleasure, breathing hard, said, "Well, then, I no longer have anything left to accomplish in this world. The people will, with time, take their revenge on the regime. I finally managed to carry out my mother's last wishes and fall in love and discover the most beautiful feminine dimension of myself. Now I am ready to die with no regrets. Hurry up, get to work before I change my mind."

Death stood up, slowly and deliberately, got dressed, his back to her, and then stood, hesitating. As if he couldn't bring himself to leave. He turned to Mahin once more. He looked at her passionately and lovingly. He sat down next to her and embraced her tightly and said, "I thank you. After thousands of years of being alive, you were the first woman to love me." Then he got up to go.

"Blessings," he said.

"So why won't you kill me?" Mahin asked.

"I have decided not to," Death said.

"But is that possible?" Mahin asked.

"Occasionally . . . rarely . . . it happens," Death said.

Then as he pulled his hood down towards his face, he said, "Once, years ago, I went up into the heights of Shahran with a driver and we drank four liters of aragh sagi together, got blind drunk, twirled our underwear around our fingers, and danced and talked and laughed so much that I decided not to kill him."

Then he paused, smiled, and said, "I think I have a particular weak spot when it comes to people who drink aragh sagi during the final moments of their lives." He laughed. Mahin too.

Before vanishing into the dark recesses of the cell, Death stopped once more and asked, "Will we see each other again?"

"If you want to, definitely," Mahin said, kindly and happily.

His Excellency Death gave a smile and vanished, and this was how Mahin realized that she would never fear death again. For that reason, as often as she could, she made her way to the front of the demonstrators at all the protests and shouted louder than anyone, "Death to the Oppressor / Whether the Shah or the Leader."

Mahin was for a time an unemployed university graduate, then for a time unemployed with a Master's, and finally unemployed with a doctorate. Like many others. But she turned over her impoverished life by publishing books and articles and translations in the field of ancient Iranian languages and culture. If her mother's two-bedroom apartment in Kakh Street hadn't been left to her, she would definitely have ended up homeless years before. After her father and mother, she had most loved her maternal uncle, Fereydoun Taban. She wanted to continue his work. Through her writing and research, she wanted to remind people that there is something valuable, something in this land which must be preserved beyond me and us, and that is the Iranshahri[72] thought and wisdom; an invisible thread entwined in the warp and weft of the legendary, classic, and contemporary texts. A thought that flowed in the works of Rudaki and Khayyam and Ferdowsi right up to Maestro Shajarian and Gholamreza Dadbeh, and whose secrets have for hundreds of years been taught clandestinely to only twelve people in each generation, so that they would be passed from person to person to reach the next generation. One of those people was her beloved uncle Fereydoun Taban.

Mahin was walking slowly next to the sidewalk and deep in these thoughts looked around her. As the demonstrators, fists clenched, feet stamping on the ground, repeated their rhythmic slogans in unison, albeit without enthusiasm, she suddenly heard a profound silence in parallel. It was a sound she had never heard before. Amid all the racket, this sound

[72] Iranshahr: Greater Iran, including the intellectual and cultural values of ancient Iran, to which individuals from various religions and ethnicities, within the geographical boundaries of Greater Iran, considered themselves citizens.

of silence was so deep and dark and real that she stood and listened carefully. She looked around her. She felt that this silence reached her from under her feet, from under the feet of the noisy demonstrators. Yet the other pedestrians continued walking along the sidewalk regardless, heeding neither the government demonstration in the street nor the sound of silence beneath their feet.

The people, everyone, at some time, in the 1980s, 1990s, 2000s, or later, had ceased to support the Islamic Revolution. The people, the very same ones who, disregarding the demonstration ordered from above, were going about their daily business on the sidewalks, had started to have doubts many years before. To mistrust. Many of them had tried to reform the situation, but when they saw that this regime was deaf and blind, they lost hope in the reforms as well, and in subsequent demonstrations chanted: "Principalist, Reformist / The Whole Thing's Over." But when they saw that no one had listened to these slogans either, they finally gave up trying. In general, they had had more than enough of the revolution and of the Islam that the regime represented, and in the last presidential elections they hadn't even bothered to vote. Enough!

For years now Mahin had been talking with her mother Azar in her head. Ever since that day . . . that first day, the day her mother was executed, on April 13, 1979. As she stood on a corner of the street listening to the sound of silence beneath her feet, Mahin thought, "Mom! It's as if all of the people have been crumpled up. Become their own waste. But I'm certain they're much better than that. Aren't I much better than this? Then so are the rest of them. We can be better. Yet what they've left of us is exactly that: cowed, fainthearted people who, because they cannot lord it over their superiors, lord it over those beneath them instead. Mom, in this country the distance between you and becoming a criminal is no more than the distance between you and your favorite clothes, your favorite hair color, your nail polish. It's the distance between you and the truth you want to speak. The distance between you and a kiss.

"Uncle Bijan's daughter Azadeh is right. When she got out of prison, she said that the workers are even more downtrodden than us journalists. Workers who protested because they hadn't received their wages ended up in prison. Or the environmentalists . . . Or the rappers. They arrest everyone for the ridiculous crimes of spying, activities against the security of the state, separatism, or even corruption on earth, film them giving a forced confession, emasculate and defame them, or, if they're obstinate, kill them quickly. What about Sattar Beheshti? He was arrested on October 31 and on November 4 they handed his body over to the poor old woman and when his uncle complained and asked how this kid was killed, the answer was 'Shut up. It's got nothing to do with you.' Or what about Kavous Seyyed-Emami? They arrested him on January 24 and handed over his body on February 8. As easy as that. Azadeh says she's following up in secret to find out exactly why environmental activists have been arrested. She's made some guesses: one of them is that environmental activists in distant regions have come across missile or atomic sites belonging to the Revolutionary Guards, or that they have encountered birth deformities due to the illegal burial of German, Austrian, and Russian atomic waste. As they were handing Seyyed-Emami's body over to his family, they said, 'He committed suicide. The medical officer has confirmed it too!'

"In the most recent general demonstrations, when people burnt down mosques and Basij bases and the offices of Friday prayer leaders out of anger and resentment, yet again they arrested young protesters and snuffed them out. They killed loads of them and flung their bodies here and there in rivers, lakes, and dams, and loads of them were destroyed in such a way that nobody has found their bodies yet. What's more horrifying than this, Mom, is the stealing of bodies. Can you even imagine it? They kill people and then they even steal their bodies. What about Kiyan Pir-Falak's mother? She took her son's body home in secret out of fear of the authorities, and using ice trays she'd borrowed from her neighbors she kept her son's body cold until she could bury him—Kian, the little boy who used to say 'In the name of the God of Rainbows'—far from the gaze of the police. Imagine if you had to knock on your neighbors' door and ask if they had ice trays for your nine-year-old son's corpse!

"Mom, these days our lives have become exactly like zombie movies. I mean, what do they do with these bodies? Some say they sell their organs. They do something to some of the prisoners that means that on release they either kill themselves or die of their own accord. Can you believe it? They give them bizarre injections . . . What about Yalda Aqa-Fazli? A girl of nineteen whose life did not reach the Yalda Night of her twentieth year. They arrested the girl at the Revolution Avenue demonstrations and took her to Qarchak Prison. When they released her three weeks later, she went straight home and committed suicide. To understand what was going on, our only option was to change the rules of grammar: the regime suicides them! The suicides that the regime carries out. When Yalda was in jail, after twelve days they gave her permission to make a call. She called her friend, and her friend recorded her voice. It trembled when she spoke, and yet there was a kind of honor and pride in it. In that shaking voice she said, 'I didn't express regret for what I'd done right up to the last moment. In my file they wrote that the criminal did not express regret. Listen, in the nineteen years of my life I've never been hit so much as I have been in these twelve days.'

"Yalda's best friend said that when she was released and she got to see her, her hands had turned black because she had held them over her face so that her interrogator's kicks wouldn't reach it. When her death was reported everywhere and people got their hands on the voice file, the regime whitewashed things again. 'The girl overdosed,' they said. Mom, these young people are beautiful like flowers . . . it's not just one or two of them . . . Their photos should've been on the covers of fashion and beauty magazines, or sports and health magazines, not on funeral announcements and gravestones . . . They were exactly like the gorgeous people in the tales of the Kings of the Peris . . . but now all of them are busy rotting in their graves. I keep thinking of the scene of Siavash's murder in Shahnameh:

His elephantine body on warm ground
They cast, fearing none;
Garui placed a bowl before him
And twisting it as one would a sheep's,
He cut that regal head from its body
And threw it down like a lofty cypress onto the grass.

"Mom, at the beginning of the revolution, they announced with pride when they killed a counter-revolutionary, but nowadays they kill so many people, they cannot admit it; they say that one fell off the upper floor, this one overdosed, that one had a burst appendix, this one committed suicide, and that one was killed by a burglar. And they say all this as if the easiest thing in this country is for young people to get killed . . . and a medical officer always confirms everything. Medical officers have confirmed the regime's secret killings with ridiculous scenarios so often over the years that I really think they must have studied creative writing and screenwriting rather than medical science.

"I feel so down every time I look at people's faces in the metro, in shared taxis, or in the street . . . I'm even afraid that people will commit mass suicide because their grief and rage and hopelessness is so great. It's not for nothing that international statistics have shown that we're the angriest and most depressed people in the world. Imagine one day you leave the house and see that thousands of people, all over the country, are standing facing the Azadi Tower, each holding a gun aimed at their head, when suddenly, just as the sun sets beneath the two bases of the tower, everyone at once, *bang* . . . Believe me, Mom, people have reached this point out of desperation. Even their kids are no longer a motivation for life and struggle. On the contrary—they kill both themselves and their children. God knows how often the news comes out of a family killing themselves out of shame and lack of money . . . Out of despair at having a normal life . . . What's worse is that children are killing themselves. Can you believe it? After all, wasn't there that eleven-year-old boy who killed himself because he didn't have a cellphone to use to join online lessons at school? Or Najmeh, that fifteen-year-old Afghan girl they said was so intelligent and sociable? These were not more shocking than the news of those two girls from Isfahan who, laughing and cheerful, filmed themselves with their phone camera before committing suicide, announcing that they would go and throw themselves off the Chamran footbridge in Isfahan. The cellphone camera even recorded the scene of them throwing themselves off the pedestrian bridge and the moment when their red blood began to flow on the gray asphalt . . . One of them, who wore glasses, turned to the phone camera and, laughing, said, 'Hello to everyone watching this video. Where are we now then? Right . . . the overpass!' The other girl, wearing a cream-colored scarf, corrected her: 'That overpass where the cars go under.' The girl with glasses continued: 'Yeah, that one. We had a bunch of stuff to say, but we didn't have time to write a will. We didn't have time to study either, let alone time for a will. *I am* a kun goshad[73] . . . *hahaha* . . . ' The girl with glasses said, 'I wanted to say I'll miss you all so much . . . I know what I'm doing may be a mistake, but, well . . . that's what circumstances require.' The one with the scarf asked, seriously, 'So where are we going? Hell? Paradise? Limbo?' The girl with glasses said, 'We'll let you know when we get there. We'll visit all of you in your dreams.'

[73] Lazy ass. "I am" in English in the original.

"And the circumstances required that they reached the bridge and hand in hand jumped off it and it was over . . .

"It's like we're all stuck in a dead-end street. One night I even dreamed of it. I dreamed that several people had gotten stuck in a dead-end street. I was one of them. To begin with they all looked at one another in astonishment, as if they were surprised that this street was a dead end. Then some of them started shouting and crying for help or even chanting slogans. As if someone might come to their aid . . . Or a miracle might occur and a street that had always been a through street would become so again. But nothing of the sort happened. Then they started pushing at the wall, but the wall stood firm. Then somebody said, 'But we can't go home. In front of us is blocked off, so come on, let's go up into the air with these balloons.' Then a bunch of colorful balloons fell out of their pocket. Everyone was delighted and they started blowing them up and then went up into the sky with them. First they sent the children and the younger people up. Those who reached the sky were happy and waved at those of us who'd stayed on the ground and blew us kisses, but then the sound of gunshots could be heard. Some said, 'It's human error, they didn't mean to fire at our children.' Others said, 'These are pellets, they're not lethal,' but Mom, they *were* . . . They blinded. People fired from behind that high, firm wall at the people who were flying and laughing cheerfully in the air, and one by one their bloody, innocent bodies fell on us . . . one . . . by . . . one . . .

"Personally, I'm past the stage of grief and depression. I'm at the stage of rage. I remembered Ferdowsi's poetry again. When the news of Siavash's murder reaches Rostam, Rostam howls with rage, throws on his coat of mail, and says:

Empty your hearts of all fear
Make the earth an Oxus with blood
By God till I live in this world
I shall stock my heart with revenge for Siavash.

"That's the mood I'm in now, Mom. As if they had killed my Siavash." Mahin stopped, her visage ablaze with these thoughts running through her, and in the midst of the indifferent, speeding pedestrians, pulled her white scarf, which had come loose, back up over her head and tightened it a little. She didn't have time to get arrested. She had to get ready for the next demonstrations. It had been a while now since her realization that this broad, long regime in its entirety, with its dozens of overt and covert and parallel military organizations, depended on this little scrap of a scarf, on this scrap of cloth.

She remembered clearly how her mother was arrested in the first protest of the compulsory hijab, on March 8, 1979, and was executed only a few weeks later, on account of that same scrap of cloth. She remembered that when they gave her permission to visit her in prison for the first and last time, her mother Azar seemed in good spirits, as usual, albeit strikingly thinner. Her mother had said, "I'm not alone. They've arrested dozens of women like me. Look around this room . . . That is Homa Darabi. That one's Rudabeh Fazayeli. That's Farzaneh Eskandari. Those two are Shams-ol-Moluk Mosahab and Mah-Laqa Mallah.[74] There are many more. They'll either kill all of us at once or send us to jail for a few years. Whatever happens to us, remember that we did something we believed in; we don't regret it at all. My only regret . . . my only regret . . . is that we can't watch you grow up."

And Mahin had cried. And in the visiting room, she had seen that the other children were also crying. And then she remembered that her mother spoke quicker than usual, so that in those last remaining minutes, she could say the most important things of all: "If you want to make me happy, be someone who

[74] Dr. Homa Darabi was a woman who on February 22, 1994, set herself on fire in Tajrish Square, Tehran, in protest of compulsory hijab. Shams-ol-Moluk Mosahab was a poet, writer, and politician, sister of Gholam-Hoseyn Mosahab, one of the first women to attend university. Mah-Laqa Mallah was a librarian and environmental activist, known as the mother of Iranian environmental activism.

does what is right. Live for what you think is right. Struggle, but don't get killed. Stay alive for as long as you can and see a great many springs and autumns. Fall in love. Laugh. Grow. Be joyful. Dance. Sing. Kiss. Forgive. Let the wind play with your hair. From this moment on it's obvious: the mullahs' biggest fear is women's freedom and consciousness. It's dancing. It's singing. Your very being a woman is itself a struggle against them. Be a woman. Be womanly. This is the right path to take: Good Speech, Good Deeds, Good Thoughts. Remember, you're not alone, although that's what it looks like from the outside. Behind the walls of this prison, there are many like me and you . . . Find them and join together. Don't stay on your own. Move forward."

And the raven-black-chadored prison warden had yanked her mother's cuffed hands and taken her behind the black iron door. The last image Mahin had of her mother was of a broad grin lighting up her tearful face, and of her handcuffed hands with which she blew her kisses; this was Mahin's share of her own mother, in her own city, in her own homeland.

Mahin had grown up and remained alone. She had listened to all of her mother's counsels, save that one. She had chosen to remain alone. Her mother had said for her not to stay on her own. To fall in love. Of course, she had friends, boyfriends and like-minded people, but before her encounter with His Excellency Death, she had never fallen in love from the depths of her heart. She had not allowed love for any man to penetrate her. She had had sex with a few people, but before meeting His Excellency Death, had never known what it was to make love. Every time she had been in bed with a man, she had said, "When I don't have access to my own body, how can I have access to my own soul and feelings?" The men often did not understand what she said. They had done their deed with her in bed and they had not even tried to take her words seriously. Perhaps because they had accepted this regime's standards or could not be bothered to question them in the slightest: girls' and boys' schools, women's and men's elevators, women's and men's dining halls, women's and men's buses, women's and men's beaches . . . Mahin talked to men in bed, explained, sought explanations, argued. She longed deeply for at least one of them to get her. She knew very well that she ruined sex for men, so much did she drag complicated religious, social, and feminist topics to bed. She never tried to charm men. To seduce them. She didn't know how. She didn't want to. Her eyes were open, and she saw that all around her were violence and pressure and threats and censorship and control. Perhaps she focused too much on bitter events, but whatever the case may be, in her opinion these bitter things were too many. Too great. They were an infrastructure. In her head she used to tell her mother: "If you had grown up under this severe and scowling regime, you wouldn't have fallen in love either."

From down below the sound of silence can still be heard, clear and irritating. Mahin knelt on the paving stones and pressed her ear to the sidewalk. A few passers-by looked at her in surprise . . . There lay the cemetery of two hundred . . . five hundred . . . a thousand intellectuals and dissident thinkers opposed to the regime, each of whom had been killed separately and in a different manner and whose murder they had then disavowed. When each of them was casually killed at home, in the street, in the car, the doctor's office or in the deserts around the city, they did not sit around doing nothing . . . Sliced-up bodies, hanged bodies, stabbed bodies, poisoned bodies found one another and gathered in that very spot and launched the Council for Dissident Victims. They didn't want to be on their own after death. So it was that officials from the Ministry of Intelligence with nothing better to do than follow up on the living and the dead among opposition intellectuals discovered their mass grave and poured hot asphalt on it, building something looking like a street and shops and planted trees—meaning, people should know when to keep quiet . . . meaning, we will not overlook even your graves, your corpses, your rotting bones . . . as if you weren't even under there at all. They . . . those two hundred . . . five hundred . . . thousand people who would later become famous as the victims of the regime's chain murders, now pressed their ears against the asphalt of the street so they might be able to hear whether someone remembered them or see whether someone close to them had been told in a dream where to locate their secret grave.

On the side of the dead, down there, there were a great many . . . there are a great many . . . There are Ahmad Mir-Alai, Ahmad Tafazzoli, Hoseyn Sarshar, Masoumeh Mosaddeq, Daryoush and Parvaneh Forouhar, Kazem Sami, Ferydoun Farrokhzad, Reza Mazlouman, Haik Houspyan-Mehr. It is a long list. Down there is a city, the city of the martyred dissident thinkers. The city of Iran's sliced-up intellectuals.

Shhhh . . . Can you hear their silence? The sound of their silence deafens Mahin . . . Karoon is only nine years old and with his little ears is listening to the noise of the demonstrators above him. He has pressed his ear to the underside of the asphalt and tells his father down there, "Shhhhh! . . . Listen. Perhaps someone is calling us . . . Does anyone in this crowd even hear us? Do they even remember us?"

On the other side of the asphalt, Mahin recalled an ancient belief. That the dead are alive only for so long as someone remembers their life as a good one, or else they die in the world of the dead as well, turning into shadows and dust. Mahin could hear their voices and whispers down there, in the direction of the silence. Karoon wanted at least to be alive in the world of the dead. Whatever else it may be, it too is a kind of life.

The chain murders had begun very early, but as always news of them got out very late. Dr. Fereydoun Taban, professor of Ancient Culture and Languages at the University of Tehran,

Mahin's uncle, was one of them. He left his office at 3:30 P.M. on January 14 to go to his old house in Zahir-od-Dowleh in Darband. Before leaving, he had rung his house, the mansion, in Zorvan from the office to speak with Jarireh, his spouse, and their children, to say that on Wednesday night he would as usual drive to the North to spend two nights at home before going back to Tehran on Friday. Jarireh had asked how the work on the book was going. Fereydoun had said it was going well. Then he had asked whether there was any news from Leyla and Shokoofeh. Jarireh had said there was none. He had asked how Mehrab was. Jarireh had answered that he was so-so. Then they had both fallen silent until Fereydoun said he should go. Drive safely, Jarireh had said. A few hours later they found Fereydoun Taban's body, skull, arm, and leg broken, by his car, in the Punak desert, whilst the only manuscript of his last book *A Pahlavi Lexicon* had been stolen from his car.

Some people say these planned killings by the government began in the first months of the victory of the revolution, with the murder of Mahmoud Taleqani in 1979, whereas others say that it started in 1988 with the killing of Dr. Kazem Sami in his office, or in 1992 with the discovery of the sliced-up body of the Armenian bishop Haik Houspyan-Mehr in the refrigerator of a shop in Karaj. Whatever the case was, the designers of the chain murders took great interest in slaughtering a wide spectrum of cultivated opponents of the Islamic revolution, ranging from Shiite clerics to Protestant bishops to Baha'i converts to atheist freethinkers, from professors of ancient Iranian culture and languages to pop singers, from journalists and writers to poets and translators, from former prime ministers to the heads of the National Resistance Movement.

As she pressed her ear to the pavement, Mahin heard: "This is Iran. The land of word of mouth . . . of whispering in ears . . . of contradictory reports . . . of secret mutterings . . . the land where people are afraid to speak against the state on the telephone or in letters. This is Iran . . . the land of rumors and things spoken into ears . . . the land of whispers, secrets, unmarked graves, silent executions, mysterious murders, subterranean tortures and chambers, locked chests, vanished files, stolen oil rigs, disappeared dollars. This is Iran . . . the land of government chain killings, mass executions, mass graves, mass arrests, and the mass suspension of newspapers. This is Iran. The land of mass assaults on student dormitories, the mass destruction of poor people's houses on the edges of the cities, the mass destruction of Baha'i houses and cemeteries and the mass arrests of women with bad hijab, of street addicts and the homeless . . . Here everything happens en masse, yet the people suffer and strive individually in silence.

"Dear listeners, right now you are hearing our voice not from National Iranian Radio and Television, but from the depths of mass graves, from underground, through the mud and dirt under your feet. I am your host, the singer Fereydoun Farrokhzad. Stop right where you are. Look under your feet. Keep quiet. Listen. Maybe just now one of us dead is jealous of the moving feet of you, the living, and is wailing in anguish. Maybe one of us is weeping in longing for your guffaws of laughter. Can you hear our voices? Hey, living people . . . down here in the darkness and solitude, we die every day, again and again, when we hear the sound of your footsteps up there, above us. We hear when you cross from one side of the street to the other, living and heedless and uncaring about our deaths as you are. We have died each time. Once when they sliced us up or strangled us and threw us out like trash somewhere in a corner of our own homes or in a desert outside of town, once more when years later they poured hot asphalt and built a street and a whole development and planted trees over our rotting bones. 'Sparrow Tongue Trees.'[75] The same trees in which sparrows build their nests en masse and the sound of whose chirping is

[75] Syrian ash trees

so loud that it doesn't let anyone hear the sound we make, the sound of silence. We have been wiped from the memory of the prison, the memory of the street, the memory of the city and history and books, and even from the memory of the cemetery. You wretched people . . . Remember us. We who gave our lives in the name of freedom, justice, love and equality, for you, for your children. We are only a meter further down. Only a meter . . . We unfortunate dead are jealous of your being alive. You wretched people . . . if only you, the forgetful, had died, and we were alive. If only you had died at least a little bit . . . if only at least one from among us . . . Karoon . . . was alive."

Chapter Sixteen

The regime's opponents said that the revolution's umbilical cord was cut with murder, kidnapping, and torture, but others said that it was none other than Akbar Hashemi-Rafsanjani who came up with the idea of the chain killings and the *Identity* show on television,[76] as well as many other plans and plots, little knowing that he would himself a few decades later be asphyxiated in the same manner in a quiet swimming pool called Koushk . . . by order of Ali Khamenei, the very same person he had himself maneuvered into the office of Leader. People say that Akbar Hashemi-Rafsanjani, whose breast was a treasure chest of the Islamic Revolution's secrets and corruptions and murders, died in the Koushk pool, but the sound of his cries for help reached no one, least of all his personal bodyguards.

Analysts and commentators on the world's great revolutions say that revolutions start by eating their own children—but whoever said this had clearly not seen the Islamic Revolution, which started by eating its own founders. Among the fathers of the revolution: Seyyed Mehdi Hashemi, Mohammad Beheshti, Mostafa Chamran, Abolhassan Bani Sadr, Sadeq Qotbzadeh, Shahaboddin Eshraqi, Karim Dastmalchi, Mohammad Montazeri, Abbas Amir-Entezam, and Father Taleqani. Father Taleqani, who came up with the idea of Friday prayers at the

[76] *Hoveyiat* was a television program produced and aired in 1996. The show's objective was said to be "confronting the Western cultural invasion." The show targeted a broad range of intellectuals, archaeologists, artists, scientists and nationalists. In this program, in order to destroy the intellectuals' image, they showed forced confessions taken from them in prison. A wide range of these intellectuals were arrested, tortured or killed by the regime.

University of Tehran, the first to oppose the plans to institute the Rule of the Jurist, compulsory hijab, and to knock down Shahr-e No, the well-known red light district. Mahmoud Taleqani had said, "The regime of the Rule of the Jurist is none other than the monarchical regime. Why did we revolt, then?" However much he himself was opposed to the Shah, Taleqani was the same cleric whose father had been as thick as thieves with Reza Shah, and the second he ended up in jail the order came for his release. In Mohammad Reza Shah's day the state of affairs was no different. Because the Pahlavi monarchs had always held his father in high esteem, they were much less hard on him than they could have been, whereas the Islamic Revolution, which he had himself set in motion against them, could not tolerate him and very early on packed him off in his shroud to somewhere in the middle of Behesht-e Zahra Cemetery.

On that day, September 10, 1979, they poisoned the old man's food, he who had supporters from all political currents with "Father Taleqani, Father Taleqani" always on their lips. His personal bodyguard disappeared, and his telephone line and water supply were mysteriously cut off. The case in which he kept important revolutionary documents, and to which he alone had the key, vanished that very same night. When the old man died, the clock was showing exactly 1:45 in the morning, and the cloth was still spread on the floor with half-eaten dishes from dinner sitting on it. This was how the revolution ate one of its principal architects in its very first months, before vomiting up his remains over the people.

Nobody knew at the time . . . how many people had to be deceived, killed, and exiled, how the fate of a nation and of the entirety of the Middle East had to be wrecked, so that America and Britain's 4,830-person list could be implemented. The long list of the country's leaders, senior officers, university professors, ministers, lawyers, businessmen, and journalists who had to be assassinated, one by one, in the name of the revolution. The British list also had the names of twenty-five clerics; a list that led to the Night of Cleric-Killing in the mosque of Ghasr Prison. How much time had to go by before the names of British and American spies were published in the documents and memoirs of people who had been behind the scenes of the revolution for us to understand that whatever it had been, the revolution was not spontaneous and popular? Rather it had been cooked up by spies like Dorian McGray, General Huyser, Bruce Laingen, William Sullivan, and William Baker.

Setting all this to one side, although the death officers of the Ministry of Intelligence were generally people of little intelligence, when it comes to killing, they possessed tremendous knowledge and creativity. Or even if they didn't possess tremendous knowledge, they certainly were creative and took pleasure in the variety of the work. A case in point: after executing that long list, they became extremely skilled at their job, no longer needing the British and American list. They became list-writers themselves and killed each dissident intellectual in a different manner, though equally brutally. They themselves used a more precise term for it: hard-killing.

There were and remain many mysteries surrounding these killings, but the strangest of these are the locks opened from the inside, and the three cups of coffee or tea. The locks of the doors to the houses of all those who had been stabbed to death at home had been opened from inside, and when the police arrived, beside the bodies of Fereydoun Farrokhzad, Shapour Bakhtiar, and Soroush Katibeh, three cups of coffee, already begun, were waiting to be drunk, while next to the bodies of Hamid and Karoon Hajizadeh, and Darioush and Parvaneh Forowhar, there were three partially-drunk cups of tea.

They kidnapped the well-reputed translator Ahmad Mir-Alayi, whose only crime was translating the works of Milan Kundera, Octavio Paz, and Borges, on his way to his bookstore, and killed him by injecting insulin into his right arm, abandoning his body in the desert after they had put a bottle of booze in his pocket to suggest that he had gotten blind drunk leading him to have a heart attack and die. They stabbed Fereydoun Farrokhzad, pop singer, wise-cracking television presenter, and dissident, in his miserable little apartment in Bonn. He had been killed with the same knife he used to slice up watermelon for his guests. The German newspapers wrote that they had stabbed him thirty-seven times with a kitchen knife in his mouth alone, as if to say, "You can't chatter away against us anymore." They kidnapped the writer and journalist Pirouz Davani on his way to his sister's house and inflicted such a catastrophe on his body that to this day it has not been found. They killed Ali Akbar Sirjani, researcher and man of letters, in prison, with a potassium suppository. They beat Professor Ahmad Tafazzoli so brutally on the way from the University of Tehran to his apartment in Darband that he died. They went so far in slicing up that helpless couple Parvaneh and Darioush Forouhar with knives that they say that the floor of their house was swimming with blood, and that they had cut off Parvaneh's breasts and placed them in her husband's hands. As for Ghazaleh Alizadeh, the most gorgeous melancholy writer, they hanged her in the woods around Ramsar and then spread the rumor that she had killed herself because of depression. Or Masoumeh Mosaddeq, Dr. Mohammad Mosaddeq's granddaughter, whom they stabbed to death after beating her violently and suffocating her, before cutting off her breasts, flinging them into a corner of the room, and noting that a burglar drawn to her jewelry had killed her. What about the photographer, Zahra Kazemi? So much did they beat and rape her in Evin Prison that she died from the assault. As the interrogators and prison wardens put it, they rape-killed her. Although her special interrogator, Saeed Mortazavi, who earned himself a promotion every year for these kinds of services, insisted that her death had come about "accidentally" during the interrogation, the doctor who had examined her, after fleeing to Canada, informed the media that they had torture-killed . . . rape-killed her. Meaning, as the interrogators put it, they had hard-killed her. Or that helpless young doctor, Ramin Pur-Andarjani, or Ebrahim Zalzadeh the journalist and publisher, or many, many others . . . Or just recently, Kiomars Pur-Ahmad, the pure-hearted director of the television series *Tales of Majid* . . . They spread a rumor to the effect that he had hanged himself, but the idiots didn't ask themselves why someone who had hanged himself would have had broken and bruised fingers. Or still more atrocious, Darioush Mehrjui and his spouse . . .

There were so many names that it was impossible to memorize them all easily. But two things were clear: firstly, that those who ordered the murders took pleasure in inventing different kinds of compound expression based on the participle "killing"—torture-killing, hard-killing, rape-killing, slow-killing, total-killing, howl-killing, dog-killing . . . —and secondly, that the murderers were creative in their cruelty, breaking skulls and noses, crushing toes, breaking fingers, pulling out finger and toenails, tearing lungs, breaking teeth, stabbing stomachs and mouths and genitals, whipping, continuous raping, inserting bottles and batons in anuses, chopping up bodies into little pieces, electric shocks, cutting off breasts, tearing out tongues, injecting insulin, injecting air, hanging, and potassium suppositories. These are merely some examples of their acting out their creative fantasies as they murdered and tortured dissidents.

As Mahin thought about these things, Wisława Szymborska's poem describing death kept turning around in her head:

"It can't even get the things done
that are part of its trade:
dig a grave,
make a coffin,
clean up after itself.
Preoccupied with killing,
it does the job awkwardly,
without system or skill.
As though each of us were its first kill."

So it was that the murderers from the Islamic Republic's Ministry of Intelligence had even managed to make Death look good.

All the same, the murder of Dr. Fereydoun Taban, Dr. Ahmad Tafazzoli's colleague and Mahin's uncle and professor in Ancient Iranian Culture and Languages at the University of Tehran aroused everyone's compassion in a different way, especially that of Mahin and her fellow students. Excepting of course nine-year-old Karun, stabbed to death beside his father, Mahin considered that Dr. Taban might perhaps be, out of all the victims of the chain killings, the meekest and least likely to kick up a fuss. He was neither a member of any political or religious party, nor did he ever participate in any political or anti-Islamic meeting, and after the revolution he hadn't had any dealings with any political activist. Perhaps his only fault was that he was Zoroastrian, and Azar and Bijan were his sister and brother. Dr. Taban was bewitched from head to toe by the history, civilization, and culture of ancient Iran, and his only concern was tracing the path of the movement and evolution of the culture and of Iranshahri thought from antiquity until the present day. That was all. Perhaps that was his great crime, which had meant that he found himself on the Ministry of Intelligence blacklist. When it came down to it, the revolutionaries only officially recognized Iran's history from after the Arab invasion, and for them the activities of people like Dr. Taban were no more than an unambiguous and mocking grin aimed at them. And yet there was something else. A secret that nobody in the family knew of—not Khanom Joon, not Mahin, and not even Jarireh, his spouse: Dr. Taban had come to blows with Khamenei in person.

When you think about it, everything began with the construction of Khomeini's tomb, except that if you think about it properly, in reality it all had to do with *Alice in Wonderland*. If that day in particular the ten-year-old Ali Khamenei had not watched the cartoon version of *Alice in Wonderland* on his neighbor's color television, then perhaps Dr. Taban would have been alive to this day and as usual on his way to the University of Tehran to tell his students how Zurvanist, Simorghi, Mithraist, and Zoroastrian thought stood in fundamental and philosophical contradiction to the thought of Islam and of the other Semitic religions.

What had happened was that as soon as Ali Khamenei had clapped eyes on Alice, he had fallen head over heels in love with her, because she looked very much like the neighbor's golden-haired daughter. When Alice got lost down the rabbit hole, which was in reality a mysterious labyrinth, she saw three playing cards, clubs, busy painting white roses red.

"Why are you painting white roses red?" Alice asked.

The three playing cards—the ace, two, and three of clubs—paint pots and brushes in hand, replied, "Because the Queen of Hearts loves the color red."

For years Ali Khamenei remained in love with Alice, this beautiful girl with her blue-and-white dress and her golden hair. Aside from her good looks, he took delight in her bravery and love of adventure, yet the more time passed, and he grew up and his thinking took shape, the more he realized that in actual fact the character from the cartoon who had besotted him was not Alice, but the Queen of Hearts. Of course, the Queen of Hearts was foul-faced and forever shrieking, but her absolute power was bewitching, what with its simple and peremptory command: "Off with his head!" What could be better than that? Why should one's thoughts be taken up with worthless enemies? Off with his head! Done! Plus, the Queen of Hearts loved everything to be well-ordered and flawless and homogeneous. More importantly, she was besotted with the idea that everyone should obey her unquestioningly, and even Alice did not have the right to assert herself in front of her.

"What are you doing here?" asked the Queen of Hearts.

"I'm trying to find my way back home," Alice said.

"*Your* way," shouted the Queen of Hearts. "Your way is always my way."

Alice, afraid, answered: "Yes, that's right. But I was thinking that—"

This time the Queen of Hearts replied with a manufactured gentleness. "Well, wouldn't it be better if you didn't think at all? This way we can save time. How about we play croquet together?"

This interest in Alice, the labyrinth, and the Queen of Hearts stayed with Ali until one day, still a young man and a clerical student, he went to the cinema with his friends and saw *Enter the Dragon* with Bruce Lee. In this film, Bruce Lee got stuck in a mirrored labyrinth along with a man with a fork for a hand. The mirrors reflected one another and Bruce Lee and the fork-handed man could not tell each other apart from their reflections. This time, the idea of the labyrinth with its metaphorical and spine-chilling force attracted him. He started thinking about how the labyrinth was a metaphor for our internal and external complexities. The fact of the matter was that Ali Khamenei liked reading. He smoked a pipe or would stand in front of the camera with a cigarette in the corner of his mouth and strike intellectual poses. He had friends among the poets and writers. He liked classical poetry more than any other literary form. If the revolution hadn't happened and he hadn't got involved in politics, maybe a middling literary critic would have emerged from him, but once he had attained the Leadership, he never looked at his fate in this way. In reality, he was quite satisfied with his destiny. In fact, he had not seen himself as possessing any special talent. In his most honest moments, he considered himself an average person, of middling qualities, who had been given a helping hand by the circumstances of the day. Although many people do not believe in luck, it was only he and Rafsanjani who knew that if luck and good fortune had not played their part, then he and the leadership of the country could hardly have been mentioned in the same breath!

In any case, on that day, after seeing the Bruce Lee film he thought to himself, "If only it were possible just once to get lost in a labyrinth and afterwards find my way out." So it was that he started watching any film that had a labyrinth in it, although of course he was careful not to display his interest in cinema and labyrinths too often in front of his cleric friends. They were working toward the revolution and needed to concentrate on anti-Shah propaganda, blowing up the Rex Cinema in Abadan, and revolutionary kidnappings, assassinations, and executions.

So it was that he hid his love for anything other than Islam and the revolution from the others as much as possible until the revolution took place, and with each year that passed he obtained ever higher positions until, as luck would have it, he ended up Leader of the Islamic Revolution. After Khomeini's death in 1989, Akbar Hashemi Rafsanjani himself chose him to be the second Leader. It was this affair that led everyone to call Akbar Hashemi "Akbar the Kingmaker." And to respect him hundreds of times more, because they had realized that those wielding this country's absolute power as well as the power behind the scenes were in his hands and not in anyone else's.

This matter of Khamenei's becoming king, that is to say Leader of the Islamic Revolution, happened so swiftly that he even caught himself by surprise, one day uttering this famous phrase in earshot of the microphones and in front of the cameras in the Islamic Consultative Assembly, a phrase his enemies would play with and incant for years to come: "We should weep for a country whose leader is me!"

He advanced so rapidly that for years he forgot about Alice and the Queen of Hearts and labyrinths, until one night—after listening to the usual twenty-minute tape that the dreadful Seyyed Ali Moghaddam used to hand to him each night, containing the recordings obtained from bugs of high-ranking officials and ordinary people—anxiety and fear and depression prevented him from sleeping. The ends of the twenty-minute cassettes were full of sighing and cursing and insults and plots and conspiracies against him. So, after his personal physician, Alireza Marandi, had upgraded his antidepressants from fluoxetine and paroxetine to trazodone and mirtazapine and he had downed several pills, he fell asleep and dreamed that he was stuck in a giant labyrinth, though it looked more like a graveyard. Around him for as far as the eye could see were corpses and black-clothed mourners sitting on the ground, weeping. Instead of putting the corpses into the graves, they had placed them on top. The dead, clad in ordinary clothes, were stretched out on top of their own graves, while the black-clothed mourners were sitting around them and weeping and lamenting. At each body's head a green flag emblazoned with "Allah" hung from a base, fluttering in a wind whose origin was unclear. The dead women's hair flowed down all around them, and they were wearing long shirts and skirts. In his dream, he wondered what kind of burial customs these were. Why weren't these people Muslims? Further off, a young man and woman were lying on top of two adjacent graves, holding hands and smiling mournfully at one another, awaiting their death. Both were wounded and bloody. Then he noticed a dead young woman stirring and sitting up with great effort. When she had sat up, she saw blood flowing from her side and, after touching it and seeing her bloody hand, seemed to recall why she had died, whereupon she frowned severely. Upset, she looked at the crowd of mourners around her, before her eyes alighted upon him, standing in the middle. The young woman got up with difficulty, before suddenly raising her fists at him in loathing and crying out, "Khamenei, you Zahhak! / We will drag you underground!" At once, the dead and the mourners stood up and cried out at him in loathing, "Khamenei, you Zahhak! / We will drag you underground!"

He woke up afraid and dripping sweat and thought about how to interpret this strange dream. How much he disliked these people. They wouldn't leave him alone, even in sleep. When he thought about it properly, this labyrinth reminded him of Islam. When it came to it, everything in this world reminded him of the clear religion of Islam. After all, wasn't it

Islam that had brought him to this high position? Whatever he had, came from Islam. He thought about how both Islam and especially the Quran were as complicated, and at the same time, as simple, as this labyrinth and this dream with its many secrets. The external meaning of the Quran was simple and transparent, and yet everything within it could be interpreted to mean different and even contradictory things. After all, it was written in the surah of the Bee, verse 103, that "the Quran is in a clear Arabic language," but then, in another surah, "the Family of Imran," verse seven, its verses were divided into two groups: the definite and the equivocal, with the former being simple and obligatory, and the latter complicated and open to interpretation. Then it is stressed that "Nobody knows what the interpretation of the equivocal verses is save God," before amending with "and of course those versed in understanding." Oh, there are tons of similar ambiguities in the Quran, which are in my opinion among its beauties and subtleties, though the idiot unbelievers call them contradictions," Khamenei thought. Some are so brazen as to go on about the Satanic verses, saying that if Satan was able to place those words in the mouths of God or the Prophet, then how do we know that the rest of the verses weren't also revealed by Satan? ...استغفر الله!...بالله نعوذ
[77] It's good that the Departed Imam issued the fatwa enjoining the killing of that greatest of unbelievers Salman Rushdie, otherwise God knows what flaws these people might attribute to the Quran.

Some others claim that there is a flaw because if Allah is the Creator of all that exists, why then does verse twenty-four of the surah, "The Believers," say فتبارک الله احسن الخالقين meaning "God is the best of creators." Therefore, the unbelievers say, there must be other gods, then, apart from Allah. They even say that "Allah" was the name of an idol in the era of the Prophet Muhammad, blessings upon him, and that he liked this idol

[77] I implore God's pardon; we seek refuge in God.

more than the other ones, which is why it is written "creators" نعوذبالله ...استغفرالله...! The unbelievers also question, if in verse ninety of the surah, "the Table Spread," wine "is among Satan's works," why in verse forty-three, "the Woman," is it said, "أَيُّهَا الَّذِينَ آمَنُوا لَا تَقْرَبُوا الصَّلَاةَ وَأَنْتُمْ سُكَارَىٰ حَتَّىٰ تَعْلَمُوا مَا تَقُولُونَ"؟[78] Or God, may He be magnified and glorified, in verse forty-five of the surah, "the Ranks," declares that the believers will be given pure wine in paradise. The unbelievers say that if wine is good, then why should we only drink it there and not here?

He shook his head angrily and reflected, "God keep me safe from these Iranian unbelievers. Your humble servant always greatly regrets that he was not born in Saudi Arabia and that now, instead of being Leader of these Iranians who know no God, he was Leader or Sultan or Caliph of the Arabs, because after all it is their own religion. Their very identity depends on it—whereas these unbelieving Iranians with their pre-Islamic history just won't put up with Islam at all, will they? They are Muslims in name only. In practice, they are unbelievers. West-toxified. They don't perform their prayers . . . They drink alcohol . . . Women and men dance and sing together . . . They constantly show off about their Cyrus's Charter of Human Rights. The dishonorable bunch live in the Shah's day at home, in the time of the revolution on the streets."

He leapt up. What a fantastic idea. What a brilliant idea. He snapped the fingers on his good hand and guffawed with laughter. An Islamic labyrinth . . . Yes, he should build an Islamic labyrinth as a symbol of the complexity and of the mysteries and secrets of Islam and the Quran . . . Since we have Islamic human rights, Islamic universities, Islamic parks, Islamic art, Islamic sciences, and Islamic banking, why shouldn't we have an Islamic labyrinth? What could be better? He laughed uproariously: "I should remember to order

[78] O believers, when you are drunk, do not stand in prayer until you comprehend what you are saying.

that the sociology of Durkheim and Marx be removed from the curriculum and in their stead the subjects of Islamic astronomy and Islamic zoology be added . . . Let our inimies mock us as much as they want . . . it doesn't matter to us. Their mockery shows we're moving along the right path . . . I must remember to call Haddad-Adel and tell him to prepare the course materials for those two subjects himself, with pious narratives and counsel and the traditions and sayings of the Prophet among the principal sources. Or books like Ayatollah Meshkini's *Counsel.* In that very book it is written that they asked the Prophet of Islam which animals are the result of metamorphosis, and the Prophet stated that there are thirteen animals that used to be humans but were turned into animals on account of their sins: the bear, the elephant, the scorpion, the rabbit, the monkey, the eel, the spider . . . For example, pigs are Christians who asked God to send them manna from heaven. God sent it to them, but they persisted in their unbelief, and God transformed them into pigs. They got what they deserved."

He scratched his head. "We even have Islamic joy . . . I mean, we commanded it, now let's see if this people knows how to be joyous in an Islamic way or an un-Islamic one. We always want what is best for them . . . We want them to be our companions and those of Muhammad and his family, Allah's blessings upon them, in paradise." He lost concentration again. This loss of concentration was the bane of his existence. His doctor had warned him that it might be a sign of Alzeheimer's. "What will happen if I get Alzheimer's and they take the leadership away from me?" He would be so embarrassed in front of his siblings. "The jealous scoundrels . . . They have informed me that this Akbar Hashemi Rafsanjani and the heads of the Guards have even thought about what happens if I die and are now thinking about how to find some doubles . . . How loathsome. Does that mean I'm so easily replaceable? Does it mean that if I die they won't build me a grand tomb, but will just bury me anonymously and then those wretched doubles will go on living in my place? Curse this life."

He lost his train of thought once more. He had to concentrate: if he, who was Supreme Leader of Iran and leader of the Muslims of the world could not build such a labyrinth, then who could? And so he excitedly called a meeting of the Assembly for the Discernment of the Interests of the State. The funds for the labyrinth would have to be allocated from the government's budget. And when it was a question of the budget, whether he wanted it or not, the affair would end up in the parliament, even though in his opinion this sort of thing did not concern the people, it was a mere formality. It was his own oil money. It was his own country . . . He laughed. "Of course, it's my own parliament too." He scratched his head. "I'll have to present this idea as if the Islamic Labyrinth is a vital national-religious project and is tied up with the very reputation of the state. Just like compulsory hijab . . . nuclear energy . . . "

Three days later, once the forty-four permanent members and one guest member were sitting in their places, he spoke with great enthusiasm and grandiloquence of the necessity of building an Islamic Labyrinth, and of how as always with this labyrinth he could punch the enemies of Islam hard in the mouth, especially America and Israel. Yet he had not even finished speaking when Akbar Rafsanjani interrupted him and made him feel sheepish in front of everybody.

Akbar Hashemi said: "You are so excited, I thought you must have been about to give the order to build the mausoleum of the Departed Imam. What could be more important than building the mausoleum of the great leader of the Shia?" And without delay he pulled out a large initial plan of Khomeini's mausoleum, all glittering and gleaming, from under his cloak and spread it out on the table. And so the Islamic Labyrinth Project swiftly gave way to Khomeini's magnificent mausoleum in Behesht-e Zahra. All forty-five present gathered round Hashemi-Rafsanjani, showering the project with praise, leaving

Khamenei and his idea of an Islamic Labyrinth all alone in one corner of the table. Meanwhile, it was none other than Akbar Hashemi who, a few minutes later, grinning with one of those habitual smirks that made his round cheeks rosy, raised his head and winked in ridicule at Khamenei, who was sitting there in a daze, the color drained from his face and his brows knitted together. Khamenei turned purple with rage and in his head said: if that's how it is, let's see how the wheel turns! And in that very moment he decided to turn into a real leader. Someone who would make people's hairs stand on end. Then he smiled hypocritically at Akbar Hashemi, all the while imagining how he would asphyxiate him in the Koushk pool—even though he would have to spend more than two decades working and waiting to make this wish come true.

Early one morning Fereydoun Taban opened his eyes in his old house near Zahir-od-Dowleh and saw that three plain-clothes intelligence officers had made their way past the threads he had run between the doors, windows, and objects in his house so that he might have a more accurate map of the hand-hewn cave of Niyasar, and were standing in a row at the head of his bed. One of the officers, despite looking polite and harmless, was cleaning underneath his fingernails with a corner of the family photograph he had removed from its frame on the bedside table. It occurred to Dr. Taban that perhaps it was dried blood he was cleaning. He sat up in bed and put on his glasses. Nobody lived in this house, with its three bedrooms and pleasant, tree-festooned courtyard, besides himself. His family lived in the ancestral mansion in the North, in Zorvan, and he came to Tehran for four or five days a week to teach Ancient Iranian Culture and Languages at the University of Tehran. The family only showed up here during the summer holidays, for fun and to visit relatives. Leyla, his little daughter, had disappeared years before. Then his son had gone off to war, and after two years without word from him, his other daughter

Shokoofeh had followed her brother to the front in order to bring him back, but she had disappeared in turn. Jarireh had gotten better since that day Mehrab had mysteriously turned up by the mansion gates, and the house was once more, at least up to a point, lively and full of excitement, although from time to time he noticed that Jarireh would take a bunch of tranquillizers and anti-depressants. What had happened was that before Mehrab had turned up, the Ball of Light and Shabro had returned home. When the Ball of Light had appeared all of a sudden in Khanom Joon's room, Professor Taban had importuned his grandmother to tell him what news the it had brought, but all she would say was, "Everyone is alive and will return safely. Even Leyla. But it's possible it will take some time." That was it. In Fereydoun Taban's view, everything had become even more dubious and unclear once the Ball of Light had come back. All in all, life had hardly shown itself cheerful and straightforward to him, but until now he had never imagined that his time would be up so soon and before he had seen Leyla and Shokoofeh again and put all the affairs of his children and the mansion and his books in order.

He addressed the three officers with his usual polite sarcasm. "Are you gentlemen the Angel of Death himself, or just his messengers?"

They exchanged glances with one another. One of them said, "We've come from the His Excellency the Supreme Leader's Household."

"As I humbly suggested," Fereydoun Taban muttered.

Another of them, pointing to the woven, colored threads suspended everywhere in the house like a spider's web between the various objects and the furniture, asked, "What are these?"

The professor scratched his head and said, "Nothing that would interest you."

The one who had been cleaning underneath his fingernails with the family photo showed it to him and said, "What a big family. These days everyone is satisfied with one or two children." Fereydoun Taban understood the threat this sentence contained, and as he was buttoning up his shirt, shook his head. Another of the officers went over to the closet and ran his hand over each and every shirt and suit hanging there until he reached the ties. "After the revolution," he said. "People use ties as donkeys' reins or make skirts out of them. Don't you have donkeys in your big mansion in the North, or doesn't Madam Jarireh wear skirts?"

Fereydoun didn't allow this insult to get to him. He also realized that they were fully up to date on everything that concerned him. The third officer took a step towards him. "His Excellency the Supreme Leader wants to talk to you," he said. "You have to come with us."

Fereydoun Taban chose a dark, pressed suit and a navy-blue tie with a prominent Paisley or bent cypress pattern and put them on. He knew that after the revolution wearing a tie had become the symbol of the counter-revolutionaries—let alone a tie with a Paisley pattern, symbol of Iran and Iranians. He had never presumed himself to be a courageous person, but he might be considered stubborn. He thought that now they were going to kill him, he might as well die looking presentable and in his favorite clothes.

A few minutes afterwards, having variously crouched down or raised their legs high to get past the threads, they all left the house and Professor Taban sat down behind them in a Mercedes-Benz W126 with tinted windows. No one spoke in the car. They headed down Pahlavi Avenue, which had been renamed Vali Asr Avenue after the revolution, passing Shah Street, renamed Republic Street, and, in a leafy cul-de-sac whose trees had been planted back in Reza Shah's day, arrived before the gates of a large mansion that had prior to the revolution belonged to the Nezam-Mafi dynasty. In front of the gates, ten or twelve armed guards controlled people's comings and goings to the Leader's Residence. He thought about the word *beyt*. It was as if they had absolutely to use Arabic words to confer sanctity on something. What was wrong with *khâneh*, "house," that they needed to call it a *beyt*? Why had they not called it "the Leader's House?" If he had not managed to stop himself, the mania of words would have come calling for him again.

Behind the gates was a large garden full of trees, and an old, large, and simple mansion. In his head he said to himself, "The people have got themselves an ass. Everybody knows that Khamenei has taken over all the former palaces of the Shah and the Royal Family, except for the ones that have been turned into museums, and that he has built all sorts of mansions and palaces in hidden nooks and crannies around the country." He had even heard that he had built several subterranean mansions and palaces underneath that same residence, as well as in Mashhad and Tabriz and Kish, complete with pools and million-dollar collections of rings and canes and horses. One of the most important types of propaganda employed by the leaders of this state was their appearance of frugality. At that very moment, one of the officers suddenly stared him in the eyes. He had a fright. "Don't say these people can read minds," he thought.

They passed through several connected rooms, furnished only with simple handwoven carpets, no chairs in sight, before reaching the back courtyard. The Leader of the Islamic Republic of Iran was sitting on a simple metal chair next to a little table, one leg crossed over the other, wearing a cream-colored cloak, drinking tea as he contemplated the great courtyard, full of flowers and trees. He was not wearing a turban, just a white skullcap. They stood three meters away from him. As if he had suddenly woken up, the Leader turned his head and saw them, and, inclining his torso toward them and smiling broadly, took two or three steps to draw near to Professor Taban and raised his famously paralyzed right hand to shake hands with him. Professor Taban hesitated. The Leader's hand was left hanging in the air. He reproached himself and finally shook his hand, but without saying a word. Khamenei did not appreciate this.

With his left hand he invited him to sit. He sat. Again, with the left hand, he signaled for them to bring tea. They brought tea. The same two or three officers stood around them. Fereydoun Taban drank a little tea in silence and inspected Khamenei's face from over the tea cup. Was this really him? He had read in books that great dictators kept several versions of the original in reserve, so that if something untoward were to happen to them, or they simply died a natural death, the copies could take their place and their power be prolonged. He thought how with these meddlesome and greedy clerics anything was possible. One of the bodyguards standing beside him suddenly turned round and stared straight into his eyes. Once more he was startled. What if they really could read people's minds?

Khamenei spoke in a pedantic manner and used many Arabic words. He said, "I am certain that your honorable self is concerned to know what you are doing here?"

"To be honest," Professor Taban said. "Right now, I should be teaching."

Khamenei frowned deeply. He had heard that this person was against the revolution, but now he was sure of it. Especially with that Paisley-spotted tie of his. Speaking directly and easily, he said, "The objective is for your honorable self to inspect an ancient site in secret and to decipher an inscription and present a translation thereof to me alone."

Fereydoun Taban looked at the Leader in astonishment and said, "It's true that my research concerns ancient, pre-Islamic tablets and inscriptions"—and he pronounced "pre-Islamic" with particular emphasis—"but why me? When there are so many archaeologists and specialists of ancient scripts?"

Khamenei did not like this direct tone one bit. Crossing his legs, he started drinking his tea. One of the three bodyguards approached, took a notebook out of his pocket, and placed it on the table next to the teapot. The notebook contained Fereydoun Taban's drawings of labyrinths. He was stunned. Khameni said, "One of the wonders of the age is that a counter-revolutionary like your good self, and a humble revolutionary as I am, have a common interest. Of course, inshallah you good sir are not a counter-revolutionary and Taghuti lover of luxury and we are mistaken in this regard." He peered at the professor with his beady and crafty eyes and gave a noxious smile. The professor however did not smile and continued staring at him. He simply said, "You are not mistaken, but what do these drawings have to do with the ancient site and its inscriptions you mention?"

Again, Khamenei did not like this boldness. Did these anti-revolutionary intellectuals really esteem him so mean in dignity? The devil take this Akbar when everybody still treads in fear of him but not me . . . He started flicking through the drawings. He examined each one of them patiently and with a serious expression, until eventually his face lit up and he started drumming his fingers enthusiastically, looking at the professor and laughing as if to say, "Good job. Will done. Bravo. Bravo." Suddenly, the outline of a smirk appeared on the professor's lips as he was reminded of these words. It had been years now that people made jokes out of the way the Leader said certain words. His "the inimy" and his "will done, will done" had become people's catchphrases.

The professor had no choice but to drink the rest of his tea to avoid having to explain himself for smirking like that. At length Khamenei said, "We have accorded your good self the necessary authority to travel to that ancient site on the grounds that, so it was reported to us, a labyrinth has been discovered there, and you are the only person to have conducted specialized and comprehensive studies of ancient labyrinths. We would like to understand with what end in mind this labyrinth was constructed, and in what period. Does it still have the potential to be used? And finally, whether it is possible to turn it into an Islamic labyrinth."

When he heard the words "Islamic labyrinth," Professor Taban coughed up the tea from his mouth onto Khamenei's cloak. He quickly dried his mouth with a tissue and apologized.

Three scowling bodyguards stepped forward but as Khamenei calmly wiped the tea off his cloak, he gestured to them to indicate there was no problem. Then he resumed. "This labyrinth has recently been discovered during the excavations for the mausoleum of the Departed Imam. We have ordered a halt to construction until it can be examined by you, in complete confidentiality, with a very small team of archaeologists that you yourself shall select."

Professor Taban, who had in this brief interval been able to catch his breath and gather his thoughts, responded boldly. "This is just our bad luck . . . any ancient site is either destroyed or plundered after your revolution."

Khamenei's brows were furrowed for all to see, and the three officers took a step closer to Dr. Taban and put their hands on the guns on their hips. Khamenei indicated with his hand that everything was under control. Then he replied: "You only have a week to carry out this mission," after which he stood up and left without saying goodbye.

When Professor Taban suddenly caught sight of himself in his bedroom mirror that night, he felt a sense of disgust. He moved closer and gazed at his pupils. He pulled aside the skin under his eyes and stared more carefully. His pupils dilated. He had to escape. He could find a smuggler and with his family leave the country. What would he do about his research and the university and his students? What would become of Leyla and Shokoofeh? He could go to America or teach as the Chair of Iranian Culture and Languages at the University of Oxford. Or at UCLA and UC Berkeley and several other places. "Actually, "this is wonderful," he thought. "Because these self-satisfied Westerners often deliberately omit important sections of Iranian history from the Achaemenids to the Sasanids from their history books so they can just focus on the glory of ancient Greece and Rome, while ignoring the influence of ancient Iran as the world's first and greatest civilized empire. Westerners are still seeking revenge for their consecutive defeats at the hands of the ancient Iranians. Of course, the fault lies with us. We have done too little. And then they've wrapped their dreadful Islamic revolution around our throats so that we are unable to flourish. So much for them and their Arabs and their Islam," he thought. "And, on the other hand, for those Westerners and their universities . . . They've caught us in a vise and crippled us from both sides." He was thoroughly irritated. He ran his hand through his salt-and-pepper hair, stared into his pupils, and thought about how he could go abroad and defeat the Western universities' censorship by publishing his ancient documents, his books and articles. Then suddenly he recalled how seven or eight of his colleagues had left for Britain or America after the revolution, and the weight of responsibility for continuing the field had fallen on his shoulders and those of two or three other colleagues. If he left too, then the field would be finished.

He ran a hand through his hair again. He was frustrated. What would become of the Sacred Fire? What should be done with the mansion and the Gowkaran tree? If the tree had grown in their house, it must have a meaning, even though he was unsure what meaning that might be. He had spoken to the tree on multiple occasions without ever receiving a reply, despite the fact that once in the middle of the night he had happened upon his grandmother, Khanom Joon, deep in conversation with it. That night Khanom Joon had been busy reciting the Avesta and as soon as she reached the passage reading "*Then I who am Ahura-Mazda created the healing plants. A great, great many times, hundreds of times, thousands of times, tens of thousands of times, from around the unique Gowkaran Tree, I send my blessings on all those healing plants that exist for the people's bodies . . . O death, I drive you away with prostrations and prayers, I drive pain away,*" the tree began to speak: "Say, what question do you have of me tonight?"

When he heard this voice, Dr. Taban, who had been busy rearranging some books on the bookshelves in the hallway behind the kitchen, drew nearer and stood, rooted to the spot, in a dark corner. Khanom Joon looked to one side and to the other, and once she was satisfied no one was in the vicinity, she addressed the tree. "I'm at ease when it comes to Leyla, but tell me what I may do for Shokoofeh?"

"Nothing yet," the tree said. "She has a difficult trial ahead of her. In a little while send one of my leaves to her in prison. She must stay alive."

Dr. Taban leapt into the middle of the kitchen in disbelief to find out what would happen to Shokoofeh, but the tree spoke not another word. Khanom Joon left the kitchen angrily and striking her cane on the floor, and without answering a single one of her grandson's questions.

"It will be impossible to leave all this behind," Dr. Taban thought. "And what about the children?" He did not despair. A feeling told him that both his daughters would one day come back safe and sound. His very sense of self depended on all of these things: on his family, on his field of study, on the mansion and the sacred fire. On this land. On the Gowkaran tree in the middle of the kitchen. At length he said to himself, "I am the descendant of the old gentry and Iran is my land. That is the final word!"

He lay down on the bed. He sat up again. Then he got up and span round in frustration. If his spouse Jarireh and Jamshid Khan and Khanom Joon were to find out that he was working for Khamenei himself, how would they deal with such betrayal and dishonor? What would his dear colleagues Doctors Parvardegar and Gharib think of him? He sat down on the bed again. He was restless. He got up and made his way past the threads to the bathroom. As soon as he set eyes on his razor blades, he thought of suicide. But if he killed himself, what would his loved ones do? Their fate would become still more miserable if he committed suicide—particularly for Jarireh, who as it was forced herself to stay on two feet by taking tranquillizers and anti-depressants and hoping for her children's return. No. He would have to wait like the rest until he was murdered by the regime in their chain killings. That way at least his death would have some meaning. That way at least another page would be added to this regime's register of dishonorable deeds.

He roamed bewildered through the rooms and between the lines of threads and reflected. His attention wandered to the labyrinth in Niyasar. Then he started thinking about the labyrinth in Derinkuyu in Cappadocia in Turkey. How similar they were. Both of them had eight floors underground, with endless staircases and tunnels, storerooms, cattlefolds, libraries, sanctuaries, wine cellars, cool cellars, wells, and even hot springs. In the storerooms they had found the residues of grains and cereals. In the cattlefolds, the remains of domestic animals and birds. He thought of how thousands of people could have lived down there for months and even years without any need of the surface world. Dr. Taban had a theory and had been working on it quietly for years. In his opinion, and contrary to what his colleagues believed, these labyrinths had not been built for escape from enemies. Nor were they secret Mithraic sanctuaries. In his opinion, they were places of refuge from the cold of the Ice Age. Only long experience of life in the Ice Age could have justified building labyrinths that were so well-equipped. That was why one end of this labyrinth was connected to the Derinkuyu maze in Turkey, and another end of it to the one in Isfahan, and yet others no doubt to those in Tafresh and Nushabad and Samen.

It is written in the Vendidad: "Ahura-Mazda said to Jamshid Shah that in order to combat the Ahriman of Cold, you must build a *var* and there gather the seed of small and large four-footed beasts and dogs and chickens and the red flames of fire. The seeds of the men and women who are the best and most beautiful on earth."[79]

[79] Vendidad, 1991, second *fargard*, section 251:55.

What did *var* mean, if not cave and a place covered by a roof? Gosh, how much he wanted to spend his life exercising his curiosity and investigating these caves and labyrinths . . . What his theory required to be completed was an ancient cemetery. There must be a cemetery in these caves or their surroundings. He frowned; these cursed people had deliberately reduced our research budget to a miniMom so they could fill the clerics' pockets or stage their pretend war against America and Israel in Gaza and Lebanon. Running his hands over the threads, scowling and pensive, he went back to his bedroom.

He lay down on the bed, and as he placed his glasses on the bedside table he wondered how he might make himself scarce until the storm had passed over. How about if he went and lived in one of the Niyasar tunnels? Yet how was it possible to remain hidden in this country where there was in every hole a mosque and bases for the Basij, the police, the Guards, and the intelligence services? After all, he would eventually have to come out of the cave to find water and food . . . No, it wasn't possible! What if he to a remote town or village? But if the towns and roads were safe, they wouldn't have sent his Shokoofeh to the front through the middle of the mountains and forests. Is this some kind of movie? He turned from this side to that throughout the night and yet found no way to escape. In the morning, he went to the university unshaven, and the first person to notice the change in him was his old colleague and friend, Dr. Parvardegar. The color drained from her face; she touched him with her hand. "So they came looking for you too?" The professor's color changed from white to purple to red and he had no idea what answer to give. She had been the one who had come to the mansion after the revolution and wrenched him out of his torpor of solitude and depression and brought him back to the university. He had never lied to her yet. He loved her like a sister. They had killed her husband not long ago. The murderers had killed him with two bullets, one to the head and one to the chest, in his apartment in Paris and left his body there next to three cups of half-drunk coffee. And this wasn't even the entirety of Dr. Parvardegar's misfortunes. Some people said that when her husband was killed, it came out that he had a French lover who had come face to face with the murderers on the staircase and had then identified them to the French police. Dr. Taban thought that he had better not worry her still further. "No," he said. "Last night I ate out and got food poisoning. But I'm feeling better now." All the same, a few hours later, Dr. Parvardegar said, "Doctor, you seem anxious. Your hands are trembling. You're as white as a sheet. Tell me, what awful thing are they doing to you? Maybe I can help." "What could you possibly do to help?" he wondered. "The less you know, the less you'll be in danger." And this was how he ended up with no option but to submit to working with Khamenei.

Chapter Seventeen

While Fereydoun and Khamenei might be alone, he deliberately left Khamenei's three personal bodyguards hanging somewhere among the obscure twists and turns near the middle of the ancient labyrinth, which he had realized was considerably older than the Achaemenid period. Along the way the discussion had gotten rather lively, and as they passed through tight, dark corridors, Fereydoun Taban, rucksack on his back and flashlight in hand, and Ali Khamenei, cloak and turban under his arm and cane in hand, yelled at one another and continued walking. "What's more, you have kept the people in poverty and ignorance while spending their wealth on promoting Shiism in the Middle East, Africa, and even Europe!" said Fereydoun. "For what? Nobody on earth could give a stuff for your stupid idea of promoting Shiism! Even the Shiites themselves! You are incapable of producing a single work of art, a single piece of science, a single engineered structure! Let alone intercontinental missiles or the nuclear energy that has made you look ridiculous the world over. When you and your lot are destroyed, nothing will be left of your time in power except a bunch of poorly-engineered highways and bridges and apartments and dams, huge prisons and cemeteries. A bunch of ill-shaped shrines and mosques with printed, upside-down mosaics. A single work of art . . . Name just one lasting work of art produced in and representing your and Khomeini's era? Name one lasting piece of poetry. Nothing authentic will remain from your era except a great and bitter lesson for the nation . . . Do you see you've been struck dumb? Do you see you have no answer?"

Fereydoun, on edge and sweating, got a grip on himself for a moment and was astonished at Ali Khamenei's silence. Over the last five days, God knows how much they had argued and quarreled and shouted at one another till hoarse. They had walked together, yelled together, eaten together, slept and urinated. From time to time, he had sympathized with Ali Khamenei when he moaned about not knowing why the tops of his shoulders felt like they were burning as if he'd been stung by a wasp. A few times Fereydoun had had to point his flashlight at them to see what was going on, but there was nothing in particular. The tops of his shoulders were a little red, that was all. Perhaps he had gotten a heat rash underneath that ill-fitting woolen cloak.

Fereydoun turned his head to see why Ali Khamenei was silent. He pointed the flashlight this way and that until eventually he located him blundering about confusedly trying to straighten his turban and hold his cloak up, all the while fumbling around for his cane which had fallen on the floor. Angered, he took a few steps towards him, and without having contemplated the action for a moment before, in one motion he took the turban from his head and flung it on the ground, while in another motion he yanked the cloak from his back and threw it down, shouting at him: "Idiot! After five days of walking in a cave, you still haven't figured out that here is not the place for a turban and a cloak?" As he was turning round to continue on his way, he gave the turban a mighty kick and off it flew. But Ali Khamenei heard nothing. He saw only lips that moved, and yet there was no way he could put up with his turban being thrown and kicked. Which is why, scowling and in two or three long leaps, he got himself over to Fereydoun Taban and with his only good arm pushed him from behind onto the ground and yelled, "Haven't figured out? How dare you treat me like this?" And though mindful that five days earlier he had lost his three personal bodyguards, he nonetheless yelled: "Hajj[80] Qasem?

[80] *Hajj* or *hajji*, a title of respect for someone who has gone on the Hajj, or major pilgrimage, to Mecca, and performed all the prescribed rituals there.

Hajj Mostafa? Hajj Kazem? Where the hell are you? The devil take you if this is what you call protection!"

Fereydoun calmly got up and stood watching him. Ali Khamenei shouted once more: "I am the Leader of this country! Leader of the Muslim world! How dare you even touch me!" Fereydoun started brushing the dirt off his knees. Over these five days they had hurled all manner of insults at one another, but they hadn't raised their hands at each other. "Shut it!" Fereydoun said. Ali heard nothing, however. He could only see that Fereydoun's lips were moving. He touched his ears. In a loud voice he asked, "What did you say?"

Fereydoun started rolling up his left sleeve, and as he did he yelled, "I said shut it! I said for once just shut up!" Ali touched his ears several times, before banging on them in the hope that he might hear something, but still he heard nothing. "I can't hear!" he said in astonishment. "You've been deaf for years," Fereydoun said. "You just didn't realize." Ali shouted: "I can hear my own voice, but I can't hear yours . . . Speak up!"

When he had finished rolling up his left sleeve, Fereydoun calmly put his rucksack, glasses, and flashlight in a corner, and as he did, said, "This is one of the miracles of this cave. It reveals everyone's true self."

Again Ali heard nothing. Fereydoun positioned the flashlight so that its light would illuminate the relatively large space they were in. But before he did, he gestured in a particular direction and addressed Ali: "This is the center of the cave. The place where—"

Ali interrupted him, pointed to his ears, and as if he had only now grasped the gravity of the matter, shouted in horror, "I can't hear . . . I really can't hear! What awful thing's happened to me?" Then he yelled in the direction of the darknesses of the cave, towards somewhere he hoped one of his three bodyguards would finally hear him: "Help . . . help . . . Qasem, Mostafa, Kazem? Where the hell are you?"

Then, as if his shoulders had started to hurt again, he placed his hand on them and said, "What disease is this that I'm suffering from? Why do my shoulders hurt? Why are they burning? Why do they have bumps on them?"

Calm and smiling, Fereydoun went over to him and once more inspected his shoulders with his flashlight. "I guessed right," he said. "I've brought you back to where you belong."

Ali heard nothing, however. Fereydoun pointed to a corner and said, "Do you see that collar and chain over there? Zahhak was held captive here for five thousand years until the sorcerers and demons freed him."

Ali's attention had drifted back to his ears. He kept banging on them and spinning round like a madman, and, as if he were talking into a microphone, he said in a loud voice, "Hello? Hello? Can you hear me? Yes, yes . . . I can hear you . . . I can hear you. Hello? Hello . . . I can hear my own voice clearly." All of a sudden as if he had discovered something truly remarkable he said, "Yes, yes. That's enough." Guffawing suddenly and turning to Fereydoun he said, "It's absolutely brilliant . . . at last I've been set free from the evil of having to listen to your whining . . . *Ha ha ha* . . . I can't even listen to those wretched twenty-minute tapes anymore." And he laughed even louder, so that for a few moments his laughter echoed through the cave . . . *Ha ha ha ha ha ha.*

Fereydoun stood still, staring at him. He grinned at his stupidity. They had walked for five days to reach the center of the labyrinth, and prior to that Fereydoun had spent days planning how and where he could jettison the three guards and thus force Khamenei to walk alone with him for five days and nights until they got to their destination. During those five days they had passed through a great many corridors narrow and broad, long and short, passageways and precincts big and small. They had ascended and descended many levels, so that Khamenei could no longer figure out whether they were in the labyrinth's upper levels or its lower ones. Fereydoun Taban, however, was acquainted with the whole place. After he had been charged with exploring this hand-excavated cave and deciphering its inscriptions, he had spent an entire month, night and day, living down there until he'd gotten to know every nook and cranny. Even though Khamenei had initially only given him a week, he had disregarded this order and gone into the cave with a rucksack and a wheeled refrigerator containing food and water, after ordering Khamenei's bodyguards to leave him provisions as well as cigarettes once a week at a specific place in the cave. Khamenei had no choice but to accept.

During that month, he had been able to discover and explore the length, depth, history, and function of the cave, up to a point, as well as locate the center of the labyrinth and read the inscriptions that had been placed down there. He had realized that the center of the maze lay under the summit of Mount Damavand and that the various arms of the cave extended tens and even hundreds of kilometers around the mountain. Those arms and tunnels were so long that he had not been able to discover them all alone. To explore them all completely would require a large national and international team of archaeologists. He had figured out that the place belonged to a period before the Achamenids, before the Mithraic cult had even emerged. Despite this, in seven niches he had found elements left over from the cult of Mithra—seven wands, seven cups, seven coins, and seven swords made of seven types of metal: lead, zinc, bronze, iron, tin, silver, and gold. He had found many other niches with curved ceilings and holes in those ceilings, through which the full moon could be seen on certain nights. He had become so bewitched by the thought and philosophy behind the cave's labyrinth that Khamenei's order and his own life and death no longer mattered to him. Why did the summit of Damavand mark the middle of this labyrinth? Why did a spiral staircase lead straight down to the depths beneath the summit? Where did it lead to exactly? Who had ordered this place be built anyway? When? Besides worship, what other activities had they carried on there? Had it not been built to protect them from the cold, from the ice of the Ice Age? What important events had occurred there? When had the last person, the last Mithraist, departed that cave? For an entire month, he had not shut his eyes except for an hour here and there by way of rest. How many little natural pools of water, both cold and hot, had he found there, sometimes sitting in them himself. He had placed markers everywhere, found various ancient objects, identifying and collecting them together. Yet the seven ancient inscriptions, and one small inscription in the middle of the labyrinth, were things that could not be easily passed over. Those inscriptions clarified a great number of murky matters. He had read them with the utmost excitement and love and had prepared film and photographs of them to deliver them to his colleagues when the moment came. The seven inscriptions explained in lapidary fashion the seven stages of the Path and their goals, while the small, central inscription contained only two words, written in Neo-Elamite script: *Zahhak's Prison*. That was all. Was Zahhak a historical figure? Why would Zahhak have been kept in the middle of a cave that had been built in one epoch for protection from the cold, then utilized for worship and for the training of Mithraist disciples, heroes, warriors, and princes? Had it been their duty to guard him? Was Zahhak eventually freed? Who had helped him?

As he was thinking about these things, Fereydoun was also staring at Ali; without his robe and turban, all he would have to do to look like an ordinary person would be to trim his beard. A lowly employee. A manual laborer. One of the workers from Khomeini's tomb. Then he drew closer to him and casually thumped him in the face and said, "Did you want to look at this labyrinth? So look." He punched him again and said, "I'm only using my left hand so it'll be a fair fight, you cripple!" Ali, who had not been expecting this at all, and on whose lips dwelt a cheerful laughter at not being able to hear others' voices, attacked Fereydoun with rage and loathing and struck him on the head and face.. They began grappling with one another. Though they were more or less the same age, Fereydoun was in better shape. Working in the garden of the mansion in the North, and occasional archaeological excavations, had always kept his body fit. Khamenei on the other hand had a body like all clerics' bodies: unused. Lazy. A body that had been used for eating, sex, reproduction, and spreading religious superstitions, rather than for labor and effort. Ali nonetheless cared about his life. He invested in preserving his life as much as he could. All of a sudden, as they tussled with one another, Fereydoun stopped hitting him. Blood was dripping from his nose and from a corner of his forehead. Ali was in no better state. Fereydoun took a breath and wiped the blood from his eyes with his right hand. Then he took a step closer to him and shouted, "Hit me."

Ali heard nothing. Fereydoun turned the right side of his face towards him and shouted again. "Hit me . . . I have to be beaten up by you." And without understanding what he was saying, Ali casually struck him.

Fereydoun fell down. He stood up and drew close to him again and said, "Hit me. Harder. Hit me. I and all of us deserve to be beaten up. Because it was our generation that willingly handed the country over to an Ahriman like you. So hit me. Hard." And Ali once more heard nothing, but hit him again anyway.

Fereydoun stood up and said, "Harder." And Ali hit him again. Harder.

After being punched and falling to the floor several times, Fereydoun stood up, cut and bruised and bleeding, and said, "And yet a fish is fresh every time you catch it, right? Now I'm going to hit you, as a representative of my generation which has realized our tremendous historic mistake. I'm going to hit you because you had no reason to abuse the people's trust. You had no reason, as leader of the people, to turn into their enemy. I'm going to hit you as representative of the people whose revolution you stole, you who have sullied the name 'republic,' squandered the country's wealth, and cruelly killed its young people and its thinkers." And he punched Ali hard in the face, throwing him onto the ground.

Consumed by fire, by wrath, by bitter regret, Fereydoun yelled: "I am hitting you because of all the ancient works you stole and destroyed. Because of the distortion of history. Because of Iran's nature, the forests, lakes and rivers you have destroyed." And he struck Ali, who had only just with great difficulty got up, in the face, still harder.

From head to toe a volcano, like Rostam's mace, like Arash's arrow, like Siyavash's sword, filled with a feeling of revenge and loathing and rage, Fereydoun pounded Ali in the face, and as he did, yelled: "Because of the dear lives you took. Because of the dear lives you have left lonely in the world. I'm hitting you because of the wealth and tranquility and happiness you stole from this people. I'm hitting you because you have besmirched the good name of Iran in the world." And he hit . . . and hit . . . and hit, hitting him so much that Ali Khamenei's half-dead body slumped onto the ground.

When he wanted to step over this half-dead body, he took a look at Ali's torn shoulders. He hadn't noticed at all. While they had been thumping one another, two snakes had sprouted from his shoulders and now their two heads were moving from side to side and hissing.

During the five days they had been in the labyrinth together, he had gradually become certain that Ali Khamenei was none other than Zahhak himself, and yet he had either not kept it utmost in his mind or had quite deliberately denied it. He wanted to get him to confess who had saved him after five thousand years, and why. The other thing he had to do was to bind him with the collar and chain. Which meant that he would have to stay alive. If Zahhak had been kept captive in this cave for five thousand years, then this time he would have to be held captive for another five thousand years in the same place, with the same collar and chain, and then for another ten thousand years as a lesson to the people and to future rulers . . . As he waited for Ali to stir so that he could be sure he was still alive, he took a cigarette from his rucksack and lit up. What a fantastic taste. He smiled. This was the most exquisite cigarette he had smoked in his life. He thought that he should form a secret army to guard the cave and Zahhak. Just as they had done thousands of years before. He looked at him, still lying there lifeless. He stood up and poured a little water from his flask onto Ali's bloody face. When his cigarette was almost done, Ali was beginning to come round and he stirred a little. But at that very moment a buzzing reached Fereydoun's ears.

He stared into the darkness of the cave depths. The noise was echoing and he couldn't be sure which tunnel it came from. What was making it? Did it sound like a noise humans would make? But there was nobody here apart from himself and Zahhak. The buzzing grew closer and closer, now sounding like muttering. He looked in the direction of the sound. From a dark tunnel with a narrow opening a nine-year-old boy carrying a torch emerged. His expression was pure, yet mournful and confused. Behind him came a brown-haired young man, along with several other men and women, their number steadily increasing. Each one of them was holding a torch. The precinct was lit up. He looked at them. Astonished, he realized that some of them looked familiar to him. Who were they? Oh, . . . you! Mr. Mir-Alayee? Ah . . . Mr. Sirjani? . . . Good God, Mr. Farrokhzad? . . . My dear Dr. Tafazzoli . . . Mrs. Alizadeh . . . Mrs. Forouhar."

He leapt up and, tears welling up in his eyes, took a few long strides toward them with excitement and boundless respect. Oh, dear me . . . Wasn't the little boy Karoon? He had seen his photograph in the newspapers. He knelt before the boy and with a trembling voice and moist eyes, asked, "Are you Karoon?" "Do you know me?" the boy replied, happily. And he turned to his father, joyful and unbelieving, and exclaimed, "This gentleman knows me! He remembers me." A lump in his throat, Fereydoun kissed Karoon on the head, before standing up and drawing near to Hamid Hajjizadeh, Karoon's father. Respectfully and with tears in his eyes, he said, "I'm Fereydoun." They shook hands. Then he went up to each of those he knew and, his emotions a mix of sorrow and excitement, shook their hands too. They too smiled at him with a combination of astonishment and affection and greeted him. Then Fereydoun looked behind himself at Zahhak's half-dead body and said, "This is Zahhak."

Those men and women, those intellectuals, each one of whom had been killed on the orders of Ali Khamenei and Khomeini and Rafsanjani and Fallahin and Ezhei and many others, those victims of the chain murders, looked at Zahhak with disgust. Yet nobody moved. Fereydoun thought that perhaps they were too sad and depressed for even the sight of the half-dead body of their murderer to make them happy. Karoon, however, did move calmly towards Ali. When he got to him, he sat down beside him and lowered his torch so as to take a better look at his bloody, puffed-up face and at the two snakes, which were growing ever larger. Then he turned to his father and said in surprise, "He looks like us. He's a human. An ordinary human, but with two snakes on his shoulders."

His father shook his head with a forlorn expression. Then Karoon, unafraid of the snakes, placed his hand on the wound on Ali's cheek. He revived. He opened his eyes. "Who are you?" he shouted. "Who is here? Why is it so dark here?"

"It's me," said Karoon in his childish voice. "Karoon. You killed me. Along with my father."

But Zahhak heard nothing. He yelled. "Hajj Kazem? Hajj Mostafa? Hajj Qasem? Where the hell are you? Somebody bring a light."

"There are lights here," Karoon said, softly. "But you don't see."

Zahhak neither heard nor saw anything. With difficulty, he half got up. He ran his hand over his shoulders and the moment he felt the two snakes under his fingers, he fell, horrified, to the floor once more. "What are these things? O God, I seek refuge in Thee from the accursed Satan!" Karoon drew close to him again and said, "These are the snakes on your shoulders. Didn't you know? You are Zahhak himself."

Ali, who had heard nothing, fumbled in the air around him, trying to touch something. His hand bumped into Karoon's face. He was scared. "Who are you?" he yelled.

Karoon said nothing. Zahhak ran his hands over Karoon's face again. He shouted. "A child? In this forsaken cave? This dreadful labyrinth? Where the hell are you, Taban? Why is it so dark in here?"

Fereydoun raised his flashlight and looked at the crowd of dead dissidents who had gradually filled up the entire space. Unlike what people said, there weren't just two hundred, five hundred, or a thousand of them. There were many more. He only knew a few of them, or had read about their murders in the newspapers: Mohammad Mokhtari, Mohammad Pouyandeh, Siamak Sanjari, Ghaffar Hosseini, Reza Mazlouman, Parviz Davani, Daryoush and Parvaneh Forouhar, Abdolrahman Boroumand, Ahmad Tafazzoli, Hossein Sarshar . . . Oh how his heart burned at seeing these beautiful murdered souls . . . Dr. Ahmad Tafazzoli, his dear colleague. The beautiful Ghazzaleh Alizadeh was there, as was Masoumeh Mosaddeq. Ghazzaleh took a step forward like an enchantress and said, "Don't tell me you don't have a smoke!" Fereydoun went hastily over to his rucksack, and as he did, said, "Of course I do. I do." In his backpack he had a whole box of cigarettes. As if he could work without them! He took the packets out, giving one to Ghazzaleh and then the rest to whoever held out their hands. They opened the packets and shared the cigarettes in silence; Fereydoun lit a few of them with his lighter, while the rest used others' cigarettes to light their own. Fereydoun lit himself another too. Fereydoun Farrokhzad came over to him, gesturing to the cigarette between his fingers, and exclaimed with his deep voice and lively manner, "This is really hitting the spot."

A little further away stood Zahra Kazemi. Tears welled up in his eyes when he saw her face and recalled reading the news after her horrific murder in Evin Prison. He looked around himself. Those beautiful souls . . . Oh . . . Those plundered souls. Each one of them was a specimen of that poem of Rudaki's: "As the two eyes count it, one person less / As wisdom counts it, thousands more."

Everyone watched Karoon and Ali Khamenei in silence, cigarettes between their lips. Ali Khamenei was still speaking and Karoun replying to him without the former hearing a thing.

"I've gone blind," Ali said in horror. "God, what torment is this?"

"You were always blind," Karoon said with his childish calmness. "It was just that you didn't know."

When the victims of the chain murders had finished their cigarettes with great pleasure, Fereydoun glanced at Ahmad Tafazzoli, Mohammad Mokhtari, Zahra Kazemi, Parvaneh Forouhar, and Fereydoun Farrokhzad. There was no need to talk. They had understood what he meant. Together they went towards Ali Khamenei and grabbed him under his arms. "Who are you?" Ali Khamenei yelled. "Leave me alone. I am the Leader of the Revolution. You are the inimy . . . Inimy. Leave me alone. Inimy . . . Hajj Qasem, save me!"

Karoon stood up and made his way, torch in hand, through the crowd, who had opened a path for him, over to the sturdy collar and chain in the corner of the cave. They dragged Ali in the same direction. Then Karoon leant the torch against the wall and helped Fereydoun Taban lift up the heavy chain. Fereydoun Farrokhzad raised the other end of the chain. The others helped bind Zahhak with the collar and chain, the snakes on his shoulders having grown large and stout.

Fereydoun Farrokhzad then came, torch in hand, over to Fereydoun Taban and said, "We are grateful to you for the great task you have accomplished. It looks to me like the responsibility for what is to be done now rests with us." And he turned to face Zahhak and smirked.

"Won't you find it tedious to stay here?" Fereydoun asked.

"Tedious?" responded Fereydoun Farrokhzad with his usual innate good humor. "We are going to enjoy our time with him. The most important task we have here is to take care of this monster, so that he stays captive for thousands of years, and the Iranian people, free. Apart from that, this labyrinth is more extensive and entertaining than you think. It has a thousand passages and tunnels leading to a thousand corners of this earth. Some of these tunnels lead to places that are no longer part of the territory of our country, like Bukhara and Samarqand and Nimruz and Baghdad and Cappadocia. For instance, another end of this tunnel is joined to the Cave of Kay-Khosro, the living king. We know a lot of people there. One of the other ends is joined to the Eternal Forest. Another end is joined to the Palace above the Tree, still another to Persepolis, and—"

"The Eternal Forest?" Fereydoun asked. "The Palace above the Tree?"

"You're right not to know about them," responded Fereydoun Farrokhzad. "The Eternal Forest lies in the heart of the forests of Gilan and is concealed from the eyes of the living, but after thousands of years a small group of people now live there so they can preserve the ancient Mithraic, Simorghi, and Zurvanist cults. This is a secret, of course, but since I know you are trustworthy and that you will be joining us soon, I have revealed it to you."

"Am I due to die soon, then?" asked Fereydoun, surprised.

"Don't say you're surprised," replied Fereydoun Farrokhzad, stealing half a glance at Zahhak. "After the stunt you've pulled here, what did you think was waiting for you outside the cave?"

Fereydoun nodded his head pensively and said, "That's true. Incidentally, what do you think will happen now?"

"Probably they won't let anything slip for a little while," Fereydoun Farrokhzad said. "They'll put a replacement Khamenei to work until eventually they can foist his son Mojtaba on people. But they've read that one wrong . . . *Ha ha ha* . . . Good things are on their way. Afterwards you'll hear people chanting the slogan, 'Mojtaba, Leader? No way / Not till your dying day!'" And he laughed uproariously in his gorgeous, sonorous voice.

"Really? When?" Fereydoun said, in disbelief and happy.

"It'll take a little while," replied Fereydoun Farrokhzad. "But I know these people won't be with us forever. I mean just now you yourself bound Zahhak in chains. That was the most important and difficult task of all. A nation, a country, a civilization is indebted to you."

Fereydoun bowed his head humbly.

Fereydoun Farrokhzad resumed. "We all were waiting for this day. All the same, even though Karoon led us this way a few days ago, we had no idea that we would see you and Khamenei here. Apparently the whole affair had only been revealed to Karoon. I promise you that from now on things will move more quickly—the younger generation sees no link between its ideals and the ideals of this rotten revolution. It'll be them, these playful, cheerful young people and adolescents, who'll finish these bastards off."

"How?" Fereydoun asked. "They've got weapons, and they consider this country and us to be Islamic booty. Killing us is licit for them . . ."

Fereydoun Farrokhzad guffawed, and said, "You won't believe it . . . The youth will upend this godforsaken regime with dancing and laughter and kissing and the embrace of kindness. They do everything forbidden by this regime. And not because of a particular ideology or anything like that . . . No! They will destroy them just for the sake of living an ordinary life; they will conquer the streets through their long hair, through dance, through their loud laughter, their songs and their drunkenness. They'll take the country back. They will take life back."

Chapter Eighteen

Another wound appeared on my back in the middle of the night. I woke up abruptly because of the burning sensation it caused. There was nowhere left on my body that wasn't wounded: my upper arms, legs, my back. My chest. My hands and even the soles of my feet. Of course, the wounds will gradually get better, and only the scars will be left, yet tiny or unexpected things make them open up again, and all the pains and memories return to my body. To my soul. A telephone call, the announcement of an anniversary, the fall of an autumn leaf into the puddle beneath my feet, hearing a piece of music, or even seeing the familiar shape of someone who from behind resembles one of us. One of them. I got out of bed and sat on the chair by the window, facing the courtyard, staring at the darkness outside. It was a quiet night. As always. As if nobody were in the world, or I were in nobody's world. I listened carefully. Nobody, no heart, called me. I sat that like that until gradually the first light of dawn appeared and the silhouettes of the tree and the courtyard and the table and the two wooden chairs could be seen.

There is an enormous and extremely old tree in the middle of the communal courtyard of this residential block. The dimensions of the yard are exactly those of the tree. Which means that every day on either side of noon, the tree's shadow is cast into the surrounding apartments. Under the tree there is a small table and two wooden chairs next to the two large washing lines where the neighbors dry their laundry. One gentle summer's afternoon, as the heat caressed the skin on one's body, she was sitting on a chair, smoking, when I went there too, as was my habit, to smoke a cigarette.

She was of medium height and had long, undyed hair with large curls. In her disheveled hair perched a peacock feather. The feather looked lost in her hair, as if it had gotten stuck there by mistake or accident, or as if it had been placed there so that nobody could see it at first blush. It hadn't been put there for the sake of display. On the contrary. Between her hairs its white barbs bestowed a dignified and pensive appearance on her simple face. She was not beautiful. Nor was she ugly. She had a face that was without defect, but run-of-the-mill, except for her mesmerizing eyes. They were wide, and rather than possessing a bewitching beauty, they had an impressive intelligence, depth, and sparkle. Overall she seemed a little careless and scruffy. A little corpulent. Yet there was a natural self-confidence in the way she acted which meant, without me realizing it, that I greeted her respectfully and, smiling, sought her permission to sit on the chair opposite her. Holding her hand nonchalantly above her head, her smoking cigarette between her fingers, she spoke calmly: "Please do." Her arm stayed raised straight above her head. There was no posing involved in this gesture, since she had been doing this for several minutes, ever since I had been observing her from behind my bedroom window. As if she were completely absorbed in some other world.

She lowered her arm and took a drag on her cigarette. As she blew out the smoke through her determined lips, she raised her head again and observed the play of the smoke and the light and shade above her. She was watching carefully, as if she saw things through the light and shadows and billowing waves that others could not. That I could not. She behaved as if I weren't there. She did not go to the trouble of considering my presence. She didn't look at me at all. I hadn't seen her in the apartment complex before now. Perhaps she was a new neighbor, although I hadn't seen anyone moving in.

She smoked her cigarette calmly and deliberately and continued to watch the play of the smoke, the light, and the shadows, still indifferent to my presence. "The weather is very pleasant,"

I said. Her attention distracted, she glanced at me out of politeness and, nodding, agreed. I said nothing, and it looked like she either could not be bothered to talk much, or did not expect to. Once she'd finished her cigarette, she left without saying anything or looking at me. Her large earrings were silver and lapis lazuli-blue in color.

I didn't see her the following day. Nor the following week. Ten days later, she was sitting there again. There were a few small spots of paint on her clothes. Like on the previous occasion, there was no question of entering into a conversation. I greeted her very briefly, just for the sake of politeness, and I heard her answer. This time, as the hand holding her cigarette rotated in the air above her head, with her other hand she removed her left earring and put it on the table. It was the same earring. Silver and lapis lazuli-blue. It looked like an earring from India or Tibet. She massaged her lobe a little. I think she is one of those people whose ears never get used to earrings. She was about to leave without saying goodbye.

It jumped out of my mouth: "Are you leaving?"

She looked at me with astonished eyes, as if she beheld me from some other universe. It was the first time she had looked at me. What eyes. What a gaze. There was some kind of indescribable sadness exuding from her wide pupils, making one want to be silent and respectful. I panicked. It was as if she wanted to say, "But can't you see?" Yet she didn't. She remained polite and simply nodded her head. I got up too. I had to be brave. I didn't know why. My heart was beating so furiously at the sight of those eyes that she could probably hear it. In order to get a grip on myself, I asked, in a voice that only came out of my mouth with great effort, "Do you live in this complex?"

Again she turned her head and looked at me. This time it was as if she wanted to say, "Obviously." But simply out of politeness, she said, "Unit 5."

She turned away from me to leave. I needed to summon up the courage again, but I stopped myself just in time. All I said was, "Have a good day." She turned round and with an innocent and cheerful expression said, "Thank you. I hope so." As if she really had something important ahead of her and she was happy from the bottom of her heart that I had wished her a good day. At the last moment, the peacock feather caught my attention. It was still there in her hair. Concealed. Like the last time. As if it were just one hair among others. I didn't see her again. I waited for her every day behind the window. My bedroom window, on the third floor, facing the empty courtyard. I would turn the light off so as not to be seen from the outside. I was used to darkness. I had spent many long periods living in the silence and the dark. But she was the opposite. I knew which window belonged to Unit 5. Before her, a girl had lived there and for a while we'd had a relationship. As always, because my relationships with women are attractive and exciting to begin with, but in the end I make them sick of me, she packed up and left without me realizing. I was both happy and upset that this new woman in apartment number five paid no attention to me. It had been a while since I'd had a relationship with a woman. I needed attention and love and excitement. That is where the very value of being human lies. On the other hand, I was afraid of myself. After all these years I was no longer satisfied with the same old exciting activities of love, sex, quarreling, and separating. Women bewitched me in generall, but I wasn't satisfied with the way I acted with them. Perhaps I might be considered a kind sort, but in my relationships with women I had been self-involved and proud. Totally maladroit. Throughout my long life I have been complimented and praised and this has turned me into someone absurd and proud who considers myself above others. That's why in recent years I have promised myself to develop deeper, more human relationships with women, or not to have relationships at all. The truth is that of late I've realized that I feel inferior to women. I'm not sure why . . . Perhaps because women are much more complex, deeper and more creative than us men. Whatever the reason, it means that when

I am with them I panic and all sorts of inappropriate things happen. Is it really necessary to repeat the same action several times? Year after year . . . Century after century . . . I'm not one for marriage and responsibility and raising children. I've had that experience . . . I don't want it, at least not in this life. Not this time.

Every night before I went to sleep I could see her light was on. Every time I woke up in the middle of the night to light a cigarette in the darkness of my room, I could see it was still glowing. Not a shadow stirred in her room. Did that mean she slept with the light on? What about her electricity bill? Or did she sit and read a book? Ah, I remember that there was paint on her clothes. No doubt she was an artist. Yet painters no doubt walk around as they paint, think, moving away from the work to take a better look before returning to the canvas.

She turned up eventually. A month has passed. Her face had a particular calm and cheerfulness to it, like someone who has successfully completed a difficult project and who is now free for a while. This time too when I saw her, she did not look at my face except out of politeness. She's probably one of those women who's had a lot of inappropriate and odd men like me come her way and now despairs of romantic relationships. For a moment my heart fluttered as I set eyes on her. I coughed once to calm down. I ordered myself not to fall in love, and not to make her fall in love with me. Let the poor woman live her life, and yet again it jumped out of my mouth: "It's been a month since you were last here."

Shit . . . I hadn't meant to show this level of attention. But it looks like old habits die hard. She looked at me and said, quite simply, "I hadn't noticed."

"The light in your room is on most nights," I said.

This time she glanced at me briefly with eyes narrowed, as if she wanted to say, "I've figured you out, you lecherous man." But she shrugged and said, "So?"

I was taken aback. "Are you a painter?" I asked quickly.

It can't be said that I saw any particular defiance in her eyes. It seemed she'd had plenty of experience brushing off mediocre people like me. All the same, her gaze had nothing pompous about it. Perhaps it might be said her gaze was more like that of people who need nothing—those people who are connected to a source of spiritual inspiration in some secret or inaccessible place within them. With no time for the common folk.

"Sometimes," she replied.

"What do you do the rest of the time?" I asked.

This time she looked at me, hesitating a little, and then said, deliberately and carefully, "If people knew that after every question they should expect another one, perhaps they would never answer the first one to begin with."

This was the longest thing I'd ever heard come from her mouth and only then did I realize how warm and profound her voice was. What a heavenly ring it had to it. I felt myself turning red and hot from embarrassment. She had flushed too. I savored what she had said for a little bit, before saying, "I'm sorry, I didn't want to upset you."

She stood up. She smiled innocently again and said, "You haven't upset me. It's just that I don't feel like talking." Then she disappeared behind the building, as usual. I hated myself. How superficial and tedious I am. There's not the slightest thing that experienced, deep women might find attractive about me, and although I am much, much older than her, I don't in the least think and act like someone who's seen the world.

I was angry with myself for several days. As soon as I had finished work, I would go with my colleagues to the underground bar one of my friends kept, so that I could forget the feeling of being common and empty with wine and aragh sagi. How flawed I am . . . How many things I still have to learn from people. This was what I had ended up doing: at the end of each night, drunk and out of it, I would take a taxi home on my own, pass out in my clothes on the bed, and in the morning, even as the stench of alcohol that had drifted through the apartment made me feel ill, I would go to the bathroom and bandage up the new wound on my body and then head off to work.

The underground bar had a good atmosphere. In this country, everything good is underground; underground books, underground music, underground restaurants, underground theatre, even underground people. It is as if people have grown accustomed to two types of life. A day-to-day life with dark clothes, heads down, from home to the office and from the office to home. And a nocturnal underground life. At night, those same women in their headscarves and long manteaux toast the health of forbidden loves with forbidden drink in their favorite hidden haunts with their friends, dancing forbidden dances to forbidden music wearing forbidden clothes. Often I sit in a corner and people-watch in silence. I like all of them. I even like the masquerade of the way they live.

Once a drunk young woman sat next to me. Even though we did not know one another at all, she said without warning, "I'm Mahtab. I work at the National Steel Office and I have only one wish in life. That one day, in my own country, in the streets of my own city, I will be able to live the way I want to." "How do you mean?" I asked. She said, "I mean, for example, one moonlit Thursday night, that I'll be able to let my hair down, and, wearing a simple sleeveless dress—this dress here for example, go dance underneath the Azadi Tower and kiss my boyfriend and recite my latest poem for him:

"It was your simple image
And my lost solitude
Like a butterfly briefly alighting on a hand
Or listening to the lightweight flight of a dandelion seed
Carrying the message, 'I love you.'"[81]

She had a deep and alluring voice. She rested her head on one hand as she was talking, while with the other she toyed

[81] Poem by Mahtab Naseri.

with a glass of aragh. She continued: "Then we would go hand in hand to the Nayeb restaurant and eat and drink our favorite foods and beverages. Then we'd go to the Azadi cinema and watch an uncensored movie. For example, imagine how cool it would be to watch Kubrick's *Eyes Wide Shut* on a cinema screen. Then we'd go to my place and have loud sex. Late at night we'd go to a club with our friends and dance until morning . . . That's it. My wish is that simple. That impossible." Her head slumped onto the table from the effects of drunkenness and she fell asleep. I saw that in the middle of the night when she wanted to leave the bar that she had put on a long black manteau and a very long maqnaeh that reached her waist.

Fall had arrived. The orange, yellow, and crimson leaves of the great oak tree in the middle of the yard were so gorgeous and sad that every afternoon as soon as I had come back from work I would go and sit under it, drink tea and smoke a cigarette and think of Mohammad. Of one of my first wounds. I rolled up my sleeve and looked at my upper arm. The wound had healed, but every year, as soon as the first leaf of autumn fell, it opened up again and started to hurt. I ran my finger over Mohammad's wound. Further down was Fereydoun's wound. I raised my arm and looked at the back of it. Ghazzaleh's wound had also started to hurt. In fall I completely forgot about the woman who was my neighbor. Fall was entirely devoted to Mohammad. On that day, December 18, 1998, he had left home and been killed on Iranshahr Street, and ten days later they had found his body in one of the villages around Shahriyar. Fall was devoted to Mohammad's voice alone, when he recited Akhavan-Sales's poem:

It embraces tight its sky, the cloud
With its cold, moist fur-lined coat
The leafless garden
Is alone day and night
With its pure, sorrowful silence.

Its instrument is rain
Its anthem wind
The king of seasons, autumn.

Mohammad's voice was rasping, because beside thinking and writing and translating, he had nothing to do but smoke. He had been born into a poor Yazdi family, and his room was so damp that the ceiling had collapsed a month before his murder and made his books and translations all wet and dirty. Although he had studied sociology at the Sorbonne, they wouldn't give him permission to work at the university. And nobody in this country could balance their outgoings and their income by translating articles and publishing books. That was why Mohammad lived in impoverished circumstances, yet they had not even been able to tolerate that and had killed him. They strangled him. He was one of those people killed in what afterwards the newspapers called "the Chain Murders." When word got out, someone was arrested for his murder at the journalists' insistence and condemned to life imprisonment, but the guilty man did not even spend a single day in jail.

Fall is Mohammad's season. The season of all the Mohammads who were killed before they succeeded in bringing about change. How many such Mohammads have we had? Was there not that other Mohammad . . . and what about Daryoush and Parvaneh? What about poor Siamak and Pirouz and Fereydoun Taban, or Ghazzaleh, and Masoumeh Mosaddeq . . . ? How many of them we have in the history of this country . . . Each one of them has turned into a wound on my body. At night and in the middle of the night I would wake up because of the burning sensation and see that a fresh wound had appeared and realize that they had killed yet another one of us . . . I has been friends with all of them. A close friend. How much fun it was in Fereydoun Taban's mansion up in the North. We would sit for hours talking about the ancient history of the world. Of Iran, Greece, Rome, Egypt, India, China. Fereydoun and his grandmother

Khanom Joon would be thrilled to bits as I told them, "Back when the people of other lands were living up trees, the Iranians were writing poetry." Sometimes something would escape my mouth and I would give him information that could be found in no extant ancient manuscript. He would hurriedly note it down and say, "What you are saying really makes sense and even sheds light on several points of confusion in history and archaeology, but where did you get all this stuff from?"

I always dodged the question. What could I have said to him? I had made friends with all of them just so I could give them a helping hand, even the tiniest one, and make it easier for them to understand this life, this dark, suffocating, complicated life. To show them the happy face of life. To soothe them. However little. For however short a time. Not a day or night went by without us reading books and poetry and blind drunk hurling insults at this regime and all its horrid crew . . . They always used to ask me why I was single. I couldn't tell them the real reason why. Or whenever they broached the matter of my past and my family, I would be forced to change the subject, because I didn't like to lie to them. I wanted them to feel that there were still good, kind, compassionate people in this world, in this country. I wanted to reduce their pains of soul and psyche, even if by the tiniest amount. But recently plain clothes agents from the Ministry of Intelligence have been on my tail, they've interrogated me several times, and although their spies have followed my footsteps to the homes and workplaces of all my friends, who have been murdered one by one, they haven't been able to pin anything on me. No image of me has been recorded by any camera. Not that that would stop them. If they could, they would no doubt kill me too.

I was feeling cold. I rolled down my sleeve. A cold breeze blew the autumn leaves onto me and onto the little table. Ah, how beautiful fall is in this country . . . and beauty is sad.

I got up to go and lie under a blanket in my room when she showed up from behind the building. She didn't see me. Her head was down and she was lighting up a cigarette. I couldn't be bothered. I went. She must have heard the sound of my footsteps on the leaves. Perhaps she saw me from behind as I was leaving, a little hunched over and listless.

Today I saw her from the window. I don't remember how many days it has been since the last time. I watched her for a little from the chair by the window. As always, she was a little casual, but not listless or grumpy, however. She was sitting on the chair I usually sat on. What was she trying to do? Was she trying to show she owned that massive tree and that modest courtyard? The table and chairs weren't mine, of course. I know they don't belong to the owner of the complex either. I've been living here for years now. Even though the tenants change here every year, I stayed put. I picked up my cigarette and went outside. Before doing so, I took a look at myself in the mirror. With my salt-and-pepper hair, long, thin nose and tall height, I had always been attractive to women. I tidied up my hair. I promised myself not to engage in any idiotic seduction. And placed a hold on excessive questioning.

When she saw me coming round the corner from behind the building, her head was raised and her eyes noticed me without expecting it. She smiled gently and took a drag on her cigarette. Generally speaking it seems like she is not too concerned with observing the usual norms of politeness. When I said hello, she nodded her head, still smiling the same smile, and said, "It's a lovely day. The autumn leaves make one sad even if one has no reason to be so." This was the first time she had initiated the conversation. I nodded, looked up at the leaves above me, and took a drag on my cigarette. "Ultimately everybody has some sadness in their being," I said.

She didn't look at me. She didn't nod in approval either. She stood up and said, "Would you care for some tea? At my place." Her tone was clear and firm, yet I didn't sense any coarseness in it. On the contrary, there was a kind of refined politeness in it even without the use of the standard polite terms "Would you like, please, how about we . . . " I promised myself I'd remain dignified, but inside I was excited. I hadn't expected this at all. How wonderful it was that the other residents weren't the type to poke their noses in, because otherwise they would have been talking about us for a while now. Maybe they have been, and I just didn't know about it. I stood up. Without waiting for my reaction, she had already set off in the direction of her apartment. I set off after her, without putting out my cigarette. Given my height, I always had either to push the branches aside or stoop down when I wanted to pass behind the back of the building. The door of her room was ajar, and a soft orange-red light came out of it. I opened the door slowly. She was in the kitchen, filling the kettle. Although it was sunset, she hadn't turned on any lights. The gentle light of sunset came in through the large window. A warm feeling, of calm and safety, suffused my body. For a moment I lost myself and was close to falling in love with her, or even worse, to breaking down with thoughts of Mohammad or with torments of my conscience at not having done anything when he or the others died, or perhaps because of the pointless arguments I'd started with my ex-girlfriend in this very apartment, or because of a thousand other things.

The wall opposite was covered by four white bookshelves. It was filled with books, and with two large earthenware vases, with a few handmade sculptures, large and small, surrounding it, as well as some strange-looking ashtrays. One of them was a tortoise shell, while another was a clod of dried earth whose middle had been crudely hollowed out. In the room there was also a suite of gray armchairs and couch over which an orange-brown throw had been haphazardly draped. On the floor there was a handwoven Bakhtiari carpet, and by the window a round dining table with four seats. Between the kitchen and the living room was a hallway leading to two or three doors. Behind the armchairs was a tape recorder and a CD holder. Here and there, some vases contained luxuriant ferns. There were two or three beautiful paintings on the walls, as well as one or two half-finished paintings leaning against the wall. I had guessed right. She was a painter. Farther over, there was a decently sized desk on which were a laptop and several books and scattered papers. Was she not a writer, translator, or editor?

"Does it look like your apartment?" she asked. I sat on a stool next to the kitchen table, and as I was taking my last drag on my cigarette, said, "The architecture, yes." Then I went over to the bookshelf and picked up the tortoise shell and stubbed out my cigarette in it. I felt at home and comfortable, thanks to the way the room was decorated and the gentle sunset light. Why wasn't my house like this? It hadn't even occurred to me after all these years to unpack my books from their boxes or to put a stereo in the living room. As she put some fragrant Do Ghazal tea in front me, she said, "It's brewed with cardamom." The scent filled the room. She had asked a question, so that meant I could ask one too. Without thinking, I asked, "What is your name?" She didn't look at me. She smiled. She sat down opposite me and blew on her tea. As if she had no intention of answering me, or even of giving an explanation. I liked what she was doing. She wasn't like any of the women I'd met in this long life of mine. She lifted her head from the fragrant steam of the tea and looked at me, smiling. I started laughing. Meaning that I think she saw my neat, white teeth for the first time. I knew that with those big, hazel eyes and thick eyebrows, I possessed the piercing gaze mature men have. Women readily fell captive to me, but she seemed different. She took hold of my feelings and my mind, rather than my instincts . . . Although right from the moment I entered her house, my instincts were also aroused. Oh, if it were possible to place a kiss on those prominent lips of hers so casually blowing out the smoke of her cigarette . . . I had to take control of myself. It struck me that she was one of those women who could throw me out of her house as easily as she had invited me there.

I shifted positions in my chair a little so that my mood would change. I took a sip of my tea and for the sake of amusement said, "Does your name begin with 'p'?" She gave a loud laugh, something I had not expected. Her laugh came from deep within. As if with her unfettered laughter she was giving me permission to relax a little. I laughed as well. "No," she said. I wanted to ask right away, "Does it start with 'b'?" But I stopped this silly game just in time. Suddenly it leapt out of my mouth: "My name is Manouchehr."

This wasn't my original name, but it wasn't a lie either. This was one of the hundreds and thousands of names I had given myself. One of the hundreds and thousands of experiences with people I had acquired in life. It wasn't possible for me to tell her who I was. I had never told anyone during all these years, all these centuries. Not a single person. I didn't understand whether it was the warmth of her presence, the soft light shining on the household objects, or the sight of the peacock feather half concealed in her hair that provided me with such an uncontrollable feeling of intimacy that all of a sudden words and memories poured forth unauthorized from my mouth: "When I was fourteen, my mother took me on foot from a village a hundred kilometers away from Khorramshahr to the city so that I could see my father for the first time. We walked for three days and nights to get there. On the way my mother talked about my father. She said people say he's a good man. She hadn't seen anything bad in him herself, apart from the fact that the day after their wedding he upped sticks and left. My mother said my father was kind, that when he saw me, he would definitely like me. Maybe he'd want to keep me there with him and send me to a good school. My mother said we shouldn't get upset if he had a wife and children. He's a man, after all. And if he didn't want her, it wouldn't matter. I could stay with him, and she'd go back to the village. I should study. Become a good, reliable, decent person. When we got to the city, we were so tired and hungry we went straight to a public bath with cubicles. It was early morning on the fourteenth day. There my mother ordered some sheep's head and feet stew and cold yoghurt drink. It was so good. I can still taste it. In the baths, with the steam all around us, we ate sheep's head and feet stew and cold yoghurt drink and laughed. With sangak bread[82] and fresh Seville oranges. It might have been the tastiest food I've eaten in my life. Then my mother called the masseuse over to scrub the dirt well off our bodies and knead and pommel us. The jingling of the masseuse's bracelets as she pommeled us is still ringing in my ears: *dring, dring, dring!* After the breakfast and the yoghurt drink and the massage, we slept right there on the platform in the baths. When we came out, we had turned into different people entirely. My mother rubbed a little rouge and powder on her face and drew a design above the right side of her lips with pure, dark-colored henna. She was not an ugly woman at all. In some ways she was quite beautiful. It was just that she squinted in one eye. It was only a ten-minute walk from the baths to the house of the man who was my father. I was so excited that my heart was beating furiously, and tears had started to flow. My mother noticed, wiped away my tears with the corner of her flowery chador, and said, 'The pain and sorrow of being far away is over. From now on you will have only good fortune.'

"After we'd knocked on the door, we were kept waiting outside for twenty minutes under the hot summer sun before they opened. They'd seen us out of the window. The sound of shouting could be heard behind the door. 'That's your father's voice,' my mother said. I pulled her arm and said, 'Come on, let's go. I'm scared.' The noise of all that shouting had ruined my excitement. I was afraid. She stood right there and said, 'It's your father. Everybody says he's a good man. He surely loves you. You're his own blood.' When he opened the door, I froze in astonishment. He was an old man. He was bald. He wore

[82] In *Sangak* means little stone. The bread is baked on a bed of small river stones in an oven.

glasses and had a Hitler mustache, and his look was angry and irritable. He was wearing striped pajamas. His wife appeared behind him. She was young and pretty and fat. The same age as my mother. All of a sudden, a whole bunch of kids came to the door. They were their children. One of the boys, who looked the same age as me, stared at me with wide, intelligent eyes and took a bite from a piece of watermelon. Cool watermelon would've really hit the spot in that heat. I was still pulling at my mother's arm. She had turned red and started stammering. My heart was pounding so fast it was practically coming out of my mouth. I felt like my complexion had turned the color of straw. They led us to the reception room. There was a large bowl of fruit on the table. Their house had wallpaper. Our house was mud and straw. There was a chandelier hanging from the ceiling of their house. In our room there was a fluorescent lamp. On the table, in a bowl, enticing, were different varieties of peaches and nectarines. I wanted to put one of the nectarines in my pocket. The man who was my father did not even glance at me. His brows were furrowed, and he was sitting on the couch. I had not seen a couch before. He didn't even invite us to sit. We stayed standing.

"'This is your son. Manouchehr,' my mother stammered. 'I've brought him for you to see him. He's fourteen now. He studies very hard.' My father didn't even lift his head. He was red with anger. The other woman and the children had vanished into another room. Every now and then the sounds of their screaming and shouting could be heard before they fell silent again. My father put his hand down the back of the couch, took out his wallet and flung a handful of notes down on the table. 'Take it and get lost,' he yelled. The hem of my mother's flowery chador fell from her mouth where she had been holding it. She turned as a white as a sheet. In a voice that sounded as if it came from the bottom of a well, she said, 'We didn't come here for money. I have cattle. I'm a farmer. I have enough to get by on. I just wanted you to see your son.' Once again, the man did not lift his head to look at me. I tugged my mother's arm. She was still staring at him. As I was pulling my mother from behind, I bumped into the wall and a frame fell and shattered. I pulled my mother harder and ran outside. Behind us the sound of my father's roar made the walls of the house shake.

That night, in the desert on the way home, we lit a fire by a mountain so that we could sleep. I was hungry but didn't feel like talking. I put my head on my mother's skirt; she was facing the moon and sobbing softly and wiping her nose with a corner of her chador. That very night, right there on my sobbing mother's skirt, I wept so much from sorrow that I died of a broken heart."

I fell silent. All these words had poured forth from my mouth without me willing them, like the gentle bubbling of a spring in some far-off meadow. I stuck my hand in my pocket to find my packet of cigarettes. It wasn't there. She calmly pushed her own packet toward me. Without looking at her, I pulled out a cigarette and lit it. The light of the match flickered throughout the room. As I struck the match, I noticed that my hands were trembling.

After two or three deep drags on my cigarette, I finally lifted my head and looked at her. She, who had until that moment it seems been staring at me, turned her head toward the window. It had gotten dark. The tea had gone cold. The birds outside the window silent. The only sound to be heard was the bubbling of water in the kettle on the gas stove. As a sigh softly escaped her mouth, she stood up, emptied the tea glasses into the sink, and poured fresh tea for me. "What became of your mother?" she asked.

I took a sip of hot tea to refresh my mouth. "She hauled my body on her back for two days until we got to the village," I said. "They washed me and buried me in the courtyard of the shrine amid the weeping and howling of my mother, grandmother, and the inhabitants of the village. She never remarried, even though one or two men who already had two wives or were widowers sought her hand. She was a proud woman. She continued tending her orchard and cattle right there until she grew old and died. They buried her next to me."

We both finished off our tea in silence. When my cup was empty, I stood up. I didn't feel like saying goodbye. Why had those words flown out of my mouth, anyway? However much I claim to, I have no control over my feelings. I think it was out of grief for Mohammad that I got this way . . . Out of grief for the autumn. I opened the door in the darkness and left.

Three days later at sunset the woman knocked on my door. Without me inviting her, she came in and said, "Shall we drink tea together?" She was carrying a tray with a kettle and a teapot, cigarettes and dates. We both lit our cigarettes. I knew she'd come to hear the rest of the story. I brought two glasses. I knew I wanted to tell her more than I told other women. Why? I don't know. There was an uncontrollable allure in her actions, her speech, her mournful eyes and her nonchalant manner that made me do something to make her want me. I could no longer pretend otherwise. I thought about her constantly. I wanted to impress her. So, as she poured the tea, I said, "It took a long time before I awoke from the sleep of death. I came out of the grave covered in soil and washed myself in a river. When I looked at myself in the water, I was still the same fourteen-year-old child. I headed home. I didn't know what I ought to do. Wouldn't my mother have a heart attack when she saw me? When I snuck into the house and saw how old my mother had become, I realized how much time had passed. She was making green herb frittata. She had grown so old that her hand shook as she poured the batter into the frying pan. My grandmother, who was over a hundred, turned her head to stare at me, standing behind the crack in the door, in the darkness of dusk, gazing at them by the flickering light of the fluorescent lamp. She couldn't even blink or open her mouth. In the mournful silence of the house at dusk the only thing that could be heard was the sizzling of the frittata in the hot oil.

When I shut the door slowly behind me, I had made up my mind: I did not intend to return to that life. It had been years now that my mother had gotten used to my not being there. So it was that I set off. I still remembered the way to the city and house where the man who was my father lived. As it had been the previous time, it was three days and nights journey, but it took me ten years to get there. I wandered confused and aimless outside the village, hands in pocket, until I reached the village qanat.[83] An old man was trying to draw water from it with great effort. When he saw me, he asked me for help. I filled his bucket with water. I wanted to continue on my way when I saw that with each step the old man took, the water overflowed and spilled. I took the bucket from him, filled it again, and helped him mount his cow. I led him to his house. When we got there, he told me, calmly but in a commanding tone, to milk the cow. I did. He made rice with squash for dinner and invited me to eat with him. As I closed the house door behind me, the scent of the peach blossoms in the courtyard made me intoxicated. After dinner I gathered the dishes, washed them, and got out the old man's bedding which was stowed in a corner. I thanked him and said I had to continue on my way. 'In snow like this?' the old man said. 'What snow?' I asked. 'It's spring and there's blossom everywhere.' 'Open the door,' he said. I opened it and was struck in the face by a biting cold and flakes of snow. The courtyard was full of snow and all the blossoms had frozen. I had no choice but to shut the door and said I would stay until it stopped snowing. The house was cold, and the stove was out. I went outside and broke up some firewood. As I was lighting the fire, tears of joy gathered in the old man's eyes and he said, 'God has sent you to me so that in my old age I won't suffer

[83] A qanāt or kārīz is a system for transporting water from an aquifer or water well to the surface, through an underground aqueduct; the system originated in Iran approximately 3,000 years ago.

from cold and loneliness.' The next day it was still snowing, and snow and sleet was getting in through the cracks in the dilapidated walls. I made cob mortar and blocked up all the cracks. I ended up staying with the old man until he died. Six years had gone by from the day I had filled his bucket until the day I buried him. I buried him under the peach tree. It was spring and the tree was once more bursting with pink blooms. Sitting under the porch, I looked at the old man's grave, which with the first morning breeze was covered in blossoms. With the first pink petal that fell on my face, I made up my mind. I gathered the old man's cows and sheep, chickens and cockerels, shut the latch of the courtyard gate behind me, and set out.

"The animals and I walked and walked until I saw a solitary cow underneath an ancient oak tree, bellowing as the sun set over the meadow, straining to give birth to her calf; under the oak tree there was also a large stone slab. I stood beside her. My cows and sheep also stood around her. Tears were welling up in the cow's wide, black eyes. It was getting dark by the time the calf was finally delivered. I sat down beside them and made a fire. It struck me that I ought not to leave them on their own. It was not long before the wolves started howling. The cow was weak and unable to walk. The calf did its best to walk but soon grew tired and lay down next to its mother and started to drink milk. It had not long since gotten dark when, amidst the howling of the wolves, the cow took a turn for the worse. I didn't know what to do. I didn't know which way the settlement of the cow's owner was. Eventually a torch appeared in the distance, getting closer and closer. It was a young woman. She was very happy when she saw the calf. She put it over her shoulders to take it home. "What about the cow?" I asked. As she was departing, the woman said, "Stay with her until I get back." I stayed. It was not yet dawn when she returned with a cart. I helped her put the cow in the cart. Her house was a long way away. It wasn't clear why the cow had walked all that way to give birth to her calf by the abandoned road along which I had been passing. As soon as we got to the house, the woman handed me a large knife and told me to slaughter the cow because otherwise the meat would be haram. I started to cry from fear. The woman understood my pitiful expression. She snatched the knife from me and slit the base of the cow's throat in a single movement. Great quantities of blood spurted over our clothes and faces. I saw a dog, then a scorpion, come and start drinking the cow's blood. The woman continued what she was doing, paying them no attention. As if for her it were natural for them to have their share of the cow.

"With her head, the woman gestured for me to bring the large iron tub from next to the well. I did. The woman was strong, and it seemed like she had resolved to make the best of life, come what may. I helped her skin the cow. To remove its head, to take out its heart, liver, and kidneys. To clean its intestines. To remove its eyes and tongue and last of all to salt its skin before hanging it out in the sun to dry. She was so skillful in doing all this that not even the tiniest piece of its body was thrown away. She even hung its hooves on threads from the wall of her house, saying, "This will bring blessings." Then she told me to light a fire in the yard. She salted large pieces of the liver and threw them on large bits of charcoal to make kebabs. Sitting down next to the fire, she said, "Sit down. Eat." I sat and ate. That same night I became her husband. Without asking me anything, she spread out her bedding and told me to lie down next to her. I lay down. Then she taught me what I should do with her as a man and a husband. Which I did. Afterwards she told me that her husband had years before joined the Russian forces when they had invaded Iran and since then there had been no news of him. She said that he had no doubt married a Russian woman and stayed there. After that her two sons had died of cholera. The woman was at most eighteen or nineteen, yet she was as accomplished as a woman of thirty. I stayed with her for four years, until she died giving birth to our first child. The baby did not emerge from her belly. It was summer when she died. I buried her in the yard under the apple tree. On a piece of wood, I wrote "A Single Grave for Two Loved Ones," and placed it at the head of the grave. The tree was laden with apples. I sat in the porch of the house from sunrise to midday, looking at their grave and wondering what to do. Eventually I rounded up the cows and sheep and hens and cockerels, shut the iron latch of the wooden gate, and set off."

I breathed a sigh of relief. It had gotten dark and the only light in the darkness was the smoldering of our umpteenth cigarettes. I said to the woman, "Have you ever seen spring in Khorramshahr?"

"I was born there," the woman said. "But years after you were there. When I was a kid there was war there."

"I was part of that war," I said.

"When the Iran-Iraq War reached Khorramshahr," she continued, "one night during the bombing my family left me behind a truck with the neighbors so that they could take me somewhere safe. They couldn't come themselves because all four of my grandparents were nearing death and there was no room for them in the truck. I never saw any of them again."

"Did they get you to somewhere safe?" I asked.

The woman took a drag on her cigarette, and as she stared at the ashtray and blew smoke out of the corners of her mouth, said, "No."

She didn't say anything else. Nor did I. A little while after she got up and left.

She came to my apartment the next time too. This time she brought some aragh sagi and two glasses. When we had taken the first shot, she kept staring at me. I realized she wanted to hear the rest of the story.

"I have no idea why I'm telling you all this," I said.

"Nothing in this world is without its reason," the woman said. "Even if we don't understand what it is."

So I resumed. "After I'd got to Khorramshahr at last, I went to find my father again. It wasn't obvious at all whether he'd still be alive after so many years, but I wanted to kill him for the way he'd insulted my mother. When I got to him, his son opened the door, the one who that day had stared at me and my mother, watermelon in hand. He was now a mature man himself and looked a lot like his father. He recognized me as soon as he saw me and shook my hand. I still looked like I was fourteen and it was obvious from his expression that he was astonished by how young I was, but he didn't ask anything. 'I'm Amir Houshang,' he said. He took me to see an old man who was breathing his last. Then he left the room, but before he did, he stood by the door for a moment and stared at me. I had the feeling he knew I wanted to kill his father. He shut the door and left. The old man opened his eyes and looked at me as if to ask, 'Who are you?' 'I'm the son of my mother,' I said. 'Because the man who made her pregnant was not my father.' He got it. A tear rolled down from the corner of his eye. I didn't feel the slightest pity. 'I've come to kill you,' I said. Meaningless sounds came from his mouth and with his eyes he implored me not to. He was terrified. 'He'll be dead in an hour's time,' I thought, 'and yet he's scared that I'll take even that one remaining hour from him.' Then I slapped him extremely hard. I slapped him so hard that his false tooth flew out of his mouth and landed two meters away. He was in floods of tears and with his remaining strength he howled . . . I stood up, spat on him and left. My spit landed on his left eye.

"When I came out, I was in the mood for a fight. I was like a drunk. I was lurching. I had left my cows and sheep to a boy selling chewing gum on the outskirts of town. 'Do you know how to look after these animals?' I asked him. 'No,' he said. 'I only know how to sell chewing gum.' 'Do you have parents?' I asked. 'No,' he said. 'Just two sisters and a little brother.' 'That's good,' I said. 'From now on all these cows and sheep are yours. Take your sisters and brothers and follow this road until you reach where the meadows and mountains and springs are. That'll take you a day from here. Keep going on this road until you reach an old oak tree with a big stone slab underneath it. When you get there, there'll be two roads in front of you. One of them goes left, the other right. You'll take the one that goes right.' The boy kept waggling his head like Indians do to say 'of course.' I realized what was going on. 'Do you know which hand is your left?' 'Yes,' he said, 'the same one my father used to hit me with every night.' 'Do you know which one is your right?' I asked. 'Yes,' he said. 'The same one my mother used to dry my tears with and give me a bite to eat.' 'When you reach that road,' I told him, 'keep going with the animals until at last you get to a house with a wooden gate whose iron latch is shut. There's an apple tree in the yard and under it my wife and child are buried. From now on that house belongs to you and your siblings. There's just one piece of advice I'll give you.' 'Tell me,' the boy said. 'In life, be kind to people, but don't trust them easily.' 'Yes, sir,' he said. I saw the flash of excitement in his eyes as he led the cows and sheep away and waved me goodbye.

"When I left my father's house, the city was silent and people asleep. I kept going all the way to the Karoon River. I sat down and saw all my future life pass in front of my eyes: probably I would find myself a job in town and a wife and some kids. And it wasn't obvious at all what kind of father or husband I would be. I looked at my hands. They were still young, but lacking in the thrill of life. I could see nothing attractive in that kind of life. Nor could I find in myself the motivation to travel and have adventures. I felt like it was all just chasing the wind."

The woman poured two more glasses. We both downed them. I got up and went over to the gas stove, made Bandari sausages in silence, brought them over with bread and fresh herbs and we ate them. As we were eating, the woman asked, "Then what happened?"

"The tales of my life are endless," I said. "It's best you don't let them take you captive."

"What if I want to?" she asked.

I looked at her. The woman got up calmly, before commandingly taking my hand and leading me toward my bedroom. As if it were her own home. She threw me down on my bed and bent over me and kissed me. How moist the kiss was . . . warm and kind and sensual . . . It was one of the best lovemakings of my life. Her kisses were strange. After a few minutes I got the feeling that I had kissed those lips before. Sensuous, moist lips and loving, deep kisses. It could even be said I felt a certain pain in her moist kisses. The pain of an old love. We did not get out of bed for seven days and seven nights, except to eat and go to the toilet and bathe. During those seven days and seven nights, the peacock feather was in her hair as always, and yet I never plucked up the courage to ask her what it was about. For seven days and seven nights we made love, entwined together. A hot, intimate, thrilling lovemaking. She did things with me that never occur to many women. She ran her hands over the wounds on my body but asked nothing. She did not even look at me inquiringly. Did she know? Her silence excited me to want to explain, but every time I stopped myself at the right moment. When with her saddened expression she stopped touching my wounds, it was she who told me to insert an ice cube into the opening of her vagina, and without letting the ice go completely inside, to lick it until she climaxed. It was she who poured cream and honey on my body, on my wounds and little by little kissed and tasted it. She was so electrifying and warm and kind in the way she made love with my body that it was like she had been in love with me for years and had waited patiently all that time apart, even though not a single romantic utterance escaped her mouth. I knew such mad and at the same time tender lovemaking with her that it was torture to imagine being separated from her body. Oh, in spite of all its sorrows, how thrilling it could be to be human!

When the madness of our lovemaking had subsided somewhat, she sat on the bed, took a sip of water, and said, "So tell me the rest of it."

As my middle finger was playing inside her vagina, I said, "I don't know which part of it to tell. I told you already . . . my stories are endless."

"I love your voice when you tell stories," the woman said. "Tell me about Khorramshahr."

"I was in the Iran-Iraq War from the very first months right up until they arrested me for the crime of being friends with a Baha'i soldier and proselytizing on behalf of the Baha'i Faith, and in the detention center they forced me to rape a woman prisoner. The interrogator told me that if I did that, he'd spare me from execution. I looked at the woman. She had fallen naked on the ground and her body was covered in wounds. Wisps of mournful music were coming from her direction. The women gestured to me with her head that it didn't matter. Save your own life."

I sighed. I felt ill as I recalled that episode. I cut it short. "When I got close to the woman, I realized that the music was coming from her body. She was a strange woman. She was brave and directed caustic comments at the interrogator. I on the other hand was fearful. I had no choice but to rape the woman . . . Although after that the interrogator didn't keep his promise and killed me with a single bullet."

I drew my finger out of her vagina and tasted the humidity that lingered on it to forget that painful memory. I liked how it tasted. It aroused me still further. If I didn't stop myself, I could slide inside her body until the end of time, but the woman had gotten up and was sitting on the edge of the bed. I should have been careful not to irritate her. Like the previous women . . . but this time was different. I was more concerned that I would fall in love with her and wouldn't be able to wrench myself away from her. Had I fallen in love before now? I had been loved by many, but in love? I had always wandered into love's environs, but fear had always seized me at some point, on a frontier so close to love, and I had taken flight. It was the same this time. Her firm breasts, her curly hair, and the long, unpolished nails she dug into my back were an invitation to a natural but thrilling life. In her wide eyes, which now seemed strangely familiar to me, there was a depth and an uninhibited and creative experience. She was an amorous soul of whose life I had not the slightest idea, not even knowing her name. Her gaze was one of those bold ones neither concerned to display its wares nor to repent of its faults. Now it seemed infinitely beautiful to me. It was beautiful because intensely simple, natural, and profound, and its power arose from its awareness of these circumstances. I realized I was unable to resist her. Oh, how I wished I could throw caution to the wind and fall in love with her. Hadn't I fallen in love with her just now? If only I could get over my fears. Stop trying to control myself and the universe. Get lost in love in the fullest sense. In a woman. Drown in this woman. With all my being. With all my eternal existence.

I sat up on the bed. We were both still naked and had no intention of getting dressed. I placed two cigarettes between my lips and lit them both. I gave one to her and asked, "Are you sure you don't want to ask me anything?"

The woman took a drag of her cigarette and said, "I don't think the things you've been telling me are lies. The rest doesn't matter to me."

She was a wise and intelligent woman and each time she opened her mouth she had me more infatuated with and bewitched by her than before. It was now dark. I had made up my mind. I wanted to leave. I had to leave. I didn't want to fall in love with her. I didn't want to—I mustn't lose control of my emotions.

I pulled the sheets over her. The room was half dark. "I want to go," I said in her ear.

"Why do you experience these lives?" the woman asked.

It leapt out of my mouth. "So that I can grasp the sufferings and joys of humanity . . . So that I can help, sometimes."

There was a faint smile on the woman's lips whose meaning I couldn't discern. Then she asked, "What's the point?"

"It has a little bit of a point . . . here and there. Maybe nothing. I'm not sure myself."

"Don't be afraid of me," the woman said. "Don't be afraid of love."

How she had read my mind. I said nothing.

"Goodbye," the woman said.

I was surprised. Other women did not separate from me so easily. Either they separated fighting and quarreling or sobbing and sighing. "Don't you want to know who I am?"?" I asked.

The woman smiled and said, "It's been years and years, centuries and centuries, millennia and millennia I've known you, my Lord."

I was caught off guard. Where did she know me from? Why did she call me "my Lord"? And why had she said "centuries and centuries, millennia and millennia?" I got dressed hastily under her gorgeous and mournful gaze. For a moment her eyes distracted me. I looked more carefully. She was smiling at me. How familiar her beautiful, sad eyes were. Hadn't I seen her before this? When? Where? Centuries ago? Perhaps thousands of years ago? Those eyes . . .

This was my apartment and technically speaking the woman ought to have left but I had made up my mind and I wanted . . . I had to flee people . . . no, her, her love! As I was about to close the door behind me, the woman with beautiful, sad eyes was still under the sheets in my bed. I came out of the bedroom and as soon as I turned my back to the courtyard window, in the half-light of the exterior I saw a tall-statured and gorgeous woman behind the big window, suspended motionless in the air, watching me. With the familiar beautiful, sad eyes and peacock under her arm and snake on her shoulder. Ah . . . She . . . was the ravishing Eblis. What was she doing here? I had my suspicions. My hand was still on the door handle. I opened the bedroom door. The woman wasn't in my room. I looked at the window again. Oh Eblis . . . *Eblis* . . . You again!

Eblis the Beautiful with her sad eyes, suspended in the air behind the window, smiled and said, "Centuries and centuries . . . Millennia and millennia . . . My Lord. يا رب العالمين"[84]

[84] O Lord of Worlds.

Chapter Nineteen

It took much longer than I thought it would. I don't know why it didn't occur to me to bring a calendar with me. I must have been on the road for about five or six months. I was tired and wanted this family mission to be finished, to find refuge and peace and quiet back at the mansion. Winter had slowed me down. Sometimes sleet and snow made me unable to leave my shelter for days. But now I felt like it would soon be spring. I longed for spring at the mansion. For Chaharshanbeh Suri, for the Nowruz Festival, for gleaming new clothes, Khaneh-Tekani[85] and the Haft Sin.[86] For parties and joyful dancing. Had any guests actually come to the mansion this year? Probably not. Who was in the mood for these things anymore? Who was left anyway? I missed everyone. Even the servants and Hasrat. How had Hasrat saved the greenhouse from the winter cold? Had he saved it? What were Mom and Dad up to, Khanom Joon and Jamshid Khan, Mandana and Mina? What if Mandana and Mina were now married and had gone abroad without wishing Mehrab and me farewell? Had Leyla come back? Was the Tree of the Incident still in the middle of the kitchen, or had it vanished just as unexpectedly as it had appeared? If I were to see Behnam, I would have a heart attack and die in his arms from longing, from excitement, from the weariness of all the things I had experienced on this journey. If I were to see Mehrab, I would hug him tight and say to

[85] "House-shaking," the traditional cleaning and washing of the entire house just before Nowruz.

[86] The Haft Sin is an arrangement of seven symbolic items whose names start with the letter "sin" ("s")/س, traditionally displayed at Nowruz.

him, "You fool, why did you abandon us all like that?" What about Bahman? Was he even at the front, or had he gone back to Tehran and opened his own repair shop? I stopped. I dismounted from Shabro and opened my backpack. The sun was unexpectedly hot and the steam from the melting snows rose up from the ground like ghosts, winding around themselves and around me. During these months of traveling, the beauty of the forests, mountains, rivers and meadows had provoked me to silence and deep reflection. How insignificant I was compared to all these beauties of nature, never repeating. A bee gently on a flower that had only just poked its head above the snow. I sat and watched it; everything had attained the summit of equilibrium and perfection. Was it not true that the aim of Creation was beauty? And if this were the case, then why did we not spend our lives in pursuit of it? My problem was still beauty . . . This journey had made me think even more deeply about it than before. Why was it strange, even for my family, when I announced I wished to consecrate my life to beauty? To understanding it . . . To producing and multiplying it . . . For otherwise what use is humanity for life, for the land, for nature?

I drank a little water from the flask and looked around me. There was no sign of another human being. From my backpack I took out, the only photograph I had brought with me from between the pages of my notebook. It was the photograph of all of us together. Whenever I longed for home, more than anything else this picture of the twelve of us calmed me down. Mom had taken this photograph of us the day we came back from the palace up the tree. I would run my fingers over my own face, over my laughter and shining eyes and think of Behnam. Stupefaction and anxiety could be seen in in everyone's faces except Mahsa's and mine. She was perpetually laughing. She was sitting on Bahman's shoulders, laughing at the camera, her hands holding on to Bahman's. Bahman was standing next to me in the photograph, Behnam behind me. I remember clearly how, just as Mom wanted to take a photo of us, Behnam had pressed his head through my hair up against my ear and said: "There's no need for me to tell you to smile in the photo. I'm just going to tell you I love you and then let's see what happens." A miracle took place and I smiled in the photograph, despite all the reasons to be stupefied and anxious. After Mom had that very day printed the photograph and given all twelve of us a copy, she said, without looking me in the face, "Love has made you beautiful." And I blushed and, all astonished, wondered how she knew. In the photograph, Mehrab was standing on my other side, as were Mina and Mandana and Azadeh. Behind us were Mahin and Mozghan and between them Iraj, while Leyla was standing in front of me. As always, one of her hands was holding mine.

As I ran my fingers over each one of them, I thought of Leyla and Mozhgan and Iraj, of Mahsa and Mahin and Azadeh. What were they up to now? Had it all turned out well for Iraj and Mozhgan in the Soviet Union? Or had they died from excessive cold and hunger in the labor camps of Siberia and the Ukraine? What if they too had ended up in coffins on the River of Farewell? Since I wasn't there to fish their coffins out of the river, who could've done it? What if nobody had taken them out of the river and they had gone downriver and reached the sea? The Caspian Sea? Was Mahin still teaching in some distant location, or had she now gone back to Tehran to go to university? How grown up was Azadeh now? A lump swelled up in my throat. I felt horribly alone. It had been weeks since I'd seen anybody, and my mouth hadn't opened once save to eat. Early on I had sometimes asked the Ball of Light to manifest itself and talk to me. In numerous places it had saved me from cold and snow. Elsewhere it had manifested itself, without me expecting it or ordering it to, to be my conversation partner and save me from depression and despair or to show me the right way to go. All the same, whatever it was, it was a ball of light . . . It wasn't an ordinary human being that could comprehend human misfortune in revolution and war and on the road. It nonetheless accompanied me in the towns and villages so I could taste a little of the flavor of daily life. I hadn't been to any city after the revolution except Rasht. On this journey however I visited plenty. Zanjan, Sanandaj, Kermanshah and Ilam and many other places. I would leave Shabro somewhere safe outside town and by day would visit the city together with the Ball of Light in the form of an elderly man, thus playing the role of my father, while at night we went back to Shabro. In the cities I saw people, silent and clad in black, standing in long lines for bread and milk and oil, while the Revolutionary Committees circulated slowly in their Nissan Patrols close to the sidewalks, their officers, guns in hand, scrutinizing each and every passerby from inside the car, as if they wanted to catch them red-handed or all of a sudden leap out, slap handcuffs on them, and take them away. The Committees' Patrols were the absolute power of the streets. I had seen so much during this time. Much of it I had written down in my notebook of memoirs, much of it committed solely to memory until the day I found the patience to write it down.

It was during one of these walkabouts that our eyes met. Which city was it in? He was thin and of moderate height, wearing a gray and black t-shirt with the number 23 on it. Despite the noose around his neck, he smiled and waved at everyone, at me who stood watching him disbelieving and powerless—as if he wanted to say, "Don't be scared, we'll see one another again on the other side of the road." He even laughed at the cleric who tried until the last moment to get him to recite the two declarations, in the Oneness of Allah and the Prophethood of Muhammad but could not. They said his name was Majid[87] and that he had shot dead a corrupt judge. They said that even

[87] Referring to Majid Kavousifar who was, along with his nephew Hossein Kavousifar, convicted of the murder of the corrupt judge Masoud Ahmadi Moghaddasi. Majid and Hossein Kavousifar were both publicly executed by hanging in Tehran in August 2007.

under interrogation he had insisted that not only had he no regrets, but that if they didn't kill him, he intended to kill so many corrupt members of parliament and judges that he would exhaust the lot of them. They hanged him before he could. In the city square, surrounded by hundreds of men and women and children who stood disbelievingly, stupefied and silent and sorrowful, unable to take their eyes off him. Off him who looked at all of us, at me, laughing and brandishing his manacled hands at us. As his body was hanging from the gallows, fluttering like the flag of the Islamic Republic. My face was covered in tears and I thought, "Life has been executed. As easy as that." I was suffocated by fear and powerlessness. Behind me somebody softly muttered some poetry and left. "Save the plundering clerics and imams / Human beings are members of a whole."[88] Yet were we really? If we were members of a whole, then why had we stood aghast and watched as he, innocent, was strung up? In his last moments, the young man who was executed had turned to us, to me, with a broad smile on his face, and said, "At least I'm dying like a man. What about you?"

As the crane slowly brought down his lifeless body, the following phrase kept going through my head: "How will I die?"

I put the photograph back in its place and proceeded. I was tired. As if the weight of life, the weight of loneliness had collapsed on my shoulders. Would it really be possible to come back from this journey alive and go to the forest again with all the kids from the family, get lost again and turn up in that mysterious palace again? But did I even resemble myself, the self of before the journey? Myself before Majid's laughter on the gallows? Myself before being raped? Myself before Kay-Khosro's cave? Wouldn't all laughter remind me of Majid's laughter from now on? From now on, wouldn't all song remind me of the

[88] Referring to Saadi's famous poem: Human beings are members of a whole / In creation of one essence and soul.

singing girl held prisoner behind the curtain? Now, although I had only been away from the mansion for a few months, I still want to naively set out, notebook in hand, and ask the residents of the mansion and of Zorvan, "By the way, what happened to love?"

I resumed my journey at a gentle pace, thinking all the while about the incidents along the way. I didn't have a great deal of force left in me. I went on for a week in that manner, until one foggy sunset, as I rounded a bend, I ran into five people sitting around a fire, their forms appearing out of and vanishing into the mists. From a distance they seemed friendly and not dangerous. I came closer. Eventually they saw me. They invited me to sit next to them and eat with them. I did so. It was like I was getting there. Like there was not actually far to go to Khorramshahr, to the war. As if to confirm that the five of them had many a memory of blood and fighting and death, each of their bodies bore on it a memento of the war, while every now and then the noise and light of explosion on the horizon cleft the mist and made everyone fall silent.

Two or three months earlier, the last time I had been in touch with Mom by telephone, she had said they had found a trace of Mehrab. The person who had told Mom about this had said that someone else had told them that someone answering to Mehrab's description had been seen in Khorramshahr. Who had seen him? We didn't know. On which front exactly? We did not know. When exactly? We did not know.

Now these five men had come back from the front and were picking over their memories of Majnoon Island. When I got close to them, one of them, who had left an eye behind in the war, asked, "My daughter, what are you doing here alone, with a horse?" He was not old enough to have been my father, yet his calling me "my daughter" made me feel safe. "I'm looking for my brother," I said. Then I asked them about Mehrab. I showed them his photo. No. They hadn't seen him. Or maybe they had. Here all the young folks look alike. Another one of them, who had left his leg behind in the war, asked, "What did you do before you came on this trip? Were you studying, working, or did you have a husband?" "To be honest . . . " I said, "I wanted to devote my life to love and beauty, but things turned out otherwise. I haven't been to university. I haven't gotten married either. I do have a greenhouse, but I'm not really sure what my job is." Another of them, who had no arm, burst out laughing and said, mockingly, "Love and beauty! What a waste of time. Who in this world needs them? Who pays money for them? People need water and food and housing." Another, who had lost his nose in the war and who kept appearing and vanishing in the fog, said, "We all got married to our cousins. We've devoted ourselves to work, family, and war. Work and family matter. Money matters. War matters. Martyrdom matters. Religion matters." Another, who had lost his ear in the war, said, "You're young. You don't get it. But listen to our advice. Earthly love is fleeting; only God's love lasts forever. Earthly love's a nest of corruption, but spiritual love will guide you to paradise." I tried to change the subject. "Do you know Omid Raisi?" I asked. "Have you heard of him?" And I showed them Bahman's photo.

They muttered to one another and at last it became clear they did know him. They spoke of him with respect. They said he was a Revolutionary Guards commander and that he wasn't one of those commanders who never set foot outside headquarters. On the contrary. He was one of those who was at the front of the fighting. I thought that it must be him. It would be just like Bahman to fight like that. As they gave me a share of the wild pheasant they had caught, I listened to what they were saying. It became obvious that they were old childhood friends from the same neighborhood. And they were thrilled to still be alive despite the war, and to be returning to their villages and their families.

The first of them, whose name was Abbas and who was

sitting on my right and had left his nose behind in the war, turned to me before commencing his tale and said, "Sister, our memories are men's memories and if someone says something inappropriate, be so kind as to forgive us." How kind and polite, I thought. He didn't have a nose, and every now and then mucus came out of two black cavities and he wiped it away with a handkerchief. He turned back to the group and said, "Well then, as we were saying . . . when I'd gotten outta there it was dusk and I was beat. I thought I'd go to Ahmad's shelter and spark up a cigarette. On the way I saw a boat upside down in the bushes next to the Karkheh River. I was passing by when I heard a sound from under it. It caught me by surprise. I thought some unfortunate animal had gotten stuck under there, I pulled the boat up with both my hands to let the animal out but suddenly I saw, O my careless heart, a Basij commander laying on top of a twelve- or thirteen-year-old Basiji, banging him . . . you can imagine I was astounded. In my panic I let go of the boat and ran off towards Ahmad's shelter. On the way I ran into Asghar. I told him what'd happened and said, 'Let's go tell Ahmad and figure out what oughtta be done.' Asghar said, 'I'm coming from Ahmad's shelter right now. He ain't there. Go back to your own shelter so if the Basij commander finds you, there's someone else with you. If he finds you, he's gonna waste you. I'll go to the Central Shelter and find Ahmad and tell him.' I realized he was right, so I went back."

Ahmad, who had left an arm behind in the war, was sitting to my right, and continued the story, all the while staring into the flames. "Right, I told Abbas to go back to his own shelter, I'll go find Ahmad and bring him to you. Abbas went. I lit up a cigarette in the darkness and was walking quickly and thinking about the wife-pimpin' Basij commander, who would twirl his prayer beads around in front of us and keep saying 'subḥân Allâh, praise be to Allah,' but at the same time was doing that awful thing to that poor kid. Then all of a sudden I caught sight of the same Basij commander sprinting towards me dripping with sweat. I was rooted to the spot. As soon as he saw me he said, 'Have you seen Abbas?' I figured he wanted to do something terrible to Abbas or at least get him to shut up come what may, so I said, 'No, I ain't. What's going on?' The fat prick had run so much sweat was pouring off all over him in sheets. Panting he said, 'Nothing, nothing . . . I need him for something.' Knowing full well what the asshole needed Abbas for, I decided to stir things up a bit and said, 'Will you let us know if you hear anything? Perhaps we can help you out somehow.' The commander peered at me suspiciously and ran off in the direction of Abbas's shelter. When I saw this, I took a shortcut through the bushes towards Ahmad's shelter to find him as soon as possible and let him know all about what was going down with Abbas so he could go help. I was running in the darkness when I stumbled on something and fell over. My knee hit a piece of rubble and really hurt and started bleeding. I looked down to see what I'd run into and saw a wounded rabbit next to a rock. It looked like the poor critter had taken a bullet that day during clashes with the Iraqis. I picked it up and thought at least we got dinner for tonight. I got up and kept limping on when I saw Farshid with a cane under his arm walking in the darkness. 'Hey Farshid,' I said. 'Where are you off to?' I told him all about Abbas and the Basij commander. Then I told him I was going to find Ahmad so we could go help Abbas so the Basij commander wouldn't just waste him. 'Let me see, what happened to your leg?' Farshid asked. I told him. 'First of all, let this rabbit go, don't you know it brings bad luck?' he said. 'No way,' I said. 'Says who?' 'What's this wound on your knee mean, then?' he said. 'Let this rabbit go before somethin' worse happens to you.' 'Man, you're right,' I said. 'Take this rabbit yourself and let it go somewhere in the bushes. It's suffering real bad.' He took the rabbit and said, 'I'll go find Ahmad, you go to Abbas. Then he gave me the walking stick he was holding and said he wanted to take it to one of the fighters who that evening had been wounded in the Iraqi operations."

Farshid, who had lost his right leg in the war and was sitting next to Asghar, resumed telling the rest of the story. "Right, as soon as Asghar handed the rabbit to me and limped off into the darkness with the stick, I felt awful for the rabbit. Its heart was pounding in my arms. I said to myself, 'Let me take it to Ahmad's shelter so I can tell Ahmad what happened and bandage this poor rabbit up as well, maybe it'll get better and I can let it go. Well, the rabbit I was holding . . . I felt real sorry for it and at the same time I was scared I'd be struck down by it. For a second I was paralyzed with fear. I was in total darkness. I felt someone behind me. I looked around but there was nobody. Nobody in front of me either. In all this chaos my flashlight battery had run out. I was walking real fast in the darkness when I felt someone was behind me again and then all of a sudden a blurry shadow appeared in front of me. I started hiccuping outta fright. However much I tried to hold my breath, I couldn't stop. I started thinkin' about my grandma who'd told me what to do when I had hiccups. One eye on the shadow that was getting closer, I took seven quick sips of water from my flask, then held my breath and counted to seven and recited seven blessings on the Prophet and his family, but the hiccups still wouldn't go away. Well the shadow was getting closer and closer. I was shitting myself with fear. I thought it must be either the enemy or a jinn . . . Had it come because of the rabbit's evil influence to finish me off? I drew my gun. The shadow was now very close. I ordered it to halt. To tell me the password. But the shadow said, 'Shut up and die, Farshid. It's me, man! Habib.' I went forward, shaking with fear. He was right, it was Habib. 'Why've you turned yellow?' Habib said. 'I kept hearing a noise behind me,' I said. 'And I felt like someone's followin' me, but whenever I turned round there weren't nobody.' Hiccuping, I told him everything about the Basij commander and Abbas and Asghar. The hiccups had gotten so strong I got a stomach ache. 'What's this rabbit you're carrying?' Habib asked. 'I'm gonna find Ahmad,' I said, 'then bandage up this poor critter, but I'm so scared of its evil influence.' 'Give it to me,' Habib said. 'I don't believe in all that nonsense. Tonight I'll cook and eat it, it'll be done.' I handed the rabbit to him. 'You got a stomach-ache, go to Abbas so you can take care of him and do something to make your hiccups better too. I'm gonna find Ahmad for you and bring him to you, then deal with this rabbit.'

Habib, who had left his left ear behind in the war, and who was sitting to Farshid's right, said, "Right, as soon as Farshid left, I was running, still holding the rabbit, towards the Central Shelter where I guessed Ahmad would be when a shadow coming from behind me fell in front of me. Now it was completely dark, so God knows how anyone could see a shadow in that darkness. I thought it was probably Farshid foolin' around and tryin' to frighten me. I turn round and shouted, '*Bang!*' so I could frighten him instead, but I saw there weren't nobody behind me. I was scared out of my wits. I drew my gun. I fired off a few shots into the darkness. There was no sound. I picked up my pace when the same shadow came from behind and fell in in front of me again. This time I didn't look just hurried up when I'm hit in the foot. My roars and curses filled the air. 'Who are you, you son of a bitch?' I yelled. In the darkness a voice in the distance said, 'Who are you? How many times do I have to say "halt . . . halt"?' That wretched shadow came forward and I saw it was our own Ahmad. 'You wife-pimper,' I said. 'Don't you know I only got one ear?' The poor guy kept apologizing. I saw that the bullet had only caused a flesh wound and had passed through the side of the foot. 'You're lucky I only got one eye,' Ahmad said. ''Cause otherwise my bullet woulda hit the target and you woulda collapsed at the knees.' We both laughed. He wanted to give me a piggy-back so we could go bandage up my foot but I said there was no need, and told him everything about the Basij commander and Abbas and Asghar and Farshid and said, 'You run to Abbas's shelter, I'll get myself there limping carrying this rabbit.' 'Okay,' he said, and ran off."

Ahmad, who had lost his right eye at the front, said, "Right, long story short I took a shortcut and ran towards Abbas's shelter. The shelter was in uproar. You were all there, right . . . and two or three other folks. You know the rest of it yourselves."

"I hadn't made it there yet," Habib said. "I was getting there, limping all the way. So, what happened?"

"When I got there, the Basij commander and Abbas were at one another's throats and Abbas's face was covered in blood and the wife-pimpin' Basij commander had his nose in his hand," Ahmad said. "Of course, Abbas seen to it that the commander was well served and stabbed him with a knife. Asghar and Farshid were having a hard time separating them. As soon as I saw Abbas's nose in that asshole's hand I drew my gun and right there let one off in his left leg and he fell down. Then I put the gun straight to his head and said, 'You move and I'll kill you like a dog. As an army commander I'm court-martialing you right now in the presence of these witnesses for the crime of sodomizing and raping a fighter of Islam and your sentence is death and loss of honor. You've stained the honor of the revolution and the sacred war and the Basij and the fighter.' Then we all took him outside into the desert behind Abbas's shelter and I told him to dig his own grave.

"He cried and howled and pleaded with that messed up body of his and dug his own grave. As soon as he'd finished digging, we heard a noise behind us. It was Habib and the Basiji kid was with him." At this point, Ahmad sighed and said, "You were all there for the rest of it and you saw what happened."

"I wasn't there and I didn't see," I said. "Now that I've heard what happened up to here, please would you tell me the rest?"

"You tell it," Commander Ahmad said to Habib.

"I was limping towards Abbas's shelter when I heard somebody crying," Habib said. "I go towards the noise and see that a fighter, twelve or thirteen years old, is sitting in the darkness, crying! All of a sudden I thought, 'What if this is the same innocent kid the Basij commander was screwing?' But I was too embarrassed to ask directly. I said, 'Come and help me get to Abbas's shelter. I've been shot in the leg. The poor kid got up and helped me. On the way I started tellin' him why I was headed there. The kid stopped and said, 'Really, you swear?' 'Yeah,' I said. 'I swear.' 'I wanna come too,' he said. 'All right, come,' I said. He didn't say nothing else and I didn't ask. Long story short, by the time we got to where the guys were, the prick had dug his grave and was sitting in it and begging and Ahmad was pointing his gun at him. As soon as we got there, the kid said, 'Let me kill him.' We were all stunned. When the Basij commander heard the boy's voice he looked up and recognized him. He begged him to forgive him. But the boy took out his own gun from his belt and right there fired a shot into the middle of his forehead. 'Now I've forgiven him,' he said. Then I noticed the poor rabbit had been shaken around in my arms so much that he'd kicked the bucket. We put the rabbit in that wife-pimper's grave and then we all threw earth over them. Keep it all to yourself. That's it."

It was now totally dark and the fog had gotten thicker and thicker. I looked at them, half-lit by the flickering flames of the fire. I was content that at the end of the tale justice had been done. I thought that they must feel the same way, but I could see that they all looked shocked, as if they had suddenly recalled something painful, looking at one another in surprise, sighing, and staring at the fire in silence. Just for the sake of saying something, I said, "What a story."

Nobody said anything. "So why are you upset?" I asked. "Wasn't justice done?"

Commander Ahmad sighed, looked at each of their faces, and at length said to me, "Because just now we remembered that just as we'd given that man what he deserved and we wanted to head back to the shelter, a shell landed right on the grave . . . in the middle of us."

My body froze solid. It shot naively out of my mouth: "I thought you'd got out of the war alive."

Ahmad looked at me sadly and said, "Nobody gets out of war alive."

I looked at them all again. Had the rabbit's evil influence gotten to all of them, meaning I was now hearing stories from the mouths of people who no longer existed, and eating the flesh of a pheasant that was not real? When I looked at them again, it appeared that their expressions had changed. They looked aghast. I remembered that strange tale that Khanom Joon had told us when we were small children. "You all told a story," I said. "I have a story too. Do you want to hear it?" They kept staring at the fire, their expressions mournful and lost. Through movements of their heads and hands, they indicated that yes, I should tell it.

"In olden times, there were three cities," I began. "Two were in ruins, while the third lacked only houses that were still standing. In this city without houses were three castles, two of which were in ruins, while the third lacked only its fortifications. In this castle without fortifications were three kings, two of whom were dead, while the third lacked only breath. This king with no breath had three sons, the first and second of whom were dead, while the third of whom lacked only life. One day this lifeless prince desired to go hunting. In the sideboard he found three guns, two of which were broken, while the third lacked only its barrel and stock. He likewise found three cartridges, two of which were broken, while the third lacked only gunpowder. The prince took up the gun without barrel and stock and the cartridge without gunpowder and went off to the stables. In the stables were three horses, two of which were dead, while the third did everything but breathe. The lifeless prince set off for the forest, mounted on the unbreathing horse. He saw three forests, two of which had withered up and burnt, while the third had no trees. He kept on going through the treeless forest until he saw three deer, two of which had died, while the third lacked only life. The lifeless prince, sitting on the unbreathing horse, fired on the lifeless deer from the gun without barrel or stock, using the cartridge without gunpowder. Then he put the lifeless deer on the back of the unbreathing horse and returned through the forest to the castle without fortifications."

Everyone was still staring at the fire, their expressions mournful. I gazed beyond the non-existent fog and fire and the five men who weren't alive at the far-off horizon of war, unsure whether it still existed or not.

Chapter Twenty

We are the people of the Middle East
Some of us are killed in war
Some in prison
Some of us die on the highways
Some of us in the sea,
Even the highest mountains . . .
Take revenge on us for their loneliness,
For dying is our profession."[89]

Smoke, shells, bullets, bodies. Smoke, shells, bullets, bodies. Smoke, shells, bullets, bodies. Behind a wrecked truck in a corner of the street was written: "We died in some other place, and this is our hell." Only Brother shouted: "I warned you before. We're different from earlier generations. The five of us siblings have an equal share in this inherited madness." As he struck his head on the wall and blood flowed down in a narrow rivulet from it, he yelled, guffawing, "What news from Mithra? Huh? Haven't you thought about the number 12 at all? Idiot . . . I'm talking to you. Haven't you thought about the number 12 at all?" Indeed, it had been some time since I had thought about Mithra or the number 12.

Before parting from the five dead soldiers, I'd asked them whether they wouldn't mind looking after Shabro for a while. They said they didn't know. That they had just arrived and didn't know yet what they were supposed to be doing. Then Ahmad, the commander, turned to the others and asked doubtfully how

[89] Poet unknown.

long they had been there. Abbas mumbled that he didn't know but that he thought they'd been there before, then turned to Habib and asked whether that wasn't the case. And Habib had said that he had the impression they'd been there for a very long time. That it was as if we woke up every day at dusk after a long sleep and left our houses, which no longer existed, crossing streets that no longer existed to come here, somewhere which might or might not exist. And Asghar wondered whether it's like every day at sunset when we wake up we think we're alive, we come here, we say the same things, and then we remember we've died. Farshid wondered whether every night we eat the same wild pheasant, which doesn't exist, before going back to our non-existent houses to sleep in non-existent beds until dusk the following day, then the day after that, and the day after that . . . Then Ahmad turned to me and said, "You see, it's a weird situation, but we can probably look after your horse for a little bit. It looks like we're stuck here for a while."

If some believe that the ghosts of Japanese military personnel killed in the Second World War continue to live in the cold, dark waters of the Chuuk Lagoon in the Pacific Ocean so that they can scare the travelers and tourists who years afterward go there simply to have a good time . . . If the headless ghosts of the dead of the Paris catacombs left by the French Revolution continue to take their victims from among the heedless tourists in the city's streets . . . If the ghosts of Lenin, Marx, and Stalin still stare out at people from their bronze statues in Szoborpark in Budapest and fill their bodies with horror . . . Then why wouldn't Iranian soldiers believe that during the Iran-Iraq war the sanctified ghosts of the martyrs and the Imam of the Age and Abu'l-Fazl in person saved them, or avenged them on the Iraqi enemy? All the same, in the all his years at the front Only Brother saw neither the Imam of the Age, nor the laughing martyrs, nor the spirits of Abu'l-Fazl and Zahra and Zaynab, nor the sweet-scented martyrs. Even as he covered his ears at explosions we could not hear and howled from a pain we could not feel and threw himself from this side to that, he would say of the child soldiers that they passed out at the noise of explosions and died on the spot. He talked about the suicides of soldiers who hadn't wanted to pull the triggers of their guns. He talked about dead bodies that had been shot in the back on the orders of various people and had just been left there for God to deal with. He talked of the hurried desert executions of Mojahedin and Communists and Baha'is at the front. Of the ambushes and spurious cases made by the Hezbollahis against politically active soldiers to arrest them. Of anonymous, unmarked, mass graves. Of mines. In the truck: mines. Under the pillow: mines. Under the feet of wild cheetahs: mines. Under the feet of border villagers: mines. Under the bed: mines. In sleep: mines. In sleep: mines. In sleep: mines . . .

Only Brother . . . my Only Brother Mehrab, with his bleary, red eyes and swollen veins, spoke of horror.

However hard it was to find Mehrab, finding Bahman, Revolutionary Guards Land Force Brigade Commander Omid Raisi, was like drinking water. I met with him in his office at the headquarters, surrounded by several other bearded officers. The moment he saw me he turned white, as if he had seen a ghost. His expression cold and frowning, without bidding me welcome, he turned to the other military personnel in his room and told them that his sister had come from Tehran on family business. The rest of them greeted me and with great warmth asked me how I was, before respectfully leaving the room. When one of them, short of stature, laughingly said to me before leaving, "What lovely music you listen to," I was reminded once more of the fact that everywhere I went, my body's sorrowful music accompanied me. I said nothing, forced a smile, and shrugged. Once we were alone in the room, Bahman came over to me with two giant steps and hugged me tight. Tall, with a serious expression and a thick beard and mustache, the mark of frequent prayer on his forehead, wearing dark green uniform with gold insignia of rank on its shoulders, he looked like another person, while, his eyes full of tears of joy and disbelief, his lips swore and cursed without stopping: "How did you wind up here you jackass . . . Wow Shokoof . . . Fuck, man, you've turned into some hot shit."

I explained briefly to him that it had been about two years since we had heard from Mehrab but that we had found traces of him in Khorramshahr and now I had come to find him. Right there and then in front of me, as if he had anticipated everything, he quickly and carefully made me a false Basij card, stamped it and handed it to me. In less than a minute, I had become his sister. "What name would you like me to give you?" he asked. "Whatever," I said. "Now that I'm Omid Raisi, you can be Nahid Raisi," he said. With the card I was able to accompany him everywhere as an assistant. He also took a Basij form out of a drawer, wrote a date from two years earlier on it, and indicated on it that I was a member of the Tehran Basij, Tehranpars District. Then he said, "Whatever ID cards you've got, hand 'em over. If you get caught somewhere you can't have conflicting documents with you 'cause otherwise they can easily slap the label of spy—hypocrite—Communist on you and then you'll end up in a whole world of trouble." I only had my identity paper with me. I told him I needed it to find Mehrab. I'd have to prove that I was his sister. "What matters is that we find him," he said. "As long as you're with me, I'm your ID. I'm the law round here." He took my identity paper and stuffed it in a drawer underneath a pile of papers and books which he then locked. Then he looked me up and down and said, "Your hijab is terrible. You gotta tie your scarf tighter. Why don't you have a maqnaeh? Why don't you have a chador?" I tied my scarf tight. He looked me up and down again. "Nope," he said. "That won't fly. I gotta get you a maqnaeh and chador from somewhere." I said I wasn't the sort to wear a chador. He laughed. "For now, jump so I can get you out of this hell," he said. "Before we do anything else, I have to call home," I said. He put the telephone in front of me. He didn't take his eyes off me the entire time I talked with my mom. He watched my lips. The movements of my hands and eyes. He smiled and shook his head in disbelief and took pronounced and excited drags of his cigarette. His admiring gaze was really bothering me, and I turned my back to him so I could talk in comfort. Mom screamed with joy at hearing my voice. I told her that I'd just arrived and that I'd found somebody who'd promised to help me find Mehrab. Mom asked who that was. I couldn't say it was Bahman. As far as the family was concerned, Bahman had been martyred some time before. I said it was a high-ranking Revolutionary Guard who, it turned out, was the uncle of one of my classmates. Then I asked how Dad was. She said he was well. I asked again: "Are you sure Dad's doing well?" And Mom replied anxiously, "But is something supposed to have happened to him?" I regretted insisting. I changed the subject and asked about the other residents of the house. Mom started talking but after I'd listened to her for a bit, I began to worry. She spoke very quietly and allusively and with much beating about the bush. I pressed the receiver to my ear and as I listened to what she said about the mansion and the children I wondered why she could not utter a single sentence directly and concisely. I felt like she was talking in a half-sleeping, half-waking state, deliriously, beating about the bush with many an allusion, and worst of all, scattered and without focus.

Under the gaze of the soldiers and officers and bearded, hirsute commanders, scowling and nosy, Bahman coolly put me in a jeep. When we got in, he looked in the rear-view mirror behind us and said, "You see that guy who looks like a bald, squashed Arnie with beady little eyes whose forehead has a mark like it lands on a shit every time he prays?"

Without intending to, I started laughing. The bald, squashed Arnie with beady little eyes whose forehead has a mark like it lands on a shit every time he prays. All that in a single sentence. Bahman hadn't changed one bit, it seemed. It had been that same short, bald man who had commented on the music coming from my body. He must've been about fifty. He was standing next to two older officers and watching us through narrowed eyes. I said I could see him. "This motherfucker is counting down the hours till he can take my place. The son of a bitch has influence everywhere." "I shouldn't have come to see you," I said. "I'm sorry. It'll create problems for you." "Holy crap . . . Now that he's staring at you like this I'll have to lay him out flat." Then he stepped on the gas, and we sped out of the headquarters.

As he was driving, he turned to look at me and, cigarette in mouth, smiled and shook his head. When we'd gone a little further, he stuck his hand into his breast pocket, brought out an old wallet, and handed it to me. It looked familiar. "This is your own wallet," he said. "The last time I was at the mansion I swiped it to have something to remember you by." It struck me that this was indeed the same old Bahman. Then he said, "Open it."

I opened it hesitantly. Stuffed in the folds were a few pages from books which looked like they had been torn by accident. I read them carefully.

Page 127/ Scott Fitzgerald

"Don't talk so much, old sport," commanded Gatsby. "Play!"

At morn
At night
We are joyful

In surprise, I opened another fold. It was another bit of another book.

Page 53

Apart from sitting, thinking, and in dreaming of grasping his heart, I . . .

As in the desire to suddenly conquer his heart . . .

I am a morning which even if from lack of sleep . . .
And should I be agitated, early morning . . .
Oneself for . . .

Wasn't it from *East Wind, West Wind*? I opened another fold. There was a piece of the *Blind Owl*:

In that moment my thoughts had frozen, a strange, unique life was produced in me. Because my life was connected to all the beings around me, to all the shadows that trembled about me, depending profoundly and inseparably on the world and . . .

"Bits and pieces plucked from the novels you were reading."

He had gone red and looked only at the road in front of him. I thought how names were the shortest form of magic spell. He had taken the name "Omid," hope. A spell which ought to have saved his life had turned into the curse of his life; Omid had meant that he wouldn't give up . . . whereas he should have given up years ago.

"In the last fold on the left, there's a bit of a photo," he said.

I found it. It was the photograph Mom had taken of the twelve of us after the night of the palace. But the edges of the photograph had been ripped off and in the middle there was only the two of us and Mahsa laughing at his shoulder.

He turned his head toward me and took a long look. I said nothing. Then he said, "Now look in the last fold on the right. It's a bit of a newspaper. Don't get upset. It's the only thing in this wallet that's got nothing to do with you, but I kept it to show you one day."

I found it. It was a black and white photograph of a middle-aged, bald man next to a short story with the headline "Search Continues for Killer of Saeed Toosi,[90] Quran Reciter." The

[90] Saeed Toosi has been referred to as Ali Khamenei's "Khamenei's favorite Qu'ran reciter." In October 2016, VOA-PNN shed light on Toosi's case in which he was accused of sexually abusing nineteen of his prepubescent Qur'an students over the years. Senior members of the government, including Khamenei, tried

name sounded familiar. In his first letter Bahman had said that one day at last he had . . . the pedophile religion teacher . . .

Still staring at the road in front, he said, "Sometimes you've got no choice but to implement justice yourself."

Then he said, "Now you've seen it, rip it up and toss it out."

I tore up the paper and threw it out of the window.

I fell silent. Bahman always generated conflicting emotions in me: fear and security.

After our silence had continued a while, in his usual cheerful, playful tone, he said, "I didn't even dream you'd come here. Did my letters get to you?" Then he took my hand and kissed it softly. I calmly extracted my hand from his. "What's the matter?" he said. "There's nothing weird about falling in love. It ain't just for a year or two."

I took a deep breath. I tried to control my contradictory emotions. I asked calmly, "Where should we go to look for Mehrab?"

He pretended not to hear. He turned red. He paused. Then at last he asked, "What's the deal with this tune?" "I don't know," I said. "It's been coming out of my body for a while." He laughed and said, "Man, you learn something new every day."

"So where should we start?" I asked again.

He looked at me, aggrieved. "You're in love with that chicken shit pretty boy? Right?" It just leapt out of my mouth: "Totally."

His face was no longer red. It had turned purple. Even so, he did not take his eyes off the road. Then in a gentler tone I asked, "Do you have any news about him?" "I do," he said, listlessly. I wanted to ask immediately, "What news? Where is he? When did you see him?" I don't know why, but a vague fear blocked my throat. What if he said he'd been killed? What about if he'd

to cover up the scandal for four years when the victims and their families filed complaints with the judiciary. Journalists were also warned not to publicize the investigation.

been put in jail or executed in the desert for the crime of being a Communist? "Ain't you gonna ask where he is?" he asked. "No," I said, staring at the road. I thought that we would find one another, alive or dead, when the time was right.

Bahman took me to Khorramshahr, "the Fertile City" turned the Bloody City. It had fallen into the clutches of the Iraqis for a whole year, before it was taken back with huge casualties. It was in ruins and could scarcely be called a city anymore. Here and there were strewn the corpses of palm trees, statues, cars, tanks and military trucks. The place had been left half-abandoned. At the entrance to the city was written: "Perform ablution before entering. This city is soaked in the martyrs' blood."

I remembered how before the revolution we had all come here for a vacation during the Nowruz holidays. The city had been full of color and light and excitement. Full of tourists and engineers, both foreign and local. Mixed, open-air swimming pools, open-air cinemas, luxury boutiques with the best Iranian and foreign brands, huge, colorful advertising banners, lush green parks and pleasure boats by the side of the river. It was so beautiful and bustling that it was known as "the Bride of the Persian Gulf." Now, however, the city was in mourning, black and crippled. The bodies of the walls, houses, offices, and the bazaar had been punctured by shells and bullets. The city had been assassinated. A shell had hit right in the middle of the forehead of the "Bride" confectionery whose pastries and ice creams we had fallen in love with during those Nowruz holidays. It was not only the body of the Bride of the Persian Gulf that had been punctured; her heart had bullets in it too.

He took me to the only boutique left in the city. I remembered that before we had bought American- and French-brand two-piece bathing suits and summer outfits there. The salesperson was the same one as before, only now he had a long beard and mustache, a scowling expression and a dark shirt. Bahman bought me a long coat and a maqnaeh that went under the chin. He wouldn't let me pay for it. Then he took me to the only restaurant in town, empty and desolate. He ordered us kubideh kabab. The handful of other customers were all men and looked at us in curiosity, while some of them on seeing Bahman's uniform and the insignia on his shoulders placed a hand over their chests and inclined their heads slightly, greeting him respectfully and asking after his health. He struck his chest in turn and said, یا حق[91].

"How did you get to this position?" I asked.

He rubbed the dark mark on his forehead and said, "By pimping and whoring. Like everyone else. Everything started with this shit-mark."[92]

"Why didn't you go back to Tehran and make a life for yourself there?" I asked.

With a totally serious expression I hadn't seen on him before, he looked into my eyes and said, "You need to have hope to make a life. To make war, no hope."

Then he started eating, surrounded by stubborn flies, and with his head down, said, "Eat up before it gets cold."

We went to the city's general hospitals and single mental hospital together. Before we did so he took his keffiyeh off the car dashboard. "It comes in handy," he said, throwing it around his shoulders. As we walked around the beds of the wounded, he explained that many of these soldiers were shell-shocked and had lost their tags. Some of them had been mistakenly declared to be missing in action or taken prisoner and sometimes it would emerge that someone had just been dumped in some corner of the mental hospital. When they were unable to identify a shell-shocked soldier, they routinely transferred him to

[91] "O Truth!" (i.e. God). An expression used by warriors and dervishes when greeting or saying goodbye.

[92] After the revolution, those who wanted to make a display of their piety pressed a small clay disc to their foreheads, leaving a permanent mark. Shia Muslims touch a small clay disc with their forehead when they prostrate themselves during ritual prayers; the disc may be made of earth from the holy city of Najaf. These people wanted everyone else to know how much they prayed.

one of the hospitals in a different city in the hope that their families might locate them there.

The hospitals were full of the injured, the wounded, and shell-shocked soldiers, but there was no news of Mehrab. "There was a counter-offensive a few days ago," he explained. Thanks to Bahman's numerous connections, we were able to meet with the hospital directors and check the lists of the war wounded from the first day of the fighting. We spent all day moving between offices and lists and the beds of the wounded; "T": Tabesh; Tabandeh; Taleshi; Tabrizi; Tavazon; Touraji; Teymouri; Tehrani . . . There was no Taban. Mehrab Taban, no!

The city's only mental hospital was also full of soldiers in love. Melancholic soldiers. Mad soldiers. Shell-shocked soldiers. Prophet soldiers. Soldiers healthy in appearance but with hearts pierced by arrows. Dead. One of them came running over to me and said, "I have just been sent on my mission, but these idiots won't believe me. Help me. Save me from this madhouse." Another mistook Bahman for the Imam of the Age. One shell-shocked soldier held his head in his hands and yelled, "Maryam, where are you? They've fired a shell . . . Get back to the trench . . . Get back to the trench. Maryam . . . Maryam . . . Those shameless scoundrels have fired a shell . . . Come take me home with you . . . Help . . . help . . . " And he struck his head hard and again and again on the iron bars of the bed. There was no news of Mehrab there either.

The city was small. We looked everywhere. I wanted to split from him there and then and go to Abadan but Bahman said, "Holy crap . . . Do you think they just give out hotel rooms like that? This is an Islamic country, sister. A close relative, a man, must be with you at all times, or otherwise they'll think yours is the oldest profession." I think I must have turned red when he said this, as he immediately apologized, but then without delay he asked, "By the way, tell me how you got yourself here in the first place? Did anyone bother you on the way?"

"What day of what month of what year is it today?" I asked.

"March 16, 1983," he replied, surprised. "Nowruz is coming up. Why?" "On that basis, it took us about five months to get here from the mountains and the forests." He looked at me open-mouthed and laughed heartily. "Man, you really are one hell of a motherfucker."

That night we stayed at a dingy, rundown old guesthouse. As we were checking in, the old man there, who had thrown a keffiyeh over his shoulders and who also had a mark on his forehead, ran his eye over the keffiyeh on Bahman's shoulders, glanced at my Basij card, then inspected me from head to toe with a lascivious, suspicious look. One of those looks that meant to say, "How much do you charge per night, you whore?" Bahman noticed the way he was looking, took off his keffiyeh so that the gold insignia on his shoulders could be seen, and then as if by accident, as he touched his waist his hand slipped toward the gun hanging there, although it didn't look like this display of power was necessary, since as soon as the old man saw Bahman's insignia and then his war card, he turned pale and stood up straight and in a trembling voice said, "At your service, Guard Commander, sir." With a scowling, serious expression Bahman asked, "Is there a prayer mat in the room?" The old man took out a dirty prayer rug from under the counter and handed it to him, also pointing out the direction of Mecca. Then he showed us to a room with two single spring beds in it and a view of slaughtered palm trees. When we were alone, Bahman flung the prayer rug the old man had given him into a corner of the room and said, "Jump into the bath. There must be hot water now. You stink." It had been ages since I had last washed. I think I spent an hour in the bath scrubbing myself. When I got out, Bahman was no longer in the room. A little while later he returned with two large falafel sandwiches and a few snacks and a bottle of homemade aragh sagi in a black plastic bag. He laughed when he saw my astonishment and said, "Did you think that just because the country's gone Islamic, folks've stopped drinking?"

He brought two glasses. He poured aragh for both of us. As if something had just come to mind, he said, "In that mysterious palace we all had a drink. D'you remember?" I did. He continued. "I always think that night was a dream. It wasn't real." "Perhaps it wasn't," I said. "There are lots of things in this world that we can't get our heads around." He knocked back his glass and said, "Yeah. Like my love for you. 'Cause it ain't obvious at all why a kid from the streets like me should fall for a proper young lady like you."

"Why are you drinking tonight?" I asked. With his head down, he said, "If I don't get blind drunk tonight I'll be so screwed up I won't be able to get to sleep." He did get blind drunk and passed out right there on the floor in his uniform and boots. But before he did he started to chatter away. He sounded like his letters. As he cut up a cucumber and sprinkled salt on it, he said, "Did you know a cucumber once saved my life?" I was lying on the bed under the blanket. I laughed. "When the war'd just started," he said, "I was in Qasr-e Shirin. I'd become buddies with the guys there. Little by little I realized one of them was one of the Hypocrites who'd been turned,[93] but in his heart was still with them Hypocrites. I was an idiot and didn't turn him in. If only I had. I pitied him. I thought he was harmless and wasn't bothering anybody. His name was Kiyoumars. We called him 'Kiya.' Once his mother came to see him at the front. I looked in our supplies and all I could find to offer her was a few cucumbers. I washed them, peeled them, cut them up and salted them and took them to his mother. A little after that Kiya became the head of our group of twenty or thirty or so. One day at dusk he ordered everybody except me to go on a foot patrol of the area as far as the lake, which we never went to at that time of day 'cause at night that was where the Kurdish Komala militias that were working with the Hypocrites and the

[93] A term that the Islamic Republic used to refer to the Mojahedin-e Khalq; the original "Hypocrites" were people who had pretended to follow the Prophet Muhammad but who were secretly against him.

Iraqis were based and they would shit all over our boys. In the mornings the area was ours. In the mornings the ordinary folks were there farming and comin', coming and going and we'd pay it a visit, but evening, night, no way. Long story short, at dusk that day, that son of a bitch Kiya made everyone go on patrol. The boys protested, said it was dangerous, but Kiya said the order come from the top and must be carried out. When everyone was settin' off he ordered me to stay put. I didn't like that one bit. I said to him, 'You son of a bitch, d'you think I'm scared?' All of a sudden opposite to how he usually was with me, 'cause we got on well, he yelled at me and told me I gotta look after the base. I had no choice but to stay and I didn't close my eyes until morning, waiting, but there was no word from Kiya or from our group. They just went and vanished without a trace."

He knocked back another glass, ate a piece of cucumber and offered a piece to me too.

"Then what happened to them?" I asked.

"They handed all those poor guys over to the Komalas and the motherfucking Hypocrites. The next morning I got on the walkie-talkie to HQ and told them. They sent a group and we went to look for them. We checked everywhere but there was no sign of an engagement or shooting and blood. It was like they'd melted and soaked away into the ground. It was obvious they'd handed those poor guys over to the Hypocrites so they'd be forced to fight for them. That was why he didn't want to take me with them. He wanted to return the favor for that cucumber."

Bahman knocked back his glass and laughed uproariously, then said, "What a stiff he was."

"Tell me more about the war," I said. He poured himself another glass and drained it off quickly. "Sometimes," I said, "I wish I were a man and could become a soldier and experience war in the raw."

"War's a shitty place, Shokoof," he said. "Full of contradictions. You see the filthiest and the most angelic human beings here. People who throw themselves on mines the night of an op just so everyone else can walk on their body pieces and advance. You see people who never let go of their prayer beads but shaft some poor boy who cannot speak for himself. Or someone who had lice swarmin' all over his back and ain't eaten hot food in his life came here and ended up in charge of divvying up rations. The prick thought he was God on earth. He gave the fighters, who couldn't say anything, tins of beans and chickpeas, and stole the tinned chicken and meat and fruit and sold it on the black market. Or some of them swipe by the truckload the provisions and clothing and sleeping bags and camping stoves people send for the fighters. The Guards and the Basij are full of these scum."

"But you yourself are a Guards commander," I said. "These things are happening on your watch."

"Yeah," he said. "Sometimes I find the strength to stop them. Some of the other commanders are in on it. Like that Squashed-Arnie I showed you. There ain't nothin' I can do. Oftentimes I got no choice but to keep shtum about it."

He continued. "I've seen people who've come to the front just to get their paws on two free car tires. Someone else came to steal a revolver so he could go kill his unfaithful mistress. Loads of them come and stay six months so they can go back to their offices and get promoted to management. There's every kind of person here. One of them's me. Here they all think that I'm one of those fanatical Hezbollahis. Look at this." Whereupon he undid his buttons. Over his old tattoo of the Shah, he had had tattooed a picture of Khomeini with his massive turban.

"So why do you do these things?" I said. "Don't!"

"Because in this world, either you gotta be strong and give orders, or be weak and take 'em," he said. "I don't give much of a damn about life, but since for the time being I'm alive I want to be strong. Both in life and in war. To be strong you gotta get up to your neck in the dirt."

"But with every lie you tell," I said, "you are killing yourself just a little bit more. Your innocence. Your convictions."

He blew a raspberry, and said, smirking, "Convictions . . . innocence . . . lucky you. It's obvious all these years you ain't stepped outside the mansion for you to have stayed all pure and innocent like this. In this country, everything's for sale. Religion, faith, prayers, leadership posts. You sell stuff so you can buy other stuff instead."

What could I have said to him? His existence reminded me of a sky with little wisps of cloud, each of which the wind blew in a different direction. I told him to give me a glass of aragh too. I drank it rapidly and ate a tomato straight afterward.

He poured us both another glass and said, "You got it right . . . I'm not that innocent sniveling kid who wrote you that first letter anymore. The war's made me grow up. Sure, there are loads of good-hearted, innocent kids at the front, but they all either die or turn into wolves like me. Simple, kind, patriotic young men. You know how much I hate these fucking clerics. Some wife-pimping cleric comes here and shows a gold key to these poor Basiji kids and says it's the key to paradise and he can guarantee with this key whoever gets martyred in tonight's operations will go to paradise. Fuck his mother. Then he gives each one of them a key. The sick-ass pimp. Those poor old kids get all caught up in what he's saying and go throw themselves on mines to open up a path for the advance during night ops."

"What do you do in these situations?" I asked.

"Nothing," he said. "I watch. Anyways it's me who stamps and signs the bottom of all the transaction letters and purchase orders for the seminary and the front."

I took a long look at him, upset. "Don't look at me like that, Shokoof," he said. "That's how it is everywhere . . . If I don't do it, somebody else will."

Then with his index finger he made a mark on the guesthouse's filthy carpet and said, "Mark my words. Notice what I'm telling you. The day after the war's done, these people, these folks who're just now getting it good—clerics, Guards, Basijis, scavengers and beggars and thieves that manage to get out of the war alive back to their towns and villages—will take this way of thinking and acting with 'em and it's them who'll be running the country. I mean they'll be puttin' the country up for auction between themselves. They'll sell it off bit by bit and it'll go to the dogs."

"What'll happen to you?" I asked.

He laughed bitterly. "Me? I'm gonna die in the war!"

Then he lit two cigarettes and handed one to me. "Smoke it, it's good for your nerves, otherwise what I say'll make you go crazy by the morning."

I took it and started smoking. "Shokoof," he said. "I wish the only problem people like me had was lying and pretending. I've seen stuff in this war that messes with my sleep. I don't have a troubled conscience for the stuff I've done at all 'cause there's a ton of rotten shitty sellouts like me here . . . and a ton of donkeys like those Basiji kids too. As long as the donkeys are here us wolves'll be here too . . . If I don't do this stuff somebody else will, but at least sometimes I make an effort to get stuff done right. Not them. I've done some good things sometimes, but them, never . . . But the problem ain't them anyways. Sometimes I got a troubled conscience 'cause of other things that've happened and I can't sleep a wink."

He blew the cigarette smoke out of his mouth with a sigh and said, "Once buying spare car parts saved me and two of my buddies . . . What happened was that they'd give me any car that was broken down to fix it 'cause I'm a good mechanic. There ended up being three of us and we went into town to buy wrenches and brakes and clutch pads and carburetors and that kinda stuff. It took a while and it was night by the time we were done. They'd ordered us not to come back if it took a long time 'cause the highway wasn't safe at night. 'Cause the Komalas and the Hypocrites would set up checkpoints using Guards' uniforms and cars an if they saw soldiers from the Guards or Basij or Army they'd have no mercy and kill 'em on the spot. Motherfuckers. We stayed the night in a guesthouse, but we were awake until morning 'cause we were afraid the locals would give us away. You see, some of them were working with the Komalas and the Hypocrites. We were wide awake and alert like dogs until morning. Holding our guns. Long story short it was finally morning and nothin' had happened. We went back to the base but it was like they'd scattered the seeds of death everywhere. There were no guards or military police or anything else movin' about. We pissed ourselves in fear. We got our guns ready and reported to HQ over the walkie-talkie. They got there fast, in a helicopter, and we started our patrol. I hope your eyes never see anything as bad as that . . . When we went in we saw that the motherfuckers had chopped off the heads of every single fighter and tossed 'em all over the place or just left 'em sitting on their chests. The whole scene was so horrible that we all passed out . . . Fuck all their mothers . . . They'd ripped off all their tags and cut their names and insignia off their uniforms too. It was a horrible, horrible scene . . ."

His eyes were full of tears and his face angry red with pain and rage. "Out of that 101-man base, only the three of us were left. That night the motherfuckers decapitated 98 of us. Enough."

He knocked back another glass. Hiding his sigh in the smoke he exhaled, he continued. "Outside the base we saw they'd chucked a bunch of bodies on top of one another in a ditch and then set fire to them with gasoline. The scene was so horrible that we just stood there with our mouths hanging open in silence. Some of us threw up and had fevers for weeks after. The three of us couldn't look each other in the face for some time after. We felt guilty. We felt like we'd betrayed them so we could stay alive. Ever since that night I keep asking myself why I had to stay alive—why they had to die."

He knocked back another glass of aragh. I looked him in the face. What was left of the innocent Bahman who had told jokes for us the night of the palace, put on a shaliteh-skirt and danced so we would laugh? I wondered whether, after having seen those scenes, he was alive or rather had died and it was just that I could not see that. He knocked back another glass and stubbed out his cigarette. Immediately, he sparked up another and said, "We were a mess for ages after. On the one hand we'd shat ourselves like dogs, on the other we wanted revenge. We went mad. After that day the three of us were always at the front of every attack and counterattack. We killed Iraqis and Hypocrites an Komalas so mercilessly you'd've thought the motherfuckers had killed our parents . . . What ain't we seen in this crappy war . . ."

"What are the other two doing now?" I asked.

"One of them was martyred in ops a year after," he said. "The other one got shell shock, and they sent him home."

The breath was trapped in my chest. I stood up, went over to him, and without thinking about it, hugged him. He lingered in my embrace a while. He sighed, raised his head, and looked at me. His eyes were moist. "Move away," he said, "so we don't make no more rods for our own backs." I was startled. I moved away and lit up a cigarette. "I keep telling you memories so I can distract myself from you," he admitted. "Do you get how it feels to be in love with somebody and for her to be that close to you, with her long hair and languid eyes and cigarette in the corner of her mouth but you can't even touch her? Can't kiss her?"

I sat down on the ground beside him. He filled another glass and drained it, handing me one too. I felt sad for him because I could sense how much he suffered. "If only you weren't so alone," I said. "Find yourself someone."

He laughed bitterly and knocked back another glass. Taking a long drag from his cigarette, he said, "For me you're like a wisp of white cloud in a black sky. A rainbow in stormy weather."

When this poetic utterance came out of his mouth, my head was bowed, staring at the ashtray; I turned to him in disbelief, just so I could be sure that it was really him saying this.

He continued, his head also down. "Every time I came to the

mansion and spied on you from behind the trees and you were reading a book or twirling a few strands of hairs round your index finger and staring at the sky. I thought that the clouds were a story for you and the sparrows beautiful words. Or the way you stared at the ground, I felt like the earth was poetry for you and the plants were the verses. Ever since we were kids I felt like you were different than the rest, 'cause you were very different than me. You didn't speak much but when you did you didn't talk about a pigeon flying alone in the sky, for example. You told us about the sorrow it felt. You didn't talk about how lovely rain was, you went out into it barefoot. I remember that night when we got lost in the forest, when it was getting dark, all of us twelve kids sat down on a big stone slab. Everyone said something about that stone slab 'cause it was black and massive and pretty. Like it'd fallen to earth from another planet. But it was only you who said stone means solidarity and connection. You said, 'Maybe the twelve of us kids should depend on each other like this stone.' Then that day when all the kids said something about their romances, you . . . Shokoof . . . it was only you who said it doesn't matter who you love, what matters is the experience of love."

As I watched his lips in astonishment, his speech now so full of feeling—and without a single swear word mixed in—that it occurred to me that perhaps I might reduce the dreadfulness of his life a little with a kiss. I put my cigarette out in the ashtray and allowed my deep sense of sympathy and compassion for him to be my guide. I threw my arms around him and kissed him. He looked at me in disbelief, but before he could answer my kiss with long kisses of his own, I said, "This was my first and last kiss. After this, you will hanker after me more than before, but I will no longer be within reach."

He kissed me and said, "This one kiss is the most beautiful thing that's ever happened in my life." A little afterwards, he gently lay down his head on my legs to fall asleep. And he did. Like an innocent little boy amid the ruins of a great war.

Chapter Twenty-One

Piece of brick, mud, twigs and leaves, lizard, *Twenty Thousand Leagues under the Sea*.

Piece of brick, mud, twigs and leaves, spider, *The Odyssey*.

Piece of brick, mud, twigs and leaves, *Kayhan for Children*.

Two shelves of the library had collapsed on themselves, with one exploded shell and one unexploded one. The latter, the size of a large water heater, had half pierced the ground and burrowed right into the heart of Will Durant's *The Story of Civilization*, next to which a lizard had lain an egg. Here and there a handful of shrubs had grown up between Ibn Battuta's *Travels*, Aristotle's *Politics*, and Tabari's *History*. On one branch, the pages of Forough Farrokhzad's *Let us believe in the onset of the cold season* fluttered in the breeze:

"Nobody is thinking of the flowers
Nobody is thinking of the fish
Nobody wants
To believe that the garden is dying
That the heart of the garden has swollen under the sun
That the mind of the garden is slowly
Being emptied of green memories."

Nowruz 1983 came and went in the war-stricken city, mournfully and without fuss. Only the few trees dotted here and there celebrated spring. Nobody donned new clothes. When once I found myself by chance standing opposite a peach tree laden with pink blossoms, shouldering the burden of spring in the city all alone, I realized Nezami too had understood this point:

"An entire spring bloomed from my one lonely tree!"[94]

For a month and a half, Bahman and I had been visiting all the surrounding towns and cities: Susangerd, Hoveyzeh, Ahvaz, Bostan, Andimeshk, Shadgan, Shalamcheh, Abadan, Shushtar, and Masjed Soleyman. But of Mehrab, not a word. It was as if he had turned to smoke and vanished into thin air, until one day, as we were returning, hopeless, from Ahvaz to Khorramshahr, the ruins of a number of large buildings caught my attention. Trees and bushes were growing out of several of the buildings' windows. I watched a pigeon fly down from the sky, alighting on a branch of a tree that seemed to be growing right in the middle of the ruins, although it was too large to have grown up in the ruin in only the two or three years the war had been on. I felt something stir and bloom suddenly in my heart. "Go do the things you need to do," I said to Bahman. "I'm going to have a look around over there." "What's Mehrab gonna be doing in them ruins?" he asked, astonished. We parted ways and arranged to meet again before sunset at the same old guesthouse.

I passed between the wreckage of two buildings and made my way to the ruined library. There were still Arabic slogans on the bullet-riddled walls, left like salt on a wounded body, from back when the city had fallen to the Iraqis, عاش الفارس العربی, and next to it جئنا لنبقی[95] Meanwhile the Iranians who had taken the city back a year later had responded thus: "We came but you weren't here." Elsewhere under that slogan was written, "It was you who wrote *fârs* means warrior."[96] On another wall

[94] Nezami, a great poet of the 12th century.

[95] "Long live the valiant Arab warrior" and "We've come to stay."

[96] TN: the Arabic letters *f-â-r-s,* vocalized as fârs (Persian fârs), mean "horseman, knight" and therefore "warrior," the meaning intended by the Iraqi troops. However, fârs also means "Persian" (a person), and the Iranian troops are playing on this ambiguity: "it was you who wrote 'Persian' means warrior."

was written in a shaky hand, “The enemy has entered the city. We will have been martyred in just a few moments. Pray for us.” On another wall still was written, “If we are killed, live in our place.”

I passed through the corridors and the reading rooms, past the metal bookshelves and the wooden boxes containing the catalog cards, stepping over twigs and leaves and mud and the dried corpses of lizards, frogs, and mice. In a corner, a dusty copy of Sohrawardi’s *The Cry of the Simorgh* lay. The last orange and yellow rays of the sunset were turning dark and silence gave the atmosphere a menacing allure. I took a look around the rooms. Amid the ruins, I stood still and listened to the sound of silence, inspected the broken bookshelves, the tables and chairs strewn about at all angles, the walls riddled with bullet-holes. I thought about the people who had once sat on the chairs and studied there. Were they dead? Or had they been driven out by war and taken refuge in other cities? Was Mehrab one of them? The doorless, windowless walls stared at me like eyeless, mouthless, rotting bodies. A green praying mantis rubbed its legs together between the pages of Dehkhoda’s *Dictionary*. A staircase summoned me to the darkness of the basement. When I reached the bottom of the stairs, I could hear talking, far away and indistinct. I picked up a piece of brick. Perhaps there was something threatening down there. I moved cautiously toward the sound. Behind the bent and crooked metal shelves and the series of books on the history of political science that had fallen on the ground, someone was lying in a corner of the room, and beside him sat a man.

I didn’t know whether I should keep going, stand right where I was, or go back. I was still hesitating when the seated man turned to face me—a bearded, thin, pallid man. Although the light was dim, I could see that he looked tired and on edge, though not threatening. I was still standing scrutinizing him when he took a giant step towards me and shouted, “You!”

I didn’t recognize him. The man was striding toward me,

coming closer and closer, and without thinking I took several steps backwards and brandished the brick threateningly. I was scared. From the dark corner he came towards me, standing by the window. When he got close, through the thick beard and mustache and unkempt hair, I saw two familiar eyes. Was it him?

It was him . . .

It was him . . .

It was him . . .

I was rooted to the spot and dropped the brick. It was him. Behnam. My Behnam.

He reached me with one more stride. He hugged me tight and spun me around and as he did, said, "What are you doing here?" Then he pushed me away a little distance and said, "Let me look at you. Is it really you? Here? In the ruins of Khorramshahr?" I was dumb and dizzy with disbelief. Then, as if he had just remembered something important, he took my hand and pulled me to the corner where a man was lying. "Come here, come here . . . Mehrab has been waiting for you."

I let go of his hand in disbelief and ran towards the other figure. This frail man lying there with his long, unkempt hair, beard and mustache, his sunken, vacant eyes and bloodied leg, bore no resemblance to my Mehrab. Those eyes were absolutely unlike my brother, Only Brother, my dear Mehrab. I knelt beside him and hugged his head tight and my tears began to flow. How had this happened to Mehrab? I looked into his eyes and covered his face with kisses. It was at that moment that I realized that there was nobody anywhere in the world I loved as much as him. My brother. My Only Brother. My one and only like-minded comrade and companion during days asleep, during days awake, the days of the temple and the forest, the night of the palace . . . Oh, how this brother was a part of my own body . . . and now he had wound up in this atrocious state. I turned to Behnam and asked, "What happened to him?" He sat down next to us and said, "I'm not sure. He got shell shock, or ended up like this under torture. It was so hard for me to find him. Sometimes he recognizes me, sometimes not."

Then, as if he had only just come to his senses, he asked, "How did you turn up here anyway?" "Bahman and I have been looking for Mehrab for over a month now," I said. The moment Behnam heard Bahman's name, he prickled with anger. He opened his mouth and was about to say something when suddenly Bahman himself came down the stairs and into the corridor. As soon as their eyes met, Behnam flew toward Bahman and they were at each other's throats. I had never seen this side of Behnam. He struggled with Bahman as if he were some battle-hardened combatant, while Bahman yielded nothing to him. After they had thrown a few kicks and punches, they began grappling with one another, all the while hurling insults I couldn't really make out. Then, even as they kept interrupting and threatening each other and started kicking and punching again, I began to pick up things here and there. That the two of them had seen each other several times at the front and that Behnam considered that what had happened to Mehrab was Bahman's fault. Then I heard Behnam say, even as he was throwing punches, "Wasn't what happened to Mehrab enough? You had to drag Shokoofeh here too?" Bahman grabbed him by the collar and yelled, "How did I know you were gonna be here, you asshole! I didn't bring Shokoofeh anyhow."

In the end I jumped between them and yelled, "It's got nothing to do with Bahman. I came to the front myself to find Mehrab. Bahman was helping me."

Then I turned to Bahman and said, "What's the story with Mehrab? Did you know he was in this state?"

"Ha! Did he know?" Behnam said sardonically, irritably wiping the sweat and blood off his face. "He was helping you? Did he tell you that he knew Mehrab was in prison? Did he tell you that Mehrab was in this condition? Did he tell you that he himself threw Mehrab in jail?"

I looked at Bahman in utter confusion. As he was wiping

the blood from the corner of his lip, Bahman moved away and said, "Shokoof, I didn't wanna tell you. I didn't wanna upset you 'cause I didn't know where Mehrab was after he escaped from prison."

"Prison?" I shouted. "Which prison?"

Pointing to Bahman, Behnam yelled, "Which prison? The Guards' prison in the desert. The gentleman himself threw Mehrab in jail!"

I looked at Bahman in disbelief, who, taking a step closer to me, began to justify himself. "It's true. I threw him in jail so I could save him. The Guards wanted to execute him for atheism and promoting unbelief. He kept talking mystical nonsense about the Third Step and other bullshit. When the Guards commanders heard about it, they put together a file on him. They wanted to execute him in the desert for heresy and unbelief. I put him in jail to buy time while I prepared to help him escape. And I did help him break out, but after that I lost track of him. I heard that he'd gone back to the fighting and gotten shell shock."

Bahman wanted to hug me to calm me down, but I moved away from him in disgust. Why had he not told me any of this?

Behnam, whose anger it seemed had not reduced one whit, moved toward Bahman again, directed a punch at his face and shouted, "How many people like Mehrab have you arrested so far? For how many people have you signed desert death warrants? Those young people who've cleared the grounds of mines with their own bodies died because of your silence. Abdollah and Davoud and Yaser were killed because of you." Bahman, with great effort, hurled him to one side and yelled, "War is war. It ain't a place for pretty boys like you. What can one guy like me do up against all these Guards and Basijis and Army folks? If I speak up they'll put me on the bodywasher's slab. Like Abdollah and Davoud and Yaser. Sooner or later they'll put you up against the wall too."

Now standing some way apart, they continued to shout

at one another at the tops of their voices. Behnam gestured up and down at his dusty and wounded body and said, "Can you see any pretty boys here? But in your face all I see is a vile piece of scum. When they were executing Abdollah and the others you should risked your own life and limb to save them. You shouldn't have signed their death warrant but you did. You just clung to your desk at HQ like some lily-livered coward."

Bahman looked at me, then at Behnam, as if he were more concerned about my judgment than what Behnam was saying. Behnam drew close to Bahman with two big strides and, flicking the insignia on his shoulders with disgust, said, "You got to where you are now with this kind of filthy business."

Eventually Bahman replied, "There was nothing I could do for them. They wanted to execute them for promoting Communism. The order came from the top. Each one of them had a file as thick as my neck . . . By the way, just 'cause I didn't grow up like you wrapped in cotton wool, does that mean I gotta die? When you're surrounded by all these jackals and hyenas, you gotta be a wolf to survive."

"No," Behnam yelled. "Don't die. But don't get everyone else killed either. Don't just fight on your own behalf. Now that you've turned into a wolf, use the situation to save everyone else . . . to save those defenseless young people."

Bahman muttered a "motherfucker" under his breath and answered with a sneer. "Everyone else? Fuck everyone else. Where was everyone else when I was on the streets and didn't have a piece of bread to eat? Where was everyone else when I was coughing up blood and being punched and kicked right and left? Everyone else? Ha!"

Behnam answered angrily but in a more level voice: "No one else helped you, but you can help them. Act like a human being for once. Didn't Mehrab and his family ever do anything good for you? Why didn't you save Mehrab? They tortured him so much in that prison of yours that he ended up like this."

Bahman spat the blood out of his mouth and said, "I pissed on the morality and the humanity of people who didn't care about me. Who say someone like me's gotta die to be counted a hero." Then he continued in a somewhat softer voice, "I helped Mehrab escape, you dick. Who d'ya think told you where Mehrab's prison was? Who arranged for the warden to take your bribe? Hmm? It was me . . . Me! You moron!"

Behnam looked at him in astonishment. He had nothing to say.

"By the way, motherfucker," Bahman said. "What have you got against me? What did I ever do to you, pretty boy?"

Behnam, coolly but with a look of disgust I had never seen before in his eyes, said, "I don't have any problem with you personally, but I am against all the things you represent: silence in the face of oppression and injustice. Collaboration with traitors and informers. Running after promotion in this filthy, murderous system."

Having calmed down, Bahman turned his back on Behnam, blew a raspberry, and as he lit a cigarette, said, "My strength ain't equal to the oppressor's, that's why I collaborate with him. Are you that strong? Be my guest . . . Ain't nobody stopping you. Go get yourself killed. I wanna stay alive. At least for as long as the war's going on."

During all this time, I had had one eye on Mehrab, lying there, half-conscious, and another on the two of them. Finally I went over to Mehrab. I kissed him. A tear rolled down from each of our eyes. He was thin and gaunt and dirty. "Mehrab," I said. "Without you the mansion and the tree and the temple and the forest lack all charm or delight." He smiled faintly. Did that mean he recognized me? Then, pointing at Behnam and Bahman, I said, "You wanted to find humanity in war. Did you?" He moved his head gently, and I did not understand what he meant by it.

Turning to Behnam, I said, "So won't you tell me finally how Mehrab came to be in this state?"

Bahman jumped in. "He musta got shell shock. I ain't seen him since he got outta prison. I asked around everywhere on the hush-hush but you saw for yourself . . . We went looking for him everywhere togethe. He'd vanished like a drop of water in the ground."

Behnam, casting a dirty look at Bahman, said, "That's not how it was. He got like this in prison."

"Don't talk nonsense," Bahman said. "He was only in prison for a week. I sent Davoud to you myself to tell you how to get him outta there. You moron, did you think the Hidden Holy Helpers helped Davoud find you?" Behnam struck a match angrily and lit a cigarette and said, "Let's say you did help him escape, it was you who put him in there in the first place . . . When Davoud and I got him out, he was already in this state. You threw Mehrab, healthy and well, into prison with your own hands, and yet you didn't know they tortured him in there? Liar."

"Impossible," Bahman said. "I gave a clear order for them to look after him. I bribed the wardens so they'd do whatever he asked. Then I went off on an op. When I got back, Davoud had been martyred. I'd lost trace of Mehrab and there was no news of you either."

"So no doubt they did this to him when the honorable gentleman was away on operations. They tortured him so much that his brain and body don't work anymore. He can't walk properly. He can't talk properly. He's forgotten everything. Only every now and then does he remember something."

I looked at Bahman, busy frustratedly smoking a cigarette. It was now completely dark and the only modest illumination came from the lights on the horizon. I wondered why Bahman had not told me. Bahman read my mind, and taking a deep drag on his cigarette, said, "I didn't tell you 'cause I couldn't find any trace of him. 'Cause I was afraid you'd blame me."

In a calmer tone, Behnam said to me, "We've been on the

run for about two months. I wanted to get him out of this region, but there are patrols on the roads everywhere. There's no way out. Unless we were to escape over the mountains and through the desert, but there was no way I could take that on alone with him in this state." He gestured to Mehrab's broken leg. "We needed a jeep and equipment."

He continued. "When I helped him escape from prison, he didn't know who I was. He kept pounding his head on the wall and talking about Mithra and the family madness. But one morning he recognized me suddenly and begged me to bring him here because he knew you'd come here. It took three weeks for us to get ourselves here."

Astounded, I said, "Until an hour ago I didn't know I was going to turn up here myself. How did Mehrab know I'd come here?"

"I don't know either," Behnam said. "Mehrab told me Leyla came to see him one night in prison and told him to go to this library and wait for Shokoofeh. Leyla also handed Mehrab a letter which he was supposed to give to you." I looked at Mehrab enquiringly. He appeared to be conscious. With his eyes, he indicated his clothes. I looked through his pockets. I found the letter. It was dirty and crumpled. It was addressed to me. Very concise.

"Shokoofeh, my dear sister, I am alive and well, and all these years I have been busy studying the Simorghi Faith in the Eternal Library and at the same time observing your life, my dear ones. I am truly sorry for having left you alone all these years. I live with that woman up the tree, the Simorgh. If I hadn't come to meet Mehrab, his death would have been certain without him having completed his mission in this life. My sister, I know you will have many questions. One day perhaps I'll be able to reply to them all. Just know that these dark, somber days will pass, but first you will have other dark, somber days in front of you. I cannot return to the mansion for the time being. My function and duty in life is elsewhere. I am writing you this letter so you may prepare

yourself. The sacred fire, the tree, what remains of the family, the mansion, and Kay-Khosro need you. Be strong. Save Mehrab. Stay alive, and as soon as you are free, return to the mansion."

I looked at Mehrab in bewilderment. What did she mean by "as soon as you are free"? Who was Kay-Khosro, anyway? What did she mean by "what remains of the mansion and the family?" Tears welled up in both our eyes. Why had Leyla written that Mehrab's death would have been certain? That they would have tortured him so much in prison that he would have died? "It's been three days since we got here," Behnam said, "and I have been constantly praying that you wouldn't come here because I'm being followed, and if they find you with me they'll definitely arrest you too. I was waiting for Mehrab's leg to get a little better to convince him that we should get out of here as soon as possible. Besides that, here they look at any suspicious stranger as if they're a spy." Then, as if he had suddenly come to his senses, he got up, came over to me and hugged me tight, kissed me, and whispered in my ear. "Every time they took me to the gallows, I had no regrets except one, that I hadn't been able to kiss you again."

At that very moment Bahman, his face enflamed with rage, without looking at Behnam, spat on the ground and cast me a ferocious look, before going over to Mehrab and saying, "I'll take Mehrab to a new guesthouse—the previous one has been under surveillance for two or three days. I know the owner of the new one. He owes his own and his family's life to me and there won't be a peep outta him, he won't dare. The "Martyrs' Guesthouse" on War Avenue. Try to get there as soon as you can. We gotta find Mehrab a way to escape."

We helped him put Mehrab in the car. I kissed my brother. I put the letter in his pocket, placed Shahnaz's Sharaf-e Shams ring on his finger, and said, "Mom and Shahnaz and everyone else are waiting for you." Then Behnam and I went back to the ruined library, but before I did I said to Bahman, "If I haven't got there by morning, then something bad's happened to me. However you can, get Mehrab to the mansion. Don't worry about me."

With a face like thunder, without looking at me, he nodded his head, but before stepping on the gas and disappearing down the end of the road, he stuck his head out of the car window and said, "You gotta stay alive, just like Leyla said. So look after yourself."

Chapter Twenty-Two

In the darkness of the ruined hallways and rooms, we picked up whatever might be useful to us. A torn rug, a battered kettle, two chipped glasses. We found a few books, none of which we had read. Behnam found Walter Benjamin's *One-Way Street*, and I picked up Marguerite Duras's *The Ravishment of Lol Stein*. In other rooms, we found still other books. Carl Gustav Jung's *Modern Man in Search of a Soul*, and one volume of Dante's *Divine Comedy*: *Inferno*. We also found a copy of Mohammad-Hassan Saheb-oz-Zamani's *The Third Line*. Even though most of the pages of these books were either torn or unreadable because damaged by the humidity, holding them in our hands here in the middle of the war and these dark ruins was a solace for our hearts. It made us feel safe. Like we were with our nearest and dearest.

In the basement, in a room with no outward-facing window, there had grown an ancient tree. It was odd. How could so large a tree have grown in these ruins? Its upper branches had grown up through the broken ceiling above us, reaching the upper story and beyond to the sky. This was the same tree that the pigeon had alighted on just before sunset, drawing my attention to the ruins. We set up camp right there. We took the bits and pieces of food we had with us out of our backpacks, and Behnam lit a fire with the scraps of paper and books. We had a cold night ahead of us. Behnam looked long and hard at the tree but said nothing. He put two cigarettes in his mouth and lit them. He gave me one and said, "I don't know whether you smoke or not, but tonight you need to." I didn't know he smoked. I took it from him and smoked it. How many times had

I ever smoked a cigarette? We turned on the tap in the kitchen, and after a little mud had come out, a half-limpid water flowed from the pipe. We ate a bit from our provisions before setting up our little tea station with the tea and sugar cubes Behnam had in his backpack. We were silent until the tea was brewed. The sound of my body's sorrowful music wound through the room. I was waiting for him to ask something. He didn't. Then, as we were drinking, he told me about what had happened in prison, and I told him about what had happened at the mansion. We flicked through a few books, read a few pages, then threw them on the fire. The first thick volume that Behnam came upon was Edward Browne's *A Year Amongst the Persians*. Most of its pages were either torn or were stuck together with the humidity. He read a paragraph. Then he flung the book into a corner. He took up another one. He read a paragraph of that before losing interest and putting the book back in its place, saying, "You see. Nothing is calming anymore. It's like I'm no longer who I used to be."

Then he stuck his hand in his backpack and retrieved a notebook. He looked at it, before flinging it into the fire. I guessed it must be the notebook containing his memoirs. Quickly, I plucked it from the fire. "Why did you want to burn it?" I asked. "Because everything is just chasing after the wind," he said. We both stared at the fire for a few minutes. "How naive I was," he said. "All these years had to pass, and all these things happen for me to get that."

I looked at him in the silence. Still staring at the fire, holding his cup of tea, full to the brim, he went on. "Our extreme opinions and behavior were a mistake. We were mistaken to take up arms. And we were mistaken to be so blindly opposed to the Shah and America. We should've made practical and specific demands that would've gradually improved the state of society."

Then he shook his head. He looked at me and said, "What a shame I understood all of this so late."

"Even if you had understood back then, you might not have been able to change anything. Communism was a mighty wave, with all its beautiful ideals and the appalling damage it left behind it."

"We were so naive," he continued. "We wanted to advance a hundred years in a single night. To be honest, did any of our leaders even know how we were supposed to attain our fine political ideals? There was no question of reason and logic and calculation. Everything stayed at the level of slogans."

I looked at him in silence. He had changed—and this change set my heart at ease. I threw a handful of books on the ailing fire. "The past turned out to be something it shouldn't have been, while our present is this. So, let's think about something good: the future."

He smiled faintly. "You start," I said.

His beautiful black eyes flashed as he gazed into the flames:

"We had all the world's words at our command and
We did not say that
That should be used
For there was but one word
One word was not put forward
Freedom!
We did not say it.
But you imagine it."[97]

Majid and his anxious smile on the gallows came to mind, and I said, "Whoever in Iran awakes to the gallows goes / I for a waking life wish, and no gallows."

Then, he smiled and said, "I want you to be my wife and for us to have a daughter called Zhiyan. In our language it means 'life'. And a boy called Zhivar, which means 'life-giving.'"[98]

"I had no idea you were Kurdish," I said. He laughed and

[97] Ahmad Shamlo, a great contemporary Iranian poet.

[98] Both names are Kurdish.

nodded. The blood had rushed to my face when I heard this surprise marriage proposal. He however, without looking at my face, as if he were talking about his most mundane plans in life, took my hand in his, and, staring at the tree, its branches half-lit by the fire's light, asked, "What about you?"

"I'll choose our son's name," I said. "I will call him Kay-Khosro. The ideal human. The just king. I hope he'll be good-looking and tall like you. But I don't want him to be unreliable like you, constantly disappearing."

Suddenly I remembered Leyla's letter. Which Kay-Khosro had she been talking about?

Behnam laughed. He lay down and made me lie down next to him. He took me in his arms and said, "What matters is that I have always been faithful to you. From the day I first set eyes on you eight years ago in the mansion courtyard till today." He shut his eyes and murmured into my ear in a sleepy voice, "Tell me again. What does the future look like, in your view?"

Then, as if preparing himself for a sweet dream, a smile on his lips, he closed his eyes.

"When I was on my way to the front, in a very remote village I saw a shepherd girl with a bewitching voice," I said. "She said her name was Sahar. When she sang for her sheep, the wind, the earth, the fire stood still in astonishment at her bewitching voice. When she sang, breaths were trapped in chests. Without knowing why, people had lumps in their throats, their hearts started beating fast, and they became kind. Groups of people arrived from the surrounding villages so that she would sing for them. It was if there was something in her voice that awoke people's consciences and provoked their hearts to compassion and sympathy—but one day the village cleric told her that she no longer had permission to sing, because her voice aroused the men. And yet the men were not aroused. They had merely discovered a tenderness of heart. But no one dared dispute what the cleric said. After that, the girl was shut up behind a tent curtain in her house, and no one even had permission to see her face. In the future I have in mind, Sahar is free to sing, and no one will determine what she can do. She will sing and people will fall in love with tender hearts."

He moved his head around on my chest as if he was deep into some pleasant dream.

He was silent. So, I resumed once more. "As I was coming here, I met a frail old woman in a town, barely literate, poor, all withered up, wearing a black chador. She wandered the streets of the city alone, carrying a wooden cross on her scrawny back, to which she had stuck a poster, and on it was written, 'You killed my Sattar! I will not depart this world until I have avenged him.' People passed on by without noticing her, or sometimes stood and shook their heads at her pityingly. Her name was Gowhar. In the future I have in mind, Sattar is alive and has a good job, while Gowhar is retired and is living out her old age peacefully."

Then I said, "Why do I have to take such a detour anyhow? My wish is for there to be no war. For people to be free however they like, eat and drink, dress, sing however they like, or dance in the streets."

I turned to him and said, "You see. The future I have in my head is very simple. I wish for an ordinary life." But Behnam had descended into a deep sleep, a smile on his lips.

I went to sleep too, but before I did, I took up the notebook containing his memoirs. I opened a page at random.

"*August 31, 1982*

"243 days have gone by since the beginning of the year, and 122 are left.

" . . . After lunch they summoned me to the command post. I set off full of happiness at being sent on a mission to the Allahu Akbar Hills. When I reached HQ, the commander told me to get my stuff and to come there by car at dinner time. My suspicions were confirmed: I would be going to the Allahu Akbar Hills. I set out for 203 again. On the way I dropped in on one of my friends, Mohammad Reza Akbarzadeh. Then I went off to the command post. A Jeep Shahbaz got there at the same time I did and said Behnam Rostami should get his stuff and come to 100 with us. I was astonished. I thought I'd go see the commander again. I went there at five. When he saw me, he said that that they'd informed him I engaged in political discussions and that I played cards with another one of the boys (Artillery 5). Then they banished me to 155 but sent the guy who played cards back to his own position after talking to him for a few minutes."

I open another page. "Last night I went to sleep thinking of Shokoofeh, but I dreamt of Uncle Vendad. He was walking, soaking wet, his clothes dripping, on the railroad line. I had never dreamt of him after the Hezbollahi forces had cruelly killed him like that on the railroad line on the old bridge and then thrown his body into the river. In my dream, I was in uniform like I was at the front. I went to see him. I embraced my uncle cheerfully. I got wet. My uncle laughed."

The left corner of my lip was moist. I opened my sleepy eyes a slit. An intense light surrounded me and around me the air had grown warm. In the light, I noticed Behnam's head close to mine. Very close. Still closer; this time he kissed the right corner of my lips. It became moist. I licked the moisture off with my tongue. He pressed me into his arms. How often throughout the years I had re-staged making love with him in my imagination. In the forest. In the temple. In the bedroom. Even, several times, while on the road. In the mountains and green meadows, under the ceiling of the sky. In the cave. But in the ruins of the library? Never! Well . . . finally . . . his real body . . . The weight of his real body lay heavily on mine and *oh* . . . Was this not the most pleasurable weight in the world? He wrapped his arms around my body. I wrapped my hands around his neck, and we entwined ourselves in one another without a word, twisted and pulled one another down . . . inwards . . . into the depths.

We drowned in a sea of kisses and bodily pleasures. We let

no breath remain to us in the depths of the sea of the soul. The sea of desire. We let ourselves suffocate in the oxygenless depths, where the bubbles of suffering and drunkenness were scattered around us, dragging us farther and farther down. To the netherworld. To the bodiless universe. To the eternal universe. I let his long, thin fingers touch every inch of the geography of my body and soul, scratch them out, throw them on the fire, and build anew. I let his hot kisses blister my skin, destroy me, and other kisses restore me once again. How many bitter regrets of body and soul had we suffered, life after life? How many times had we fallen in love, and then fallen in love again, and more in love, life after life? As were thus rolling, body and soul, we passed over the *Complete Poetry of Hafez* and the *Book of Lovers,* and I let him press his manhood into my womanhood exactly when half of my shoulders were lying on Khayyam's *Quatrains* and half my leg on Attar's *Conference of the Birds*. My moans wound through the lofty, half-dark space of the ruined library, hung from the branches of the tree, and flew upward and out through the broken ceiling. Toward freedom. In our lovemaking we attained not only the madness of love, but the madness of freedom too. Freedom from bonds and chains . . . from must-dos and must-do-nots. Freedom from fears and traditions . . . from the patrols of the Committees, prisons and hangropes . . . In each other's bodies, we lived the freedom of love. The freedom of becoming one.

Chapter Twenty-Three

How much do you charge a night, you whore? Which opposition group leaders do you sleep with? If you don't talk, I'll torture you slowly till morning and you'll be begging . . ."

How many hours I was hanging there, I do not know. He first performed his ablutions, before falling furiously on me with the whip. So much did he talk of the pure Islam of Muhammad, before flogging me, and so much did I curse his prophets and imams and god, before he beat me black and blue, that I entirely lost track of time . . . The sound of the blood dripping from my body onto the floor passed over my body's mournful music and wound around the cell:

Drip.
Drip.
Drip.

It was a basement in the depths of nowhere. I was brought down long staircases until we got there. Fifteen or twenty meters down. Sometimes people's voices could be heard in the distance, as well as the slamming and grinding of iron hinges and doors. I tried to pay attention to the music of my body, to focus on that. On that music that reminded me of the mansion and of Behnam, but the pain . . . the pain . . . the pain burned me right to the marrow of my bones.

As dawn broke, we were still in each other's arms in the ruined library, the tree still smoldering from within, when a shout separated our entwined bodies: "Hands up or I shoot!"

We turned round and looked. It was that little bald man from the Guards. The same one who'd been looking for an excuse to undermine Bahman. The little man turned to me, and pulling my identity papers out of my pocket, shouted, "Are you a spy for the Hypocrites or the Communists?" As I was about to untangle myself from his body, I suddenly wondered what had happened to Mehrab and Bahman. Abruptly several Guards, guns in hand, entered through the door and through the broken ceiling and sprayed the walls with bullets. I wanted to throw myself on Behnam to protect him, but he anticipated me and threw himself on me instead. He was hit by a bullet. Another bullet struck my leg. I dragged myself on top of him, held him and weeping, kissed him. With his last remaining strength he said, "Don't cry. As always . . . I'll see you again soon."

They say that pain and suffering are necessary to create awareness; I can attest to the fact that pain made me aware that it is not possible to be a lion among pigeons unless one is a dead lion. I can attest to the fact that pain made me aware that my body is weak in the face of whips and daggers and kicks and rape. Very weak. I . . . can attest to the fact that awareness is painful.

My flesh had been sliced up under the whip, while my arms, which had been bound behind my head and suspended from the ceiling, appeared to have come out of their sockets. Meanwhile, blood was still dripping from the leg that had been struck by a bullet. All the same, I was in a strange state. I was in pain, and I was not. I was burning and I was not. As if, because of how intense the pain was in my heart, my body had grown insensible. My Behnam had died . . . My brain had become numb. Behnam's breath had turned into an innocent smile and mingled with "I am your restless lover" and in my arms had turned into a sigh . . . one last sigh. His last exhale had touched the skin of my face. The skin of my lips . . .

I was in floods of tears.

I was in floods of tears and once more started screaming and yelled, "If only . . . if only . . . if only there were a God."

I could not hear what that little man was saying at all. I could not hear the music of my body. The noise of my screaming resounded, in my cell spinning and spinning in my brain. "If only . . . if only . . . if only there were a God." The more I screamed and cried, the louder the sorrowful music of my body got and the more it aroused the bald little man, whose name I now knew to be Rahmati, and who was more of a Ministry of Intelligence interrogator than a guard, causing him to torment me still more. In some way, I wanted him to torment me. To hit me. To chop me up . . . Oh, Behnam . . . Oh, Behnam . . . Were they not wasted, those black, playful eyes of yours? Were they not wasted, that height and fine stature and beautiful face of yours? Were they not wasted, that voice . . . those simple and humane values of yours?

As soon as my disordered thoughts had grown numb, the sound of his heavy boots resounded through the empty, dim, cold cell, and could be heard above the sound of the sorrowful music of my body. Vague . . . distant . . . whip in hand, he struck it against me, this way and that. My thoughts and feelings blended with what was coming out of his mouth. "Did you sleep with Behnam and with Omid Raisi? The moment I set eyes on you I knew you were a wolf in sheep's clothing. What's your relationship with Omid?" The sound of the whip . . . the sound of dripping blood . . . "How long have you been in contact with him? Who do you spy for? What do you know about Omid? Who does he spy for?" The sound of the boots mingled with the sound of the music of my body. *Oh Behnam, if only I could lie in your arms but once more* . . . "Answer, you whore . . . I'll do something to make you start talking again!" And his whip beat on my body like a stick on a drum. Hit me . . . hit me . . . harder . . . *I want to die. If only Eblis could come and help me die sooner. If only the Ball of Light were here.* The whip . . . the whip . . . after that, I remember nothing until a bucket of water on my face brought me round again.

My eyes would only with great difficulty open halfway. They were swollen, while the pain had spread throughout my entire body. The sound of water and blood mingled together dripping . . . dripping . . . dripping from me wound its way into my ear. I was still alive. His distant voice once again reached my ears. "Your life is in my hands. I want you to surrender yourself to me. For you to desire it . . . If you surrender yourself to me, I'll free you tomorrow morning. Because in this town, I'm the plaintiff and the interrogator and the judge. I'm your god too. But if you don't give yourself to me, I'll send you to the Center and from there to Tehran and by the time it gets there your file'll be this big . . . " He must have pointed with his hand to his thick neck. "And I don't have any sway there, so they'll try and execute you at the double. For the crimes of espionage on the frontline, forging documents, spreading unbelief, vilifying the Prophet, insulting the sacred matters of Islam, and sorcery. The prescribed penalty in Islam for sorcery is death. The prescribed penalty for sexual relations without marriage is stoning. The prescribed penalty for insulting sacred matters is death. The prescribed penalty for spreading unbelief, death." He guffawed and said, "By now you've been condemned to death four times over." Then he brought his odious, ugly face close to mine and said, "How does this tune come out of your body, you witch? Put on Baba Karam[99] for us so we can jig a little, you whore." He laughed hysterically and went on. "When you were putting out for Omid, were you taking requests? *Ha ha ha* . . . I want you to give it to me 'cause you want to, so why don't you put on a romantic tune for us? I'm your god and my will is that you eat my cock 'cause you wannit, and you, ohh, don't that

[99] A popular dance tune.

taste good?" My face was struck by his putrid breath. He ran the whip up and down my body and squeezed the middle of my leg firmly and said, "Just like you ate Omid's . . . "

I tried to think of something pleasant. Why not? Didn't I used to think that beauty was the cure for all the world's wounds? Hadn't I wanted to consecrate my life to it? It was spring outside. Wasn't it? The blossoms . . . Somewhere outside this dark pit blossoms were certainly opening at right that moment, heedless of me. As I imagined the reflection of the light of the rising sun on the white-crimson blossoms of the wild apple tree, a smile appeared on my lips. Then I saw a vixen playing with her cubs. They were clambering over each other and the morning breeze was ruffling their bright orange-black fur. I raised my head with great effort from amid the wounds and the drops of blood and looked at his vile face with its lascivious gaze locked on me. I started to laugh. At the sight of this ugly, jerry-built face and its lewd gaze . . . At this foul-smelling mouth and at my agonizing, blood-dripping position in his contemptible hands. At this cell, my and my family's idiotic naivety, my body's music. At that beautiful and heedless blossom busy blooming, those innocent playful foxes . . . At this humiliation and sexual complex of his . . . It was like some surreal scene. Like death grinding its teeth. Like a mocking impression of life . . . I laughed . . . I laughed . . . I laughed, and even as my wounded and bloody jaw was gripped by pain, the sound of my peals of laughter wound around the cell and slapped his odious, bearded face. The Guard-interrogator, the little man scowled, and as he was about to slap me in the face, I gathered up all my forces and spat in his, adding, "It's obvious Omid's really got under your skin . . ." And I laughed longer and louder, while he whipped me more and harder. And as he did, I thought that now Behnam was dead it was good that I would die here in the depths of the cavity of the misshapen mouth of life. In the dark, putrid pit of war . . . And that would be it. I thought how good it was that I had been able to send the Ball of Light back to the mansion in time. I had whispered into its ear that it should go find Shabro and return home with him and tell them that Mehrab and Leyla and I were all alive and well but that it might take us a while to get back. And the Ball of Light had leapt out through the gap in the window of the car that had been driving through the desert for an hour to take us to this fearful basement in the middle of nowhere. The interrogator whipped me again and I laughed still louder. Let him kill me. I wasn't even particularly sure whether my life was following the right course or not anyway. What an opportune death.

In a semi-conscious state, I saw him put a chair underneath my legs, draw closer to me, then set another chair beside me, onto which he climbed to unfasten the chain on one of my arms. Then he started stripping me. I screamed with what remained of my vital force, thrashed about, spat and kicked, but he just hit me harder. "What happened to your Islamic morality then?" I yelled. "Did it all just turn to smoke and vanish into the air faced with a woman's body? Like your prophet with his forty wives, you're just a common old lecherous ladies' man."

He punched me hard in the head and howled, "Don't let me hear the name of the Most Noble Prophet come from your dirty lips, you whore!" Then he thumped and kicked me in the side several times and ripped the clothes from my body, before saying in a completely calm and collected voice: "In the Islamic sharia it is stated that a virgin's place is in heaven. Even though I know you're a whore, I wanna be sure you're going straight to hell and will burn in its fires."

Then he descended calmly from the chair, walked around me and gazed at me up and down with his dirty, beady eyes. He came close, and amid all my thrashing about and shouting, he laughed loudly and licked my body. He sniffed it. He spat on it. He stuck his fingers into its orifices. Into the openings of my wounds. I screamed. I screamed . . . I was whipped and whipped. I passed out.

When I came to, I saw that he was standing by the door. Then the cell door opened and the prison warden, scrutinizing my naked body, pushed a blindfolded boy, fourteen or fifteen years of age, inside. The horrid little man, the interrogator, took off the boy's blindfold. On seeing my naked, suspended body dripping blood, the boy crawled horrified into a corner of the cell and held his head in his hands.

"Get up and fuck this whore," the interrogator commanded.

The boy shook his head in horror. Impossible! And he pressed himself against the wall, crumpled up, his head hidden in his hands. The little man threatened the boy in a louder voice, and again the boy did not obey. This time the little man pulled the boy to his feet and in a swift movement pulled down his pants and raped him in front of my disbelieving eyes. The boy howled in terror and pleaded, but there was no use. My stomach was turned upside down and I vomited.

Once he was done, he threw the boy into a corner and kicked him hard a few times, then said, "Now do you understand what screwing means? So get up and go screw this whore, otherwise I'll screw you again." Again the boy, howling with tears, did not stir.

"If you fuck this whore," the little man said, "I'll make sure you're not executed, and you only do five years in jail." The boy slowly and tentatively raised his head. I noticed a modest light of hope in his expression. He looked at me with a bloody, crying, scared face. I nodded my head slowly to indicate approval. I wanted to die, but at least let this boy live. I suddenly wondered if the Ball of Light had been here, what would it have done? Would it have helped me, or would this have been another appalling life lesson? I grinned at the thought. At the thought of the life lessons that would come to an end, at the cost of my life . . . Ah Khanom Joon how naive you were . . . How stupid I was to have set out on this path.

The interrogator, who had noticed my nodding my head,

shouted angrily. "You mean you're prepared to surrender to this little Baha'i boy whose cock is the size of a date stone, but not to me? You wanna show what a good human being you are, you whore?" He yelled at the boy. "If you don't fuck her right now, you'll be put to death tomorrow morning. It's your choice." Blood was dripping through my eyelashes. I lifted my head, again with great effort, and nodded to show the boy my approval. The boy stood up slowly and hesitantly, got up on to the chair behind me, and, crying, undid the zipper of his pants with trembling hands. He fiddled with himself a little but out of stress his member would not swell. He was shivering. The little man started talking about sex so that the boy would get a little aroused. Apparently, he was successful. A few minutes later the boy pressed himself against me and like that did his deed, crying and on edge. As he knocked my body back and forth, my pains intensified, but I didn't make a sound. The boy was still shivering and crying even when he was done. The entire time the lewd little man had been watching with a hysterical grin and fiddling with himself. Once the boy's business was done, he kicked him into a corner of the room and said, "To hell with your screwing. You call yourself a man?" Then he returned to touching me as he slowly and deliberately stripped off. The boy tried not to look, but the filthy little man ordered him to look up and learn how to screw. "This is what screwing means . . ."

As the man got onto the chair behind me, I lifted my head with what remained of my forces and muttered into his ear, "You don't know who George Orwell is, but he has a theory about odious creatures like you. He says that sexual deprivation causes excitation and rage so uncontrollable that they turn into dictator worship or the desire to make war on the world and destroy it. You don't know him, but he knew you well."

He thumped me in the head and raped me in the most violent fashion possible.

The boy covered his eyes and, crying, addressed the man.

"You are dirtier than Satan. Satan is nothing compared to you. I hope you burn in hellfire."

When he had finished his business with me, he calmly unfastened the chain on my arm so that I slumped lifeless on the floor. I heard him getting down from the chair, wash himself, whistling, in the basin that was in the corner of the cell, before putting on his Guards uniform. Then he picked up his handgun from the table, went over to the boy and emptied a bullet into his head.

Chapter Twenty-Four

She was a large, sad woman who talked to dogs and slept with cats. Before she turned into a giant and before Gisuo's hair was soaked in blood as it was, and before Niloofar and Elaheh wound up in prison, everything was proceeding as normal. They were four old friends. Housemates. Single. Journalists and social and political affairs editors and sub-editors at four non-state newspapers. Until one day the cassette tape of her father's last will and testament, recorded among the Turkoman tribes, mysteriously reached her at the editorial offices at the end of the eastern cul-de-sac of Golriz Street, Jordan Avenue, Tehran. In fact, it was as if it had suddenly appeared on the desk out of nowhere. She put the cassette in the tape player. "Cheerful Songs by Soussan" had been crossed out and over it was written in a crabby, froggy hand "Final Message from the Accursed Deputy of the Accursed Prime Minister of the Diabolical Regime."

It was her father's voice. Her heart began to pound furiously. Hot tears welled up in her eyes. The voice she had forgotten years ago was clearing its throat and then, amid the crackling of the tape player and the background noise, he spoke of their collective efforts to prevent the foreseeable disasters after the revolution—things that no one knew at the time but that, decades later, everyone had come to recognize.

She had been working as a newspaper journalist for three decades. For years she had felt sorrow and sympathy for the pain and suffering of this people and had smoked cigarette after cigarette in the dark recesses of the neighborhoods of Mahalleh

Ghorbat and Khak-Sefid, of the brick kilns of Pakdasht and in Zurabad in Karaj and wept at her own state, at the state of her father and his sister and of this people. She was ever present, wherever there were protests against this regime's corruption and thieving. At demonstrations, at sit-ins, in prisons, and even beside the bodies of the victims of the chain murders. She was the first journalist to get to the body of her very own uncle, Fereydoun Taban, in the desert around Pounak. It was she who had informed his wife Jarireh of his death. A little afterwards that terrible event had taken place at the mansion. She could never forgive herself for that appalling event. She constantly asked herself what would have happened if she had not told Aunt Jarireh. Would she have still been tempted to kill herself? After she had learnt that Aunt Jarireh was afflicted with the madness of suicide, she herself had been so tormented by her conscience that she wanted to punish herself; so, she overcome her fears and from then on not only photographed and reported on demonstrations and sit-ins, but also joined the ranks of the protesters. She had to release thirty or forty years of rage somewhere. Where better? She clenched her fists and chanted slogans with all her rage and disgust: "Death to the dictator. Death to Khamenei." She wore a mask so that the anti-riot police would not be able to identify her, but some of her colleagues figured out what was going on and were angry with her. They asked her why she was exposing herself. They told her that a journalist's duty was to report on protests, not participate in them. One of them even said to her, "Don't say you're planning to make an asylum case for yourself." She was angry with them for misunderstanding her like this, but she turned a blind eye and kept working. The good thing was that Niloofar and Elaheh and Gisuo did understand her. Friends, housemates, and colleagues for years now, they understood very well what she really thought and felt inside. Perhaps because they knew her secrets.

The editor-in-chief had asked her many times why she kept

going to sit-ins and strikes when she knew they weren't permitted to print reports about most of these events. At night she would return home and write down the details of the things she had witnessed in her journal. And so it was that in her twenty- or thirty-year career as a journalist she had seen so many dead bodies that she had nightmares about them. The bodies of writers, journalists, university professors, poets. Of priests, Baha'is, Yaresani dervishes, atheists. The bodies of rough sleepers, slum dwellers, the poor, and, most importantly of all, of her own father, his sister and brother, and his wife . . .

It was early morning the day the cassette tape reached her, and the rest of the journalists hadn't come in yet. Nobody could know she was the daughter of Bijan Taban, First Deputy to the Shah's last prime minister. But who had sent her this old tape?! Whoever it was knew her and her father. Her colleagues were opposed to the regime's violence, but not so much that they would want to destroy it from the roots up or that they could accept a leftover from the Shah's regime in their midst. She quickly wiped away her tears, and the only thing that occurred to her was to make three copies of the tape and place them, along with a letter, inside three copies of the Quran that the previous week an employee of the Islamic Propaganda Organization had foisted upon them and squeezed into the editorial office bookcase, which she would then take to the post office and mail to three of her journalist friends who had sought asylum in France, Germany, and Britain, respectively. As documentation of the crimes of this regime, so that one day perhaps an international court would condemn them.

For several days she was caught up in all the feelings provoked by her father's message when one day one of her contacts in the police informed her that a twenty-two-year-old Kurdish woman by the name of Zhina Amini had been brought in by one of their officers and subsequently died under torture. There had been plenty of stories like this before. What about Zahra

Bani-Yaqoub? Or Zahra Kazemi? The news of the tragedy had always been suppressed or at least reduced to a three-line item at the bottom of the page between reports about road accidents or a gas canister exploding in someone's house. Or, worse still, it had been turned into a joke. She was always irritated by the fact that political tragedies quickly became jokes and passed from mouth to mouth.

She remembered a joke she had heard recently. After the Guards had shot down Flight 752 from Iran to Ukraine and killed 176 innocent people, the regime had announced that it was due to human error. A little later the army fired on one of its own frigates in the Persian Gulf and killed forty of its own officers, and the regime once again said it was due to human error. Instead of people getting angry and protesting, they came up with a joke: the IRGC attack in the air, the Army attacks at sea, and Saypa and Iran-Khodro take responsibility for all casualties on the ground.[100]

The first thing she thought was "Don't let this tragedy get turned into a joke." She had to do something. She picked up the phone to tell Niloofar and Elaheh and Gisu what had happened. They would have to do something. It was true that before this poor young woman, many others had been pointlessly and cruelly killed, but this time something had changed. In reality, what had changed was not the substance of the tragedy. It was her. She herself had changed. After seeing her Aunt Jarireh's body. After hearing her father's voice on that scratchy old tape, something had started growing inside her. It had started to bubble and boil. She felt that enough was enough. Enough of all this oppression, all this killing, all this silence. Something inside her was getting bigger and bigger until it would explode. She told her friends that they should try to get this story to be

[100] Saypa and Iran-Khodro are two state-owned car manufacturers, here blamed for the high accident rates on the roads.

the main headline on the front pages of their respective newspapers the following day. If they didn't allow that, then at least for it to be the second headline. That she knew that they probably would not, but they should at least do their best. Each of them wrote a separate full report about the killing of the young Kurdish woman Zhina Amini and took it to their editors-in-chief and put their feet down: "Either print it or we resign. Enough silence."

Azadeh took the report to the desk of the editor-in-chief of *Sarmayeh*. With a firmness she had not hitherto suspected in herself, she said, "You have to publish this." The headline she had put was "Was She Guided?" When the editor saw the beautiful, innocent woman's photograph, he was saddened. He was a Kurd himself. The blood boiled in his veins and he directed a Kurdish insult at the Moral Guidance Patrols. He had to do something. He lit a cigarette. He put his feet on the desk and gazed at the smoke in the air for a few moments. Azadeh was pleased. She knew that this was what the editor did whenever he wanted to take a dangerous decision. Then he brought his feet down from the desk, stood up excitedly and said, "Whatever happens, happens . . . We'll make it the main headline." Azadeh screamed with happiness. She called her friends to let them know. The three of them all reported in total disbelief that their editors had likewise accepted to make it the main front-page headline. It seemed it wasn't just her . . . There was something bubbling and boiling inside everyone. It was like a bowl full of tears and sighs and groans—a single teardrop was just enough to make it overflow, and Zhina Amini's death was that final tear. That final sigh.

It was morning on that day. The newspapers had been arranged next to one another in the newsstands, and on their front pages large photographs of Zhina Amini's beautiful face, a doleful and innocent smile on her lips, the main headlines "A Guided Death," "Was She Guided?" "Fatal Guidance," "Tragic Guidance." Azadeh looked at Zhina's lips. How much they reminded her of the Mona Lisa's. Was it a smile or sorrow? Had those lips ever been kissed? How many kisses, how many smiles she would never know . . .

What ought to have happened, happened. The news flared up like a fire under ash, and its flames reached every part of the country. The inhabitants of Saqqez and Sanandaj were the first to start demonstrating and chanting slogans: in Kurdish, *Jin, Jian, Azadi*. Then the people of Gilan. Then those of Tehran. The Balouch. The Azeris. The people of Mashhad and even of Isfahan, Bushehr, and Yazd. All of a sudden across the country people chanted the same slogan in unison: *Zan, Zendegi, Azadi* . . . Woman, life, freedom . . . The country was united in rage and disgust at the regime. For the first time, women took off their headscarves and burned them in city squares, while men took great pride in protecting them so the forces of repression could not arrest them. Over a single day of half-formed freedom, such an enthusiasm and solidarity and affection formed between people, between the men and women they had kept apart for decades in the name of Islam as not closely related and therefore strangers to one another, that they wept tears of joy. Young women and men stood with open arms beside the street and hugged passers-by, while next to them they had written on a piece of cardboard: "Free hugs for the sad nation of Iran." Kurds and Baluch, Azeris and Ahvazis, who had been made for decades to fear each other under the label of separatist, chanted loving and fraternal slogans for one another in the streets, while finally when night fell, a young couple displayed their courage and, lit up by the automobiles that had stopped and sounded their horns at great length in protest at the killing of Zhina Amini, kissed one another lovingly on Revolution Street in Tehran so that their kiss would be the first of the Revolution of Freedom.

How happy Azadeh was that day. She had achieved mighty things. She had triumphed over censorship at last. At the demonstrations she chanted slogans until night, clapped and stamped her feet, and hand in hand with young women and men danced, sang, and set fire to her headscarf and long coat. Alongside other girls and women she had even cut her hair short in mourning for Zhina, in a symbolic move, like Farangis and the girls of Iran and Touran had in mourning for Siavash, and, as she had done so, she had shouted the slogans "clerics get lost" and "death to Khamenei, you Zahhak" so much that by the time she wanted to go back home that night, her voice was completely hoarse. They had cut the internet again. They always did this during general demonstrations. All the same, she had taken as many photos and videos as she could so she could send them whenever possible to her colleagues in the media on the other side of the border. She hadn't been able to call her family or friends or message them. They had cut the communication lines inside the country as well. She ran all the way home so she could talk to Niloofar and Elaheh and Gisuo and find out what had happened to them that day. She knew that as always they would make their way home sooner or later to recount the day's thrilling events to one another. More than anyone, she wanted to talk to Gisuo. Gisuo had been like a little sister to her all these years. She was calm and kind and fragile and ten years younger than her. For that reason, Azadeh always felt she had to support and take care of her. Gisuo had been arrested twice previously, and Azadeh had once gone to visit her in prison using her sister's identity papers and wearing a chador. When Gisuo had caught sight of her in the visiting room, she had almost screamed from happiness and given everything away. That day Azadeh had secretly given her a very small voice recorder and told her to record the sounds of the prison. That they would then write them down together. For the sake of the historical record. Yes, Azadeh was also a Taban. Throughout history, all the Tabans had been possessed by the madness of memoir writing.

That particular day, the revolutionary excitement did not last long, as on her way she saw repressive and anti-riot forces with their bulletproof black vehicles that they had recently purchased from China, Russia, America, and God knows what other Western countries, heading toward the center of the demonstrations . . . She was flooded with anxiety. She knew what would happen. She knew that these joys, these enthusiasms, solidarities and sympathies, these peaceful, beautiful demonstrations and protests, this short-lived and furtive freedom would once again be suppressed. Beauty would once more lose to ugliness and peace to violence, freedom to captivity. As she ran towards home and found a way through the anti-riot forces, armed to the teeth, all the beautiful things she had seen that day gave way to her memories of the ferocious repression of the previous peaceful demonstrations, calm demonstrations, silent demonstrations, the demonstrations of the rose. Hadn't people given the forces of repression roses during those demonstrations? They had taken the flowers, yet a few minutes later pulled the bolts and tatatata, tatatata . . . People fell like autumn leaves onto the street. And hadn't they repeated that in the massacre in the cane fields? So that for years to come no rain would wash away the blood of the Jarahi cane fields.[101]

When she got home, sweating and breathing heavily, none of the others were in the house. She was worried. After all, at least one of them should have gotten home by now. It was past midnight. No doubt they'd all stayed at the newspaper offices to follow the news. She called the editorial offices of *Etemad* from the house phone. In quiet residential neighborhoods, the telephones were still connected. They told her Niloofar had been arrested. She was terrified. She rang the editorial offices of *Mellat*. They had arrested Elaheh too. She called the editorial offices of *Azadi*, the security forces had raided the offices to arrest Gisuo, but the people there had helped

[101] Referring to the mass killing of protesters by the Islamic Republic in the Jarahi district of the port city of Mahshahr in south-western Iran during the November 2019 protests; the neighborhood had formerly been the site of sugar-cane cultivation. Hundreds of people were killed in this massacre.

her escape by the back door. Cold sweat sat on her spine. She knew that it had been dangerous to publish this story, but not so dangerous that they would arrest them all that very day. She called her own editorial office. The deputy chief editor was still there. He told her that the editor-in-chief had been arrested. And that she should not show her face there for the time being. That she should flee the house—they were after her. Azadeh left the house. She had to do something. She had to look for Gisuo. She was inflamed with emotion. Her palms were sweaty. There were sudden pains in her heart. She went into the street. She'd been on the route of the demonstration only an hour earlier. The demonstration was on its way to Freedom Square from Revolution Square. The roads were blocked by demonstrators and drivers were honking their horns. She ran from Revolution to Freedom . . . What a long way . . . But she ran . . . she ran . . . she ran . . . She knew that Gisuo would be there. Gisuo loved Freedom Square. She hated Revolution Square. She always said that the revolution did not bring us freedom, but thinking of freedom always brings us back to the atmosphere of the revolution. That was why she was in the habit sometimes of walking barefoot under the Freedom Tower, in between the tulips and over the grass.

When she got there, everywhere was in tumult . . . Hundreds of thousands of people had gathered and were chanting slogans unrelentingly. She fought her way through the crowd and stood under one of the legs of Azadi Tower, the Freedom Tower. There she was caught by a terrible surprise . . . Gisuo's dead body was lying on the ground under the right leg of the Azadi Tower, surrounded by people. She was wearing a white t-shirt and jeans. It was obvious that in support of the protests she had taken off her scarf and manteau and set them on fire. She was laid out like Sleeping Beauty and her long black locks were wet with blood. Azadeh ran towards her, cradled her head in her arms, and like a demon, like a volcano, like a sky full of pain, full of black clouds, roared such a roar that the clothes on her body were suddenly torn asunder and the four columns of the Azadi Tower shook. In the blink of an eye, her height and the dimensions of her body were doubled.

And she wept . . .

And she wept . . .

And she wept . . .

So many tears flowed under the protesters that they covered the ground below the Azadi Tower and flowed down the grooves of the mosaics toward the street. As her head rested on Gisu's small chest and like a cloud in winter she poured forth tears of lamentation, for a moment Gisu gently stirred, opened her eyes, smiled vaguely and said, "At last I felt what it was like to have the wind in my hair, Azadeh." Then her head fell back, and she died.

With Gisuo's bloody corpse in her arms, standing two or three meters in height and her clothes torn to pieces, Azadeh walked from Freedom Square to her home. On the way, people assembled around her, furious and saddened and walked behind her and chanted slogans and shed tears and sang for her the melancholy song "Baray-e . . . "[102] *Oh . . . oh . . . Do you see the tulips in Freedom Square? In this land, how cheap death is, freedom how dear? Freedom . . . Freedom has taken life once more, and yet it is lifeless still.* She wept and like a lion, like a stormy sea, like Mount Damavand, span up into the air in pain and disbelief, and as she walked and wept profusely, her body grew in every direction. On seeing this sad woman, now giant-sized, people grew sadder and more furious than before, and in unison, tearful and disgusted, came up with a new slogan, yelling it out: "Khamenei, you Zahhak, / We will drag you underground." The very same slogan that Khamenei had dreamt of years before.

When Azadeh reached her front door, she stopped. Her eyes

[102] Baray-e ("For . . . "), by Shervin Hajjipour.

full of tears, she looked at the people behind her. They had realized they should not follow her any further. The tearful crowd bid her farewell, before returning to the center of town, all the while chanting, enraged, "For every person killed / A thousand more have their back," and dragging large trash bins into the street and setting them on fire.

Azadeh went into the house. As soon as she had laid Gisuo's body on the ground, she heard a sound come from it. She placed her hand on Gisuo's jugular vein. It wasn't moving. She held a mirror in front of her mouth. No condensation appeared on its surface. Where was this whispering sound coming from, then? She brought her head close to Gisuo's, and suddenly she heard her friend's last words, her last message. "Artillery, tanks, machine guns work no more / Go tell my mother her daughter's no more." Azadeh drew her head away, then pressed her head against her again. She heard no further sound. Was this not the last thing Gisuo said, her final murmur, before death? She called Gisuo's mother to tell her to come and remove Gisuo's body in secret and bury it somewhere. She told her that Gisuo had been thinking of her in her last moments and about the rhyme that had been in her head. When she talked on the phone, she realized her voice had become very loud and deep. She felt like it made the walls of the house shake. Gisuo's mother and father got themselves there at speed, their collars torn, and crying. Everyone knew that the regime's officers stole corpses and quickly disposed of them somewhere so that they could easily disclaim responsibility later on. They had begun doing this after the 2019 demonstrations and the Jarahi canefields massacre. In the middle of the night, when the family had taken Gisuo's body, Azadeh left the house without looking behind her and went off in the direction of the mountains in the north, with no particular end in mind. With ill-matching clothes, long strides, and a mind which heard nothing except a vague buzzing.

In later years, she spoke with nobody, or if she did, her voice was deafening like thunder. After Gisuo's death and the arrests of Niloofar and Elaheh, her only friends were the homeless dogs and cats who had one day started gathering around her of their own accord. To begin with she paid them no attention, but as their number increased day by day she remembered that the regime's hostility extended even to dogs and cats and that it did not permit anyone to keep a pet. So she let the outcast animals stay by her side. For years she moved in this manner from mountain to forest, from forest to desert, and from desert to cave, killing time while waiting for the next demonstrations. On numerous occasions a woman was seen at demonstrations, four or five meters in height with long locks and clad in ill-matched pieces of cloth, surrounded by stray dogs and cats, standing at the front of the ranks of demonstrators, crushing bulletproof vehicles with punches and kicks, while her dogs and cats bit the police and tore them to pieces. Despite all this, no one has been able to trace her to date, since she dismantled all the closed-circuit cameras the regime had purchased from China and Germany by squeezing them with two fingers. No bullet was effective against her burly chest, and with every step she put several police officers and guards and plain clothes officers out of action. She also pushed people aside so she could get to the martyrs of the revolution, press her head against theirs, and listen to their last messages and final murmurs before passing those messages to their families. With each painful message she obtained from those slain opponents of the regime, both her woe and the dimensions of her body increased, and in this way, as she continued her fight against them, she grew bigger and bigger, stronger and stronger.

Chapter Twenty-Five

If only a law existed
That mothers must become leaders in the world . . .
Because mothers pass on their own share
So that nobody goes hungry, sleeps hungry.
Mothers are like the prayer bead thread.
They join everyone together.
Mothers are sick of quarreling, blood and war, of death.
They do not let blood flow from anyone's nose.
If they light a fire, it is for cooking,
Not war!
If the law of the world was that mothers must be leaders
They would take meatballs to the neighboring country as a gift of welcome
Or they would take colorful summer shirts
So that some continent would come out of mourning
If mothers were leaders in the world . . . "[103]

Such was Jarireh, the mother of the family in the Tabans' historic mansion. All that was good, she blended together. All that was bad, she forgot with a cup of tea and candied seeds. From the moment she got up in the morning, she was mindful of raising wages and Nowruz cash gifts and welcome gifts and souvenirs and presents for the newborns among her relatives near and far and the servants and the gardener and even the villagers of Zorvan. By night she had passed a thousand times from room to room and house to house, carefully attending to

[103] Adrin Bahmani

the affairs of the mansion and of the women of Zorvan. She would remember, for example, that such-and-such new bride in Zorvan had died in childbirth and on the fortieth day after the death would visit her family with a plate of halva and several meters of colored cloth, blue and green, so that they could change out of their mourning attire. With the help of cheerful melodies, she put sorrows back where they belonged. She swept the shadows of depression into the corners. By moving the furniture around, she laid down a challenge to the absent members of the family, as if to say: here are your places, waiting for you. Whenever spring came round and Nader and Reza were cleaning the drainpipes, she was mindful of the fact that the nests of the newly-arrived laughing-doves and swallows and wagtails ought not to be disturbed. She was even mindful of the orange blossoms. She was careful that during the spring harvesting not a single petal be spoiled by clumsy hands or feet.

But more than anything else, she was mindful of Khanom Joon and Jamshid Khan. "They are the pillars of this mansion," she would say, "and if they weren't here, this mansion would collapse on itself." So attentive was she to their food and health that if she herself did not take their blood pressures once a week and test their blood sugar levels, she would become anxious and agitated. She knew that Jamshid Khan's food had to be low in salt so that his blood pressure would not rise, and Khanom Joon's high in garlic, so that the occasional aches in her legs would subside. She knew that when he was working, Fereydoun would drink milky tea with cardamom and cinnamon, saffron tea at family get-togethers, and sour cherry tea in summer. She knew that he got insomnia on moonlit nights and that unless she made love with him under the full moon in hidden corners of the forest, he would not be able to get to sleep. Jarireh would have been mindful of a great many things if they hadn't assassinated her husband like that and if they hadn't brought her Mehrab back from the war like that, completely insane.

When early one morning in the spring of 1983 they found Mehrab, wounded and semi-conscious at the mansion gates, Jarireh screamed so loudly from happiness that she disturbed the sleep of the inhabitants of Zorvan, although very soon, once she had seen the state he was in, she lost herself. Her strength had been gradually worn down by the long lack of news about Leyla and Shokoofeh, but when Fereydoun was killed, her ability to resist was completely overwhelmed; all day she rolled from side to side in bed and thought about life and her nearest and dearest, while death noxiously and noiselessly crawled ever so slowly over every inch of her body and soul and made itself at home. She thought to herself that in the old days death used to arrive apologetically, shamefaced. It didn't just turn up whenever it felt like. It had a protocol. It stuck to its principles. Knocked on the door. It let the residents of the house know beforehand; with sickness and fatigue . . . With some dry coughs or shooting pains in the left arm. With old age and disability. Or even with a dream. Death . . . The demon of death had rules. It stuck fast to old traditions. Whereas these days, it had set all shame aside. It didn't knock, but it stuck in the key, turned up when it felt like it and suddenly conquered the house, just as it had conquered Azar and Bijan and Fereydoun, unawares.

Jarireh stared at the ceiling above her bed, her eyes sunken, her disheveled hair uncolored, and thought, “If I am in this state, then what kind of state must my mother-in-law Zarrin be in?” In recent years, each time she had seen her, she had been thinner than before; at Azar's funeral, skinnier than at Bijan's funeral; at Fereydoun's funeral, thinner than at Azar's. They had taken all three of her children from her and placed them on the breast of the cold earth. These misfortunes break a person. Tears gathered in Jarireh's eyes. She rolled from side to side again. She no longer even had the strength to look at Mehran, the mad apple of her eye, let alone her three other children . . . To distract herself from all this bitterness, she lay in wait for the indistinct and distant sounds Mehrab made in his bedroom on the other side of the living room. Several years had passed since Mehrab's return home, and this was still the state he was in. He got neither better nor worse. Sometimes he was well, and often not. When he was well, he was really well. He became the Mehrab he used to be. With a glint in his eye, kind and straightforward; with his tall height and a smile on his lips he would go into the courtyard and attend to the flowers, spend time with the servants, the gardener, his sisters and their children, and lark about. On a few occasions he had even gone to the kitchen and helped Maryam, Shahnaz, and Shafiqeh cook, or helped Hasrat water the flowers in Shokoofeh's greenhouse, or for a few moments drank tea with Jarireh and talked of those far-off happy days and their grand family parties. Shahnaz adored his tall stature, just as she had before, and made him his favorite sweets and pastries, which they would then eat together. That very day Jarireh had heard that Mehrab had kissed Shahnaz's forehead as he was popping one of her sweets into his mouth and told her, "I know. In my previous life, you were my mother!" They had both laughed.

For Jarireh, thinking about Shahnaz always made her feel a mix of jealousy and peace. She knew that Shahnaz worshiped Mehrab just like a mother, and this made her jealous, yet she also had the peace of mind that came from knowing that whenever she finally succeeded in departing the world, Shahnaz would be there. Shahnaz would always be by Mehrab's side. Better and more responsible than she was, even.

The clock on the wall, a souvenir of the Qajar age, struck eleven. Hours had passed since Maryam had knocked on the door and invited her to the breakfast table. After Fereydoun's death, the servants' wages were occasionally delayed. In the very first year after the revolution, she had been purged from her management position in the Mazandaran Province Organization for Children's and Adolescents' Intellectual Development, and no longer had permission to work. She no longer thought about work. Each time she had wanted to pay the servants' delayed wages by selling some of the house's antiques, one of them had realized and insisted she stop. The servants would say that it was thanks to her that they had land, rice paddies, and sheep. That they had enough to get by on. That for years she had provided for them far more than they had a right to.

Shokoofeh's greenhouse had made it through some difficult winters, and with Hasrat's help it was still functioning, though not as well as it might or ought to have done. It covered its own costs, and a little more. That was all. Despite all their financial problems, Jarireh had once told Hasrat that the greenhouse should function adequately until Shokoofeh returned to take care of the flowers. But when would Shokoofeh return? Would she return at all? How often during these years had she reproached Khanom Joon. Indeed, because of the lack of news about Shokoofeh, she did not in the slightest feel like taking care of Khanom Joon. Everything was her fault. Had she not insisted, would Shokoofeh have been spared this dangerous journey? Tears ran down from her eyes, sliding over her cheek and ear and onto the pillow. *What a mistake I made . . . With my own hands I sent my beloved daughter off to the mountains and forests and the war. I served my innocent daughter up for the vultures of this regime to devour.* It was true that the Ball of Light had a few years earlier told them that Leyla and Shokoofeh were alive and well, but then why had so many years gone by and they still hadn't come back? If Shokoofeh wasn't dead, she had certainly been taken captive by the regime's mercenaries . . . If anything else were the case, then why hadn't she come back yet? *What kind of mother am I that I could not take care of my darlings? What kind of mother am I . . .* And her tears flowed, and her pillow was soaked through.

For the thousandth time, as she did every morning, she counted on her fingers how long it had been since Mehrab had come back. Then she counted up how long it had been since Leyla had disappeared in 1976, and since 1980 when Mehrab had gone off to war, and since summer 1982 when Shokoofeh had gone off to the war after him and then never returned. When had they executed Azar? In fall or in spring? When had they assassinated Bijan? In winter or in fall? Exactly what day was Fereydoun's assassination? Had Azadeh informed them about his death? Who had found Mehrab next to the garden gate? All the dates got mixed up together, and as always made her more confused than before. Why did fall always remind her of Fereydoun anyway? Why every year was her heart full of foreboding on the first day of fall, at the sight of the first yellow and orange leaves, and why did grief conquer every inch of her being? Why did everyone leave their departure until fall? Why did nobody ever return in fall? Each time she got around to reckoning up the time that had passed since her dear husband's death, a lump came to her throat and then bitter tears choked up her airways and she lost count. She always had the same problem. Whenever she cried deeply, her nose would become blocked, her airways constricted, and she would throw up. She would have been close to throwing up again had she not gotten to the bathroom in time and washed her face and blown her nose vigorously. She sat on the edge of the bed, her face dripping wet, her nose red. The water dripped onto her nightgown, the one she had once purchased with great excitement for her nights of lovemaking with Fereydoun. She ran her hand over the side of the bed where Fereydoun had always slept. *Oh, Fereydoun . . . oh . . .*

She tried to think of something better again, as the psychoanalyst had advised. How about she think about Mina and Mandana's wedding day? Or her grandchildren's birthday? Or perhaps it would be a better idea to think about her favorite words? Heart . . . heart . . . heart . . . light-hearted, heart and soul, heart-ravishing, heart-thrilling, mild-hearted, hard-hearted, heart-stopping, heart-wrenching, heart-searching, heart-piercing, heart-sinking, tender-hearted, heart-happy, cheerful-hearted, heart-in-mouth, heartburn, lion-hearted, heart-warming, hearty, heart-ache, heart-break . . . heartbroken . . . heartbroken . . . heartbroken . . . heartbroken . . . *Oh, Fereydoun . . . Oh . . .*

She had ordered that no one touch his bolster cover. And especially not his clothes in the closet, or the books and notes in his study. Nothing should be touched. She started sobbing again. "The only things I wanted from life were writing, light, and love," she thought. "And you provided me with all three. Amid all the memories and books and index cards and your special kinds of creativity, you hid a little sliver of light that you gave to me alone that day we fell in love with each other at my nineteenth birthday party." She thought about the way he used to laugh. To kiss. *Oh, Fereydoun . . . Oh . . .*

Mehrab's distant, indistinct cries could be heard from his room on the other side of the living room. Jarireh held her head in her hands and squeezed hard. Mehrab was shouting again, about how the Iraqis and the Guards and the locals were attacking the Temple of Mithra. About the Third Step and about how he was on his way . . . he was on his way.

Ever since he had been found mysteriously one morning by the garden gate, he had lived in alternating states of madness and sanity; now prophet, now shepherd; now poet, now illiterate; sometimes, when those feelings of madness, prophethood and poethood got the better of him, he went to the temple, where he would either retreat or perform military drills using ancient techniques learned from God knows where. For some time, nobody knew where he was, until one day Mina and Mandana betrayed the secret of the discovery of the Temple of Mithra to Jarireh and Khanom Joon and Jamshid Khan, following which those disasters ensued . . . , The news gradually made its way from the members of the family to the servants and even to the inhabitants of Zorvan, and people went to every corner of the Taban family forest, openly and in secret, carrying shovels and picks, in the hope that they might find treasure and ancient objects. When a little while afterwards Mehrab found out, he was angry and went half-naked to the village square and started threatening people, and then it was, "death to

Khamenei" and "mine . . . mine . . . shell . . . shell . . . take shelter . . . take shelter . . . the Iraqis are attacking. They've killed Mithra . . . help . . . help."

A little after that, in one of his mad states, Mehrab ran off shouting in the direction of the temple and sat on its entry hatch and did not move for several days and nights, come wind and rain, sunshine and moonlight. On a few occasions he even came to blows with covetous treasure-hunters arriving from villages near and far and threw them off the family property. It was during that time that something came to him in a dream. In a half-waking, half-sleeping state, a lantern in one hand and a shovel in the other, he went behind the great statue of Mithra and the Bull and started digging like someone possessed. He found a chest half a meter down. He opened it. There was a sword inside it. Something was written on it in an ancient script he had not seen before. A little while later that he fell into a deep sleep in the temple, though soon afterwards he was started from sleep by a hand shaking his shoulder. In front of him were standing a Handsome Young man and a Beautiful Young Girl with a crown of flowers. Both were clad in ancient clothes: the Young Girl attired in a simple, long, cotton dress and silk scarf, a crown of wildflowers on her head, a torch in one hand and a belt in the other, a smile on her lips. Mehrab stood up. He looked about him. All around the cave were standing young men and women dressed in ancient attire, looking at him with welcoming expressions. Mehrab's sixth sense told him that he was present at some kind of ritual.

The Handsome Young Man was waiting for him, sword in hand. Without knowing why, Mehrab picked up the ancient sword he had earlier found in the chest, and in the half dark space of the temple, lit only by the torch, started fighting with him. Although the Young Man was very skillful, Mehrab was more skillful still, eventually putting the Young Man to the floor and holding his sword against his throat. The Young Man stood up and smiled at Mehrab. The Young Girl went over to Mehrab and handed him a belt. Everyone else took a step closer to them. The Young Man tied the belt around Mehrab's waist, then hung the sword from it. Then the Young Girl placed a crown in the hands of the Handsome Young Man. Mehrab knelt before him. The Young Man placed the crown on Mehrab's head, but Mehrab respectfully removed it, proffered it to the Young Man with both hands, and said, "I am devoted to the service of Mithra and have no need of a crown. Mithra is my crown."

The young man took the crown back, a smile on his lips, and fastened a bronze bracelet around Mehrab's wrist. The following words were engraved on the bracelet: "Mithra is my crown." Those standing around the temple took another step closer. Mehrab could see joy and smiles in every face. They all looked familiar. They looked like the elders and scholars and sages and poets in history books. Everyone chanted in unison, "May he triumph. You are now a warrior. You have ascended the Third Step."

So it was that the very next day Mehrab suddenly became fully conscious, to be afflicted by the Madness of Article Writing. He started writing scholarly, well-documented articles, some of the information for which he took from the ritual of a few days earlier, some from his own earlier specialized research, and yet more from the evidence of the Mithraic temple and the ancient sword. He took photographs of the temple, the sword, and the ancient script on it, and sent them off with a letter to Dr. Parvardegar at the University of Tehran, requesting that she examine and decipher it. Dr. Parvardegar's reply offered plenty of hope. He added it to his article, and when the latter was finished, he sent that too to Dr. Parvardegar to read, if necessary correct or complete, and if acceptable, to publish it in the university journal.

During the weeks he was busy writing the article, Mehrab was his old self again; he was in a good mood, he recalled everything, and sat for hours in his father's study, concentrating on his research and writing, attempting to decipher the ancient script on the sword. Or, along with Khanom Joon and Jamshid Khan, his mother and his sisters, he attended to the affairs of the mansion, told jokes, and occasionally recounted some of his memories from the time he had been absent from the mansion. Two months later the Zorvan mailman handed him a package; it was the university periodical containing his article. Not only had his article, with its novel theories about the Third Step of the Mithraic Cult and the decipherment of a script more ancient than cuneiform, been published in its entirety, but Dr. Parvardegar had also written another article complementing his, suggesting that Mehrab Taban's theories might not only elucidate hidden aspects of the Mithraic Cult and give Mithraic Studies a new lease of life, but that it was also worth dwelling on his proposed decipherment of the five thousand year-old script. Thus, Mehrab finally breathed easily having, it seemed, discharged an important office in life, and was able to go back with a tranquil mind to his mysterious life oscillating between the two poles of prophet and shepherd, poet and illiterate.

As Jarireh lay on the bed, frustrated and helpless, it occurred to her that someone should give Mehrab his medicines soon. Then, as the ring of the telephone echoed in the drawing room and mixed with Mehrab's roars, she remembered her own parents, who would go months without answering the phone, or hang up the moment they heard it ring. They had told her she should either be on their side, or that of her corrupt royalist fire-worshiping husband. Then she remembered her ill-fated sister Narges. Of how she had joined the Guards after the revolution and she and her permanently drunk husband were busy drawing up files for this and that person and in that way adding to their wealth by the day, as well as making money from the name of their poor martyred son, Bahman. She remembered how just a few months earlier Narges's awful husband had come into the mansion courtyard in a Guards Nissan Patrol together with four Guards officers and shown her their search and interrogation warrants. In front of their eyes, they had turned the house upside down and loaded whatever remaining ancestral gold and jewels and items of value they could find into the Patrol and taken Narges for interrogation too. But before they left, they smashed up all the vats of wine they had kept hidden for years under the eaves in the attic or in the courtyard storeroom and wrote that down in her file.

She could not believe that Asghar, her drunkard brother-in-law, was now sitting opposite her in the interrogation room with a prayer mark on his forehead, hirsute, with long beard, a keffiyeh around his shoulders and prayer beads in hand, labeling her and her family corrupt royalists and unbelievers. Asghar, her brother-in-law, struck a revolutionary and angry pose, yelling, "Your file's a thick one. You are fire-worshippers. While downtrodden Muslims are living in misery, you unbelievers and corrupt royalists are drinking the people's blood, surrounded by all those valuable things, and worshiping fire. So tell me, where've you hidden the fire, then? Where's Khanom Joon's Ball of Light? You've been condemned to death for the crimes of fire-worshipping, unbelief, and witchcraft."

Jarireh, sitting opposite him, handcuffed, wearing a headscarf she'd been forced to put on, said, grinning, "Even if nobody else doesn't, I know that you're always drunk, and you can't get to sleep at night without a bottle of aragh sagi."

"The Islamic Revolution has guided me on to the right path," he said. "I've repented and now I'm in the service of the Imam and the dear revolution."

Jarireh grinned once more and said, "In service of the Imam and the revolution, or free money and theft in the name of the Imam and the revolution? How many people have you concocted dossiers for and sent to the gallows so you could suck up their possessions and wealth? You have a rented house and car repair shop, so how could you have become the owner of a four-story apartment building overnight? Where did you get those twenty hectares of land? What about those five shops in the middle of town?"

Her brother-in-law slammed his fist on the table and shouted, "Shut your mouth! You with your fire-worshiping counter-revolutionary husband. It's a good thing they killed him. He deserved it. After all, isn't the country Islamic now? What was all that wine doing in your house? Why've you still got all those pictures of kings and butt-naked women dancing all over your walls? You're condemned to death for the crime of royalism."

The interrogation went on for twelve hours straight, until the morning of the next day Khanom Joon and Jamshid Khan arrived with the deeds for a five-hectare section of the garden and swapped it for Jarireh's liberty. The minute he saw the deed in Khanom Joon's hands, Asghar's behavior changed. He became kindly and polite, and addressing Jarireh and Khanom Joon and Jamshid Khan, who had been looking at him up and down with repugnance, said gently, "You're very fortunate I've taken on responsibility for your file, because otherwise your mini-Mom sentence would have been life imprisonment."

"Come with us this very instant to the Registry Office so we can transfer this deed to your name legally," Khanom Joon said. "But before you do that you must burn our family's file in front of our eyes."

The horrid little man was by now a master at this sort of thing. "Don't you worry at all," he said, and an hour later, as everyone was coming out of the Registry Office, he set the file with its hundreds of pages on fire in a quiet cul-de-sac. Before he did, however, Jarireh said, "I want to see what our crime was." She opened the dossier and scrutinized the list of names of people who had signed complaints or witness statements against them. Both of her sisters. Both of their husbands. Both her brothers and both their wives. And worse still, some Zorvan villagers whom she had always helped in time of need and whose daughter's trousseau she had paid for. In these documents they were accused of unbelief, witchcraft, gambling, fire-worship, holding debauched parties, proselytizing for Zoroastrianism, dealings with Baha'is, Jews, and Communists, counter-revolutionary beliefs, not observing hijab, wine-drinking, and a great many other things. One of the charges was that she was the spouse of Fereydoun Taban. There were a great number of documents relating to Bijan and Azar. They saw, with the utmost surprise, that there were even a few sheets filled out testifying against Mehrab. In them, he was accused of spreading unbelief and counter-revolutionary ideas in public and at the front. Some people from Zorvan had signed underneath. She knew that because Mehrab had stopped the treasure-hunters, they had taken their revenge on him in this way. They set fire to all the sheets at the end of the cul-de-sac. When the final sheet had burnt, Jarireh said, "I wish never to see any one of you suffer ill-fortune again," before getting into a car with Khanom Joon and Jamshid Khan to go back to the mansion. Yet before they did, her ill-fated brother-in-law poured out his last drops of poison. "Your parents have passed on a message for you, never to call them again. They said as far as they're concerned, you are dead."

Eventually the telephone ceased to ring and Jarireh, rolling from side to side in her bed and drowning in her thoughts, could hear Mehrab's roars once more. She held her head in her hands. Would Mehrab, her darling child, ever get well? Suddenly she got up, determined. She would have to finish things off. She could not bear to remain in this state any longer. She took out the rope she had hidden under the bed the previous day. She placed a chair under the ceiling fan and tied the rope around the hook above it. How many times had she killed herself since Fereydoun's death? She had lost count. She had tried every possible method of suicide, but in the busy mansion there had always been someone to save her. This time, however, nobody could save her. Everyone was preoccupied with Mehrab. She locked the bedroom door from the inside. The sound of Mehrab's roaring had grown louder and louder. She heard feet running on the staircase and in the living room. She put her head through the loop. As she was pushing the chair away from under her feet, she tried to think of something good: of Fereydoun's laughter.

Mina and Mandana, tired and ailing, were once more sitting by Jarireh's side, massaging her feet with concern and kindness. As soon as Jarireh came to, she screamed, pulled at her hair, slapped Mina and Mandana in the face, and shouted, "If you like me even the tiniest bit, let me die." She wept bitterly until she eventually went to sleep with the aid of a sedative. Khanom Joon and Jamshid Khan were always watching her from a distance. Jamshid Khan had thought to himself on many an occasion, "Who said everyone must be strong? Jarireh isn't strong. She's gotten weak, fearful, she's sick of everything that's gone on around her—Fereydoun's murder, Mehrab's madness, Azar's execution and Bijan's assassination, Bahman's martyrdom. Her sisters' and brothers' and parents' betrayal. Shokoofeh and Leyla's disappearances." Yet he did not know that Jarireh had not repeatedly killed herself because she was weak. Rather she had done so to free herself of her miserable fate, of the miserable news, of the miserable incidents with no end . . . Jarireh killed herself so that one day she would not have to hear the news of Shokoofeh and Leyla's deaths as well.

Ultimately Jarireh's obsession with suicide reached such lengths that she even committed the act in front of others. The doctors and psychoanalysts said, nonsensically, that she was trying to attract attention. Who was it who said that someone who, amid others' laughter and tears and even their ordinary conversation, picks up a vegetable knife and, while talking to them, and even in front of their sons-in-law and grandchildren, slices open their veins, intends to attract attention? No. She really intended to leave.

Once when Khanom Joon, Mina and Mandana had gone to

Jarireh's bedroom to talk to her, Jarireh had said, "Killing myself is the best thing I can do. I won't miss this wretched life for even an instant."

"What about us then?" Mina and Mandana had asked, tears in their eyes. "What about our children? How can you do this to us?"

Jarireh had taken and kissed their hands. "I love all of you," she had said. "But why won't you see that I am tired? I've had enough for ages. I'm already dead. It's only you who don't get it. I'm tired of opening my eyes every day and realizing that I'm still alive. I want to go to sleep for a long time, for ever. That's all."

"What your life lacks is a spiritual perspective," Khanom Joon said. "Something to give your material life coherence, purpose and meaning."

"But don't you see that it's been ages since I've believed in God?" Jarireh asked, scornfully. "Nobody believes in God anymore. Don't you read the papers? Don't you see all this oppression and injustice? Don't you see that even my parents have turned into oppressors? Who now believes in God? God is dead, but the news hasn't reached you yet."

Then, as if she had suddenly found new energy, Jarireh jumped up and, standing in the middle of the room, said, "I feel something's missing. Something has gone missing from people's lives, from all our lives, something nothing else can replace. I don't think it's just about the people missing because they didn't come back from the war, or this regime has killed them."

Jarireh was plunged in thought. She sighed and went on. "What's missing from life is light. The light of joy. The light of life. The light of hope. The light of love."

Then, as if she had made some important discovery, she smiled colorlessly at the rest of them and said, pointing at the corner of the room, "Yes. That's right. Darkness has triumphed over me and over us. The shadows attack me from the dark corners of the house. They overcome me. I . . . we . . . to get to the light, we have to move away from this darkness. That's why we kill ourselves."

Everyone watched Jarireh pouring out her soul in silence and sorrow. At last Khanom Joon said, "Who said God is dead? God is Fereydoun. God is Bijan. God is Azar. God's name changes every day. God is hope. God is the innocent souls kept captive in the prisons . . . God is all the blood spilled for this country, for freedom, for better days ahead. God isn't dead. It's just that God now and then appears in the body and soul of such-and-such a person and then vanishes. His name changes, but He is everlasting. He is multiple. It is your sight that's dead. You need sight. A sight that would show you that all these beings who have come into life only to leave are connected and bound to one another by a hidden chain. And this connection has meaning. It is our job in life to discover this hidden chain between things and people and give our own life meaning and direction."

Jarireh, however, still seemed drawn to her new way of thinking and discovery. "These days even schoolchildren kill themselves," she said "Even old men and new brides, people who have just gotten out of prison, and even the disabled soldiers back from the war kill themselves and set themselves on fire. If it were at all possible we should start an organization for people who kill themselves so we could assist one another. Assist one another in committing suicide."

Then, looking here and there about the room, she started speaking to imaginary people, like someone possessed by madness. "My dear . . . come here . . . come closer . . . let me help you die . . . You too . . . I'll help all of you." Then she turned back to Khanom Joon and with a serious expression said, "It is possible to die easily, without all this torment and smugness and these morality lessons. If people help each other to live, why not to die? Do you know how many people have killed themselves over the last year in this country? I've collected all the statistics. They're in that notebook. In the drawer of my dressing table."

Jarireh pointed to the dressing table. Mina got up hesitantly, found the notebook and flicked through it. Every page of it had been carefully divided into five columns. A column for name and surname. Date of birth. Date of suicide. Place of suicide. Reason for suicide. Mina shuddered when she saw the lengthy index of the dead, then passed the book on to Mandana for her to look.

Jarireh resumed. "When you are asleep . . . when you are laughing and eating or having a good time with your children and your friends, people are killing themselves. I've called it 'the National Depression.' Can't you see? We are a dead nation, yet no one has the guts to admit to it."

Then, as if she had lost control of herself, she stood in the middle of the room, her face pallid, her hair disheveled, in that long, loose, cream gown, and as if she were acting a part for the benefit of spectators, she put her hands over her lips and addressed the invisible people in the room. "Shhh . . . shhh . . . Nobody has the right to laugh. Nobody has the right to be cheerful. Dancing is banned . . . Wine is banned. Love is banned. Singing is banned. Thinking is banned . . . Freedom is banned. Writing is banned. Poetry is banned . . . Shhh . . . We'll kill the lot of you . . . We'll strangle the lot of you . . . This is an Islamic country . . . We'll hang you all in the city squares . . . We'll flog you . . . Do you think this is a joke? You yourselves wanted it. You voted for it."

Then, as if she had come to her senses again, she stood up straight, looked at the girls and Khanom Joon, sat down on the bed, and said, "So it's just me you're fixated on? I'm only one of the eighty people who die in this country every day by their own hand. This very day, right at this very moment that you're keeping me alive by force, seventy-nine other people are killing themselves. Go stop them."

Khanom Joon cast a regretful glance at the notebook and said, "If only you and the rest of the people you've listed in there and whose bodies are now food for ants and snakes knew that you are the result of the millions of years of challenges that created beings have confronted until one day, out of millions of egg cells and zygotes, you stuck to your mother's womb. Maybe then you'd appreciate life properly."

"I have accepted my life," Jarireh said. "I have lived for as long as I was useful. In any case, how do we know what Mehrab says isn't right? Perhaps we experience numerous lives. Perhaps we'll have the chance to be born again. If Mehrab lived several centuries ago, how do we know I won't be born anew in several centuries time? Hmm? Anyhow, nothing useful will come from me again. My work in this life is done. Two of my kids have gone on to have a comfortable life, my Mehrab will never get better, and it doesn't matter to him whether I'm here or not at all. My Leyla and my Shokoofeh are certainly dead, it's just that I haven't been told yet. There are no other possibilities. I've been a useless mother. A spouse without value. Rejected as a sister. As a daughter, forgotten. I'm happy killing myself. Why don't you get it?"

Mina and Mandana took their mother's hands and kissed them. "It's really you who have to change the way you think," Jarireh said. "Don't cry so much. Just imagine that I want to go on a trip around the world. Imagine that I am cheerfully packing to go see Fereydoun. To see Leyla and Shokoofeh . . . Azar and Bijan. Why don't you look at it like that?"

"You've been disconnected ever since Fereydoun died and no word came from your children," Khanom Joon said. "You've lost your ties to life, to your family, yourself and even to nature. Someone whose ties have been cut off cannot see how things are connected. Someone whose ties have been cut off is like an isolated piece of a raincloud. It only rains when these pieces are side by side."

"I have no objection to this state of affairs."

"Mom, since you insist so much on killing yourself, we'll kill ourselves with you," Mina and Mandana said.

Although hearing this startled her, Jarireh said, "I've realized that whether we're present in this life or not doesn't matter. Without us, the trees are greener, and the water flows more. The clouds rain whenever they feel like, with or without me."

Khanom Joon struck her cane hard on the floor. "You've got that wrong. Being present or not is necessary for those around you, around anyone, or even for nature. Just as Fereydoun's presence or absence has gotten you in this state, your not being here could have the same effect on your children and grandchildren. When you praise the beauty of a flower, that flower grows more beautiful. It means that we all depend on one another. We are one."

"Khanom Joon, kindly leave," Jarireh said, dismayed. "I am sick of wise counsels. You don't see I am counting down the moments until I can go. I've even lost track of the suicides I've been recording."

Khanom Joon stood up angrily, and, leaning on her cane, turned her back to leave. "Goodbye then," she said emphatically. "See you at the Resurrection."

Up until the day when, in the Registry Office of His Excellency Death and Her Highness Life, Khanom Joon, Mina and Mandana helped their mother's soul pass from this life, Jarireh had, according to Mina and Mandana's precise calculations, attempted to commit suicide one hundred and ninety-three times. Since in the Taban family everyone had for hundreds of years kept a book of memoirs, Mina and Mandana had one too, but devoted to their mother's suicide attempts. Recording the date, type of suicide attempt, and various details. The two of them had practically given up on their daily life so that they could keep Jarireh under regular observation. Until that most particular of days when everybody helped her, Jarireh tried every possible method of suicide; her noose was thoroughly frayed, pills had not worked, somebody had come to her rescue each time she had slit her wrists, and in the end her attempts to drown herself in the Sea of Mazandaran and to fling herself off the highest tree in the forest had also led nowhere, because there was always someone observing her, even when she was hanging herself behind a locked door or opening her veins in the bath. Mina and Mandana had given everyone spare keys to all the rooms in the house.

Incomplete love, incomplete marriage, incomplete motherhood, and incomplete suicide had turned her into a melancholic, obsessive, and superstitious woman who did not even believe she had the strength to die. Once, busy talking to everyone even as she was hanging herself, everyone looked at her, astounded and paralyzed, unable even to expel the air trapped in their chests. She was talking nineteen to the dozen about some television program or other at the same time as she was putting her head through the noose, when someone wanting to buy flowers entered without warning and screamed on seeing that strange scene, at which point everyone recovered their senses and went to Jarireh's rescue.

Her entire body was cut and bruised. Had that ominous day not arrived, the sympathy that the mansion's residents had for her would gradually have given way to a sense of having had enough of her. That day, despite what Jarireh's brother-in-law Asghar had promised her when he had burned the file in exchange for five hectares of the garden and told them he no longer had any business with them, a Patrol turned up in the courtyard with three Guards and a summons for Mehrab. It turned out that Mehrab had on several occasions, without the family's knowledge, gone to Zorvan, barefoot, hair disheveled, and shouted in the middle of the square that nobody had the right to steal from the Sanctuary of Mithra, and to emphasize his point had chanted "Death to the Dictator" several times, before turning to the villagers watching him in astonishment and saying, "Do you think your children have been martyred in the war? No. They've killed them. They've raped them. They've shot your children from behind. They've sent your children over mines. I've seen all this with my own eyes." After which, he had grabbed several people by the collar and made them witness: "Don't you remember going to Sangar-e Parviz together, but then they killed you . . . they killed you." Then he had wailed and hit himself and, all curled up, started crying and saying, "Take shelter . . . take shelter . . . the Iraqis are here. . . Mom . . . Dad . . . help . . . mine . . . mine . . . they're taking Mithra . . . the Guards are here . . . they're killing Mithra . . . Help . . . help . . . Death to Hezbollah . . . Death to the Islamic regime."

On seeing the summons for Mehrab that fateful day, Jarireh exploded with rage and shouted, "My child's gone bad in your war and now you won't even ignore his madness? A madman isn't a criminal. He hasn't hurt anybody." And at that very moment Mehrab came into the courtyard, carrying a bottle of wine, wearing only a pair of Y-fronts, laughing and dancing, and shouted at the Guards: "*Ha ha ha* . . . Death to Khomeini. Death to Khamenei," and as he was laughing and dancing and running, took off his underwear. He placed it on one of his fingertips and started spinning it round and saying, "I am Khomeini," and then started doing an impression of Khomeini: "Say *Allâhu Akbar* . . . say *Allâhu Akbar* . . . Weep . . . Weep . . . It is the month of Muharram that has kept Islam alive. Weep . . . Don't let something happen that people think something has happened . . . *Ha ha ha* . . . " And he pressed the bottle to his lips and glugged away at it.

The Guards pointed their guns at him and drew the bolts. "Halt or else I fire," one of them shouted at Mehrab. "It's the blessed month of Muharram," another one shouted. "Put your clothes on, you shameless man." Mehrab, as naked as the day he was born, offered his chest to him and said, laughing, "Are you trying to scare a child? Come on, you idiot, hit me. Is there anything left of me anyway? I've been left behind in the war . . . Can't you see?" At that very moment Shahnaz threw herself recklessly in between them, opened her arms wide so that her own body formed a shield for Mehrab's, and said, "By this holy day, forgive this child. This child is out of his mind."

But Mehrab came out from behind her and started dancing and singing again. "Isn't dancing banned? So come kill me. Isn't being cheerful during Muharram a sin? So come kill me . . . *Ha ha ha* . . . Isn't drinking wine forbidden? So come kill me." And he started glugging away at the wine again, but in such a way that most of it spilled over his head and face and chest.

Again, one of the Guards shouted, "Halt . . . Otherwise I'll kill you . . . Halt . . . Give yourself up," and before Shahnaz or Jarireh could place themselves between the guns and Mehrab, his naked and innocent body was host to five lead bullets.

After that, everything happened very fast. Jarireh, Khanom Joon, Jamshid Khan, the Sisters, Shahnaz and the rest of the servants threw themselves, screaming and striking their heads, on to Mehrab's bloody body. Jarireh cradled Mehrab's head and Mehrab smiled innocently and sweetly at his mother with his last remaining strength and said, "Laugh, Mom. Laugh. These people are afraid of our laughter and joy." And then his eyelids shut fast. Jarireh howled . . . howled . . . howled. Then, as if she had come to, she leapt up, raging like a volcano, and ran into the house, all the while laughing uproariously. She took the dagger that was the memento of Jamshid Khan's youth from the wall of the drawing room, and ran to the kitchen, where she picked up a lighter and a jerrycan of oil, which she sprayed over the curtains. Over the carpets. She threw the bookshelves to the floor and sprayed oil and then threw the lit lighter on them and *BOOM* . . . And all the while she was laughing uproariously and talking to herself in a loud voice. "This country doesn't need love and culture and art. This country's thirsty for blood . . . Blood!" The laughing faces of the Safavid and Qajar kings and dancing women were burning as Jarireh ran back over to Mehrab. Suddenly everyone noticed the smoke and flames emanating from the mansion and amidst all that, someone shouted, "Shahnaz!" Everyone turned round, and on the balcony of the upper floor Shahnaz had removed the headscarf she had worn all her life, and in one hand held her long, gray plaited hair and with the other was cutting it off with scissors and throwing it to the wind. Then she went onto the railings, and letting out a great, mournful wail, threw herself off the balcony to the ground.

For a moment, everybody was paralyzed.

Silence . . .

Nobody knew what to do. Watch out for Jarireh, stay by Mehrab's laughing corpse, go to Shahnaz's corpse, or save the mansion? In the end everyone headed in a different direction. Khanom Joon and Jamshid Khan ran toward the mansion. The servants ran towards Shahnaz, while Hasrat and Mina and Mandana stayed with Mehrab and Jarireh. At that very moment in a rapid motion Jarireh plunged the knife she had been holding pressed tight against her body into her womb. She pulled her womb out using her hand, and in front of Mina and Mandana and Hasrat's horrified eyes, pushed Mehrab's head into her stomach, as if she desired to return her Mehrab to the womb and say, "Come back to me . . . Come back to my womb . . . Where nobody can harm you any longer."

Chapter Twenty-Six

Mehrab, Jarireh, and Shahnaz's bloody bodies lay under white sheets in the burnt remains of the drawing room awaiting morning and burial in a simple ceremony next to Fereydoun, Bijan, and Azar—but as it happened matters did not wait until morning, since that very night Khanom Joon was spoken to in a dream. She ordered the servants to saddle the horses and to ready everything for a day's journey. When the servants wanted to accompany them, Khanom Joon refused them permission. She said that she had to take Mehrab and Jarireh somewhere, and that once they had returned, the ceremonies would be carried out as planned. No one dared object. However, Mina and Mandana and Jamshid Khan did set out behind Khanom Joon without asking why. When they reached the River of Farewell, the full moon spread a silvery vagueness above them, above the river and the forest.

Khanom Joon dismounted and told them to wait. Then she ordered them to place the bodies on the ground. Mina and Mandana spread out the mats, Jamshid Khan lit a fire, Khanom Joon handed out the little pieces of food prepared earlier, and they sat waiting in silence. Gradually the silhouette of a boat became visible in the distance. Khanom Joon and Jamshid Khan went down to the riverbank, their canes striking the ground, before standing to attention, heads held high, despite the difficulty of holding their frames erect. In accordance with Khanom Joon's dream, they waited for life's chief, Death . . . and yet the person who came to meet them was none other than their son, Fereydoun.

The boat was old and wooden and had a little cabin.

Fereydoun, standing up and directing the boat toward them with the long oar, was dressed in simple, casual clothes, contrary to his usual practice. He wore a white shirt with rolled-up sleeves, gray canvas pants and sneakers. As soon as Fereydoun had brought the boat to a halt by the bank, everyone went in silence to meet him. He hesitated for a moment before stepping out of the boat on to the shore, looking doubtfully at the cabin. Then, apparently having made up his mind, he put his foot on dry land. First, he hugged his grandparents tight, then kissed their faces and hands affectionately, before saying, "If only there was a way I could recompense all your many troubles and kindnesses." Next it was Mina and Mandana's turn. He drew so tight to them in hugging and kissing them that their tears became mingled. "I'm so proud of you for being so strong," he said.

Then he turned to the dead bodies. He walked over to them and lifted the sheets. A moment later Mehrab and Jarireh opened their eyes. Both were dressed in fresh, white, Zoroastrian clothes. As soon as Jarireh saw Fereydoun, she wanted to hug him tight, but Fereydoun turned his back on her. Mehrab stood up and went towards his father. Fereydoun hugged him tight and kissed him. "You are a champion," he whispered in his ear, then moved away from him. His expression was stern. There was not a shred of joy in it. Again, Jarireh wanted to throw herself happily and excitedly into his arms, but Fereydoun once more moved out of the way and with a cold expression said, "I really didn't expect you to act so irresponsibly."

"Your death and the children's crippled me," she said, hurriedly justifying herself. "I was thoroughly sick of life."

"You should've turned into the pillar of this family and mansion, in my place," said Fereydoun. "They should have been able to lean on you, not had you make them suffer. The point of grief and sorrow is not to produce suffering. You've gotten that wrong. The point of grief and sorrow is to wake people up. To make right what has made you grieve."

Fereydoun was angry which was obvious from his tone. Jarireh listened, head down and shocked. Fereydoun went on. "You should have fought with what made this family and this land grieve, rather than letting grief overwhelm you and aiding the forces of evil, the forces of darkness and the enemy."

"Alright," Jarireh said, ashamed. "But I was dead without you, it was just that nobody saw me die."

"Your duty was to pass on all the culture and customs we had taught you to our children and grandchildren," said Fereydoun.

"I was just as dead as you were," Jarireh said, sobbing and weakly. "I was just as incapable faced with life as you were."

Mehrab was standing in a corner, leaning on a tree and watching them. Mina and Mandana went over to him and hugged him. At that moment, a man and a woman emerged from the wooden cabin. Both were strikingly beautiful, tall of stature and clad in white from head to toe. Fereydoun extended his right arm in the man's direction and introduced him respectfully. "His Excellency Death."

Everybody was rooted to the spot in silence. Then Fereydoun pointed to the beautiful, tall lady, and, with a respect that was obvious, said, "Our chief, Her Highness Life."

Breaths were trapped in chests. No one had heard of an angel called Life before. There was plenty of talk of the Demon of Death and Eblis and the Angel Soroush, but the Angel of Life?

Both were standing in the boat. Her Highness Life did not take her eyes off Jarireh, in this respect completely the opposite of His Excellency Death, who was entirely absorbed by everyone else. Eventually the beautiful, white-clad man, wearing a cotton summer shirt and pants and white sneakers on his feet, took a step toward the edge of the boat. His hands were in the front pockets of his pants. His attitude was familiar and humble, yet dignified and authoritative, like some mournful aristocrat. Eventually he raised his head and looked carefully and respectfully into the faces of each of the living and the dead. First at Khanom Joon, then Jamshid Khan, then Mehrab and Mina and Mandana, and last of all, though differently, at Jarireh. A kind of reproach was visible in his gaze. Eventually Jarireh could bear it no more, and said, "Enough. I know I was weak and didn't manage to lessen my family's pains one bit, but rather added to them. So, leave me alone and let me stay dead in my own way. That's it."

Her Highness Life, her hair blacker than night, reaching down to her waist and showily contrasting with the white of her long shirt, addressed Jarireh in a voice that sounded like the twittering of swallows or the murmuring of springs: "The most fortunate and happiest people are not necessarily those who know the least pain or most success. They are those who have found the way to help themselves and others. If someone helps themself and others, life places at their disposal whatever they have need of for that kind of life, and in that way, they turn into the most fortunate of people."

Jarireh cast a helpless look at the beautiful lady. She sat down on the ground, furious, took her head in her hands and said, "What beautiful words . . . But what a shame that grief has penetrated to the core of my bones and turned me into someone completely different. What hopeful words . . . But what a shame that reality is devoid of hope."

She stood up and took a step towards Her Highness Life. "It's not my fault that the life you're responsible is so hard and arduous," she said, pleading. Then, looking at His Excellency Death, she continued. "And the death for which you're responsible so calming and easy."

His Excellency Death and Her Highness Life looked at one another in astonishment. At last Her Highness Life said, "For everyone, life is a brief opportunity to make meaning." Then His Excellency Death continued, addressing her. "And death is a lengthy opportunity to experience life without meaning."

With a spirit no one had seen in her for some time, Jarireh stood firm and said, "Ladies and gentlemen, enough of these attempts. I've died. Have you forgotten? I killed myself only yesterday. Show some respect for the departed. Recite the prayers for the dead for me. Farewell." Whereupon, casting a furious glance of farewell at the others, she stretched out beside the river on top of the autumn leaves and drew the white sheet over herself.

As she did, Her Highness Life turned to the others and said, "Fifty-three years of her life were left. I grant them to you." And she looked at Khanom Joon. Khanom Joon lowered her head in respect and acquiescence.

Then His Excellency Death, with a voice that was deep and warm, like the beating of a stork's wings, addressed Jarireh, lying dead on the ground. "We've heard what you have to say." Then, looking at Her Highness Life and nodding his head slowly in confirmation, he continued. "We have forgiven you and we now give you permission to arise and join your husband."

Thereupon Jarireh's ghost stood up slowly and looked at its body. Then it looked at everyone. Khanom Joon and Jamshid Khan gazed back sorrowfully and reproachfully. Mina and Mandana wept. Fereydoun took Jarireh's hand, helped her board the boat, and hugged her. Jarireh and Fereydoun seemed calm.

Next Mehrab lay down next to Jarireh's body and drew the sheet over himself. Fereydoun extended his arm again. Mehrab's ghost separated from his body and boarded the boat. Mehrab looked at everyone, smiled, and said, "Tell Shokoofeh how much I love her. Tell Leyla how much I missed her." Then, turning to Her Highness Life, he said, "You owe me another life. I must raise myself to the Seventh Step." Her Highness Life nodded in confirmation and said, "In this life Shahnaz, who had no blood relationship with you whatever, was able to love you more than her own soul. In the next life, she is deserving of being your mother." Mehrab smiled.

Then as His Excellency Death took up the oar and the boat moved slowly off into the thin mist, Her Highness Life stood smiling at those who remained mourning on the banks.

CHAPTER TWENTY-SEVEN

Enkidu, may the paths in the Cedar Forest
Weep for you, nor day nor night elect for silence
May the peaks and mountains and hills
We traversed together weep for you
And may they praise your name with a thankful song!"[104]

I gave birth to you in prison. A boy who might have been at the same time Behnam's child, that of the fifteen-year-old boy from the prison, or my interrogator's. My son, it is as if you are the essence extracted from this nation's contradictory soul. Noble and vile. Idealistic and amoral. Good and evil. Despite all that, I have always told you that you are Behnam's son. The only love and man of my life. I named you Kay-Khosro in memory of the cave of the Living King. May the Divine Glory always be with you, and your life be in service of the goodness, freedom and prosperity of this land.

By the time I was freed from prison, you were fifteen and living in the men's ward, without ever having been found guilty of a crime . . . Without you ever having set eyes on streets, shops, ordinary people, cinemas, bookstores, mountains, rivers, and seas. Until we set foot in the mansion together, you had never set eyes on wildflowers, woodpeckers, or squirrels. Everything you knew of life in your childhood you had learnt from the black-and-white televisions in the cells, or from the stories I had told you. For as long as you had permission to be with

[104] Adapted from Gilgamesh's lament over Enkidu in the Persian translation of *The Epic of Gilgamesh*.

me in the women's section, until you were nine, I brought you up on dreams of the mansion and the forest and Shabro, with edifying tales of Jamshid Khan and Khanom Joon, the Ball of Light, memories of Mom's photography, Dad's opinions and books, and Mehrab and Leyla's kindnesses and empathy. On the dream of playing with Auntie Mina and Mandana, the dream of the traditions of the people of Zorvan and Gilan, the wonder of the Gowkaran tree, the Temple of Mithra, and the Sacred Fire. During all those years, all the women in the ward mobilized themselves to show you whatever they found crawling or twitching in any corner of the cells and ward and courtyard of Evin Prison, talking about it for hours. Do you remember? You must. By the time we were released, you must have seen hundreds of sparrows from afar or up close, while twenty-four pigeons had come so close to you in the courtyard that you were able to stroke their feathers. You had seen dozens of butterflies and honeybees and you had fifteen flowerpots—flowerpots you had made from the bottoms of drink bottles and in which you cultivated red and orange and pink geraniums. You played with ants and saw several spiders and grasshoppers and praying mantises here and there, next to the beds. Three times you saw mole crickets, mice or rats fifty-three times. Once one of the women prisoners smuggled in her kitten for you and let it spend several nights with you. Do you remember? I cannot be selfish and claim I brought you up single-handedly. No. That's not how it was. All the women on the ward brought you up. They changed your diaper, winded you, and Parvin and Massoumeh even nursed you. Before her execution, Parvin rocked you on her knees every night so you would sleep, while Farzaneh used to make you a puree of potatoes and milk before she was exiled. Before she was released, Bita, who we discovered was a distant relative, used to tell you stories of her house in a mysterious and distant village called Razan, and of her brother Sohrab who had been executed right there in Evin, and her thirteen-year-old sister Bahar, who was a ghost and was always fluttering around their remaining family in order to protect them. Before they were executed, even Khadijeh and Zahra sewed you a patchwork blanket made of scraps of cloth they had gotten their hands on here and there. I brought that blanket with me to the mansion as a prison souvenir. On execution nights, our cellmates would all sing loudly and in unison so that you wouldn't hear the bullets, to distract you from the terror that reigned over the cells: "Winter's over at last . . . Spring's flowering at last . . . The sun's red rose has come back and night flees at last / The mountains are meadows of tulips . . . Alive are the tulips . . . In the mountains they're planting the sun, flower after flower at last."[105]

I taught you to read when you were four, using the *Shahnameh*. I asked the librarian to acquire a few children's books, since the number of children being born in the prison was growing by the day. By the time they separated you from me and took you to the men's ward, we and your five playmates had already read the *Shahnameh* twice from cover to cover and had reached the story of the Avenging of Siyavash when they took you from me. The first weeks were really difficult, and I suffered constant anxiety that they would molest and hurt you there, but my mind was gradually set at rest, because they sent you to the political prisoners' ward, and the adults and writers and university professors who were there became your close companions. Over time the two of us got used to the situation. Did we have any other choice? You had permission to visit me once a fortnight. We were able to chat a little, eat something, and I could see how you were growing up and becoming more and more aware. You would say that prison was your school and university, with a whole bunch of writers, poets, journalists, and sociologists. You were right, although you would know nothing else about life until the day we were freed. You had never seen a

[105] A poem by Saeed Soltanpour, "Winter's Over At Last." During the revolution, it was turned into a song and sold on cassette. An album including the song, entitled "The Flames of the Sun," was released in 1979.

rainbow. You did not know what pleasure it was to ride a horse in the garden, or how much fun family parties were. You did not know what it meant to stretch out under the canopies of the trees and glimpse the light passing through them. You did not know what kind of pleasure it was to grow up among brothers and sisters, grandparents, or uncles, aunts, and cousins. You had never seen a greenhouse in your life. In your life, you had never seen the rising and the setting of the sun and moon. Kay-Khosro, my son, you grew up in a cave. In a labyrinth called Evin.

During all those years, I had no word from anyone. What state was the mansion in? Mom and Dad? Had Mehrab made it back there? Had the Sisters gotten married? Had Leyla come back? Were those mysterious leaves that had sealed the wound on my arm one night in prison not the work of Khanom Joon and the Ball of Light? Was the fact that my file, as thick as the judge's neck, disappeared overnight, not also their doing? Then why in all these years had the Ball of Light not shown itself to me? Why had it not brought me news of the mansion? Was Bahman still alive, or had he died in the war, as he had wanted? It had been years now since the end of the war. Beset by prison's unending heartaches, I wondered whether we would ever gather again around the Gowkaran tree and eat its fruits as we used to do, talk and laugh. When had been the last time I'd laughed from the bottom of my heart anyway?

Thus, fifteen years after your birth, we set foot in the half-burnt ruins of the mansion and came face to face with the remains of the family, at one time ten people, floundering between life and death. Birds had made their nests everywhere in the mansion, leaving their droppings everywhere. All the servants had left except Hasrat, and the mansion was half-ruined and burned down. After Mom's suicide, Mina and Mandana and their families had sought asylum in Germany. They had buried Mom and Mehrab and Shahnaz next to the graves of

Dad and Uncle Bijan and Auntie Azar. The greenhouse was desiccated and ruined and Hasrat drifted around the mansion like a wandering ghost, doing his jobs to the extent of his powers. Khanom Joon and Jamshid Khan passed the bulk of their time moving between the intact and destroyed and half-dark rooms, and only set foot in the courtyard with great difficulty. Yet the tree in the middle of the kitchen had not moved an inch. It was the same as it had always been. Laden with fruit. Leafy. Thriving. Home to a thousand birds. The tree stood firm, as if none of these disasters had afflicted the mansion.

Do you remember that when we set foot in the half-burnt drawing room for the first time, you looked at the smoke-damaged and broken frames of the calligraphy and paintings and tilework, before looking with concern at Khanom Joon and Jamshid Khan, and then at me, and saying, "Is this the same mansion and family you told me stories about every night?"

"This is what remains of them," I said.

"So we have to live in these ruins?" you asked.

"Exactly," I said. "And our job is to make them flourish again."

"How?" you asked.

"We'll figure it out," I answered. "The most important thing we have to do is to get you ready."

"To do what?" you asked in surprise.

"To inherit," I said. "You are the inheritor of this mansion, this sacred fire, this tree and this dynasty."

"But I've never had a childhood," you said. "I want to be young, at least."

"You will be," I said. "Look around you. Everything has been prepared. This garden and this mansion and this tree possess everything necessary to give your childhood back to you. I promise you: life will restore to you whatever it has taken from you up to now."

I was fast asleep in the smoke-damaged, dusty room that had been the favorite of my childhood when I was woken up by kisses on the tresses of my hair. Was it him?

It was him . . .

It was him . . .

It was still him . . .

It is always him.

As he had years ago, he took my hand and led me out of the mansion without a fuss. Passing through the courtyard, he took me to the same spot. To the middle of the forest. To the place where with the first kiss I had sacrificed the sheep of shame beneath Eblis's feet. I was so happy to see him that I could not breathe. He squeezed me tight against him and kissed me and said, "It's taken you a thousand years to get here. It's taken so long."

He was dead, and I could tell that from his pallid color, but it did not matter. In this land we had all lived together for centuries and millennia. Sometimes our dead were more alive than the living. I pressed him tight against me and said, "It's taken me a thousand years to hug you again." Like he had done that year, he placed my hand on his heart and said, "Do you remember?" "Always," I said. Then he said, something suddenly appearing to darken his expression, "Our son . . . Kay-Khosro . . . I saw him today . . . Isn't he gorgeous . . . Hasn't he grown up? I always wondered if you'd gotten pregnant, and what would've become of you and the child. I was worried about you." "Did you see? He's tall like you," I said. He laughed. I went on. "We're still alive. That in itself is a miracle." "It is," he said. "And I've had fifteen years to plan for that miracle. Come with me."

I followed him. He took me to the temple. He had been waiting for me in the Temple of Mithra all these years—waiting for me to get myself back to the mansion, dead or alive. Throughout all the years he had been observing the mansion crumble, he had passed his time establishing relationships with the ghosts of the surrounding area. He had learnt the ways and customs of the afterlife from them and come to understand that, however much he might be alive after having died, death nonetheless marked the end of many of his abilities. The statue of Mithra and the Bull was still standing, as solid as ever. He led me in front of the statue, took my hands firmly in his, and said, "Right here, in this holy and ancient place, I ask for your hand in marriage. Will you marry me?" And without even waiting for my reply, he removed the wooden ring he had hollowed out with his own hands a thousand years before by the River of Farewell from the necklace around his neck and placed it on my hand. I too unclasped my necklace. I had kept the ring all these years by whatever means was necessary. Kay-Khosro, do you remember? In prison they kept asking me what the wooden ring was. I put it on your father's finger and we kissed. Both of us knew we belonged to one another, dead or alive.

The wedding celebration was held at the mansion, but not right away. Years had to pass. We had to let you experience childhood, adolescence, youth . . . We had to let you enjoy yourself, understand beauty, feel joy, be smitten with hope. We had to let the importance of the mansion, the tree, and the history and culture behind them penetrate deep into your veins. First, though, Khanom Joon and the Ball of Light arranged matters so that everything would be far simpler than we had imagined. Overnight, the mansion resumed its former beauty and splendor. The tiles and paintings were restored, and the objects still left in the house were put back in their proper places and in good condition. Of course, many things had been broken or burnt during those years of dispossession, but what remained still bore with it the culture and history of the mansion, and powerfully too.

"In all these years the Ball of Light was here," I asked Khanom Joon, "how come it hadn't already done all this?"

"The Ball of Light was here, but not hope," she said. "Now you are here. Kay-Khosro is here, and so is hope."

During all the long years that followed, as we readied you for your great responsibility, your father came and went and spent time with us. You certainly remember. Behnam's and your first meeting took place very soon after our return to the mansion. You were picking pomegranates from the Gowkaran tree for me to open when Behnam entered the kitchen unnoticed, carrying a bunch of wild primroses. You looked around in surprise and said, "Oh . . . Such a dizzying wild scent. What is that fragrance?" Without showing himself, Behnam said, "I picked them for you." You looked around, confused, before turning in the direction you'd heard the voice come from and saying, "Don't tell me you're my father." Behnam appeared a few paces away from you and said, "That's me." The two of you stared at one another. It was as if you were both troubled and did not know who should take the first step. I had been busy opening up the pomegranates, and I stood up. I wiped my hands on my apron and, putting a hand on each of your backs, I said, "Don't worry. In this mansion, the dead and the living can embrace."

So it was you both took a step forward and embraced. Your relationship with your father soon became even warmer than I had anticipated. Behnam had so much to say to you. About love. About war and freedom. About his memories with me.

I am writing these things here so that you'll remember them afterwards when you read this notebook. What I've told you here is the epic of your life . . . The heritage of the mansion . . .

So it was that you, father and son, spent your time with one another day and night. Right at the beginning we discovered that you were obsessed with the scent of flowers. Often you marched off in the direction of the forest and returned an hour later with a bunch of wildflowers. In all your prison life, you had never seen a wildflower. In fact, you had never seen any kind of flower aside from geraniums—that was why the shapes, colors, and heady scents of violets, primroses, tulips, and wild saffron made you tipsy. Do you remember? Once you went off so far with Behnam that you got to Vevli Forest, the Silk-Tree

Forest. The Persian silk tree, whose otherworldly, heady scent intoxicates the entire forest, the animals, the birds, and even the ghosts. When you came back that day, you were holding a bunch of the whitish, pinkish silk flowers, and as you smelt it you tottered like a drunk, while your father supported you under your arm and you both guffawed with laughter.

Years later, our wedding celebrations lasted for seven nights and days, in accordance with family tradition. We had by then crossed the threshold of middle age . . . You must remember that all the family came. Dead and alive. From our great ancestors to distant relatives we had never even seen . . . From my mother's side only the handful of relatives who had not betrayed us and the country were invited. How thrilled we were to see our beloved dead: Mom, Dad, Mehrab, Uncle Bijan and Auntie Azar. Mozhgan and Iraj. Unfortunately, their fate had been what I had guessed it would be. Their coffins had flowed downstream on the River of Farewell, without anybody recovering them from the water, burying them, and saying, "May God have mercy on you." Bahman was there too. Mahsa was sitting on his shoulders as usual and they chatted away and laughed together. When, amid the confusion of the guests all coming and going, he spotted me wearing a wedding dress, he hesitated for a moment, before waving at me with Mahsa's hand, which he was holding, and smiling kindly. He had been killed years before in the war. Just as he had predicted. Mina and Mandana came back from abroad. A Mina and Mandana who bore no resemblance to their former selves. They were mature and focused. Ready to stay. Ready to build.

Azadeh also came for the wedding ceremonies. Now a woman of giant size whom no Guard, soldier, or undercover officer had ever managed to get their hands on . . . And what about Leyla . . . Who would ever have believed she would turn into that beautiful young woman with long, flowing, white locks who stole everyone's hearts? When I saw Mehrab I hugged him so tight that he almost disappeared into my body. Ancestors near and far, on my father's and my mother's side, also came. The same ones who years before had come with Uncle Bijan and Auntie Azar to convince us to flee the country. They were still every bit as talkative and given to jokes and nostalgia. As usual, Mom had set up her photographic equipment. All the servants, dead or alive, had come back to the mansion and were busy working and living with all their former enthusiasm. Shahnaz was there too. Cheerful and thriving. She looked young again and still more energetic than before.

The first three days of the week-long celebration were taken up with greetings and dancing and drinking as well as the nuptial ceremony in the presence of the mobed Jamasp and the sacred fire. From the third through the fifth days there began the arguments about politics and religion and culture . . . The reviewing of memories and catastrophes. You witnessed some of these yourself. But many of them, not. I watched you from afar, getting on well with the young people from friends and family. What pleasure it gave me to see you pursuing a normal life. Between the third and fifth days, we talked of the pains we had suffered and the loved ones we had lost. We talked so much that by the end of the fifth night the grief and sorrow had reached a climax, lumps in throats had turned into tears, and eventually started flowing downhill. The people of Zorvan, who knew nothing about our wedding celebrations, were thoroughly perplexed to know where this salty flood had come from, flowing down from the hill where our garden was onto the meadows and paddies, and thence to the village and the houses. On the sixth day, all manner of dancing was added to the heated political discussions and to the griefs and sorrows, and so it was that on the morning of the seventh day we all concluded, dead or alive, blind drunk, united and of one accord, that the best way to combat the regime was to gather together in the main square in Rasht and to dance and party and drink there, in front of the City Hall. Practically speaking, that is, to act against the security of the State. An open action against the laws of sharia.

It was around noon that we set out, the dead and the living, for town. There were some people who from the start did not join us in our craziness, and we accepted that. They had the right not to. It was a matter of life and death. You, Leyla, Khanom Joon, Jamshid Khan and the rest of the grandchildren and sons-in-law stayed at the mansion. You had to stay. That was the plan.

The only unexpected event prior to our moving off toward City Hall Square in Rasht was the appearance of Eblis. As always, she bewitched all the guests with her height and loose hair, her grace and her simple, ruinous beauty. As always, she was carrying the peacock, and the snake was on her shoulders. She stopped in the doorway as she was entering. I went up to her and said, "What a long path had to be trod between our first meeting and today."

She said, a smile on her lips and stroking the peacock, "And this will also be our last meeting." And she set out with us. Some in cars, others on foot or flowing through the air. Some, like Azadeh, went taking massive strides, carrying several people in her arms or on her shoulders. At around six in the afternoon, we all gathered in the square in front of City Hall. One of the dead had stolen two or three loudspeakers from the pick-up trucks selling herbs and vegetables and handed them to the living so they could connect them to the large sound system they had brought with them. Suddenly, City Hall Square was booming with the sound of Manouchehr Sakhaee. "A flower in the bride's hair, *yâllâh* . . . kiss the groom, *yâllâh* . . . the groom has kissed you . . . he's plucked the bud of your lips . . . tonight he's scattered seed . . . for the dove of his heart . . . tonight he's scattered seed."

I put my hand over my mouth and let out a long wedding ululation, as was the northern custom, and everyone else joined in, before dancing and laughter suddenly made the city square explode. I, in my white wedding dress, my hair loose, and Behnam, in white linen shirt and pants, danced in the middle of the square, surrounded by friends and family, all the while sipping from our bowls of wine. Eblis too, bowl of wine in hand, observed us with a smile, and from time to time she too bounced around a little in time with the music. We had blocked off the road and people in their cars were stationary all around the square, staring at us as if they were seeing aliens. The women of our party were wearing low-cut party dresses and miniskirts, while the men embraced them and kissed them passionately, laughed and danced. We had arranged right from the start that whenever the anti-riot guards arrived, we would continue with our action against the security of the State and Islam. Meaning that we would continue to get drunk and dance. To laugh and sing. We had arranged not to fear death and to concentrate our attention on dancing and joy alone. To concentrate our attention on life.

We had all been drunk for seven nights and days, so it was hardly odd that we had become so bold and courageous. As the old Persian saying goes, "Drunkenness and truth." In our drunkenness, we wanted to show the truth of our life. Hadn't that been Mehrab's final request to Mom? In the last moment of his life, he had laughed and said, "Mom, laugh. Laugh. These people are afraid of our laughter and joy." All we wanted was to be ourselves and carry out Only Brother's final request. Amid all the ululations and dancing and music, Behnam pulled me into his arms and said, "Are you sure this is what you want to do? You're not afraid? They'll get here soon."

"I'm sure," I said. "But to be honest . . . I am afraid! For Kay-Khosro more than anything else."

"Kay-Khosro is strong," he whispered in my ear. "Mina and Mandana's kids are here too. Khanom Joon . . . Jamshid Khan . . . And as you yourself have always said, for as long as the mansion and the tree and the Simorgh are there, our path continues."

He was right. We rested our heads on each other's shoulders and chests and in the middle of that noisy, raucous tune, we swayed gently to the sorrowful music of my body like the leaves of a poplar rustling in a spring breeze.

With my head resting on Behnam's chest, I caught sight of the pedestrians. They stood on the sidewalk watching us, dumbfounded. The giant Azadeh was dancing in away there in the middle, waving at the pedestrians and blowing them kisses. Some of the pedestrians were laughing, some dumbfounded, some frowning. I saw a student music group stop on the sidewalk when they saw us, look doubtfully and hesitantly at one another, and finally, appearing to have made up their minds, take out their instruments and sit down and start playing along with our wedding song. Several other people stopped where they were and without thinking started jigging their shoulders to our song and smiling. I laughed and gestured with my hand for them to come join us. "Come and dance!" Then I left Behnam and went toward the crowd.

"Look, we're not doing anything wrong," I said to the pedestrians.

I gestured to my wedding dress and continued. "Today is my wedding day and this is my city too. I want to celebrate my wedding in my own city. What's wrong with that? You are invited to my wedding too. Come. Come and let's eat and drink and dance together."

Several adolescent girls and boys promptly accepted and danced hip-hop style to the song "A flower in the bride's hair, *yâllâh*," while the rest of the young people passing by caught onto their excitement and joined in. Eventually the girls took off their headscarves and spun them around their heads, ululating and dancing. Then some middle-aged and young couples came over, laughing, and the celebration really took off. Little by little, people put their shopping baskets aside, removed their headscarves, flung their manteau into a corner, and joined us, dancing and laughing. A few people even filled their goblets and drank to the health of me and your father. A little after, some old women and men joined the group and started to dance, too.

All of a sudden, I noticed that among the passersby, there was one who did not take his eyes off Eblis, who was standing still in the middle of the commotion of the crowd and staring back at him. I went up to Eblis. "Do you know him?" I asked.

She took my hand and led me over to him. When we had gotten very close, finally the passerby was able to tear his eyes off Eblis and cast half a glance at me too. "يا رب العالمين"[106] Eblis said to him, smiling, "what are you doing here? This is the lovers' assembly."

The Lord of Worlds, God, who it seemed was only now able to extract Himself from Eblis's spell, replied, "That's exactly why I'm here."

When God spoke, His voice was deep like valleys and oceans. With that height, salt-and-pepper hair, penetrating eyes and clear expression, how simple, beautiful, and at the same time splendid He looked. All the same I noticed several wounds on his arms and neck. I was thinking how well God and Eblis suited one another when Eblis extended her hand towards Him and said, "So dance with me then."

At first God looked doubtfully at Eblis's hand hanging there in the air, then at me, and finally, having made up His mind, took her hand. Eblis led Him to the middle of the throng and the two of them started dancing, all the while gazing utterly besotted into one another's eyes. They weren't dancing to the music of "Bride, kiss the groom, *yâllâh*" with its 6/8 beat, but rather seemed to be dancing along to their own inner music: a gentle, rhythmical, romantic, galactic music.

No voice could any longer be heard above the din. The noise of our joy was so loud it made the town deaf. After all, it was a wedding celebration, wasn't it? That's what a wedding is anyway . . . We weren't doing anything wrong. We wanted to be

[106] O Lord of Worlds.

joyful, and we were. Everybody was either dancing or embracing and kissing one another. Nobody was watching anymore. Everybody was in the middle of the square. The cars were shining their headlamps on us and giving prolonged blasts on their horns to accompany our celebration. By the time I went back to Behnam, having danced with various people, twilight was upon us, and I said, "Kiss me. Kiss me hard." And he did. It occurred to me that his moist kisses in the square would be my most beautiful memory of life.

Manouchehr Sakhaee was singing that tonight he had scattered seeds / for the pigeon of his heart for the thousandth time when the black bullet-proof cars arrived bearing the anti-riot forces, clad in black and armed from head to toe. They surrounded the entire square. The drivers started honking their horns even more in protest. We turned the music up, louder and louder, so that even if we wanted to, we would not be able to hear the riot police's warnings and threats. Some people stopped their drinking and dancing as soon as they set eyes on the anti-riot forces, vanishing into the back streets, but to our tremendous surprise we saw that many adolescents and younger people had stayed behind and kept on drinking and dancing, caring even less than before. Someone had lit a fire in the middle of the square and the girls and women, dancing around it, threw their headscarves and manteaux into it and cut their hair in protest at the presence of the anti-riot forces. We took one another's hands in support, forming a ring around them and dancing. United and of one mind. Eblis and God joined us too. We didn't hear what the Special Guard were saying, but we could see that they were holding a megaphone and saying something to us. It didn't matter. We were drunk. Drunk with truth. Drunk with belief in what we were. We were drunk with life, and nobody had the right to take that away from us. So we danced . . . We danced, and with Behnam's hands tightly knotted with mine, we started falling . . . One by one, at first . . . Then more of us . . . more . . . Like autumn leaves . . . Like autumn leaves, you couldn't tell which fell first and from which tree . . . We danced and fell to the ground and died. We danced and died, because this dancing and this dying were our only tools against them. Swearing by love . . . swearing by God and Eblis who stood watching us, weeping; our warm blood was our only weapon against their cold hearts.

We accomplished what we had to do. What we had to do was to stain their hands with our blood, blood that even a thousand washes couldn't wash away. For our bodies to weigh down their shoulders, the city's, the country's, the land's shoulders even if they turned around a thousand times and could not see us there. And so it was that with our dancing, our blood, and with our loud peals of laughter in the city square, we took our part in a revolution that will one day, sooner or later, triumph. One day in the future, our bloody dance will continue in the free and joyous laughter of our children and grandchildren and great-grandchildren, even when we are forgotten.

About the Author

Born in Iran in 1972, Shokoofeh Azar was the first Iranian woman to hitchhike the entire length of the Silk Road. She worked as journalist and field reporter in Iran, covering human rights issues. After several arrests in connection with her work as a journalist, on advice from her family, she fled Iran in 2010, and was granted asylum in Australia, where she has lived as a political refugee since 2011. She is the author of essays, articles, and children's books. Her first novel, *The Enlightenment of the Greengage Tree*, was shortlisted for the Stella Prize for Fiction and the International Booker Prize and was a finalist for the PEN America Award and the National Book Award for Translated Literature. *The Gowkaran Tree in the Middle of Our Kitchen* has already received two awards for a manuscript-in-progress, one from the Australia Council for the Arts and the other from Creative Victoria.